PRAISE FOR TIMOTHY S. JOHNSTON'S
THE WAR BENEATH

"If you like novels like *The Hunt for Red October* and
Red Storm Rising, you will certainly enjoy *The War Beneath*."
—*A-Thrill-A-Week*

"If you're here for thrills, the book will deliver."
—*The Cambridge Geek*

". . . an engaging world that is highly believable . . ."
—*The Future Fire*

"This is a tense, gripping science fiction/thriller of which
Tom Clancy might well be proud . . . When I say it is gripping,
that is the simple truth."
—Ardath Mayhar

". . . a thrill ride from beginning to end . . ."
—*SFcrowsnest*

". . . if you like Clancy and le Carré with a hint of Forsyth
thrown in, you'll love *The War Beneath*."
—Colonel Jonathan P. Brazee (RET),
2017 Nebula Award & 2018 Dragon Award Finalist

"Fast-paced, good old-fashioned Cold War espionage . . . a great escape!"
—*The Minerva Reader*

"One very riveting, intelligent read!"
—*Readers' Favorite*

THE
SAVAGE
DEEPS

THE RISE OF OCEANIA

ChiZine Publications

FIRST EDITION
The Savage Deeps © 2019 by Timothy S. Johnston
Cover art © 2019 by Erik Mohr (Made By Emblem)
Cover design © 2019 by Jared Shapiro and Errick Nunnally
Interior design © 2019 by Jared Shapiro and Errick Nunnally

Distributed in Canada by
Fitzhenry & Whiteside Limited
195 Allstate Parkway
Markham, Ontario L3R 4T8
Phone: (905) 477-9700
e-mail: bookinfo@fitzhenry.ca

Distributed in the U.S. by
Consortium Book Sales & Distribution
34 Thirteenth Avenue, NE, Suite 101
Minneapolis, MN 55413
Phone: (612) 746-2600
e-mail: sales.orders@cbsd.com

Library and Archives Canada Cataloguing in Publication

Johnston, Timothy S., 1970-, author
    The Savage Deeps / Timothy S. Johnston. -- First edition.

(The rise of Oceania ; 2)
Issued in print and electronic formats.
ISBN 9781771485067 (softcover).--ISBN 9781771485203 (PDF)

    I. Title.

PS8619.O488W37 2018   C813'.6   C2018-904662-7
                                              C2018-904663-5

CHIZINE PUBLICATIONS
Peterborough, Canada
www.chizinepub.com
info@chizinepub.com

Edited by Leigh Teetzel
Copyedited and proofread by Klaudia Bednarczyk

Canada Council   Conseil des arts
for the Arts   du Canada

We acknowledge the support of the Canada Council for the Arts which last year invested
$20.1 million in writing and publishing throughout Canada.

ONTARIO ARTS COUNCIL
CONSEIL DES ARTS DE L'ONTARIO
an Ontario government agency
un organisme du gouvernement de l'Ontario

Published with the generous assistance of the Ontario Arts Council.

Printed in Canada

TIMOTHY S. JOHNSTON

THE
SAVAGE
DEEPS

THE RISE OF OCEANIA

Books by Timothy S. Johnston

ChiZine Publications

THE WAR BENEATH
THE SAVAGE DEEPS
FATAL DEPTH (forthcoming)

Carina Press

THE FURNACE
THE FREEZER
THE VOID

TIMELINE OF EVENTS

2020
Despite the fact that global warming is the primary concern for the majority of the planet's population, still little is being done.

2055
Shipping begins to experience interruptions due to flooded docks and crane facilities. World markets fluctuate wildly.

2061
Rising ocean levels swamp Manhattan shore defenses and disrupt Gulf Coast oil shipping; financial markets in North America become increasingly unstable due to flooding.

2062–2065
Encroaching water pounds major cities such as Mumbai, London, Miami, Jakarta, Tokyo, and Shanghai. The Marshall Islands, Tuvalu, and the Maldives disappear. Refugee problem escalates in Bangladesh; millions die.

2069
Shore defenses everywhere are abandoned; massive numbers of people move inland. Inundated coastal cities become major disaster areas.

2071–2072
Market crash affects entire world; economic depression looms. Famine and desertification intensifies.

2073
Led by China, governments begin establishing settlements on continental shelves. The shallow water environment proves ideal for displaced populations, aquaculture, and as jump-off sites for mining ventures on the deep ocean abyssal plains.

2080
The number of people living on the ocean floor reaches 100,000.

2088

Flooding continues on land; the pressure to establish undersea colonies increases.

2090

Continental shelves are now home to twenty-three major cities and hundreds of deep-sea mining and research facilities. Resources harvested by the ocean inhabitants are now integral to national economies.

2093

Led by the American undersea cities of Trieste, Seascape, and Ballard, an independence movement begins.

2099

The CIA crushes the independence movement.

2128

Over ten million now populate the ocean floor in twenty-nine cities.

2129

Tensions between China and the United States, fueled by competition over The Iron Plains and a new Triestrian submarine propulsion system, skyrockets. The USSF occupies Trieste following The Second Battle of Trieste.

FEBRUARY 2130

Present day.

"I love the sea, born of an inconceivable deluge, because it is made of water. Water, as fluid as our souls, shapeless, enslaved to none but to gravity. Water, welcoming our bodies in a total embrace, setting us free from our weight. Water, mother of all life, fragile guarantor of our survival."

—Captain Jacques-Yves Cousteau, Ocean Explorer, Inventor, and Innovator

13 February, 2130 AD

PRELUDE: THE APPROACHING STORM

Location:	The Gulf of Mexico
Latitude:	27° 34' 29" N
Longitude:	54° 56' 11" W
Depth:	25 meters
Vessel:	USS *Impaler*
Time:	2300 hours

THE MASSIVE WARSUB HOVERED SILENTLY NEAR the seafloor. Her maneuvering screws were set to station-keeping and an anchor stretched to the sandy bottom. It was night in the world above, and the ship's hull shimmered in the murky sea. Fish darted about and kelp swayed just under the vessel. In the half-light filtering through the water, infantry in scuba gear practiced hand-to-hand combat on the bottom, and troops riding swift scooters flitted about. These small vessels had needle guns mounted to their stabilizers, and one by one their operators fired simulated rounds at each other. The murmur of ordered commands from facemask speakers and screams from officers angry at troops not following instructions echoed in the waters closest to the offending soldiers.

The troops reset for another try, and repeated the war game scenario.

Above the nightly training session, the 250 meter–long warsub was in silhouette with the full moon directly overhead. Small bubbles escaped from soldiers' masks as they wrestled with trainers and as they cried out in pain from perfectly applied wristlocks and arm bars. Torpedo tube hatches on the hull of USS *Impaler* opened and shut repeatedly during weapons drills.

It had been months of such training exercises; the USSF clearly expected trouble.

Soon.

Inside the warsub, in a small cabin near the bow, Captain Heller and First Officer Lieutenant Commander Schrader sat at a steel table. They had been discussing the crew's preparedness and the infantry's training for over an hour before Heller finally pushed aside his notes and set his pen down.

He leveled his hard eyes on Schrader but said nothing.

Schrader shifted under the glare. He had served with the captain for years now and knew the man well. Normally he was calm, bordering on cold, but there were times when his emotions flared like a storm and had the potential to engulf everything and everyone around him.

Schrader worried that something had stirred within the captain lately. Trieste City had consumed him for months. A year earlier, the undersea city had attempted yet another bid for freedom. George Shanks, who had headed up Trieste City Intelligence, and Janice Flint, the former mayor of the city, had launched a battle in the waters around the ocean colony. Many USSF sailors had died in that fight, along with Triestrian citizens and crews from Chinese subs. In the end, Trieste had surrendered and the USSF had arrested Shanks and Flint, but the colony had become a continuing source of concern for Heller.

Eventually Schrader managed, "Sir?"

Heller sighed. "Truman McClusky is on my mind."

McClusky was now mayor of Trieste, though he had taken part in The Second Battle of Trieste, and in fact had been a major cause of it. He had led *Impaler* on a grand chase around the world's oceans, sunk Chinese vessels, attacked an Australian undersea city, killed French and Chinese and American sailors, and yet still he was wandering the travel tubes and cabins of Trieste freely. In fact, the citizens of the city had elected him as mayor shortly after The Battle.

Even though Trieste was now under USSF control, the military still allowed her people to elect an official to act as a liaison between the USSF and the colonists. The title "mayor" was only a word, though, and didn't hold much meaning.

"Why's that?" Schrader asked.

Heller removed his round wire-frame glasses and rubbed his bald head. The sinews in his forearms rippled. He was in his standard USSF blue uniform, but as captain he permitted himself one modification—he kept his sleeves rolled up. "Yes, McClusky is only a figurehead. The people need to feel as though they have a say in issues. We didn't want them to feel humiliated following The Battle. We don't want this fight for freedom they can't win to bubble up again. I don't want McClusky to try anything."

"But we've beaten them twice." In fact, Schrader thought, the first time it had happened, the CIA had killed McClusky's father. The impact that had had on the son hadn't escaped him.

"Still," Heller said, "they are continuing the nonsense."

"Hoping for independence?" Schrader snorted. "That's ridiculous. With us right here?" He gestured around them, referring to the city just a few hundred meters to the east of their current location. It was a silly motion; they were in the cramped confines of the captain's office. "We'd crush them again."

"Obviously." Heller frowned. "If we ever decided to arrest or kill Mayor McClusky, we would need proof of his treason, otherwise it would cause an uproar with the citizens of the city. They probably elected him to protect him. They worship the man, especially since his father's assassination in 2099." He paused, and then said, "Early in The Battle, the Chinese undersea forces fled."

"But the Chinese lost a lot in the—"

Heller held up a finger. "No. I'm not referring to the Chinese Submarine Fleet. That's controlled by mainland China. It's an important distinction. I'm referring to the forces of the Chinese underwater cities. Sheng City and New Kowloon, for instance."

Schrader considered the information for a few moments. "They don't have many reserves. They were scared of losing warsubs and sailors."

Heller took a deep breath and exhaled. "Perhaps." He studied Schrader's eyes. "Or they left to prepare for another day. Perhaps the Chinese undersea cities were working with Trieste. Something connected the two colonies." Another pause. "Or someone."

Schrader could tell that Heller was still trying to figure it out. And anything Heller put his mind to, he would achieve.

It was inevitable.

Heller said, "Let me introduce you to some people." He pushed the intercom button on the bulkhead behind him and whispered a command. Then he sat in silence.

Schrader watched him but said no more. He knew Heller liked that he didn't push, that he knew when to watch and listen.

The muted sounds of the sub echoed in the cabin as they waited. A few clangs, the sigh of the ventilation system, commands over the loudspeaker related to the ongoing training on the seafloor.

And then the hatch slid open and two men stepped over the threshold. A USSF seaman escorted them in.

"That'll be all, Seaman Abernathy," Heller said. The hatch slid shut. Then to Schrader: "These are my two spies at Trieste."

———••———

SCHRADER'S FACE ERUPTED INTO SURPRISE. HE knew Heller had been watching Trieste closely, but hadn't known exactly *how* closely.

The first man through the hatch was Robert Butte. The last name was pronounced "Beaut." He was an important government official and well-liked by the citizens there.

Heller looked at Schrader and smiled. The blood had drained from the XO's face. "You know Robert, obviously."

"Yes," Schrader said, still staring at the man. "And you are the USSF's spy at Trieste?" He shook his head in surprise. "The deputy mayor? McClusky's right hand man?" The fact the second most powerful person in the undersea city was a USSF informant must have been Heller's crowning achievement in the year since The Battle.

Heller then pointed to the second man. "This is Rafe Manuel. He works in Trieste City Control with McClusky."

Schrader now turned his attention to the second man. "You are also informing for us?"

The man nodded. He was Hispanic with dark eyes wrinkled at their corners. "Yes, Commander Schrader. I work with the mayor and deputy mayor there. I—"

Heller interrupted. "You told me over coded message that you had some information about what McClusky is up to."

Manuel swallowed. "Yes. He has been sending subs out to the Atlantic. These subs don't come back."

"What do you mean by that?" Schrader asked, perplexed.

Heller responded. "He means they're going to some secret location. A hidden base perhaps, and the independence movement at Trieste is doing something there. I mean to find out what."

Schrader stared at the men standing before them. Heller was clearly convinced there was still an independence movement, and Schrader was too smart to question his captain about it right then. But it did surprise him. "Do either of you know what it is?"

The reply was in stereo: "No."

"Do you know where this base is?" Heller asked Manuel.

"Not precisely. They go north. That's all I know."

"North." Heller growled the single word and stared at the man. Manuel could only stare back, but his discomfort was clear.

"That's right," he finally replied.

"But why do all sonar reports show the ships going *south*? Around the curve of South America and out to the Mid-Atlantic Ridge?"

Manuel shook his head. He hesitated and his eyes flicked away for a heartbeat. "I can't explain that."

Heller turned to the deputy mayor. "Can you explain it, Robert?"

The man seemed surprised. "I didn't even know this much, Captain. Rafe here works in Sea Traffic Control. He sees the tracks of the subs. I don't."

"And McClusky has never spoken of this mystery to you?"

"No."

Robert Butte stood ramrod stiff now, and locked eyes with Heller.

Heller looked away and seemed to process this information. "I trust you," he said finally. Then he slid out from behind the table in one lithe motion and stepped toward Manuel. "On the other hand, I believe that you're lying to me." His voice was coarse.

Manuel backed away slightly, but it was difficult in the small cabin. "I'm not—"

In a flash Heller snapped out a hand and locked it around the man's throat. He squeezed and reeled the man toward him. Manuel was wiry and thin, and no match for *Impaler*'s captain. "I'm telling the truth," Manuel gasped.

"Right. The ships are going *north*. Do you still claim that? Do you not realize we have ships equipped with sonar too?" His teeth were bared and his arm flexed horribly.

Then in one sudden movement he spun the man around and stepped behind him. He kicked at the back of Manuel's knees, which buckled instantly. Heller held the man in place as he forced him backward precariously. "You've been spying for us, but you're working for McClusky, *aren't you*?"

Schrader sat frozen, riveted on the scene, perplexed and shocked at Heller's sudden display of force. The deputy mayor also seemed astonished.

Silence descended on the cabin as Heller forced the man backward. Gasping air was the only sound now. Manuel's forehead beaded with sweat as he struggled, but it was useless. Heller had his knee in the man's spine as he pulled Manuel backward. Creases traced across the captain's forehead, and his face had turned red. Either in rage or exertion, Schrader couldn't tell.

Manuel cried out—

And a tremendous crack echoed through the chamber.

Heller stepped away and shoved the man's limp body to the deck.

But Manuel wasn't dead. His eyes jerked about in confusion. He was probably realizing his spine had snapped, Schrader thought . . . that Heller had just broken his back with his bare hands.

Heller started to kick him in the face. Again and again the sound of wet thuds filled the cabin. And then he started to stomp on him. And through it all he yelled between gritted teeth, "You were trying to deceive me! You were spying for *him* and telling me that you were working for *us*!"

He yelled it over and over. Eventually he grabbed a shelf bolted to the bulkhead to provide balance as he slammed his right boot down on the man's forehead. Manuel was gurgling now. His words were mere gasps masked by blood bubbling out from his nose and from between shattered teeth.

Three more tremendous thuds pierced the cabin and Heller screamed something unintelligible.

He stepped back, breathing hard. Schrader stared at the man in shock. He had been so calm and calculating one second. And then—

And then—

Heller exhaled one long breath and struggled to gain control. It took only five seconds. His breathing returned to normal and his expression showed absolute serenity. Then he turned to the deputy mayor, who had pressed himself into a corner. Despite being a large man—easily 220 pounds—he was terrified. Heller said, "You see what happens when people disappoint me." He pointed at the mangled mess twisted on the deck at his feet. Air still escaped from its lungs, but slowly.

There was no air being inhaled anymore.

The captain continued. "He lied to me. He was trying to deceive me."

A pause. And then Butte said, "I will only tell you the truth."

Heller grinned. There was sweat trickling down the side of his face. He brushed it away absently. "Good. I want to know where those ships are going."

The deputy mayor swallowed but maintained eye contact with Heller. "I'll do my best, Captain."

"You better." He pointed down without looking. "This is not a fate you should want for yourself."

There was no response.

"I've also heard that there is a new recruit coming to Trieste."

Butte frowned. "People arrive every month to become Triestrians."

"Yes, but this one is coming for some other purpose. He is coming to help with this independence movement. Find out who he is and why he wants to help."

Butte nearly snorted but obviously thought better of it. He collected himself in time and said, "Do you have any other information to help? Age? A name?"

"No. That's your job." Then Heller turned to Schrader. "Dump this carcass out the moonpool." He punched the hatch control and stepped over the threshold, leaving bloody footsteps behind him. There was brain matter mixed in with the blood. "Clean this up," he barked as his steps rang into the distance.

Outside, Seaman Abernathy was standing guard. His face was a rigid mask, but it was clear that he had heard the commotion.

The hatch closed.

Another command echoed over the comm system, but neither Schrader nor Butte paid any attention. They looked at each other.

Neither could believe what had just happened.

"Good luck," Schrader whispered.

The pool of blood on the deck continued to spread outward.

TRIESTE CITY UNITED STATES CONTINENTAL SHELF

30 KILOMETERS WEST OF FLORIDA

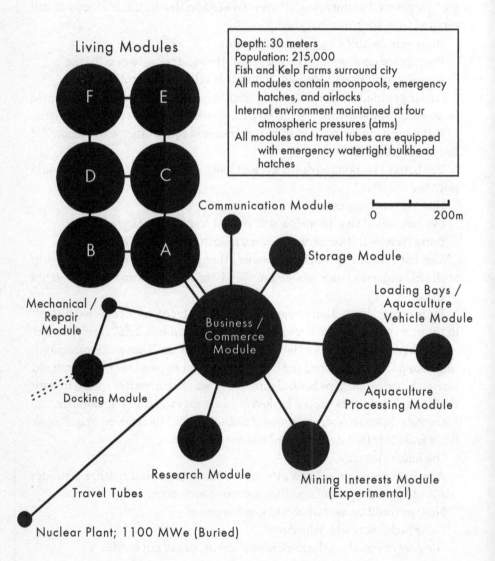

Living Modules

F   E

D   C

B   A

Depth: 30 meters
Population: 215,000
Fish and Kelp Farms surround city
All modules contain moonpools, emergency
    hatches, and airlocks
Internal environment maintained at four
    atmospheric pressures (atms)
All modules and travel tubes are equipped
    with emergency watertight bulkhead
    hatches

Communication Module

0   200m

Storage Module

Loading Bays /
Aquaculture
Vehicle Module

Mechanical /
Repair
Module

Business /
Commerce
Module

Docking Module

Aquaculture
Processing Module

Research Module

Mining Interests Module
(Experimental)

Travel Tubes

Nuclear Plant; 1100 MWe (Buried)

part one:
secrets

CHAPTER ONE

THE BODY WAS ON THE DECK at my feet. There were five of us surrounding it, staring down with shocked expressions. The smell rising from the corpse was nauseating and I noted hands drifting toward noses to block the odor. I'd dealt with plenty of death in the past—some of it at my own hands—but I hadn't dealt with rotting bodies before.

"It's unquestionably a murder," the person at my left said.

He was Cliff Sim, Chief Security Officer for City Security at Trieste. Generally speaking, the United States Submarine Fleet enforced their rules at our colony, and City Security took care of internal issues.

Like this one.

The corpse was male. But apart from that we couldn't really tell much. His face had been completely smashed and there were only pieces of skin left. Gray and tattered and rotting. I could see inside the skull in a few places and even some bright white bone was visible. The skull was empty.

The insides of his head had spilled out.

"Could a seacar's thruster have done this?" I asked. "Or perhaps a surface vessel?"

We lived thirty meters underwater, under a constant four atmospheres of pressure. We were always venturing outside in scuba gear or in seacars, and sometimes we even jumped into moonpools for recreation, venturing to other modules without air tanks, and so on. We couldn't swim to the surface, for we lived in a saturation environment. If we did . . .

Death by The Bends.

A horrible, excruciating way to die.

We were prisoners of these deeps. Prisoners in our modules and seacars. We loved the life and what we had accomplished so far, colonizing the continental shelves of the United States, but there were many hazards always nearby.

"No way," Grant Bell said. He worked at City Control with me. His voice was usually calm and confident. Now it wavered. "Those aren't slices on his face. Something's crushed his skull."

"Still. Screws aren't sharp. The edges are blunt." But I knew it was a stretch. A thruster would have cut the head clean off. I remembered returning to the city the day after The Second Battle of Trieste last year. Almost two thousand mangled bodies had drifted in the waters surrounding the city. Their final moments of life had left their faces twisted in the anguish of a crushing and watery death. Some had been missing limbs. Some had been dismembered.

Some had been pulverized beyond recognition.

As I'd powered the seacar *SC-1* into the Docking Module following our surrender, I'd had to thread between the bodies. Clotted blood had tinted the waters, and I'd known our screws were further chopping the corpses and drifting limbs and leaving a trail of chum behind.

It had been a tragic scene, but all those Triestrians had died for the dream of independence. A dream I was going to bring them.

Or end up just like them while fighting for it.

I'd hidden my revulsion at the time. I'd had to appear as the confident leader of Trieste.

For better or for worse, after that battle, I'd suddenly become the beacon of hope and freedom my father had been.

I pulled myself back to the present and considered what machinery we had around the city that could have done such a thing to the man at my feet. The kelp processing facility perhaps, where we prepared the plants for export. But no. It was definitely murder—I was just trying to come up with some other possible explanation.

I didn't want to believe it.

His legs and arms were twisted about haphazardly. A puddle of water was expanding around him, his clothes were in tatters, and wisps of brown hair protruded from the remaining bits of rotting scalp.

I turned to the two men who had brought him in. "Where was he?"

"Drifting near the Docking Module. Obscured and trapped in the grasses."

"What were you doing out there?"

"Working out."

Both men looked extremely fit. They wore scuba gear with masks pushed onto their foreheads. Their flippers were on the deck beside the moonpool. They had pulled the body up, hauled it over the edge of the pool into Living Module A, and then had immediately called City Control. Grant and I had been on shift and had come with Cliff from security.

I continued staring at the body. Murder at Trieste. But why? We were all working for the same goals—to expand our reach into the oceans while the climate catastrophe on the surface continued to grow.

There were over two hundred thousand souls in Trieste, and we worked without many luxuries. We were fishermen and farmers and laborers and engineers.

And politicians, such as myself, though I actually preferred the occupation *spy*.

"Thanks," I said to the two men. "Go continue the workout." I gestured at the corpse. "His family will thank you. I'll let them know what you've done."

"Thanks, Mac," they said in unison. They donned their masks and flippers and disappeared out the moonpool with a splash.

I stared at the body for a few more moments, thinking about the abrupt reality of this situation. This morning I had been dealing with the kelp farmers complaining about excessive tea exports topside. Now this.

I saw some movement inside its head. "What the hell?" I lowered myself and peered into the skull and—

"Fuck!" I yelled as I fell back. There was a crab scurrying within.

I stared in horror at the creature. It was feasting, and probably had been for a few days.

—••—

GRANT WAS STARING AT ME.

At Truman McClusky, former agent of Trieste City Intelligence and current mayor of the city. I hadn't especially wanted the job, but circumstances had forced it on me. We had lost the fight for independence the previous year—a battle Mayor Flint and TCI Director Shanks had initiated without consulting anyone else—and as a result, the USSF had killed thousands of Triestrians, occupied our undersea city, and now watched everything we did, closer than ever before.

"What do you think?" Grant asked me eventually.

I sighed, after taking a few moments to collect myself. "We need to find out who that is." I pointed at the corpse. "We need to know who killed him and how." *And I need to know why he seems so familiar to me*, I wanted to say.

I just hoped it wasn't who I thought it was.

That would be a disaster.

———••———

TWO HOURS LATER WE WERE IN the doctor's office in the central module. Cliff was still with me; I'd sent Grant back to City Control to continue his duties directing the considerable sea traffic around the city. Seacars, transports to and from the US, swimmers, cargo subs on approach or departure, and nearby USSF warsubs powered around our waters like fish. It was getting crowded out there, making Grant's job tougher and more stressful than ever.

The doctor was an older woman with white hair and a stern expression. She'd treated me before for injuries when I had worked as a laborer. She didn't have the best bedside manner, but she was skilled. Her name was Stacy Reynolds. She said, "The body's been outside for maybe two days. It's obvious something crushed his head. That's the cause of death. Internal organs are fine."

"What crushed it?" I asked.

"A boot." She stopped and cast a hard look at me. "With a foot in it."

Cliff grunted. I said nothing for a few long heartbeats. Then, "How can you tell?"

"The imprint here." She pointed at some skin around the ears and where the forehead should have been.

"Can you identify the boot?" Cliff asked.

The doctor sighed. "I'm not a forensic pathologist. We don't have one here, though I do have a student right now who did an internship back in Denver. He might be able to help. I can see a tread mark or two but can't tell the foot size."

"Is it USSF?" I asked in a curt voice.

She stared at me and hesitated.

———••———

I GAVE CLIFF INSTRUCTIONS TO BEGIN an investigation and to try and keep the USSF out of it.

"Sure, Boss," he said in a curt, businesslike tone. That's what he called me. I didn't mind. He used to be in the USSF, and I knew he liked the chain of command.

I then marched to City Control, on the uppermost level of the city's central module. It was the Commerce Module, the largest one at Trieste, and one of the nicest in all of the oceans. It rose four stories from the seafloor, and we'd dug down into the earth for five. Nine stories in total with a skylight for a roof that allowed the sun's light to penetrate right to the deepest level. A balcony surrounded the atrium in the center on each floor, circled by restaurants, bars, hotels, and offices. Vines and shrubs and even trees grew on the balconies, helping provide oxygen, and the shimmering light from the sun flickered over everything. It was daytime above.

The view from the surface was one that many of us hadn't seen in years, and some of us in fact had *never* seen.

There were more people born underwater now than ever before.

We felt this future might well be a success, as long as we could keep the USSF off our backs. They might have occupied us, hoping to squash the desire for freedom, but it was still there, perhaps even stronger than before.

It was a mostly silent desire, but I knew it was there.

When I arrived at City Control and entered my office, I called Kat and sat back, waiting. Muted voices from the control stations outside drifted in. Sea Traffic Control, Pressure Control, City Systems Control, Aquaculture and Mining Control . . . People were hard at work, making sure we continued the struggle and kept ourselves producing things needed by the countries of the world.

Triestrians generally didn't complain about hard work, I thought. We *liked* it.

It meant progress.

A minute later Katherine Wells entered the cabin and approached my steel desk. It was utilitarian, much like everything else in the colony. Our offices were sparse and our private spaces even more so. We were all working for the same goal, and we'd sacrificed materialistic things to achieve it.

I watched Kat as she entered. She and I had started a relationship just before The Battle—that's what everyone called it now—last year. She was an expert in undersea engineering and seacar design, and her desire for independence for the undersea cities of the world had taken hold of me too; her passion for sea life was one I found extremely attractive. She was African American, tall, fit, and had a lush voice. She could also fly off the handle when crossed, something I'd experienced more than once in our adventures so far.

Kat stopped and looked at me. Her eyes were soft. "Don't forget the meeting with Meagan this afternoon at 1600 hours. We have something to—What's wrong, Mac?"

"Rafe's dead," I said with blunt force. No cushioning the blow.

Her mouth fell open. "Say again?"

"Murdered."

I could see the thoughts racing through her mind. "The USSF?"

"Probably."

She sat in the chair before the desk. It was creaky and scraped the metal floor when she pulled herself closer. "They found out?"

"I'm guessing."

Rafe had been spying for me for the past few months. He had been telling me what *Impaler*—the USSF warsub that seemed to hover endlessly outside the city conducting war games—had been up to. He'd been training over there in his role as sonar operator at Trieste.

"I was stupid, I guess," I muttered.

"Why?"

"I suggested he give up some false information. Stuff to protect you and Meg. Obviously didn't work."

She looked away and considered that. "What did he say?"

"I have no idea."

"Why not?"

"I told him a few things to try. I'm not sure which he used." I sighed and stared at the ceiling. "I was stupid," I repeated. Rafe had been a good man. He'd come from El Salvador two years earlier to learn a trade and help the undersea efforts. He'd been an efficient sonar operator, and had been learning more every day.

And then this.

"You're sure it's him?"

"He was messed up. Took me a while to recognize him."

"You saw his face?"

"He didn't have one."

Kat paused. "What happened to him?"

"You don't want to know."

"But how do you know it was him?"

Because it was the worst thing that could happen to us, I wanted to say. I needed to operate Trieste City Intelligence in the shadows. Our struggle for independence had to be covert. No one could find out. The USSF was always watching. And if they uncovered it . . .

They would crush it.

As they had crushed Rafe's head and face.

I had to swallow the bile in my throat.

"What have I done?" I whispered.

Kat's voice turned to steel. "You've done what has to be done. We have to lead this fight from here. The people are expecting us to win this."

"We didn't win last year," I said.

"That was because you knew to back off so we could fight another day. And that day is coming."

I stared at her for a few minutes, at the set of her jaw and the fire in her eyes. She was right, of course. We had started on this path months earlier—I had to see it to the end.

It was just hard losing another man.

Especially in such a ruthless and cold way.

"Do you know who might have done it?" Kat asked me.

I exhaled and my body tensed. "I think so."

—••—

AN HOUR LATER I LEFT MY office and joined the command staff in City Control. It was a large circular room filled with screens displaying life in Trieste. Consoles arranged in concentric circles monitored everything about the environment and the enclosures in which we lived. Air pressure inside and water pressure outside. Temperature. Salinity. Power generation in our nuclear plant, buried to keep it safe after the USSF had destroyed the first one. The fish farm fences—walls of bubbles that effectively kept fish trapped—and kelp farm production. Sea Traffic Control was there too—showing all traffic in the Gulf and Caribbean as it was relayed to us and displayed on a large map—and the communications center responsible for coordinating messages within the city, with the mainland and nearby ships, as well as with mining operations in the deeper waters nearby.

I stopped and took it all in. It was hard to grasp even after all this time—the dangers and pressures of living here—but we all felt the optimism and excitement on a regular basis.

There were ten people there staring at me. No one said anything.

They had heard about the death.

People died underwater. It happened more frequently than we cared to admit, because every death gave others ammunition for the argument humans shouldn't live below the surface.

But people had died in the quest to colonize the solar system, and those endeavors continued.

It was the notion of *murder* that affected people so.

I watched their pale faces.

"He's been identified," Kristen Canvel, on duty in Systems Control, said into the silence.

I nodded and waited for her to confirm my suspicions.

"Rafe Manuel."

I glanced around. Just a few days earlier Rafe had been in that very room, performing regular work as a sonar operator. Jaden Kahn was at that station now, staring at me with wide eyes. I pursed my lips.

Kristen said, "There was no water in his lungs."

"So he died inside and someone dumped him outside?" Claude Lemont said with anger in his voice.

I cleared my throat. "Yes, that's right." I paused. "Cliff is on this. He'll find who did it. I promise."

And then I turned my back and stalked out.

—••—

I WANDERED AIMLESSLY AROUND THE ATRIUM and passed people going about their daily work. There were children on break from school, walking with their mothers and fathers and babysitters. There were restaurant workers and scuba repair people and farmers on their way to start their shifts outside where the slightest malfunction could kill in an instant. There were puddles everywhere, from swimmers just in from outside and strolling around in wetsuits, carrying dripping gear. Above was that remarkable view, the expansive skylight, thirty meters of water, and then the sun at its zenith.

I watched it all as I marched past, listening to people talk about their lives and work underwater.

By the time I passed through the Commerce Module, I had become used to the concept of Rafe's murder and the fact the USSF had likely done it as punishment for spying on them.

It was a part of this life. It was a harsh thought, but it was the truth.

The espionage business was a tough racket. I'd been a part of it for the bulk of my adult life. Since the CIA had killed my father to stop his quest for independence in 2099, I'd felt drawn toward *intelligence*. Through all the missions I'd been on for TCI, to Chinese and French and German undersea cities, I'd known it was a dangerous business, that people died.

Hell, while imprisoned in Sheng City, tortured for four months, *I* had expected to die and never see Trieste again.

I'd given in to the pain and suffering then. Had given up on everything for years afterward.

But that was part of the pressure of living underwater and fighting for your city. The four atmospheres was only a portion of it. The weight of thirty meters of water above our structures was another.

There were many other contributing factors as well—too many to count. And I, as mayor of Trieste and director of TCI, had to learn to deal with setbacks and just soldier on.

Quietly. Calmly.

With calculated plans.

I'd get revenge for Rafe, but I couldn't sacrifice the city for it.

It would just take some time.

I could be patient.

CHAPTER TWO

I SPENT THE NEXT FEW HOURS marching through the city, mulling the situation over, without really knowing where I was going or what I was doing. I exchanged pleasantries with most people who passed—they all knew me, after all—but didn't invest much thought into the words.

I was on autopilot.

The travel tubes connecting the modules were three meters high with curving bulkheads and conveyer belts in the center of the decks. The ceilings had long skylights to let light in. The blue waters above shimmered and children moved about as I passed, with necks craned to catch sight of a unique fish or perhaps even a shark. At night it was also a beautiful scene. The city's lights illuminated the nearby region, which attracted fish and species of all types.

Soon I found myself standing at a particularly large viewport on the west side of a living module. It was a communal gathering area for people to relax and recharge in between work shifts. There were some people there currently, and they watched me, curious. I nodded at them before turning to look at the waters we lived in.

We were under a constant four atmospheres of pressure for a number of reasons. Firstly, the increased pressure in the city kept the ocean pressure above at bay, so our structures didn't have to resist the tremendous weight of the water. It also allowed us to have moonpools in every module—open water where we could enter and exit the ocean easily without having to pass through airlocks.

If the pressure inside ever dropped, however . . .

I shuddered. It would mean an immediate series of alarms and emergency airtight hatches slamming shut, and City Control would initiate an evacuation procedure for all citizens in the affected module. The water would rise in the moonpool and begin to flood the module's corridors, cabins, and ladder wells.

Another reason for the higher pressure was that every sub, seacar, and living structure in the oceans also maintained four atms. Colonies and countries had standardized this around the world, otherwise moving from one vessel to another, or one vessel to a habitation structure, would be a nightmare of decompression and recompression. It would make living underwater even more dangerous and laborious than it already was. As it was now, leaving Trieste and going to the one-pressure atmosphere of the surface would require a hundred-plus hours of decompression time.

I stared into the ocean and watched a multitude of vessels and divers churning about, leaving trails of bubbles which rose slowly to the surface. It was a wondrous view I never tired of, but it was a reminder of a dangerous life. There was no escaping that. My history as a spy for Trieste City had been full of incidents where I'd had to kill to survive or I'd nearly died in the line of duty.

Behind me, a pair of gruff voices broke into my thoughts. I turned and had to suppress a curse. Two USSF sailors wearing their blue uniforms were pushing through people also looking out the viewport, leaving behind them a wake of angry citizens. I noticed some of them glance at me as if pleading for help, and I knew I couldn't let it pass.

"Hey," I called out. "Watch where you're going."

The two men stopped and turned, expressions hostile. "Why should we care about you?" They began to approach, their postures rigid.

"I'm the mayor," I said in a neutral tone. "And you better stop advancing toward me or we're going to have a problem."

They stuttered to a stop and glanced at each other. They clearly knew me by reputation, but I could see the thoughts churning through their minds. Around us people had grown silent; they were watching the situation intently.

"You think being mayor makes you above the law?"

"What law are you referring to? The one that says the USSF gets to rough up my citizens? I've never read any such law."

"No," the taller of the two growled. "The one that says the USSF has authority over this city."

I snorted. "Authority over our exports, commerce, and safety. Not stepping on people's civil rights."

I noticed his hand twitching toward the holster at his side. He was standing five meters away, but I could sense his anger. I could see it in his eyes.

Around me the people had grown impossibly still. I could barely hear the machinery and the ventilation of the city. This was escalating and I definitely didn't want it to go any further. I didn't want to hurt anyone, besides which, I wasn't even armed.

"You wouldn't shoot the mayor, would you?" I asked.

The shorter one was broader and more heavily muscled. He had a five o'clock shadow and a widow's peak. He paused for what seemed an eternity. "No," he finally said. "At least not with so many witnesses." He nudged his partner and the two pushed their way past the crowd, rougher than before.

I sighed, realizing I hadn't exactly solved anything. I'd just made the soldiers angrier.

But still, the people nearby flashed me smiles and there were even some chuckles.

Maybe I *was* a politician, after all.

I turned back to the port and my eyes immediately settled on USS *Impaler*. She was a couple of hundred meters away, not connected by umbilical. Just drifting there silently, a menacing sight. She was over 250 meters long and lined with torpedo tube hatches, bay doors for smaller subs and infantry, grapples, and mines. The dark hull seemed to absorb the sunlight, and was marred by a multitude of small geometric indentations to disrupt incoming sonar pulses and limit other vessels' range of detection.

I snorted as I watched it. There was a reason she was there, not the least of which was to scare us into submission.

My watch chimed; it was approaching 1600 hours. I spun on my heel and turned my back on the warsub as I marched away.

—••—

IN MY OFFICE IN CITY CONTROL, Kat and Meg were already waiting for me. With them was a third person: an older fidgety man with white hair, a beard, a stooped posture, and spindly fingers. His fingers were the first thing I noticed, actually. They were long and bony and reminded me of giant white spider legs. He had large ears and very pale skin. His eyes were darting about, taking in every detail of my bare office. I wondered why—there wasn't much to see.

I turned to Meg. She was my twin sister. She had fled Trieste at eighteen and ended up at the Australian city Blue Downs. She'd learned a trade there—repairing subs—and had become proficient at it. When I'd appeared at the city in the damaged and experimental sub *SC-1*, or *SCAV-1* as it was also known, Meg had led repairs and had come with me back home. Back to Trieste. When she had found out I had joined the fight for independence she'd been furious, but after I'd explained the situation, she'd signed up too. We had new technologies the superpowers didn't have yet, and we'd hoped that would give us the edge in the coming fight. She'd been at The Second Battle of Trieste last year.

And now she and Kat were my main allies in the fight for independence.

"Hi Meg," I said. She had blonde hair, a freckled face, a brilliant smile, and her knowledge of ocean vehicles and mastery of her trade was unmatched. I knew men found her extremely attractive, and it wasn't just because of her appearance. Her knowledge of ocean vehicles and the trade in which she worked only added to her allure. It was nice seeing her smile so much now, I thought absently. Back in her teens, while we had both lived in Trieste in the family modules, she'd almost never smiled. She'd been too angry, too torn up about Dad.

"Hiya, *Mr. Mayor*," she replied with a grin. She liked to tease me about my position. She knew why I'd taken it, and why the people of Trieste had elected me, but it didn't stop her from ribbing her brother now and then.

I glanced at the visitor. "And who is this?" I wondered if the meeting Kat had arranged with me was really about The Ridge. She'd said it was, but the facility was still secret. Surely this newcomer had no knowledge of it.

"This is Doctor Manesh Lazlow," Meg said. "He's here to help."

I studied him some more. He still hadn't taken notice of me or shown any indication that he realized people were speaking about him. I remained silent to see if he'd react.

A smile spread across Meg's face. She found Lazlow endearing.

Eventually the old man noticed we were waiting for him. He finally set his eyes on me. "Truman McClusky!"

"That's me," I said, frowning.

"Of course I recognize you!" His voice was vigorous and didn't exactly match his nervous and frail appearance.

"How's that?"

"Oh, I've studied the undersea colonization for my whole life. I'm eighty years old now! I have wanted nothing more than to be a part of this grand undersea adventure for as long as I can remember! I know who you are and also know a great deal about your dad."

I paused. "And now you're here." I shot a look at Kat as if to say, *What the hell?*

"Yes!" the old man said. "And I'm here to help you."

I began to grow uneasy. I wondered how much this man knew and what exactly Kat and Meagan had told him. "Uh—"

Kat immediately sensed my nerves. "Don't worry, Mac. Lazlow is here to help us at . . ." Her voice trailed off and I gestured at her not to say more.

I considered my next sentence carefully. "And how can he help our efforts here at Trieste?"

Lazlow chortled through dry, cracked lips. He was obviously still getting used to the underwater environment. It was a dramatic change from the surface and some people took longer to adapt than others. The pressure could get to some. The lack of consistent natural light to others. And the lack of comfort sometimes also drove visitors back topside. But Lazlow, despite his jittery mannerisms and lack of ability to focus on just one thing, seemed genuinely happy to be in Trieste. "I'm an acoustician!" he practically yelled.

"You are an expert in sound?" Meg had introduced the man as a doctor, and I'd assumed a medical field.

"Yes!"

My brow flattened. "We do spend a lot of time listening to the oceans around us."

That took him aback. "Well of course you do! It's how you detect vessels in the area and track their paths! It's how you identify subs and seacars. It's how you manage to translate messages sent from kilometers away through different densities and salinities. It's how you—"

"I understand all this," I said, cutting him off. "But why—"

"We recruited him," Kat said.

That stopped me. I hesitated and stared at Lazlow. He had a wide-eyed expression on his face now, one of simultaneous wonder and bemusement. Haltingly, I said, "You recruited him." I was just stalling now, wondering exactly what to say. The doctor seemed frail and was quite old, not really suited to our brand of work. "Look," I finally said. "I don't want to prejudge here, but this is a tough life. Existence is tenuous. And you are—"

A fire flared in the old man's eyes. It was sudden contrast to his earlier appearance. "I'm eighty and as I said, I've spent my *entire life* thinking about this! And thanks to these two here—" he snapped a gesture at the two ladies, so viciously that I thought his arm would break "—I've finally achieved my dream!"

I held my hands up. "Okay, okay, Doc. I understand. You have some knowledge that could help us out."

"It's more than that, Mac," Meagan said. "It's going to *really* help us out."

I mouthed, "Is it the noise bomb?" The two of them had been working on a stealth deterrent for ocean travel.

She shook her head.

I sighed. So, here was an acoustician to help us with . . . detecting ships from farther away? That could benefit us. But our immediate need was actually fortifying our defenses without the USSF finding out, developing more powerful subs, faster subs, vessels that could go deeper, and a way of countering the SCAV subs that the USSF was sure to unleash on the oceans soon. The SCAV subs could go in excess of 400 kph underwater, when the previous generation of high-speed vessels could only hit a maximum velocity of eighty. And Katherine Wells, my girlfriend, had been the one to finally invent a crewed vessel to break that barrier. The USSF had gained the technology from our subs after The Second Battle of Trieste, and were no doubt working feverishly to reverse engineer the secrets of the micro-fusion drive that flash boiled seawater to steam to propel the ships at remarkable speeds.

At that moment the hatch to my office opened and Deputy Mayor Robert Butte strode in. Big and imposing with a genial smile and a pleasant manner, he was the perfect politician. He could work his way around red tape and speak easily with the laborers who made Trieste a success. He was well-liked by almost everyone. He could tell a joke at a moment's notice and wine and dine the most powerful corporate leaders and politicians. He knew something about everything in the city and truly seemed to love Trieste. He often spoke about how he would never live anywhere else in the world. This city was his life and everything he did was for her people. I had chosen him shortly after my own election because of his love of the city and his easy ability to lead by example, among other reasons.

"Sorry to interrupt," he said. Then Butte's eyes settled on the old doctor, and he offered a broad smile. "Hello, I'm Robert."

Lazlow seemed caught off guard, but only for an instant. He held out his hand. "I'm Doctor Manesh Lazlow."

"Is someone sick?" Butte grinned. "Did your fondness for kelp vodka finally catch up to you, Mac?"

I watched the man silently for a minute before I shook myself out of it. I grimaced. "That's not something I care to try again. No, Lazlow is coming here to live. To help us."

The other's eyebrows lifted. I could tell what he was thinking: *At his age?*

"He's an expert in sonar," I said. I realized it would be better to tell as much of the truth as possible. The more you hid, the more likely you were to reveal something secret. "He's an acoustician. He'll be helping train our controllers."

Something suddenly occurred to me. "And since Rafe is gone . . ." I trailed off, leaving the obvious implication.

Something seemed to flash across his face, as if the mention of Rafe had hurt in some way. Perhaps they'd been closer than I'd thought. They'd worked together in City Control, after all. In fact, Butte had worked there during Mayor Flint's time as well. He'd been in the communications division. "Perfect," Butte finally said, smiling again. "Then you'll be in high demand here."

Lazlow smiled but didn't say more.

Kat and Meagan stared at each other uneasily.

—••—

"WE SHOULD HAVE LOCKED THE HATCH," Kat hissed later. Butte had left to take care of city business, and the four of us were alone once again.

"It's okay. Robert is fine. He doesn't know anything." I paused. "Hell, I don't even know anything, come to think about it. Why do we need an eighty year old acoustician?" I raised my hand to cut off Lazlow's splutter of protest. He was sitting in a chair before my desk, cleaning his glasses and staring around him at the bare walls again. "I'm not even sure he can handle this. A saturation environment can be demanding."

"Nonsense," he said. "I've been here for five hours now. And the seacar I took to get here was pressurized the second we boarded. That's an additional few hours. I'm fine."

"Still."

Kat said, "He's spent his life working on something, Mac. I don't want to say here—" her eyes shot to the hatch, and she lowered her voice "—but he will be a big help at The Ridge."

I pursed my lips. "You want to take him there."

"Yes."

I watched Lazlow, wondering if we'd just said too much. I pulled Kat aside and whispered, "How much does he know? You weren't supposed to—"

"Don't worry," she said. "He doesn't know where he's going to work. All he knows is that he wants to help out the colonization. And his ideas are . . . *brilliant*."

Meg was chatting with Lazlow and gesturing around as she described life in Trieste. Something told me Lazlow already knew everything she was telling him.

"How brilliant?" I asked.

Kat smirked. "Just wait."

"You're not going to tell me?"

"Nope."

"You just want to take him out there and put him to work."

"That's right."

I paused and considered it. "He might die. Our medical facilities aren't very good there."

"He's not *that* frail."

I stared at the skeleton of a man folded into the chair. "If you say so."

—••—

AN HOUR LATER THE SUN WAS setting and the ports had faded nearly to black. The lamps had come on outside and fish were scurrying around, chasing prey and darting away from seacar thrusters. Departing vessels were soon lost to sight, hidden by long strands of kelp swaying in the currents and the inability of light to travel very far under water.

Kelp grew a meter a day under the right conditions. We grew and harvested it, then shipped it out for methane production. We used to sell it to other countries, but now the USSF just took it for themselves.

I was in my cramped living compartment in Module B, one of the living areas for single people in the city. Despite the fact that Kat and I were dating, we weren't married, and therefore lived separately in similarly tight spaces. Families with children warranted more room. And sound proofing.

My bunk was a recessed coffin in the bulkhead. There was a small desk with a keyboard and screen across from it along with a low stool. A few shelves for clothes and one for personal items, and that was about it. All in all it was about four square meters. The bathrooms were communal in the single-person modules. It was rough, but I didn't mind. Knowing what we were accomplishing made up for the living conditions.

Besides, sex in the narrow bunk with Kat made things especially great.

Sometimes I thought my cabin could use some sound proofing too.

I smiled at that and abruptly a beep from my comm called to me. I answered it and a face appeared on the screen.

"Cliff," I said. "Any news?"

"Yes. And it's not good." The security man's forehead creased as he chose his next words. "Rafe was not in Trieste at the time of his death."

I frowned. "But the doctor said he died inside and then someone dumped his body outside."

"That's right. The last time he was seen in Trieste was two days ago, however. I've been looking through his computer files. He got a call and left the city."

My heart pounded. "Let me guess—"

"He was called to *Impaler*."

"By whom?" My words were ice.

"The logs don't say. It's from a generic address. Could have been anybody."

I said nothing for a long moment as the thoughts ground through my brain. *Impaler*. He'd been called there and two days later we'd found his body.

Cliff interjected. "There's more, Boss."

My brow creased. "Go on."

"A video. From the Docking Module. He boarded a small transport."

"Let's see it."

Cliff tapped a few keys on his end and my screen filled with an image of the bays and docks of the module in question. It was the size of a football field, with fifty berths for vessels of varying types. Warsubs were too big to dock there; they had to connect to Trieste via umbilical.

There were many people on the walkways surrounding the open water berths. Seacars descended and rose to the surface as I watched, and the screen suddenly zoomed in on a far corner where two USSF sailors stood next to a waiting transport. Sure enough, a group of men approached and boarded the small vessel, Rafe among them.

I cleared my throat as the reality of what I'd just witnessed sunk in. Cliff was back on the screen, watching me with narrowed eyes. "Did you just see that?" he asked quietly.

"I did indeed." I paused as the ramifications swirled through my head. Then, "Keep this to yourself. I'll deal with it from this point on."

He blinked. "You don't want me to—"

"No. He was killed on the warsub." It was a statement, not a question. And there was no way we could investigate it any further, for the USSF had too much power in Trieste.

But they weren't in charge of me.

"I do, however, have another job for you," I said.

He stared at me, grim, as I gave him the orders.

CHAPTER THREE

I'D PLANNED A VISIT TO THE other American undersea colonies, Seascape and Ballard, and had scheduled my departure for later that evening. I had one more thing to take care of before I left.

My bags were already on *SC-1* waiting for me, so I simply slid the partition on my compartment shut and walked down the narrow corridor to the ladder. It was 1800 hours, around dinner and the start of the third shift in the city, and the place was bustling with people coming and going either to work or out to the entertainment district in the Commerce Module. They nodded or spoke to me as I passed them, and I shot them all smiles with murmurs of good will and encouragement for the work that everyone was doing. Very rarely some would openly talk about independence, in which case I would quiet them with a finger to my lips. The people of Trieste were concerned about the USSF and the turn that the city had taken since we'd surrendered the year before. I had plans for them, but couldn't yet say. I simply gave them a knowing smile and a wink.

But if the USSF caught me doing it, even that could be enough to potentially arrest me.

I wondered if my people would rise up if Heller ever developed the balls to take me in.

I followed the masses to the Commerce Module. At that point many split off, either to other travel tubes and to waiting shift work—perhaps at the

Docking or the Agricultural Modules—or to the restaurants and bars in the atrium of the large central module. To try some kelp vodka, perhaps. The thought made me shudder once again.

At the lowest level in the atrium I found a bar not often frequented and settled silently into a secluded corner. The interior was dark and the ceiling low. Deep chairs surrounded circular tables. There were no decorations on the walls. The place had but one purpose: drinking after a tough shift. I ordered a beer—also made on site but significantly better than some of the other options—and waited.

—••—

FIFTEEN MINUTES LATER TWO PEOPLE ARRIVED and sat across from me. The first was a woman with dark spiky hair and hard eyes. Her name was Maple—decidedly unique for an underwater citizen. The second was a tall, lanky man with obvious muscle tone. He smiled at me, showing rows of bright teeth. He was Bruce Lavin.

I grinned at them. "Good to see you two."

"Good to be back," Maple said in a soft tone, looking around.

"It's safe here, don't worry."

"How do you know?"

"The owner is an old friend." This seemed to mollify them, and they nodded and settled deeper into their chairs. I was happy they were so concerned; they were agents of Trieste City Intelligence, after all. *Never be complacent*, I thought to myself. An operative was always on duty. Always looking out for trouble.

I only had seven such people working for me. When Shanks had been in charge, just before The Battle, there had been forty. The USSF had somehow found out about TCI and Shanks, and I had to limit our exposure, which meant I couldn't build the ranks back up. The slightest mistake could send everything spiraling downhill.

Two more drinks arrived for the newcomers, we clinked glasses, and shared another smile. I'd called them the day before, asking them to meet me. They knew what was coming.

Outside the pub, two USSF sailors stopped and began a conversation. I could see them through the window, but I knew it was dark enough inside that they would not be able to see us.

I watched them from the corner of my eye.

"What's the job?" Maple said through tight lips. She took very small sips of her drink.

"New technology. It's French."

They nodded.

"And you want it."

Bruce had spoken. It wasn't a question. I could see the gears in his mind working, wondering just how he was going to steal it. He could speak French, which would help.

"Yes." I gulped the last of my drink and ordered another with a raised finger. "It's called a syntactic foam. It's used in the hulls of subs. It allows them to go deeper."

"How'd you find out about it?"

"A year ago I came across a Chinese sub. I'd thought it was a standard *Jin* class vessel. A *Fast Attack*. The crush depth is . . ." I trailed off to see if he could finish it for me.

He said without hesitation, "Two thousand one hundred and fifty meters."

I smiled. "Good."

"And you were testing me there."

"Yes. And you passed." We clinked glasses again and I heard Maple curse at her partner under her breath. "Anyway," I continued, "the *Fast Attack* that tried to sink me descended to three thousand nine hundred meters."

The two swore softly.

"Yeah. It's a newer version. I found out shortly after that the CSF is replacing their current *Fast Attacks* with this one. They call it the *Mao* class."

"And the syntactic foam is the reason?"

"It's only foam during application. It hardens between the inner and outer hull, but it contains microscopic acrylic spheres which become an intermediate layer."

"And it resists water pressure better because it's made of tiny spheres, allowing their new *Fast Attack* subs to go much deeper." Bruce snorted and shook his head. "Seems so obvious, since the original deep water subs were spherical."

"The foam was actually developed in 1955," I said. "We use it too. But the spheres in the foam the Chinese have resist water pressure incredibly well."

Maple frowned. "You said to steal it from the French."

I leaned forward and lowered my voice. "The Chinese got this technology *from* the French. And I have a contact in the Chinese cities. He gave me the location of the French facility which manufactures this new foam. It's in the Indian Ocean near the Seychelles."

Maple sighed. "You make it sound simple, Mac."

Outside, the sailors were looking through the window, trying to make out the patrons. After a moment, they continued their conversation and started on their way past the establishment and out of sight.

I shrugged. "I know. I was in this business a long time ago too. I did this type of thing for years." I watched Maple in silence for a long couple of heartbeats. I knew what the end result would be, but I let her come to the decision by herself. This way she wouldn't feel forced to do something she didn't want to do.

But she loved Trieste and would do anything for the colony.

Same as Bruce.

Same as me.

A moment later she glanced at her partner and smiled. "What about it? Want to get some foam?"

A grin split his face too. "No doubt." And then he turned back to me. "What do you want it for?"

"I want to know why it works better than ours. Why their hulls can withstand more pressure than previously. I only need a small sample." Meg would be able to figure it out.

Hell, *SC-1* could take a lot of pressure, but did it through the sheer thickness of a titanium-alloy hull combined with an inner layer of our less capable syntactic foam. The Chinese and French, on the other hand, had successfully made their hulls thinner, lighter, *and* stronger. And with the SCAV drive . . . "We need every advantage over every other competitor in the seas. You know that. That's the deal, that's the business of TCI."

I leaned back. I wondered why the French had developed it and then willingly given it to the Chinese. It puzzled me, but a part of me realized that it may have been related to the Johnny Chang incident from last year.

Outside, the two USSF sailors returned and walked slowly past the window, going the other way this time. They glanced in, but didn't stop.

Inwardly, I swore at them. I wondered again why they were there. Were they just looking for a place to drink and cause more trouble in the city?

Or were they acting on orders?

We were actively engaged in a Second Cold War against the United States, China, and France, with the resources underwater being the stakes. Meanwhile the climate catastrophe of global warming was punishing the land nations of the world. I wanted to use TCI to not only make Trieste better, but also to start putting together a community of underwater cities to claim the oceans as our own.

To start the free nation of *Oceania*.

And to do that, we needed the best technology.

The best people.

And the best weapons in the oceans.

—••—

I SENT MAPLE AND BRUCE ON their way with the coordinates, without knowing exactly when they would return. That was also part of the game. They would call if they could, but often my agents couldn't check in for weeks at a time. Sometimes a call never came, and I had to assume my people were dead or captured. People had thought I was dead when Sheng City had captured me, and only a prisoner transfer brought me back to life.

I'd quit the business after that, but only for a short time. Now I was not only back, but I was in charge of TCI—as well as the independence movement.

And it didn't escape my notice that the two previous leaders of the independence movement had either died or disappeared.

I gulped the last of my beer in a cold and lonely silence.

—••—

I HAD TO TAKE A CALL from Captain Heller of *Impaler* before I could do anything else. My assistant informed me and I found a private comm tucked away in a corner where it was dark and Heller couldn't see precisely where I was.

"This is Mayor McClusky," I said in a flat voice.

"Why aren't you in your office?" He was staring at me with a hostile glare. Behind him, I could only see steel bulkheads and rivets.

"Working. That's my life. What do you want?"

"Your agricultural and mining quotas are too low. We need to send more topside."

My stomach dropped. "Dammit it, Heller. We're already producing—"

"Don't even think of refusing me, McClusky."

I stopped abruptly and stared at the man on the screen. He was wearing his round wire-frame glasses, his sleeves were rolled up showing powerful forearms, and his thick neck betrayed his musculature. I remembered dealing with him once on *SC-1*, powering home from Australia, when he had threatened to kill me unless I turned the seacar over to him. He'd fired on us then, and we had escaped only by the skin of our teeth. The incident had led to the Second Battle of Trieste and the USSF occupation, but I had been happy I hadn't given in to him then.

Ever since, however, he'd been hitting us with demands like this one.

"We need more workers." I sighed. "Increasing productivity—"

"You'll do it with the people you have. Heller out." He cut the transmission.
"Fuck."

—••—

AN HOUR LATER I MARCHED TO the Docking Module and threaded down
the multitude of docked vessels toward *SC-1*. Technically she belonged to
Kat, who had designed and supervised her construction, but she insisted I
use her every time I went out to sea. The SCAV drive was the fastest in the
oceans, and Kat had said it made her feel better I was piloting it. That I could
run in an emergency.

Her speed was why Heller had tried to take the seacar from us.

The Docking Module's ceiling was fifteen meters high and the cavernous
expanse was the size of a football stadium topside. Only instead of a playing
field, it was open water interlaced with docks and catwalks and berths for
seacars and subs. Sloshing water created a low drone of white noise that echoed
throughout the chamber. The docks were steel grating, so I could also see the
water below my feet as I marched to *SC-1*.

The vessel was moored by a rope at bow and stern. She was a beautiful
seacar, with two thruster pods attached to each stabilizer. There was a vertical
stabilizer as well; the control surfaces were similar to an airplane's. The
blunt bow contained the seacar's forward torpedo tube—complement eight
torpedoes—and could also generate the bubble that would extend around the
vessel and allow supercavitation to occur. The micro-reactor in the engine room
that flash boiled seawater to steam was the real reason *SC-1* could achieve such
high speeds. The exit port for the steam was at the rear of the main fuselage.

Seeing the seacar brought back mixed memories. The chase around the
northern oceans of North America, south through the Aleutians, and all the
way to Australia before the voyage to Central America and the pass-through
into the Gulf, where The Battle had taken place. We'd been through a lot
during that time. Almost died a hundred times, though Kat and I had still
managed to fall in love.

I cast the two lines off and climbed on top of the hull, lowered myself down
the short ladder, and closed the hatch above me.

And found Kat waiting in the living area.

—••—

"Were you going to leave without saying goodbye?" There was a smile on her face.

I couldn't help but chuckle. She could be sneaky when she wanted. "I was taking care of some business. I was going to call you."

She cocked her head. "What kind of business?"

"The TCI kind. The foam we were discussing."

She nodded. "Good. I hope we'll have it soon."

I shrugged. It was impossible to predict. "And what are you doing here?"

She put her arms around my neck and pulled me down for a long, wet kiss. Her tongue tickled my lips and danced around inside my mouth. "This," she said, breathless.

—··—

We fell to the small couch in the living area and her skintight jumpsuit rapidly ended up on the carpeted deck. She moaned softly in my ear as I caressed her breasts and nibbled her neck and ears. My tongue stroked across each nipple and then down to her abdomen. I was still fully dressed, but didn't care. I glanced up at her; her eyes were closed tightly and there was a sheen of perspiration across her breasts and neck. Her fingers were in my hair, gripping tightly and guiding my head.

My tongue touched her moist pussy and she instantly cried out.

I wondered if people on the docks above could hear what happened over the next thirty minutes.

But I didn't care.

—··—

Soon I departed the Docking Module moonpool, having left Kat behind on the docks to wave at me as I sunk below the surface and disappeared from view. The landing lights on the ocean floor led me safely away from the module, and within minutes I was out in the open water. The yoke was leather, easy to grip, and it felt good. In my left hand I controlled the lever for speed, in my right the ballast control. Foot pedals operated the vertical stabilizer and movement to port or starboard. The yoke controlled the ailerons much like an airplane. I had made the buoyancy neutral and piloted with the control surfaces. After five minutes I spun *SC-1* around until the entire illuminated city was in my view, and then I brought the ship to a stop.

Beautiful.

It was the only thing I could think as I looked at Trieste. The lights and the glow around each module. The bright blue floodlight identifying the top of the Commerce Module. The lamps of subs and seacars. The kelp farms swaying in currents. I could even see people in scuba gear out either working or swimming for recreation. The suffering on the surface had pushed us to the shelves, and Triestrians had worked hard for what we had. The scene before me was proof of it. I couldn't let it fall to the USSF.

There was a lot of weight on my shoulders. The stress of managing the city and leading her people. Of possibly sending my agents out to die. If that happened, their families would never even know what had happened to them, and I would have to deal with that as well.

———••———

MY FIRST STOP WAS BALLARD CITY, located roughly fifty kilometers off the coast of Louisiana. The Mississippi had been eroding arable farmland from the continent for centuries, if not millennia, and depositing fertile soil in the Gulf of Mexico. The undersea colony was located off the Mississippi Delta, and its primary functions were kelp and fish farming. I had an appointment with her mayor and it would only take a few hours to get there from Trieste. I could have activated the SCAV drive and been there within minutes, but I enjoyed piloting the oceans, and didn't mind the leisurely nighttime journey. I dealt with too much paperwork and deskwork now anyway. The business of mayor was far different from *Operative First Class*, which I'd been for so long.

Stapling pages had replaced hand-to-hand combat.

The thought made me shake my head.

Until a sudden *ping* hit *SC-1*.

———••———

I WAS WELL AWAY FROM TRIESTE now, so there would be no help from there. I checked my sonar and located a variety of ships in and on the ocean in a thirty kilometer radius. There were hundreds of vessels. The scope identified the sender of the active pulse, however, and my heart caught in my throat at the label that hovered over the red symbol.

It was a French warsub.

The computer compared the sounds with its vast database and displayed the name *Chasseur*, of the French Submarine Fleet.

Hunter.

It wasn't odd that a FSF warsub was out here. They had a right to patrol or voyage through any ocean they wanted. But they'd sent the ping for a reason.

It was located only twenty-three kilometers away, one of just a number of vessels out in the dark sea. But the *Liberty* class vessel, with three high speed thrusters, was heading directly for me, at a speed of seventy-six kph.

—••—

SHE HAD FIVE TUBES AS WELL as mines, and a very high top speed, which she was currently running at. My hand flicked over the SCAV drive, and I wondered if I should just do what Kat wanted me to do in situations like this.

Turn on the drive and run.

But I could wait a bit longer. Find out what they were doing. What they wanted with me.

My thoughts drifted to the two operatives I'd just sent out to a French base in the Indian Ocean. *Go steal me some secrets,* I'd told them. And now here was a French sub, churning toward me at high speed.

My sonar signaled a sudden noise nearby, and then—

An explosion off my starboard bow lit the ocean and something odd happened. It hadn't been a large blast—minor by torpedo and mine standards— but it had been *bright.* I'd squinted against the sudden onslaught.

But then along with the turbulence and tossing and shaking came an abrupt and instantaneous *silence.*

Silence in a vessel or undersea facility meant danger.

There were no ventilation fans running anymore. No ballast pumps adjusting the trim of the vessel, keeping it level. No thruster noise, no generators.

Nothing.

I stared at the dark console in shock.

SC-1 was dead.

CHAPTER FOUR

I PUSHED BUTTONS THAT SHOULD HAVE activated thrusters and lights. I tried to send my own active sonar pulse. Dead silence. It was so quiet I could almost hear the blood rushing in my ears. In frustration I pushed the throttle lever forward and immediately slammed it into reverse to see if I could trigger something in the engines—

But no.

I sat back and exhaled. I had to just accept it.

Still, I'd never experienced anything like it. Even the emergency lighting was out, and that was a separate, battery-powered isolated system! The main computer didn't control it. Nothing could explain this situation. Nothing could—

And then I swore.

There was an explanation, but I had never considered the possibility underwater before.

An EMP.

Electromagnetic Pulse.

Something feared on land because it could catastrophically eliminate any technology in one swift stroke. They weren't used underwater as far as I knew.

The printed circuits on circuit boards were so close to each other—they had to be, in our world of miniaturization—that a strong pulse of EM radiation, such as what a nuclear bomb emits at point of explosion, would fuse the circuits together and effectively short circuit anything with a CPU or motherboard.

I closed my eyes and replayed the events in my mind.

A flash of light followed by a surge of turbulence. I'd been near torpedoes before—*extremely* close to their blasts—and this one hadn't been that large. But it had been *bright*.

I pursed my lips. I didn't think *SC-1* had a defense against such a weapon. If I made it out of this, I'd have to mention it to Kat and Meg, and get our engineers working on shielding our subs against EMPs like the military did with planes and other important installations on the surface. In a nuclear war, military strategists had theorized that EMPs would be precursor to an incoming wave of missiles. And since the pulse would have wiped out any defensive computer systems . . .

It would leave the targeted nation defenseless.

A French *Liberty* class warsub had pinged me from twenty-three kilometers away. About a minute later, there had been a close explosion. There had been no other objects near me at the time, and certainly no fast-moving torpedoes. Such a weapon would have cut through the water with a loud whine and been impossible to miss. And it definitely couldn't have come from the warsub. They had only identified me a minute earlier. It had been too far away. And, as far as I was aware, there was no such thing as a stealth torpedo.

But it must have come from a nearby vessel.

Could there have been a stealth ship nearby?

No. Impossible. They had to have known where I was going to be before *Hunter* had pinged me.

It was possible someone had told them when I was leaving Trieste and where I was headed. My departure hadn't been a secret. But I still didn't think a sub could have crept up on me or followed me without me noticing.

I looked up through the canopy. The moon was there, sparkling on the surface. Who could have—

Damn.

That was it. A plane or helicopter or jumpship of some sort.

When *Hunter* had pinged me, they must have immediately signaled their partners overhead. A minute later, a missile had detonated in the water right next to me. It was the only thing that made sense.

I swore. It explained the noise right before the detonation. It had been a splash.

My heart thudded.

Which meant they could still be directly above.

I performed a quick calculation in my head. *Hunter* was traveling at seventy-six kph, which gave an ETA of eighteen minutes to my current position.

They would be here soon, and I had to be prepared. *SC-1* was dead in the water.

— •• —

I WAS DRIFTING NOW, JUST OFF the bottom. At the mercy of the currents, powerless and unable to do anything. I couldn't fire a torpedo or even send out a Mayday.

Something caught my eye at the surface. Splashes in the water that didn't quite match the dancing moon beams cutting through the waves.

"Oh, shit."

Six figures in scuba gear arrowed toward the bottom.

Toward *SC-1*.

I knew why the French were upset with me.

And I was finally going to have to deal with the ramifications.

I rose from my seat and my muscles tensed. I hadn't fought anyone in months, but I was prepared. I was always prepared, after my life as a TCI operative. I had trained for combat both inside as well as outside our facilities. It came easy to me now.

The problem was, those six swimmers who were coming straight for *SC-1* were probably also highly trained.

— •• —

IT TOOK ME ONLY THIRTY SECONDS to throw on a tank, mask, and flippers. Life in the oceans meant we had to be able to suit up fast in emergency situations, or die.

I didn't worry about a wetsuit; I knew I could put one on later if I survived this. But I did take the time to grab three items. The first was a weighted belt so I didn't float to the surface and become a victim of The Bends. The other two were a holster with knife for my left thigh, and a holster with needle gun for my right. The two Velcroed on quickly, and I turned to the moonpool. The hatch was hydraulic but the electronic buttons would not work. I had to turn the levers on the pipes to activate it. The water sloshed in slightly as the hatch retracted, indicating that the outer pressure closely matched the vehicle pressure of four atmospheres. One of the reasons why I usually piloted at a depth of thirty meters, actually: you could always exit quickly in an emergency through the moonpool.

And this was definitely an emergency.

I looked at the ocean floor just a few meters under the ship and hoped to hell the divers were not yet close enough to see me exit the seacar. Grabbing the regulator and shoving it into my mouth, I tested with a quick breath, and jumped in.

Abandoning *SC-1*.

—••—

I SANK QUICKLY TO THE SANDY bottom and looked above me. The seacar was directly overhead and obscured the view of the surface. The moonpool looked like a rectangular mirror. I wanted to keep it in sight, so I picked a direction and, hugging the bottom, swam swiftly away. It was dark, luckily, and I hoped I blended in with the shadows. There were some sea grasses growing nearby, and I picked a clump to hide behind. Spinning around so the moonpool and the bottom of the seacar were still in view, I waited.

—••—

IT DIDN'T TAKE LONG. TWENTY SECONDS later the figures appeared. Two at the bow, swimming over the canopy and peering in to see if I was in the control cabin. *No luck there*, I thought with a sense of grim satisfaction.

Two at the stern, moving slowly and searching the area around them.

And one from each side of the fuselage.

They had approached the seacar perfectly. These were highly trained and coordinated soldiers.

My mouth went dry.

Within another few seconds four of the men had disappeared through the moonpool and up into *SC-1*. The other two descended to the seafloor, directly under the vessel, and watched for trouble.

Sentries.

I only had a few seconds to act. The ship was the size of a topside recreational vehicle. The four divers would only have to search the control cabin, living spaces, bunks, the airlock, lavatory, and engine room before they realized I was not there. Then they'd start searching outside.

And, of course, time was still ticking.

The French warsub was on its way.

I unholstered the needle gun and took aim at one of the divers. He was sideways relative to me, parallel to the seafloor, presenting a much larger target.

The gun had a square barrel. The rounds were like stainless steel spaghetti noodles. Each shot held five needles. They would pierce the water like miniature missiles and impact the target simultaneously.

And if I hit the guy in the chest, he wouldn't live much longer than a few minutes.

They would cut through arteries and organs like knives through tissue paper, causing instantaneous sucking chest injuries, feared on land but even more fatal under water.

The lungs would bring in water through the chest wound with each breath the guy took.

I fired.

—••—

THE NEEDLES WERE SO FAST AND it was so dark outside despite the moon above that they were impossible to see. But I knew I'd made the target. One second the guy was floating calmly a foot above the bottom, and the next his back had arched violently, his arms out in obvious agony. A stream of bubbles erupted from his facemask and he clutched at his chest.

A cloud of red surrounded him.

I'd hit an artery with that shot too.

His partner instantly spun around and pressed himself to the sand. He'd heard the commotion; the divers had full facemasks so they could speak with one another. As his partner writhed in final death throes two meters from him, simultaneously drowning and bleeding out, he searched the area around the seacar.

He also clutched a pistol in his hand, but I had the advantage here. He didn't yet know where I was. I took aim, held in my breath, and fired.

Snap!

The shower of needles hit him right in the facemask, punching through the glass and piercing his eyes and face. He shuddered and convulsed in uncontrollable spasm—a seizure caused by sudden brain trauma. The way he'd been orientated—floating parallel to the bottom and facing in my direction— meant that the five needles had penetrated deep into his brain and probably even stabbed into the top of the spinal column.

Not even waiting for the convulsions to end, I kicked my feet furiously and shot toward the seacar. I wasn't going to let them get the upper hand here.

Catch them by surprise, I thought.

Be the aggressor.

And as I'd learned working for TCI: kill or be killed.

—••—

I PRACTICALLY EXPLODED UPWARD THROUGH THE moonpool and pulled myself up onto the deck. There was light in there now from a portable unit the divers must have brought with them. In the living area a man in a black wetsuit was peering past a curtain into one of the recessed bunks. I fired another round of needles—not quite as effective or accurate in the air, but they could still do some damage, especially when they hit someone in the neck, as mine had just done. He pushed himself away but was too late. He gurgled and clutched at his throat as he writhed on the deck, blood spurting.

I pulled my flippers off, pushed the mask onto my forehead, and peered around for the other three men. Two were in the control cabin at the front; the last was most likely in engineering.

A noise came from behind and I spun quickly. The man was big and he managed to knock the gun from my grasp and into the moonpool. But he was too close to me and, as he brought his own gun to bear, I blocked it easily with my left hand and hit him with a right cross.

It was a ridiculous situation—I still had my tank on my back and my mask on my forehead, and was engaged in a hand to hand fight inside the seacar!

I had quit TCI for seven years after my release from the Chinese prison and months of torture. During that time I'd worked at Trieste in a laborer's job, and it had toughened and strengthened me more than I'd thought possible. That strength came in handy now as we exchanged a furious series of blows. He clenched his teeth and his eyes flashed in rage as I blocked one strike after another, and landed elbow after elbow to his jaw and both temples. A dazed expression filled his eyes, they rolled up into his head showing only white, and he fell to his knees and then forward into the water.

A series of ringing footsteps came from behind me, and it was obvious the last two in the control cabin had heard the commotion and were sprinting toward me.

I spun toward them and they pulled to a stop.

"What do you want?" I snarled. I slipped the tank from my shoulders and dropped it behind me with a clang.

"You've just killed French nationals," the man said in a very familiar accent.

I snorted. "You've disabled an American vessel off the coast of the States. Why?"

"Not American. *Triestrian.*"

"Why?" I repeated with ice in my voice.

"We're here for McClusky."

"What for?"

"For crimes against France."

So I'd been correct. Somehow they'd known I was the one responsible. Still, there was no way I could admit it. Not and still lead Trieste to freedom in a war against the world's superpowers.

I exhaled. "That's absurd. Why not contact me through diplomatic channels? I'm the mayor of the colony for fuck's sake." I gestured at the two bodies. "Look what's happened." As I said it I reached down and grabbed the knife at my side. I kept it hidden by slightly twisting my body as I pointed at the corpses.

"This isn't going through diplomatic channels."

I squared my shoulders and stared at them. The one who was speaking was the same size as me. The other was slightly smaller. I knew I could do this.

I'd done it before.

I moved to the side and put the moonpool between myself and the two men. They raised weapons and took aim.

Then I threw the knife and ducked at the same time. It sounded like an impact with wet meat. I dove to the deck and rolled to the gun lying where the second assailant had dropped it.

Shots hissed out, bullets propelled by compressed air—

And a second later it was all over.

There were three bodies on the deck, one face down in the moonpool, and two on the seafloor in a cloud of red.

I swore.

—••—

THERE WAS STILL GREAT DANGER. THE approaching warsub. Slightly more than ten minutes had passed, which meant I might have eight remaining, but I knew I'd have to get moving before then and hopefully hide on the bottom somewhere. The question was, how would I do such a thing with no power?

But it had occurred to me that I *did* have power. It was computer control that was out. The batteries still had a charge. The screws could still turn. The flaps and control surfaces could still move. But I would have to do it manually now, and hope I could limp the rest of the way to Ballard.

If I could escape *Hunter*.

Strapping my equipment back on and leaving the bodies where they were,

I dove into the water and swam to the port side thruster. One would have to do for now; I simply didn't have time to wire both before the enemy vessel arrived on the scene.

The thruster pods contained banks of batteries to add additional power to the thrusters. Despite the blunt nose of the seacar, she could still hit a speed of seventy kph and it was due to her large numbers of batteries. I would have to stretch a wire from them to the thruster and manually connect it. Once done, the screw would turn. An EMP couldn't stop a machine that did not have a computer.

The problem was, once the screw started, I'd be *outside* the ship. I'd have to get back in somehow or be left behind.

The access panel opened quickly—I had become more proficient at repairing *SC-1* than I had been during the chase for Johnny Chang, that much was certain—and I grabbed a bundle of wires that led from the batteries in the thruster pod. I opened a second access panel, exposing the thruster's motor assembly, and quickly connected the leads to the motor. I had effectively bypassed the computers in the control cabin where the circuits were hopelessly fused.

An instant later, the thruster started turning.

"Oh, *shit!*" I blurted into my facemask.

The seacar started churning away from me.

I desperately reached out and grabbed the edge of the housing that surrounded the screw. It was slicing the water only a foot from my face, and the turbulence nearly tossed me off the sub. If that happened, I would disappear into the dark depths and drown after depleting my tank's air, for I could not go to the surface.

I clung to the thruster housing, feet dangling behind me as the seacar powered away from the scene, three dead French divers tossing about madly in the wake, and I wondered how the hell I was going to get back into *SC-1*.

CHAPTER FIVE

ELEVEN MONTHS EARLIER, A CHINESE OPERATIVE of Sheng City Intelligence named Johnny Chang had infiltrated Trieste and stolen Kat's design for the SCAV drive. George Shanks had pulled me back into TCI to track down and retrieve the invention. Because of my tortured past with Johnny Chang, I had decided to not only catch him, but kill him.

But that hadn't happened. Eventually he and I had realized that the best course of action would be to work together. To use the SCAV drive to begin a new quest for independence for the cities of the seas. The technology represented an incredible leap forward in ocean travel and warfare. It was a paradigm shift in aquanautic engineering.

During the chase, however, I had killed French citizens. Johnny had been trying to sell the technology to a French government contingent. I had interrupted the sale, destroyed the French seacar *Patriote*, and then fired on a French warsub.

And now here I was, trying once again to escape from the French, who wanted revenge for those I had killed. *SC-1* was cruising aimlessly in a large circular course because only one thruster was operating, I was clinging to the screw cowling for dear life, and there was a French warsub only minutes away.

They were probably watching the events right now on sonar, wondering exactly what the hell I was doing.

—••—

I HAD BOTH HANDS ON THE housing surrounding the port thruster screw, which was churning the water only a few feet from my face. The tension in my hands was mounting; I couldn't hang on much longer.

Pulling with every ounce of energy I had, I hauled myself up and placed my feet on the cowling. Then I straightened and grabbed the edge of the stabilizer. The turning screw was a blur right next to me.

I remembered the scene after The Battle, as I'd piloted between all the bodies. I hadn't been able to avoid them all. I'd mangled some of them, I was sure of it.

Perhaps this was karma.

What had I expected, anyway? The thruster to start up nice and slow and give me time to get back to the moonpool? *There's no computer control now, idiot!* I scolded myself. Once I'd made the electrical connection, the thruster had engaged at whatever power the batteries could provide.

The batteries.

That gave me an idea.

The cable between the thruster and the battery was flapping against the thruster pod. I had connected it straight to the leads in the engine. If I could just reach it . . .

I stretched as far as I could. It was a meter from my grasp, and I was fully extended, "standing" on the screw housing, only inches from certain death. The housing was only a couple of millimeters thick, and it was cutting painfully into the flesh on the bottoms of my feet.

It was still too far.

I groaned.

That warsub was only minutes away. *Move dammit!*

Grabbing the stabilizer attaching the pod to the fuselage, I pushed off and scrabbled with every ounce of remaining strength for the cable. There was nothing to hold on to, however, and I started moving back toward the spinning screw—

But I'd grabbed the power cable, and ripped it toward me.

Disconnecting it from the batteries.

The screw stopped and *SC-1* drifted to a slow stop.

I had to take several deep breaths. *Combat breathing. Collect yourself, Mac.*

But despite my exhaustion, I couldn't help but feel grim satisfaction. It had worked. But I had to get the vessel going again. Only this time, I would rig up a rope that belayed me to the hull near the moonpool. Then I could restart the screw.

My heart was practically bursting through my chest.

—••—

LESS THAN TWO MINUTES LATER I'D done it. The screw was going again, and I stood in *SC-1* dripping and exhausted. I could barely stand.

A ping echoed in the sub and it startled me. They were nearby, and they knew where I was.

The ballast tanks on *SC-1* were computer controlled, but as with older generations of subs, there were also banks of valves and gauges to control the tanks in case of emergency. I could trim the tanks—or level the seacar—and blow the tanks or take on water by turning the proper valves. They were located at the aft end of the living area, and I ripped open the panel and began turning them, taking on ballast.

SC-1 grew negatively buoyant, heavier than the water it displaced, and descended.

Running back to the moonpool, I watched the bottom to see how close we were to the seafloor.

But as we fell, the water in the moonpool began to rise.

Damn!

The pressure outside was increasing. *SC-1*'s living area was flooding.

There were other valves to control the air pressure in the sub, and I hurriedly turned them to blow some air into the living compartment.

The water was now lapping up the deck and touching the carpet near the couches where earlier Kat and I had made love—

I had to shake my head to pull myself back to the current emergency.

The air screamed into the cabin.

The water in the moonpool lowered.

I exhaled. I also had to pop my ears.

The moonpool hatch had to be closed now. The hydraulic valves allowed it to shut, and then I readjusted the air pressure to bring it down to four atmospheres.

Another ping.

Shit!

I couldn't tell how deep we were now, with the moonpool hatch closed. I had to just guess.

I kept us negatively buoyant for another thirty seconds, then switched to neutral.

The course was another issue. The warsub knew my direction and speed. I needed to change it—but without navigation control.

I knew what I had to do.

I sprinted through the hatch into engineering, bringing the portable light with me, and located the hydraulic pipes on the bulkhead for the seacar's control surfaces.

A few pulls on some levers, and I managed to reverse my course, putting us into a port turn.

I would give myself five minutes of this, then change course again.

Then I would cut power—somehow—and bottom the boat.

And hope the French couldn't find me against the topography of the ocean floor.

—••—

THE ONLY WAY TO CUT POWER was to pull the cable from the batteries. I had left the rope to the stabilizer in place earlier, and I had to once again venture out to the thruster pod. But I first had to equalize pressure with the outside once more, and then open the moonpool hatch.

Water sloshed in again, though this time it was because we were under power. Usually moonpools were only used during station-keeping, otherwise it would result in a flooded compartment and shorted circuits.

The thought made me laugh inwardly. *Shorted circuits.* The seacar's computers were currently fused beyond repair anyway.

Water rushed in, reaching the rear bulkhead in the living area. I'd closed the hatch to engineering to protect it, and so there wasn't a catastrophe.

Yet.

Increasing air pressure pushed some of the water out, but not much.

I grabbed the tank, strapped it on, and with a tight hold on the rope, jumped back outside.

—••—

MY FEET DANGLED BEHIND ME PRECARIOUSLY. I pulled myself hand over hand until I was back at the thruster pod. The sea was dark, and it was hard to see anything. Usually there were running lights on *SC-1*, but even those were out.

My hands were starting to lose their grip. My body was trembling and my throat was as dry as sandpaper. This was pushing me to my limits. I knew I was almost there though.

Hand over hand.

One inch at a time.

Finally I brushed against the power cable, grabbed with my right hand, and gave it a savage jerk.

SC-1 slowly drifted to a halt.

I swam with everything I had, entered through the moonpool, increased the pressure in the seacar once more, then sprinted to the ballast auxiliary controls to take on ballast.

And sank.

SC-1 hit bottom a few seconds later and I held my breath.

Without the landing skids extended, I had now become part of the seafloor.

—••—

THE MOONPOOL WAS STILL OPEN. THE ocean bottom now filled the opening, and it was wet and green, which made me frown, but only for an instant.

It was kelp.

I had stopped over a kelp field.

Despite my exhaustion and trembling muscles, I grinned.

The stuff was probably all around me, obscuring the shape of the seacar.

A stroke of absolute luck.

I breathed a big sigh of relief and fell to the couch, still soaking but too exhausted to think about dressing, with the open moonpool only five meters behind me, and closed my eyes.

—••—

OVER THE NEXT FEW HOURS THERE were a series of pings. Once I even heard a ship's screws nearby. They had passed very close, perhaps even right over me. But the kelp was my savior.

As I lay there on the couch with my eyes half closed and my hand on a gun, just waiting for someone to pop up through the moonpool, I wondered if I had it in me to navigate this tenuous situation. My informant, Rafe Manuel, killed by someone on board *Impaler*. Doctor Manesh Lazlow, recruited to Trieste for some mysterious reason and soon to depart for The Ridge with Meg and Kat.

And to top it all off, the French were after me once again. They weren't really trying to hide it either. I wasn't sure how they'd figured out I had been the one to kill their people during the meeting with former traitor Johnny Chang, but that had to be the reason they were after me.

Eventually I rose from the couch and sat in the dark on the lip of the moonpool, dangling my feet into the water. It was chilly and helped wake me up. Small fish swarmed my toes and nibbled my skin. The kelp brushed against me, swirling in the currents, and small waves sloshed against the edge of *SC-1*'s hull. It was beautiful. Life underwater was beautiful. Every Triestrian, everyone who lived underwater, thought so, especially with the chaos topside.

There were riots. People in the streets throwing stones, bottles, garbage. Cities flooded and abandoned and left to rot in the swamps. Famine. Disease. Wars.

We just wanted to escape that chaos, to struggle for ourselves, not for governments who treated us like refuse. Triestrians were Americans, but still the USSF treated us like second class citizens. They always had, and it had never made sense. We had been working to help their families topside, to help the American economy, not to undermine it. That treatment had pushed us ever closer to independence and me toward my father's path.

I'd have to be smarter than he was if I wanted to win the fight without causing Trieste more hardship, and I would have to keep the USSF from discovering my plans.

But first, I would have to survive the FSF.

INTERLUDE:
THE ACOUSTICIAN
ENIGMA

Location:	The Gulf of Mexico
Latitude:	27° 34' 29" N
Longitude:	54° 56' 11" W
Depth:	25 meters
Vessel:	USS *Impaler*
Time:	1300 hours

"YOU HAVE TO STOP BRINGING ME here," Robert Butte snapped at Captain Heller.

First Officer Schrader studied Butte in silence. The three of them were once again in the captain's small office, and it was clear that the deputy mayor was upset.

The office was cold and uncomfortable. There wasn't much space, and there were no friendly faces.

"A message over the comm system is dangerous enough," Butte continued, "but telling me to go to the Docking Module is stupid. They have video surveillance there, you know."

Heller's face turned to steel at the word *stupid*. "Your safety is *your* business. Disguise yourself. Take appropriate measures. It's not my concern."

"If I get caught, it should damn well concern all of us here!"

Heller shrugged. He didn't care.

Schrader shifted in his chair and watched the two men. Butte was obviously in distress, but it occurred to the XO that it might be because he was terrified after what had happened to Rafe Manuel in that very cabin.

Butte's arms were on the table with his fists clenched. His posture spoke volumes. Schrader leaned back and watched; he didn't want to inflame the situation.

"They found the body," Butte said. "They're on edge about it."

The captain made a dismissive gesture. "It doesn't matter."

Butte looked like he was about to explode. "I'm on the front line, dammit! I'm—"

"Shut up."

Silence descended on the cabin like a shroud.

Schrader felt Butte's frozen expression of anger would make a good death mask. The captain merely stared at the Triestrian without a trace of emotion. He was cold, heartless.

The tension between the two men crackled.

Schrader finally felt the need to talk, to defuse the situation. They needed Butte's help, after all. Not his fear and resentment. "Maybe I can offer something."

Both men tore their eyes from each other and turned their collective glares on the XO. It made Schrader uneasy, and he swallowed. But still he forged on. "What if, next time we need you, you go out a moonpool in your gear. You can hitch a ride on a personal scooter, which we'll leave outside your module, or we can have a transport there. You can board through an airlock or grab a handhold. *Impaler* is close enough to the city." He stopped and both men continued to stare at him. "It'll be a more secretive way to get you here." He shrugged, as if the solution was simple.

Butte shot a look at Heller and then back to Schrader. Then he nodded. "It's better than what we're doing now. I'm game."

Heller snorted. "I don't really care. You can figure it out, as I said."

Schrader said to Butte, "I'll take care of it next time."

"Good." The deputy mayor seemed to relax slightly, and his eyes softened.

"What information do you have?" Heller asked, all business. "Do you know where McClusky is sending his subs?"

"No. I don't know anything about that yet."

Heller scowled. "Then what the hell—"

"You asked me about a newcomer to Trieste. I think he's arrived. It's a bit of a mystery, frankly."

Heller hesitated for a heartbeat. Butte's words had caught him off guard. Then he spoke, and his voice was like gravel. "Go on."

Butte sighed and shot another glance at Schrader, as if seeking a friend for support. Then, "He's an old man. An academic, a professor."

"What field?"

"He's an acoustician. He's eighty years old."

"Name?" Heller was all business.

"Doctor Manesh Lazlow."

Heller looked away for a moment. Schrader also considered this. An acoustician. It was a necessary field in the undersea colonies, but the importance of this man was still unclear. "It might not be him," the XO said.

"True," Heller replied. "But it does seem odd. The deputy mayor here is correct. Why recruit such an old man?" Another long pause. And then, "Did McClusky say why he was there?"

"He implied it was as a replacement for Rafe Manuel."

"I see."

It made a little bit of sense to Schrader, at least. But still, the old man had been recruited long before Heller had murdered Rafe.

"I'll have someone look into his background," Heller growled. "And you," he said to Butte, "will continue to learn about him. What he's really doing there. Keep your eyes out for anyone else as well, in case this isn't the person we were waiting for." He appeared to mull something over for a minute, and then, "Do you have anything else for us?"

"Maybe." Butte hesitated.

"Go on." Heller's voice was ice.

"Mac met with two people yesterday. After the meeting, they went to the docks and left. I followed them."

"Interesting. Do you know who they were?"

"No."

"Do you have—?"

"I know the serial number of the seacar. You can have it."

"Good. Now continue your work at Trieste. I want more information about this Lazlow person."

Butte nodded and glanced back and forth between the two USSF officers facing him. "All right. But make sure next time I come, it's secret. My life is on the line here."

Heller grinned for the first time during the meeting. But the smile was a façade, Schrader thought; it didn't reach his eyes.

"Yes, it is," Heller said. "Isn't it?"

PART TWO:
THE DEEPS

CHAPTER SIX

FINALLY, THREE DAYS AFTER THE EMP attack and the French attempt on my life, I arrived at Ballard City off the coast of Louisiana on the Mississippi alluvial fan. I had spent two full days in *SC-1* sitting powerless in the kelp bed, waiting patiently. Had I been too brash and tried to leave earlier, I would have ended up in French hands. I'd most likely be dead already. I'd spent the time wiring the starboard thruster and rigging up a simple switch system that didn't involve a circuit board of any kind. Navigation would be difficult, but there was so much traffic between the mainland and Ballard I knew all I'd have to do is approach the sealanes and someone would help get me to the underwater colony.

When I arrived at the city, towed in by a good Samaritan and his private seacar, I arranged transport for *SC-1* to the Mechanical/Repair Module. The maintenance crews were shocked at my story, and before repairs started, I knew I'd have to contact Kat and Meg. *SC-1* contained secrets we wanted to keep for ourselves.

For the time being.

Kat's face erupted into joy when she saw my face on the screen. I was in the master repairman's office. Covering every available surface were engineering manuals and seacar schematics, and I'd had to cram myself into a tiny cubicle to use the comm.

"Mac!" she cried. "Where have you been? We've been worried sick! We've had search crews out—"

"I'm okay," I said with a sheepish grin. "Had a run in with an unfriendly warsub."

She immediately grew concerned. "Who was it? Chinese?"

I waved away her concern. "We'll talk later. For now, the big problem is *SC-1*."

"What did you do to my seacar?" Her eyes flashed.

I sighed. "I think it was an EMP. Nothing electronic is working."

A deathly silence descended over us. Then, "Did I just hear you right?" She glanced away as she processed that. "It would explain the USSF activity."

I leaned forward at that.

She said, "A few hours after you left, they scrambled troops and departed the city. Control noted multiple contacts approach the area west of Trieste and begin a search. Something spooked them."

I snorted. "The EMP was probably it. It was a small blast, but bright. It had an immediate effect on the seacar. I had to bypass every computer and wire the thrusters directly." I neglected to mention the six French divers I'd had to kill.

She shook her head. "It's a good thing you're so industrious."

I offered her a slight smile. "Kind of like that time we were stranded four kilometers down."

"Don't remind me."

"I have to meet with the mayor now. Then I'll go to Seascape. In the meantime, I need to know what to tell the repair people here."

Her eyes flashed again. "Damn. You're right." She looked away. "We should only fix the systems that operate the conventional controls. Don't let them in the SCAV compartment, and don't let them touch the fusion controls. Just the navigation, thruster, and life support."

"Are those separate computers?"

"Yes."

I considered it for a heartbeat. "Maybe I should let you speak with the repair crew."

"Better yet, let me get Meg on it. She probably knows them personally. I'll get her down here too."

We said our goodbyes, but not until after she'd professed her grief and worry over the past three days. She seemed truly broken up. It had been a tough time for both of us, but it was over now.

Kat had filled a spot in my life I hadn't even known was empty. For so many years I'd been on autopilot, working for the city and ignoring the politics going on in the world. But I'd regained a purpose. There was a drive inside me now, more than just about seeing the city succeed. It was a need to create a future we all believed in. It was dangerous, but I knew Kat would always be at my side.

—••—

AN HOUR LATER I WAS SITTING in Mayor Grace Winton's office just off Ballard City Control. It was a similar setup to Trieste, but her office was far more luxurious than mine. There was a huge port behind her desk with an incredible view of the farming efforts underway around the city. I could see a harvesting sub working at slicing and bundling kelp just a hundred meters away, and the upside down waterfalls of bubble fences containing millions of fish.

Her office was actually painted a bright red—*painted!*—and filled with comfortable couches, bookshelves, and even pillows. My eyes widened when I saw it, but I wasn't there to judge. I was there to offer her something.

Winton was African American and in her early fifties. I knew her only through reports on the underwater colonies, when news crews did stories on the functions of the three cities in the Gulf. Ballard focused on fish and kelp farming, and they provided food to the mainland. Winton had a calm and peaceful demeanor, a soft voice, and warm eyes. She grabbed my hand in a firm shake.

"Mayor McClusky. So nice to finally meet you. I know all about your history and your father. He was a great man."

I nodded and sat in the leather chair before the wood desk. "Thank you, Mayor."

"Grace, please."

"And I'm Mac."

"Good!" She offered a genuine smile. "I'm happy that you made the journey here. Though we were supposed to meet a couple of days ago."

"I'm sorry. Seacar trouble. It's in your Repair Module right now."

"Is it serious?"

"It might be. I have to go to Seascape right after this, and my vessel might not be able to make the journey."

She waved the issue away. "We'll lend you a city vehicle while we're repairing yours."

"Thanks."

She leaned back in her chair and locked eyes with me. There was something churning behind them. She seemed so personable and friendly, though there was clearly a professional side to her too. Then she said, "Tell me about The Battle last year. What was that idiot Janice Flint trying to do, exactly?"

I took a deep breath and wondered what to say. I realized if I was ever going to achieve what I wanted, I had to just come out and say it. Glancing around, I changed the topic. "Is this office . . . *safe*?"

There was a long pause as she stared at me. Her eyes grew harder, but she wasn't mad.

She was curious.

"My security chief checks regularly. We make sure the USSF isn't too aware of political things here." She hesitated, then, "Why?"

"Because The Battle and the former mayor of Trieste are precisely why I'm here. I want to talk to you about independence."

—••—

GRACE WINTON PRACTICALLY FELL OUT OF the chair when I said it. But she remained quiet and let me speak.

"Janice Flint and George Shanks had built a fleet of attack subs. Secretly. Right under the USSF's nose. Unfortunately, they made their move way too soon. It was reckless. I was involved in The Battle, but I convinced our people to surrender."

"And now the USSF occupies your city."

"Yes. They're a pain in the ass, but I'm still planning." I trailed off and watched her as I spoke. Her face remained impassive. I continued. "I'm actively working for independence. I'm coordinating the efforts. I'm hoping for help from the Chinese cities."

Her jaw dropped at that.

"And I'm hoping for help from you," I finally said.

She looked away. "What kind of help? It sounds like madness."

I sighed. "I know. The USSF is powerful. But I think what we need to do is present them with an option that doesn't involve too much death."

"Too much death. . . ."

"We need to show them how strong we are. We need to work together and present ourselves as one."

"Both our cities?" She looked flabbergasted.

I leaned forward. "No. *All* of them."

She frowned. "There are twenty-nine major undersea colonies. You mean to go to each one and arrange—"

"I do, though I don't plan to visit each personally, but there are surrogates out there working right now. Quietly."

She paused and it was clear that thoughts were roiling through her brain. "Do you operate an intelligence service?" Her voice was quiet.

I nodded. The danger here was very real, but I knew I had to be honest if I was ever going to attract allies in this fight. "Telling you means I could get arrested, so I'm putting my faith in you right now. In the fact that we are both undersea dwellers. In the fact that the USSF and the US treat our cities like factories and our citizens as slaves. We have it within our power to fight for freedom. I mean to do it again, and soon."

"But your dad . . . Shanks and Flint, just last year."

"They were all naïve. I'm not."

She stared at me for a long heartbeat, then burst out laughing. "Do you realize how silly that sounds? I'm sorry Mac, and I do respect you, but—"

"I have a sub that can go four hundred and fifty kilometers per hour, Grace. With torpedoes that are even faster."

That stopped her. Her brow furrowed. "You're serious."

"Absolutely."

She stared at me as she processed it. "That would explain the noises we heard during The Battle."

"Yes. Shanks had a small fleet of them. We're preparing for another attempt. But this time we'll do it right. And there will be more than one city resisting."

"But—but—" She stopped. Then, "You're giving me a lot to think about."

I rose from the chair. "I'm not here to get an answer now. I wanted to speak to you in person and offer you something to let you know our intentions."

"Our?"

"The movement at Trieste. I couldn't contact you over the comm about this. This is too big."

"You can say that again." She blew her breath out and just stared at me. And then she said, "Shit."

I grinned. "Problem?"

"You've hit me with a whopper this morning, Mac."

"You know my family history. You know my reputation. If you make the decision to join us, we're going to do it right."

"But you don't know what the USSF will do. We're vulnerable here."

"We are. But if we present a deal that offers them something in return, they may not want to fight at all."

She considered that. "And what is the offer you have for me?"

"I want to give you the secrets to the SCAV drive."

Her eyes widened. "The fast submarine?"

"That's right."

"You'll just hand it over."

"The plans, engineers to train your people, and even working vessels."

She stared at me, then laughed again. "You don't disappoint, McClusky."

I smiled. "Thanks."

"Let me think on it. I will have to talk it over with some people."

This made me uneasy.

Her voice lowered. "If it makes you feel more comfortable, I'll give you something in return. We have an intelligence service. I am a part of it. And there is an independence movement alive and well here too." She raised a finger at me. "But if you ever tell anyone that, it would mean arrest and occupation for us too."

"Don't worry. I figured as much. But just so you know, the USSF knew about our intelligence agency."

Her jaw dropped. "You're serious?"

"Captain Heller of *Impaler* had known for years."

"And they were just waiting to see what happened?"

"Yes. When we showed our hand with the SCAV drive, he made his move on us."

She shook her head. "So that's what The Battle was about. The news reports said it was a dissident faction, but that's all they said."

"It was about a lot more than that. And now you're part of it."

She raised her hands. "Not yet. Let me talk to some people. Then I'll get back to you." Then she smiled and said, "And now, would you like a tour of our marvelous city?"

—••—

THE TOUR WAS FASCINATING. GRACE ACTED as if nothing odd had transpired at all, that everything was just business as normal. She had a good poker face, and she was friendly and passionate about life underwater.

The city was very much like Trieste, but their focus on agriculture meant they had more processing modules and transports running constantly to the mainland. Trieste had mining interests as well as additional business space in the Commerce Module, but the differences between the two cities ended there. The people I saw in the travel tubes and the modules Grace Winton showed me were the same as Triestrians. Hard working, rugged, and *happy*. It was nice to see.

As we passed a fish processing and flash-freezing line in a huge module on the outskirts of the city—it was a cavernous module with assembly lines and rows upon rows of workers gutting fish, freezing and packaging them—a man bumped into me and pressed something secretly into my hand. I hid it and kept my face impassive.

The man had a medium build, was average height with nondescript hair, and he was not wearing anything that made him stand out in any way.

He did not look back as he walked away.

He would have made a good TCI operative.

Later, in private, I unfolded the note and read it with interest.

> Meet us in Trieste on Feb. 23 at 1700 hours. It's about your dad.
> We have information.
> The same place where you recently met your two operatives.

The date was five days away, the anniversary of my dad's death, and the day Triestrians celebrated his life.

—••—

THE SEACAR WINTON LET ME BORROW was a basic model made by Ford. It didn't have the highest top speed, but it would at least let me blend in with the rest of the submarine traffic linking Ballard to Seascape and I simply fell into line in the sealane and made the day-long trip without much effort.

Seascape was beautiful. Its primary function was tourism, and it did its job marvelously. Expansive viewports made of a durable but transparent material covered most exterior bulkheads. The ceilings of the upper levels were mostly skylights. The natural light in the city was stunning. With a focus on tourism, there were a multitude of activities to choose from, such as scuba diving and swimming with dolphins and underwater scooter races and even a type of target practice pitting people against each other. This colony had something else unique as well—an enclosed high-speed conveyer connecting the city directly with the mainland. People venturing to Seascape simply had to pressurize upon departure, sit on a couch, and ride the conveyer through a transparent travel tube sixty kilometers off shore to the underwater city. When the tourists were ready to return, they would stay at a "decompression hotel"—really a spa—until they were ready to resume life topside.

It was a ridiculous luxury in an age of economic and climatic collapse topside, but I figured there was still an upper class to fill such places as Seascape. I could tell just by looking at the people in the colony that they were not laborers or workers like at Trieste or Ballard. These people were more fragile, to say it politely.

But even so, the wonder in their eyes was obvious, their excitement at being underwater palpable. It was fun to watch the tourists experience the ocean depths.

The central module was much like ours, though as I had heard from many others, the atrium was not as nice as Trieste's. Ours was a city of agriculture, and we showed this off by covering our balconies with vines and trees and plants. Seascape's beauty lay in their ocean vistas through transparent bulkheads. Besides, tourists didn't venture underwater to see plants.

When I finally negotiated my way to the mayor's office, threading my way through mobs of wealthy tourists, I found myself in Seascape City Control in the central module. An assistant's face erupted into surprise when I introduced myself. "You were supposed to be here days ago," she said.

"Seacar trouble," I said. "Sorry."

She grunted in reply as she ushered me to the mayor's office, which was even more luxurious than Winton's had been. I spent thirty seconds taking it all in before I noticed the man sitting at an oak desk before a bulkhead-spanning viewport looking onto an indoor water park. I blinked when I saw that. Pools, water slides, splash pads for kids—all under a massive transparent dome. Outside the dome, fish of all types swarmed and swirled.

"Incredible," I breathed.

"I'm glad you like it," the man said. He was African American with a bald head and a goatee. His expression was stern and there was no warmth to his words or his appearance.

"It's beautiful," I said. "I've heard stories . . ." I didn't know how to finish.

"We've worked hard on the city."

"We all have. All the undersea colonists. But this is a different type of work."

"Yes." He frowned. "You're not being facetious, are you?"

I waved it away. "Not at all. I'm all for anything to encourage countries to continue colonizing."

"Even though it's tourism?"

"I think it's great." My forehead creased. "But are there enough tourists? With all the surface problems right now?"

He gestured behind him, out the window. "Look at that. There's a waiting list to come right now too."

I watched families playing below, splashing and frolicking in swimming pools enclosed within a bubble of air. I didn't know what to say.

"What can I do for you, Mac?"

I shook myself from my reverie, turned to the man, and extended my hand. "Truman McClusky."

"Reggie Quinn," he replied. "And you don't have to introduce yourself. I know who you are."

I made a mental note that still the man hadn't smiled. "Yes. I'm happy to meet you." I glanced outside again. "And I'm glad to finally see your city. It really is . . . *incredible*." I was having trouble finding another word to describe it.

"Thanks."

I studied the man. He was all business. I swallowed. "I'm here to discuss something that might interest you."

He stared at me for a long, long heartbeat. He tapped on the wood table while his eyes remained locked to mine. He didn't blink. "I'm going to say this once, and then you are going to get up and leave my city right now."

The words felt like a punch to the gut. His face remained fixed. He was serious.

I frowned. "We'll see, I guess."

He shook his head. "To be blunt, I don't want what you're selling. We're happy here. We have no reason to dislike the USSF. We're not interested in joining you."

My stomach dropped. "You haven't heard me out yet."

"I don't have to. I know your reputation. I wondered why you wouldn't speak about this over the comms. It didn't take long for me to realize it had to be something you were scared the USSF would find out. So you came to speak in person."

"But if you'd hear me—"

"I knew Janice Flint and George Shanks. I've had a strong suspicion about what The Battle was about last year. And as I've said, we're happy here."

"For how much longer?"

He blinked and gave me another icy glare. "For as long as we're here."

"No," I said in one drawn-out breath. "That's not true." I leaned forward. "You're only happy for as long as you have them." I glanced at the tourists outside. "Then what are you?"

He rose to his feet slowly and set his hands on the table. He leaned toward me. "Get out, McClusky. Leave right now. And if you don't, I'll make sure you'll wish you had."

—••—

WITHIN MINUTES I WAS IN THE seacar and on my way back to Ballard. Once there I would wait for the repairs to be finished on *SC-1* and then continue to Trieste. During the whole journey I mulled over what Reggie Quinn had said. If I couldn't interest another American city in this quest, how could I possibly attract a Chinese or French one? Why would they join a fight that would leave undersea dwellers dead and cities potentially flooded and smashed?

For the first time in a year, I wasn't just worried about the path I was leading Trieste on.

I was afraid.

CHAPTER
SEVEN

SC-1 HAD BEEN PUT BACK IN working order by the time I returned to Ballard—though only the navigation, life support, conventional thrusters, and the ballast controls had been fixed. The fusion reactor, containment facility, and the SCAV drive hadn't been touched, and those control screens remained blank. Kat and Meg would repair those once I returned to Trieste.

I couldn't help but grin as my home appeared. The landing lights on the seafloor directed me into the Docking Module, and I made my ballast neutral as I negotiated the entryway and located my berth. I shut down the thrusters and moved the ballast levers in the central console to positive. SC-1 rose to the surface of the moonpool and I cut power, leaned back, and exhaled. It had been an eventful journey, and a big positive was that at least one of the mayors had been receptive. Perhaps Reggie would come around. One day.

I found Kat in her cabin in Module A, and she embraced me as if we hadn't seen each other in weeks. It had been only six days, but it felt far longer.

"Why didn't you tell me you'd arrived?" she asked between kisses. "I would have met you at the dock!"

"I wanted to surprise you."

"You succeeded!" She kissed me passionately, then abruptly pulled back and her eyes narrowed. "How's my seacar? Where is it?"

I laughed. I wasn't sure if she was happier to see me or to have *SCAV-1* back safely. I entered her living space and pulled the partition shut behind me. It was cramped, but we were both able to sit on her bunk to catch up.

"Don't worry," I said. "She's fine. I got back okay."

"Now tell me what happened. It wasn't the Chinese?"

I lowered my voice and said, "No. It was the French."

She hesitated. "They found out."

I nodded. I relayed the entire incident to her, during which she swore multiple times.

"Shit, Mac," she said. "You're lucky you made it back at all."

I snorted. "Thanks to the kelp bed."

She looked away and considered that. "They probably knew generally where you were. But they couldn't find you. Then when the USSF ships arrived on the scene—"

"They had to run. I waited for days just to be safe. Sorry I couldn't contact you."

"I still can't believe they detonated an EMP."

"It was small. I bet it wouldn't have hurt subs a hundred meters away. I don't think an EMP travels far underwater."

She considered that. "You're right. It probably had to hit pretty damn close to be effective."

"Which it did."

She pulled me into her arms. "I missed you." Then abruptly, "Now, tell me about the two mayors. What did they say?"

—••—

AFTER I'D SUMMED UP MY MEETINGS, she swore yet again. "That idiot Reggie. He doesn't see far into the future. He only sees tomorrow. Or next year. But pretty soon that city isn't going to be faring so well."

I sighed. "Well, I can't blame him. His people have a good thing right now." Kat's eyes flared again and I had to raise my hands. "Now calm down. We just have to wait. Work on the other cities."

She huffed and looked away.

"I have something else to tell you." I pulled out the crumpled note from my pocket. "Look at this."

She gasped as she read it. "It could be a trap."

"By who? The USSF? They could just arrest me if they wanted."

"But the people would rebel. They worship you, Mac! You represent more than just the undersea city, more than just undersea life. You represent your father's legacy. You're the future."

I stared at her. "Easy now. I'm not the second coming." The way she was speaking made me uncomfortable.

"It's true." She sighed. "You just don't see it. Or you choose not to. But when you speak to people, their eyes light up. When you walk away, they watch as you leave. You're more than just a man to them."

"What does that mean?" I shifted on the bunk.

"I don't mean you're more than a man. I mean you represent an *idea*. You represent what the future *may* hold. Don't give up on it."

I snorted. "I'm all in on it. I'm not giving—"

She snatched the paper from my grasp. "If you go to this place, it might be the end. It could be the USSF entrapping you. It might be a meeting with real criminals, just to make you guilty by association. Or it could even be a way to capture you."

"I'm safe here."

"Oh sure." She grunted. "The French could have arranged this. Have you thought of *that*?"

I sighed and realized she might be right. It could be a setup. It seemed pretty simplistic though. A note, pressed into my hand by a stranger.

Looking down, I read it again. The meeting was the next day. I didn't have much time. "What if I arranged a different place? A safer meeting?"

She looked at me, confusion in her eyes. "What do you mean?

—••—

AN HOUR LATER I MET WITH Meg in the Repair Module, where she was overseeing the work on *SC-1*. She had a pained look on her face as she reviewed the engineer's report with her Personal Communication Device. Then she noticed me and flashed a quick smile before her expression turned dour once more. "The SCAV drive is going to be down for a while."

"The EMP did quite a job on it I'm guessing."

"You have no idea. The computer controls are custom. It's a fusion drive! They're not off-the-shelf components like the ones on Shanks's ships. It's going to take some time."

I looked around at the Repair Module. There were three berths with seacars undergoing structural work. Two berths had vessels with some sort of internal maintenance going on, and four berths were empty. "Well, it could be worse."

"Not much. The amount of damage is extensive. We're going to have to rebuild the—"

"I'm sure you and Kat will get it done just fine."

She stared at me. "You don't understand, Mac." She'd lowered her voice and glanced around. "We were scheduled to go to The Ridge soon."

That caught me off guard. "Do you want to take another vessel?"

"Are you kidding? Katherine Wells in something other than *SCAV-1*?"

I grinned. "Yeah, I guess you're right."

"By the way, are you going to fill me in on your trip?"

"It was . . . interesting."

"I'm sure." She gestured at the ship. "This is going to be some story I'm guessing."

"Yeah."

And then another voice said from behind me, "I'd like to hear it too."

I spun on my heel and faced the newcomer. My heart thudded in my chest. It was Johnny Chang.

—••—

I HADN'T SEEN HIM IN A year. Since we'd been involved in the heated chase through the Atlantic and Pacific. The fight at the French base on the guyot. The fighting in Blue Downs and the Second Battle of Trieste.

After we'd fought the USSF, I'd sent him out in one of Shanks's supercavitating vehicles to act as our emissary to the Chinese cities. I'd received one message from him about the French syntactic foam, but otherwise he'd been quiet.

He had a grin on his face. His hair was longer, as if he'd been too busy to have it cut. But other than that, he looked the same. Broad shoulders, fit, athletic. Small wrinkles at the corners of his eyes, with real warmth in his smile.

We embraced heartily. "Where have you been?" I asked. "You haven't—"

"Later," he said. "Let's catch up someplace a bit more private."

I nodded. "Sounds good."

He looked at my sister. "How are you, Meg?"

She scowled. "Mac's damaged the seacar, and now I've got to get it fixed yesterday."

He glanced at *SC-1*. "I thought you were a good mechanic."

"I'm not used to fixing fusion reactors."

He blinked.

"It's a long story," I grumbled. "Come on, let's go get something to drink."

—••—

JOHNNY AND I MADE OUR WAY to a restaurant in the Commerce Module. Not the most private place, but certainly not one where the USSF would expect me to have a clandestine meeting with someone involved in our struggle for independence. Johnny kept looking around the entire time, clearly happy to have returned to Trieste. He hadn't seen it in a year after all, and before that he'd been working for Sheng City Intelligence. We'd considered him a traitor at the time.

Over a beer I filled him in on what I'd been up to: repairing the city following The Battle, burying the nuclear plant, rebuilding the Storage Model, managing city affairs, governing, dealing with political issues, and trying to keep the USSF off our backs. And on top of all that, sending TCI operatives out on missions and trying to prepare for the fight for independence.

"Now it's your turn," I said in a quiet voice with a glance around. "We've all been dying to know how you've been doing."

He grinned. "I've visited all six Chinese undersea cities. I've demonstrated the *Stingray*'s abilities to their leaders."

The *Stingrays* were Shanks's supercavitating ships. Small, fast, highly maneuverable, well-armed . . . They had proven to be more than effective in battle. Johnny still had the one I'd given him. No doubt the USSF had the others, and had been reverse engineering them for months. It was only a matter of time before we'd begin to see their offspring in the oceans.

"And . . ." I prompted, hoping against hope that he'd give me good news.

He shrugged. "Mixed feelings. They're scared, Mac, and rightfully so. They all loved the ship though. They're desperate to get the drive."

"But we'll give it to them if they join us." In fact, we had already promised them the technology during The Battle; they had left because of it, a fact that had probably perplexed the USSF as well as the Chinese Submarine Fleet. We would have to give it to them eventually, just to keep our word and maintain good relations. Just doing that might be enough to lay a strong foundation for an eventual partnership.

Johnny grunted. "More than once I was scared they'd just kill me and take it."

It was a good sign they hadn't, at least. "Did they study the ship when you weren't around?"

He frowned. "It's possible, I guess. But they'd need months with a working model to reverse engineer it. Or the plans."

I sighed. I'm not sure what I expected, but it was a start at least. "We can only give them time, hope they see things our way."

I looked away and took a gulp of beer. I would have to think this through. We had to expect some pushback.

"Tell me about what efforts you've been making. What are you working on?"

He had no idea what I'd been up to. I glanced around subconsciously. Even now, if a US sailor recognized him, it would mean trouble.

"I've been preparing a few surprises. I've been rebuilding. And gathering allies. Quietly."

"And the USSF?"

"They're a pain. They've been bothering us even more than usual. And they're always watching us." I paused, and then, "And they killed a man I had informing."

"You're sure?"

"Pretty."

"I'm sure they're watching you too."

I nodded. "I bet." I said no more.

He studied me silently for a long heartbeat.

CHAPTER EIGHT

JOHNNY AND I TALKED LONG INTO the night. Soon enough our paranoia over who might be watching us disappeared and we enjoyed drinks and laughter and reminisced over the past when we had been partners and things had been better. During missions to other undersea cities of the world, infiltrating colonies, stealing secrets, or smuggling defectors back to Trieste. *To better times*, we'd toasted and clinked glasses of kelp beer, followed by grimaces as the horrible stuff burned its way down our throats.

It was still better than the kelp vodka, I had to remind myself.

And far better than imports from topside, even though they may have tasted better.

We also spoke of the adventure with *SC-1*, the fighting over the Aleutian Trench, and the battles with Chinese operatives and the Australian security forces of Blue Downs when we'd had to escape to get Kat and her invention safely back to Trieste. Johnny spoke for hours about the Chinese cities and his struggle to get people to listen to him and to agree there was really no better hope in the oceans than the rise of Oceania. He desperately wanted to see it happen—my passion had convinced him—and it became quickly obvious he would do anything to see the nation appear on the maps of the world. The problem, he confessed, was that the undersea colonies were too vulnerable. Even a moderately-sized conventional weapon could destroy an undersea city easily and quickly. The risk was great.

I understood the feeling. It had plagued me for years as well. The USSF, or any aggressive power, should they want to kill us, could tap into our air supply and poison us, bomb an exterior bulkhead, hit us with a torpedo, nuke us, hit us from the air or the surface, or easily infiltrate with enemy combatants and take over that way.

It brought to mind the Chinese attackers I'd fought the year previously. Five of them had tried to kill me in Trieste—in the Living Module.

We were not just easy targets—we were fragile and vulnerable.

But there were ways around some of those attacks. Airtight bulkhead doors and tighter security around air feeds from the surface and closer monitoring of subs approaching the city. But security underwater could never be perfect.

As far as the Chinese cities were concerned, I knew we just had to offer them something that would make the risk worth it. The economic benefits alone would be a great advantage to all the undersea colonies.

I had to figure something out.

By the time Johnny and I parted for the evening—I had a bunk set up for him in the same module as mine—I'd come up with an idea for my meeting the following day. I'd showed Johnny the note and described the interesting, albeit amateurish way in which I had obtained it, and he agreed to my plan.

My head hit the pillow in my narrow bunk and, as images of a free Trieste swam through my mind, sleep smothered me, carrying me to a place where my family was still together, my mother was not bitter and angry and crying herself to sleep at night, my sister had not run from Trieste to escape her past, no one had assassinated my dad, and Johnny had never betrayed me to the Chinese and forced me into a prison cell for four of the worst months of my life.

Through the dream I found myself nearly waking, startled at the thoughts going through my mind, but lulled back to sleep by the hum of mechanical activity always working to maintain our way of life, and wondered if my dreams were elements of my past I wished had never ended . . . or pieces that I hoped to reclaim for my future.

—••—

THE FOLLOWING DAY WAS FEBRUARY 23.

The day the city remembered the assassination of Frank McClusky.

I was usually miserable on this day. My dad had been so confident in his plans, so focused on his mission to detach Trieste from the States and forge ahead on our own. He'd started sending our produce directly to other countries and ignored the demands by our own colonizers to send the goods back to the mainland. The CIA had infiltrated the city, caught him in a travel tube, and killed him easily. Bullet to the head, travel tube flooded just in case. The cascading weight of thirty meters of water as the integrity of the tube gave way under a small explosive device had mangled his body. Not that it mattered anyway. The bullet had done the job.

They had killed the entire city council along with him, although not in the same travel tube. They'd killed some while they slept, poisoned others, sunk others while out in their seacars.

Now, thirty-one years later, our city still remembered the day with a somber memorial followed by outright celebration. I found it hard to walk around and deal with Triestrians patting me on the back, shaking my hand, congratulating me simply for having a dead dad, as if that were a great accomplishment.

But I dealt with it, as we all have to deal with things in life.

The fact that the person who wanted to meet with me had picked *today* of all days was disturbing, to say the least.

In the early afternoon I spoke at a function that was broadcast to the living modules and closed circuit system throughout the entire colony. People didn't take work off—that almost never happened—but everywhere there was a computer monitor or a television screen or a control readout of some kind, Triestrians could access the memorial and watch us recount the day that had changed us forever: February 23, 2099. The end of not just one man and the entire city council, but of a dream. There were shared glances and hidden flashes of hope in eyes as I spoke about my father and the desires we all shared of the future—I was smart enough not to use the word *independence*, however, for that would have been utterly stupid—so I focused on the needs of every undersea dweller to continue life in the oceans and bring hope to the masses suffering on the surface of the planet.

There was much underwater we could offer to the citizens of the planet; the ocean represented *hope*. It was the next frontier, and it bothered me when people didn't accept that. Sure, space was there and we were exploring new resources in The Belt and beyond, but the oceans were within immediate reach.

I also noted, with anger and resentment, the contingent of USSF officers who arrived from *Impaler* and stood close behind me during the speech. They were pretending to represent the US at the event, but of course I knew better.

One of them was Seaman Abernathy, whom I had met before. I wondered absently how he had drawn this job. He was such a low-ranking sailor.

The hair on my neck was on end as I spoke, for they were at my back for the better part of an hour.

Later, after the crowd had dispersed and the celebrations were just starting to get underway, I returned to my living compartment. In the drawer over my bunk, I removed a PCD hidden under some clothes. My other informant worked on USS *Impaler*. No one could trace the device to me; Cliff had set it up months earlier, but didn't know what it was for.

Seconds later a male voice said, "Go ahead."

"Any news to report?" I asked.

There was a pause. And then, "They know about the newcomer."

I frowned. "Who?"

"A Doctor Lazlow. They know he's there for a reason."

I snorted. So their informant had told them. I still didn't really know why Kat and Meg had brought him to Trieste, but I trusted them. "Anything else?"

"They know there have been some subs sent out to the south. They don't know where they're going."

"If they figure it out, let me know."

"Will do."

"What do you know about the death of Rafe Manuel?"

There was a long pause. And then, "I'm not going to say anything about it."

I hesitated and considered that. It made sense. Informing was one thing. Incriminating a fellow USSF officer was something else entirely.

"I understand," I whispered.

We cut the connection and I replaced the PCD; we couldn't talk long for fear my informant would get caught. I sat back in my bunk for a few long minutes, wondering how I could use the information.

In the same drawer there was a folder with a sheaf of dog-eared, handwritten papers. Clipped to them were photographs and other notes, hastily scrawled on small scraps of paper and attached haphazardly to the files.

These had belonged to George Shanks.

It was one of the few things I'd saved from his office in the heady hours during the initial USSF occupation. The other important files—names of our operatives, dates of missions, and so on—I'd destroyed. This file, however, was different.

I flipped through it until I found the record I was looking for.

—••—

IT WAS ALMOST 1700 HOURS.

And nearly time for the mysterious meeting.

Johnny was going to the location in my place. He would vet the person who wanted to meet me, and only if it seemed safe would he bring him to my location: a small lounge in the agricultural processing facility where workers prepared kelp for export.

It was a lounge I was familiar with, having worked the farms for years after leaving TCI, and I knew I could trust the people there. From their point of view, it was well known that I found that particular day of the year challenging, and perhaps I just needed some time on my own away from the parties.

I gave the directions to Johnny, sat in the small lounge with one viewport, two uncomfortable couches and a rickety table, and waited.

The other workers left me alone, as I'd expected.

Thirty minutes after the arranged time, the hatch slid aside and Johnny entered.

There were two people with him.

———••———

THE FIRST WAS A MAN IN his seventies with lines in his face, a receding hairline, a strong jaw, and piercing eyes. His arms were toned despite his age, and his skin was pale from living underwater, likely for decades.

The second was an Asian woman in her sixties. She had soft features, short hair, and a self-assured walk that betrayed her confidence and high level of self-esteem. She wore no jewelry or makeup, and her hair was not entirely black or gray. Salt water had faded it like bleach. There were streaks of blond.

They were like us. They lived and struggled underwater.

They stopped in the small lounge and stared at me. Johnny closed the hatch behind him and also watched, a perplexed look on his face.

Then both strangers smiled.

"Hello, Mac," the woman said. "My name is Jessica Ng. This is Richard Lancombe. We worked with your father thirty years ago here in Trieste."

———••———

MY HEART NEARLY EXPLODED. THESE TWO had been well-known members of my father's group of freedom fighters back in 2099. Both had been assumed dead following the CIA intervention.

They had been his most trusted advisors, in fact.

I simply stared at them. I didn't know what to say except, "Bullshit."

Richard offered me a warm smile. "I know it's a lot to take in. But to make a long story short, we escaped the day the CIA invaded Trieste."

"Where have you been since?" I finally managed. I fell back to the couch and hunched forward, listening to them and shifting my gaze back and forth, from one to the other.

"At Ballard. We couldn't leave the underwater cities. We had to continue the struggle to survive on the seafloor, of course."

Jessica said, "We couldn't abandon the fight that your father died for. His hopes for the future."

"What hope?" I asked, but I was just stalling because I didn't know what to say. Johnny too was shocked, and he just watched quietly from the corner of the lounge. He knew their reputations as well. He knew the history.

"For independence, of course." She looked at me with a frown as if I were dim.

"I don't entirely believe you."

"Of course not. You've heard of us though."

"But I've never seen a clear photo. Just grainy, distant, out of focus ones."

"We were always careful. Avoided video surveillance, which was hard in an underwater city! But if we were out in public, we wore disguises. Hats, masks, and so on."

I shook my head and continued to stare at them. "And why choose now to reveal yourselves to me?" I wanted to scream at them. For thirty-one years I had lived under the shroud of a murdered father. Dead because he'd annoyed the US government and the USSF. I had suffered a lot, as had Meg. Hell, she had run from the city because of the attention the citizens always gave us. Today was only the worst of the 365 that we experienced every year.

"Because we realize that Trieste and all the undersea cities are at a crossroads, Mac," Lancombe said. "It's time for us to reenter civilization, so to speak."

I snorted. "What, have you been living under a rock for the last three decades?"

Jessica shrugged and offered a sly smile. "In a sense, yes. We haven't gone by our names for that entire time. We have new identities. We live as a married couple, though we're not."

I blew my breath out in a rush. "And what do you want to talk to me about?"

"We want to help you, of course."

I frowned. "Why now? Why not last year?"

"Last year it wasn't you leading the fight. It was that moron George Shanks. We knew him too. Worked with him when your father was alive. He was stupid and brash. We realized he was going to fail, so we ignored his pleas for help."

I suppressed a tight smile. At least they had Shanks pegged correctly. Then something occurred to me. "What a minute—Shanks knew you were alive?"

Jessica said, "Maybe. He obviously never found our bodies so he kept trying to contact us. But he didn't know where we were or our new identities."

"We never replied," Lancombe said. "We let him wonder."

I shook my head. "I can't believe this."

"We haven't got to the most incredible part," Jessica said.

I remained silent and stared at them. "Go on."

They looked at one another, then turned to me.

Lancombe said, "We wanted to offer you help in the fight. But we also wanted to finally tell you the truth about your dad."

"What about him? He was dumb. He thought he could anger the USSF and the States and that they wouldn't retaliate. He didn't think they could get to him. He thought he was indestructible or something." I threw my hands in the air. "I've had to live with it all my life. It's why I joined TCI. It's why I'm the mayor now. It's why I'm leading the fight here at the city."

I realized belatedly that these two could actually be trying to entrap me, as Kat had warned. After all, I didn't actually know them.

But still, something told me to trust these two. A hunch. They seemed genuine, and my history as an operative had strengthened my gut over the years.

Jessica eyed me, confused.

"Just look at what happened!" I continued. "He was too vulnerable. He should have prepared better defenses."

"That's what we've been thinking about, for all this time," Lancombe said. "Don't fool yourself. We may have disappeared in 2099, but we're still very much interested in the fight."

I turned to the man. "And you don't think he was naïve?"

"Not at all."

I snorted. "Then you don't know anything about independence. About the USSF. About our enemies in the ocean with us. About what they'll do to win this battle."

"Like send five Chinese operatives to kill you in your own living module?"

Jessica added, "Or detonate an EMP right off your hull to infiltrate your seacar and kill you?"

My jaw hit the deck. "How do you know about those events?"

"We watch. We listen. We have people keeping us informed and up-to-date, the same as you."

I sighed. "Well, for what it's worth, congratulations." I hesitated as I stared at them. Johnny had remained completely quiet; he just didn't know what to say.

Lancombe continued, "The thing is, you're the one who has it wrong."

I sat up straighter and felt the blood rush to my head. What the hell did he mean by—

"Your dad saw it coming all right. In fact, *he let it happen*."

—••—

"WAIT A MINUTE." I PAUSED AND took several deep breaths. My father had seen the coming catastrophe on the surface. He'd brought the family to Trieste and by 2095 had become mayor of the city. He had also, unknown to us at the time, been involved in the failed bid for independence.

The fact that I was now on the same path didn't surprise me.

It haunted me.

I had been fourteen at the time of his death. It had destroyed Meagan. Our mother died in 2111, lonely and bitter and fearful of the future.

What Lancombe and Ng were saying was just not possible. My father would not have just allowed himself to die. He wouldn't have just sat around to let someone kill him.

"That's exactly what he did," Jessica said. "I'm sorry, Mac, but your dad knew the fight was hopeless. At least, it was in 2099. He was preparing for a future when the odds were more in our favor, and he set the cards up for that. Rigged the deck for you."

My mouth hung open. Then, "What are you saying? That he committed suicide?"

Lancombe shook his head. "No. Not at all. But he sacrificed himself for the greater good." He gestured around him. "Look at what's going on in this city, right now. The celebrations. Why do they even happen? Why do Triestrians look up to you? Why do they follow you?"

Now the blood drained from my face. I began to feel faint. I remained silent and listened.

"It's because of what your dad sacrificed. He knew he was going to die that day, and he allowed it to happen. It was so this day would come. The day that you and Meg could lead Trieste in a fight that has more chance of succeeding now than ever before.

"He sacrificed his future to give you yours, Mac. And now we're here to help."

CHAPTER NINE

KAT AND MEG WERE STARING AT me, mouths open, disbelief in their eyes.

"But no one's heard from those two since the uprising," Meg whispered.

I fixed my gaze on her. I hadn't considered the effect this would have on my sister. Dad's death had hurt her more than it had me. Now here were two people who not only claimed to have known him, but who had worked closely with him in his fight against the USSF.

"It's them," I said. "I don't know how I know—"

"But there are no clear photos."

"—but I feel they're telling the truth." I looked around at the inside of *SC-1*. The hatch to engineering was open, and beyond that, the entryway to the micro-fusion drive was also ajar. Meg and Kat had been hard at work. They still weren't done, but they were making progress.

We were standing in the carpeted seating area near the two couches; a few meters aftward was the moonpool and toward the bow were the two recessed bunks, the hatch to the lavatory, and the opening to the control cabin and the two reclined pilot chairs.

Meg was frowning. "But how can you be sure?"

"The events that have led to this. They've been watching."

"For the past year?"

"For the past *thirty*. They've monitored everything. They know things no one else should."

She looked perplexed. "How?"

"They have informants too."

Kat said, "They could be USSF, Mac."

I sighed. It was a possibility, which was why I was about to do something that would shock all of them. Johnny was with us as well, and he'd been uncharacteristically quiet. He knew the impact dad's death had had on me. Johnny had been my best friend, after all. He knew me well.

"They might be informing for the USSF," I said. "They might be good actors. But if they're not who they say they are, it's better to get them out of here."

"What are you saying?"

I gestured to the engine compartment. "How soon will the seacar be ready to go?"

Kat blinked. "The conventional controls are fine. We can depart right now. But the SCAV drive will be another—"

"*Days,*" Meg snapped. "And we need to fix her completely in case we get into trouble." She stared at me, at the look in my eyes and the set of my jaw, and she tilted her head. Her blonde hair swished behind her. "You're thinking of going right now, aren't you?"

"Going where?" Johnny asked.

I glanced at him. "To The Ridge. We've been planning it for a few weeks now. We have to check in on things."

Kat said, "We also have to get Lazlow there."

That caught me off guard. "The acoustician? Can't it wait?" I had wondered if we should make sure he could physically handle life underwater first. Besides, I still didn't know why Meg and Kat wanted him at The Ridge.

"I told you, we recruited him to help us."

"Can't he just use the equipment in City Control?"

Kat smirked. "That's not why he's here."

I considered that for an instant, then waved it aside. "All right. All right." I sighed. "Yes, I want to leave now, in this seacar. We'll take Jessica Ng and Richard Lancombe."

"And Manesh Lazlow."

"Fine."

"I want to come too," Johnny said. He was grinning, and inside I shared his excitement. To get out into deep water and spend more time with my old friend. It would be fun.

I hoped.

I added the numbers in my head. Seven people in a seacar with only two bunks. There were two couches as well, but still the living arrangements would be tight.

And Jessica was in her sixties, Lancombe his seventies, and Doctor Lazlow was eighty.

I couldn't help but laugh. "It'll be an interesting journey, but we need to leave now."

"Why so soon?" Meg asked. She was exasperated. She'd been elbow-deep for hours trying to replace computer components and circuit boards.

"To get these two out of Trieste. To keep them from harm." I pursed my lips and looked at Meg. "Besides, we knew Dad better than anybody. If they're lying about this, we'll know. This will give us a good opportunity to check."

Meg said, "But what about the SCAV drive? It's not—"

"Bring your tools and the things you need. Kat can help. We'll repair *SC-1* on the way." It was a five day journey anyway. We'd need something to fill the time. Besides, the living compartments would be too tight for all of us to stay in there. Some of us could work in the engine compartment and fusion cabin. "Get your stuff, Johnny. We're going on another adventure."

He had a look of pure joy on his face.

—••—

I GRABBED A BAG FROM MY cabin and packed it for a journey of at least two weeks—I would have to wash clothes at some point and so only took a few quick-drying items, which was the norm around the colony—and marched to City Control. Grant Bell was at Sea Traffic Control and I sat next to him.

I had known him for years. He was on our side in the fight for independence. He'd been with me the day the two swimmers had discovered Rafe Manuel's body floating in the sea grasses outside.

"Grant," I asked in a quiet voice, "if I wanted to take a seacar south, then out to the Mid-Atlantic Ridge, but wanted to trick the USSF to think I was going north, what's the best course you'd take?"

I had an idea about the range of active sonar in the fleet, but I wanted to select a course that wouldn't give us away and would help protect The Ridge.

He leaned back, chewing a pencil, and frowned. He pushed his headset up. "I'd go north toward the Azores. Wait until any pursuing ship was a hundred kilometers away, then continue on the path until you could put another—" he frowned "—fifty between you, I'd say."

"Then turn south?"

"No. That would be a mistake. If you turned south and someone was approaching from here, you might still enter their active range. They'd tag you with a ping and it'd all be over."

I considered that. "So you'd go southeast."

He grinned. "Exactly. Bearing 135 would work. Do that for— How fast are you traveling?"

"Seventy."

"Do that for at least twenty-four hours, just to be safe." He glanced at me and lowered his voice. There were other city controllers in the darkened room, of course, monitoring systems. They were sitting at their own consoles, however, engaged in their own work. "Then go due south until you're past our latitude. At that point, you should be okay." He screwed his face up in thought. "But keep in mind, with acoustic signatures, the USSF can detect every ship within their passive range."

SC-1's passive range was thirty kilometers. "What's the USSF passive range?"

He shrugged. "Say fifty just to be sure."

I exhaled and slapped his shoulder. "Thanks, Grant. I'm leaving within a few hours. We'll take your route. Keep this between us."

"Got it." He grinned. "Good luck, Mac."

—••—

TWO HOURS LATER WE HAD ALL gathered in the tight confines of SC-1. Lancombe and Ng were on one couch, Lazlow on the one opposite. The ventilation system was humming in the background, and the lighting was on full. Everyone was looking around with concerned expressions; I knew they were wondering how we would manage for days in such a small vessel.

Meg was staring at the two people from our father's past. Her eyes had narrowed and I wondered for a moment or two if she was mad at them. She'd always resented the path he had taken, after all, and later, when she'd found out I had followed the same journey, she'd been furious. For a while anyway. She had come around and was now part of the movement. Still, I couldn't predict how she was going to react.

Lazlow was also fixated on the two of them. He was intensely curious. And, for their part, Lancombe and Ng were probably also wondering who the elderly doctor was.

"Perhaps some introductions?" I asked. There were nods all around. I gestured to the two freedom fighters. "Let me introduce Jessica and Richard." I left it at that to see if—

Lazlow interrupted. "Ng and Lancombe?"

Lancombe smiled. "Yes. It's us. Though we haven't used the names for decades." His forehead creased. "And may I ask who you are?"

"I'm Doctor Manesh Lazlow. I'm an acoustician. And of course I know who you both are. No one found your bodies after the action in 2099! I've studied the undersea cities and their histories extensively."

Meg said, "People thought you were dead." She'd addressed the two elderly freedom fighters, and had completely ignored Lazlow.

No one spoke for a long few heartbeats. Then finally Jessica said, "We made sure to keep it that way, actually. We didn't want the USSF to catch us, after all."

"And how did you survive while dad died?" Her voice was steel and her eyes fire.

I cleared my throat. "I haven't told you something, Meg. Something huge."

She turned to me and put her fists on her hips. "Out with it, Tru, now!"

I didn't know how to cushion the blow, so I just said it. "Dad wasn't assassinated."

"Bullshit," she snapped.

I held up my hand. "He *knew* it was coming, Meg. And he allowed it to happen." Her jaw dropped, and no one said a word.

—••—

AN HOUR LATER WE PULLED AWAY from Trieste under the cool thrum of the thrusters and the hiss of the water as the seacar sliced westward, away from the Gulf of Mexico. I made our depth thirty meters and moonlight from above filtered through the forward canopy as we powered along at seventy kph.

Behind me, Jessica and Richard were quiet, focused on their surroundings, while Lazlow was like a kid in a candy store, peering out the small portholes with a massive grin on his face. He pressed his thin fingers to the transparent material and studied the water outside, perhaps searching for fish, or just experiencing the thrill of being underwater and moving away from civilization and toward the dark crushing depths of the Atlantic.

Jessica and Richard rose to their feet and asked if they could see engineering. Meg was already back there fixing the systems, and called for them to join her.

I knew eventually we would have to have a long conversation with them about Dad; that would come in time.

It took five hours to thread our way through the Florida Strait, and then we turned our course northward, bearing forty degrees.

—••—

THE DAY WAS GROWING LATE; THE dinner hour was long past, and none of us had had a bite to eat in over eight hours. Johnny threw some rations together in the tiny living area, which was more difficult than it sounded because there were so many of us. We'd had to bring extra rations and water, along with three extra folding chairs, and we sat together for our first meal.

I couldn't help but watch the two old freedom fighters during the bland meal of stew and bread and water. They seemed happy with the meal, however, and actually thrilled with the situation as a whole. When I'd asked them to come with me—it was more of a demand, actually, but I'd couched it as a *request*—they hadn't complained at all. They didn't even know where we were going, but they were willing.

Lazlow just accepted it as another step in his journey to help our movement—I still wondered what the hell he was going to do at The Ridge—and Johnny was just happy to be along for the ride. Kat was of course content to be with *SC-1* and me, and to have time to work on the systems and get them back up and running. She'd been busy showing Lazlow around the colony, escorting him everywhere because he wanted to see every nook and cranny, and, after days of that, had been ready to cut him loose.

Meg was the only one who showed any anxiety about the situation, but I knew it was because of Richard and Jessica.

As I thought it, I noticed them watching me.

"This is quite a seacar," Jessica Ng said.

"It's hers." I pointed at Kat. "She designed and built it."

"Seems unique." They glanced at each other but didn't say anything else.

"Why don't *you* tell me about it," I said.

Richard chuckled. "Testing my knowledge, Mac?"

I shrugged. "You claim to have informants."

"Not everyone involved in the fight for independence died in 2099. Just the senior leadership. There were hundreds of others helping, and most of them are still alive. Working in the three US cities, or perhaps in other places around the oceans."

"And you have stayed in touch with them?"

He raised a finger. "Not all of them. Just a select few." He paused, and then, "And I know this sub has a supercavitating drive. I was hoping to see it in action."

I watched him silently. Then, "You may get a chance. It's down right now though."

"Ah. The EMP. Of course."

Meg's eyes widened. "You told him about that?"

"No. They knew."

She looked at them. "A supposed informant?"

Jessica offered a small smile. "Yes. The USSF scrambled a good portion of their subs in the Gulf when that happened. It wasn't exactly secret."

A silence descended over us, and I noticed they hadn't said who their contact in the USSF was.

Meg said, "Why do you say that Dad let himself die?"

No one spoke. There were a few coughs and lowered eyes.

I watched my sister and studied her body language. I couldn't tell if the notion bothered her more than the concept of assassination. "Does it matter, Meg?" I asked in a soft voice.

"Damn right. Before today I thought he'd died fighting for an ideal, at least. But now I find out that he just let someone—*let someone*—kill him." She let out an exasperated sigh. "I just don't understand it all."

Lancombe set down his plate and looked at her. "He did something wonderful, Meagan."

"Wonderful?" She looked disgusted.

"He knew we didn't have a chance. He knew we were too vulnerable." He flicked a glance at me. "He also knew that families in the city would die if it came to outright war." He snorted. "So he set the table for a meal people wouldn't eat for thirty years. He had hoped it would be you and Mac. But he'd set it up for the next fight for independence." He looked around. *"For now."*

Meg's jaw dropped and she stared at the two on the couch. Then she shot a look at me. "Are you hearing this, Tru?"

"Yes."

"And you think they're honest? You think Dad really did that?"

The others were watching silently, as if they were embarrassed to intrude on a family's airing of dirty laundry. I hesitated, then let out a long sigh. "I do, Meg. It makes sense." I gestured at them. "They knew it was coming. They had an escape planned. They got away."

"To fight another day," Lancombe said.

"And you've been planning for thirty years?" Meg asked, eyes narrowed.

"That's right."

She sighed and leaned back. "Well, I guess I'm anxious to hear what you've come up with." There was another brief silence as autopilot kept us on course and the electric thrusters vibrated the deck at our feet, the ventilation systems hummed in the background, and the seacar cut through the dark nighttime water, lit by the moon far above.

"Tell me about Dad," she said in a quiet, barely discernible voice.

CHAPTER TEN

WE WANTED TO TRAVEL IN THE North Atlantic gyre, a current flowing northward from the tropical areas of warmer, less dense waters to the cold areas of the northerly latitudes. We essentially kept the wind at our backs. I descended to 200 meters, right at the limits of the euphotic zone. The light level was effectively zero at this point. Plugging the course into the nav screen between the two seats in the control cabin, I studied the timeline it provided.

From the Florida Straits to Bermuda it was roughly 1800 kilometers. This leg of the journey would take twenty-five hours. I decided to roughly double it and continue on that heading for an additional twenty-seven hours. The southeast leg of the journey would take another twenty-four hours—as Grant had recommended—and then the due south portion to The Ridge's latitude would be another twenty-nine hours. Then I'd need an eastward voyage of twenty hours to reach The Ridge, which lay in the tectonically active and unstable portion of the Mid-Atlantic Ridge system—technically in the rift portion of the massive geologic feature. It was a deep zone in the Atlantic where tectonic plates diverged and spread in opposite directions. The movement occurred constantly with magma rising from the mantle to form new crust. Each year the plates at this location moved apart three to five centimeters, though it occurred in impossible-to-predict stutters. As a result, earthquakes were common, and combined with the depth of the facility at 4000 meters, it was strategically placed to avoid detection.

I didn't think anyone would be searching for it in such a dangerous location.

Leading a vessel straight to the facility was the last thing I wanted, and after hearing the news from *Impaler* about the USSF tracking our subs going southward to the mysterious destination, I realized this circuitous route was certainly the best option. It would take us just over five days to make the journey, but it was a minor inconvenience in the grand scheme of things.

The turbulence was constant, the seacar rattling and bouncing in the undersea currents, and I worried that some of the passengers might become sick. Lazlow, Jessica, and Richard to be precise. All seemed to bear the journey just fine, however. Lazlow had thrown himself into this willingly and was loving every second of discomfort, and the other two had spent their lives underwater. Still, I thought, a stable steel deck of the underwater colony Ballard was far different from the bouncing and shaking of a small seacar forging through the Atlantic depths, but they didn't show even a shred of annoyance at it.

Meg and I spent the evening speaking with Richard and Jessica about our father. Meg listened with wide eyes to stories about his troubles as mayor and the obstacles he'd encountered due to the USSF and their restrictions. The reasons why he had led the fight for independence. Of course we were generally familiar with the history of it all, but there were stories about the struggle that were not public knowledge. USSF abuses of Triestrian citizens for instance, such as violent assaults like muggings and rapes. There were also instances of goods taken directly from our processing modules and sent straight to the mainland to profit the corrupt officers in charge of the undersea colonies. Admiral Taurus T. Benning, it turned out, had been one of the worst offenders. He'd built a fortune in Texas, mostly off the backs of the undersea colonists.

I shook my head at that news. I'd had no idea.

Benning had been in command of the entire Gulf and Caribbean USSF forces during the Second Battle of Trieste—I had surrendered to him at its conclusion. He now seemed to be more focused on The Iron Plains in the Pacific Ocean—a contentious area of the seafloor, claimed by both the States and China, just east of the Philippines—leaving Captain Heller the prominent officer in Trieste's region.

Richard and Jessica also spoke about day-to-day issues father had had as mayor, stories that made me sit up and take notice because I was now dealing with the same problems. Labor issues on the farms, keeping the kelp harvesting going despite mechanical breakdowns, even an attempted uprising by a group who'd wanted independence far earlier than 2099.

"Your dad negotiated with them after he stopped it," Richard said. "He folded those people into his own plans. Kept them happy."

The lights were down in the living area, and Kat had already fallen asleep in one of the bunks, and so Meg kept her voice low as she asked, "There were other attempts?" She was incredulous. We had never known.

"Yes. They were even more haphazard and insane than ours," Jessica said.

"Were they aware that dad was going to sacrifice himself?"

Lazlow, who had been paying close attention to the discussion, said, "These details would stun modern day historians. No one had any idea about any of this."

"There's a lot people don't know," Jessica said. "The city council would never have agreed with Frank's idea. You see, your dad's plan was actually to pause things until we were really ready. It was a hard freeze. He knew we weren't well enough equipped. He did it with only the knowledge of a few people."

"They killed the whole city council though. Dad didn't warn them?"

Jessica looked away and Richard lowered his eyes. "No. Your dad sacrificed himself, but he never told the council. They were on our side in the fight, but your dad didn't think they'd die as well. He expected an occupation that never really came—not until last year, that is." Richard sighed. "Had your dad known what Benning was going to do, he would have come up with something else."

We grew silent and considered that for long moments. Until then, I hadn't known who had ordered father's death.

Admiral Benning.

I'd remember that.

There were a few yawns, and we realized how late it was, and how long that day had been.

We fell asleep as *SC-1* cut through the waters of the Atlantic, toward Bermuda and a circuitous path leading to a mysterious future.

—••—

AT TIMES DURING THE NEXT DAY, I found myself sitting in the control cabin with Johnny at my side. He couldn't hide his joy, and I shook my head at him several times before he finally pointed it out.

"What's wrong?" he asked.

A shrug. I wasn't as thrilled as he was. "You?"

"Tell me you're not happy right now."

I considered that. After what I'd learned about my father, and how uncertain the future was, it was hard to be happy.

But I knew what he meant. We had a long history together, of adventures and battles and covert operations in the various undersea colonies of the world. It was a shared history, and when he had betrayed me it had hurt worse than death. But he'd made up for what had happened months ago now, and I'd found myself missing him since he'd left to negotiate a truce of sorts with the other Chinese cities.

He grinned at me. "We make a good team. This is going to work out."

"I hope so."

He gestured with his chin behind us, to Lancombe and Ng. "Do you believe them?" His voice was a whisper; the hatch behind us was open.

I considered it for a heartbeat. "Yes. They could be acting, but if they are, they're damn good. I think they have a lot to offer."

"What, exactly?"

"Defensive strategies. Tactics. They've been thinking about this for thirty years."

He shook his head. "Amazing that they hid themselves for so long."

Johnny and I piloted the seacar past Bermuda over the next hours, and there wasn't much to do and not much conversation either.

But I had to admit, I did love every minute of it.

—••—

THE NEXT DAY ALL HELL BROKE loose.

Meg and Kat had been working in the fusion room, repairing scorched circuit boards, running tests, and attempting to get the containment and control systems back up and running for the SCAV drive. They were still days away, but the hope was that by the time we reached The Ridge, *SC-1*'s systems would be fully operational.

Lazlow had spent the morning sitting in the lounge speaking with the two veteran freedom fighters, and I sat in the control cabin, in the left seat, watching systems, one eye on the sonar and one out the canopy—although the only thing to see was swirling plankton and the odd fish only briefly illuminated in our running lights before they flashed away, out of sight—and kept an ear open as I listened to the three talking behind me. Almost every story was one history did not know, and it gave new insight into both our current struggle as well as my dad's.

There were some ships on the sonar screen, which showed a thirty kilometer radius around us. Most were surface vessels, although there were subs and seacars about, but nothing out of the ordinary. Subs going to Europe were at a similar depth to us in the northerly Gulf current, and southward-bound ships were much deeper, trying to catch a current to give them an added speed boost. Most seacar depths maxed out at 2000 meters, however; *SC-1's* crush depth was 4000.

A blip appeared on the screen behind us. It was at the outer limits of our passive range, but its speed was seventy-six kph.

It was a warsub of the FSF.

It was a *Liberty* class vessel, and it took our onboard computer only a few seconds to identify it.

Hunter.

It was the same warsub that had chased me in the Gulf while on my way to Ballard. The same one that, as I'd theorized, had called in an EMP to strand me long enough for a French task force to try and take me out.

I swore. We couldn't currently outrun her. She was thirty kilometers behind us, and each hour she would gain six kilometers. That meant she'd be on us in five hours, unless they had help waiting for them either in the sea or in the air. I hoped they wouldn't be brash enough to try another EMP, especially with the US watching carefully after the last episode.

"We've got a problem," I said. The others responded instantly and clustered at my back. Kat slid into the chair on the right and pulled herself up to the controls. She toggled on the VID screen—that virtual heads up display that converted all signals to white shapes on a blue background—and the canopy around us lit up. The others gasped when they saw it. Lazlow in particular had a look of astonishment on his face as he peered around him. Vessels on the surface appeared on the canopy, as well as a few seacars in our lane and on a similar heading.

I glanced at the navigation screen. We had another fifteen hours on this course before the course shift to the southeast, and I wanted to leave the French far behind.

They wanted me very badly, I thought. *Damn.*

"We have only a few options here," I said. "First is to get the SCAV drive going *now.*"

"Not going to happen," Meg said in a curt voice.

I snorted. "Okay. Good to know. Option two is to turn and fight. We have four conventional and four SCAV torpedoes."

"How fast are the SCAVs?" Lancombe asked.

"A thousand kph. We developed them within the past few months."

He whistled.

"That would most likely guarantee a kill," I said, "but they're already after me for killing French sailors and government officials."

"They won't let up," Johnny murmured.

"No." I considered the situation for another few heartbeats. "Option three is to go deep and hope to avoid them."

"What's the—" Kat started to ask, but I cut her off.

"It's 1900 meters. But they'll just circle and shoot down at us, drop mines, and so on." I chewed my lip. "Option four is to bottom the boat. It's still shallow enough here. Depth is—" I glanced at the fathometer "—2300 meters, give or take. We could try to blend in with the bottom." It's what I had done last time. And it had worked. But it had taken days of waiting, and in the end the USSF had scared the French away.

"Any other options?" Lazlow asked.

"Option five," I said. "We try to damage them and then run."

"That would mean more potential injuries. You can't guarantee the warsub wouldn't sink to crush depth or that French sailors wouldn't drown."

"True." I paused. "We have one more option."

"What is it?"

I glanced at Kat. "We've developed a new avoidance strategy. It's called a noise bomb."

Lazlow grunted. "Can you explain?" He was an acoustician, after all. I knew it would interest him. In fact, when I'd first met him, I'd thought this weapon deterrent might be the reason he'd come to Trieste.

"It's a three-pronged system. We let the pursuing sub get closer to us. From a rear hatch, we launch a torpedo at them. It detonates behind us, but it's not an explosion. It creates a high pitched noise for five minutes to disorient their sonar."

"Five minutes won't—"

"I haven't explained the other two aspects to this. Simultaneously, we launch two torpedoes. Each goes in a different direction. They broadcast the normal noises of *SC-1* at a reduced speed. Fifty kph. We then lower our own speed to fifty, change course, and hope they pick the wrong one to follow."

Lazlow grinned. "And the five minute noise bomb confuses them enough so when it finally lets up, they see three identical tracks and don't know which to follow."

"It'll give us a chance to get away anyway. And since we've been on the same course since Bermuda, they might not choose ours."

"We're not even going in the direction we want anyway," Meg said.

We didn't want to give our true course away, but I held my tongue.

"What about size?" Lazlow asked, his wrinkled face tight with worry. "Sonar will show that those are torpedoes and we're the real seacar."

"The decoys trail objects that reflect sound; they'll send a similar size and profile as *SCAV-1*."

A silence descended on us as we considered the six options. But there was really only one, which we all finally agreed on.

Option six.

The noise bomb.

—••—

WE ONLY HAD ONE, AND IF it didn't work, we were in serious trouble.

A systems check showed all three torpedoes were functioning and ready for launch. Kat had programmed them; two decoys would cruise at bearings 11 and 263 respectively. *SC-1* would lower speed to fifty and take a heading of ninety-seven. So the French would have to decide between three tracks: follow the heading back to the mainland, follow the one going roughly north but more or less on the track we'd already been on, or follow the one approximately eastward. That would be ours.

If they chose ours, we'd have to try to evade and it would force me to damage the warsub with a SCAV torpedo and hope no one else would die.

The comm suddenly beeped, and I stared at it in shock.

"Attention *SC-1*," a female voice said.

It sounded vaguely familiar and my brow furrowed. "What the hell?"

"Attention. Do not try to run. This is the FSF sub *Chasseur*. Cease your operations immediately and heave to. We mean to board you."

I swore. It was an outright lie. The French soldiers had told me they meant to kill me. Asking us to "heave to," or stop and allow them to connect an umbilical so they could board, was a lie.

But still . . . that voice. There was something about it.

I reached to thumb the mic on—

And Kat grabbed my hand. "Are you sure? You want to reveal that you're on this seacar right now?"

"I think they know already. And if I remain quiet, they're still going to do what they're going to do. Might as well find out what they want."

She stared into my eyes and after a long and drawn-out heartbeat, she gave a small nod.

I switched the comm on. "This is Truman McClusky. What are your intentions?"

There was a pause, and then, "McClusky. I've told you my intentions. Now stop your vessel."

Smiling to myself, I did as she asked. "What do you want me for?"

"You know already. You're wanted for the murder of multiple French citizens."

I frowned. The voice was so damned—

Of course. I knew who it was. "Hello again, Captain."

She hesitated. "Stay where you are."

"How did you find out that I was the one at the guyot? Who told you?"

"That doesn't matter."

I had an idea, but didn't want to reveal my cards. "You're either very stupid or very brave," I said, "to detonate an EMP off the coast of the United States."

"We will do what it takes to catch a criminal."

"And what are you doing on that ship? *Hunter.* Last I heard from you, you were captaining a *Requin* class warsub. You tried to take me before at that French base, but I got away."

The change in her tone was ominous. She was trying to hide her anger, but could not do so. "You fired on my vessel. You killed government officials in a French base. You're a dangerous criminal. I will take you in or kill you, Mayor McClusky."

I blew out my breath in a rush. "You were stupid back then. You let me get too close. It gave me an out. Are you sure you want to test me again?"

"There is no test here. You're going to pay."

As you probably paid for the loss, I thought. She'd most likely been through hell after the incident. Forced to find out who had piloted this seacar, who had fired on her ship. The FSF had moved her to a sub less than half the size with eleven fewer crew as punishment.

"Why aren't you on the same warsub?" I asked in a quiet voice. "What happened?"

"None of your fucking business," she ground out.

Beside me, Kat covered the mic and grimaced. "This is one pissed off woman."

She was indeed. But Kat understood why it had happened then, why I'd done it. *SC-1* had been involved in a desperate hunt to stop Johnny Chang from giving away the secrets to the SCAV drive. I had done something necessary in order to capture Johnny and protect Trieste's future.

There was no going back now.

"I can't do what you're asking," I whispered into the mic. "But good luck to you."

CHAPTER ELEVEN

THERE WAS A BRIEF BURST OF yelled, unintelligible orders and then the comm signal cut out. I glanced at Kat. "You're right. She's pissed." I wondered what the French captain's life had been like since our confrontation at the guyot. She'd probably had to crawl home in a damaged vessel facing an extremely hostile crew. Then an inquisition by her government as they'd tried to piece together what had happened, why there were dead French citizens, and why a civilian seacar had bested their warsub.

And, just as important, why they had lost the secrets to the SCAV drive.

I'd arrived just as the transaction had been taking place, and stopped it just in time.

Hell, I thought, *she could start an international incident over this, if not outright war between the States and France.*

The passive sonar showed the warsub now at a distance of twenty-eight kilometers.

Our own speed was zero, our thrusters at station-keeping. The sonic bomb deterrent was prepared and ready. We would wait until they were twenty kilometers away, then launch the bomb. When it reached the halfway mark between our two subs, it would detonate. At that point, we'd launch the other two torpedoes. The decoys.

We watched the countdown slowly. The others were sitting in the living area, not making a sound.

All except Meg, that is. She remained in the fusion room, working feverishly on the SCAV drive.

Kat noticed me craning my neck to peer down the length of the seacar, and she shook her head. "We're still a good two days away from fixing it. She's just doing what she knows."

"She's good at it," I said. I remembered how she'd repaired *SC-1* after the damage the Chinese had inflicted on us over the Aleutian Trench. She'd fixed the seacar's structural issues as well as system shorts and flooding in only a night of work.

"She is," Katherine agreed. "I just hope we can get out of this."

I grinned. "Come on. You don't trust me? After what we've been through?"

"That is one hell of a motivated person out there." She sighed. "It would be a shame to see it end here though."

I glanced at the sonar screen. There were other contacts around us, but none friendly.

Friendly.

I wondered if we could even consider the USSF friendly in a situation like this. They were most likely after us too, trying to figure out the location of our secret base, and wondering exactly what we were doing there.

Twenty-six kilometers.

I put my hand on Kat's arm and smiled at her. It had indeed been an incredible year. We'd been through a lot, and I didn't want this adventure to end here either. There was still so much to do.

She leaned in and kissed me, with the other passengers watching behind us.

"Easy now," Johnny said, laughing.

I pulled away after a minute and glanced at him. "Any ideas?" I shot another look at the sonar.

Twenty-five kilometers.

It was almost time.

The FIRE button in the torpedo control panel between the two seats was staring at me, glowing like an angry sun.

Johnny sighed. "Not really. If this noise bomb of yours doesn't work . . . we can go deep. Maybe catch an inversion layer if we're lucky."

He was referring to a layer of cold, deep water. With a radically different temperature and salinity, such boundaries could reflect sounds and effectively hide a sub. Inversion layers existed in every ocean and most deep seas, and in the Atlantic one would be very deep, in the southward moving cold and dense gyre. But at our location still so close to the US continental shelf, I doubted such a layer would be present. They were usually where depths pushed five kilometers or more. Right now the depth was just over two kilometers.

"We can try," I said. "But—"

"Yeah, I know. It's doubtful."

"We could just blow them out of the water. Use a SCAV torpedo or two. But that would cause a major problem for us." Before, when I'd been forced to fire on her ship, I'd warned them to evacuate the areas of the sub I'd been aiming at. I'd only done it to disable them. And on top of that, they hadn't known my identity. Now, there was no hiding it.

"Still, if that's our only option."

I sighed.

That FIRE button was still staring at me.

Twenty-three kilometers.

"It's almost time," I hissed at the others behind me. "Get ready. We'll be firing once, on a heading behind us. It'll detonate within a few minutes. Then we'll fire two more simultaneously. At that point we'll accelerate to fifty kilometers per hour, set an easterly course, and watch them very closely. Hopefully they won't follow."

Twenty-one kilometers.

My heart was pounding and my hands were tight on the yoke.

"Don't worry," Kat whispered. "It's going to work."

If it didn't, I'd be pissed. We'd put a lot of work into the noise bomb.

On a sudden whim, I clicked the mic and signaled *Hunter.*

What are you doing? Kat mouthed to me.

I ignored her. "Attention *Hunter*," I said. "This is Truman McClusky."

After a moment. "Go ahead." It was the captain again.

"I wanted to say that I'm sorry for what happened to your last sub."

"How considerate of you," she snapped. "Are you surrendering?"

"No." I hesitated, and then, "Never. But I was wondering . . . why do you want me?"

She paused, and then, "This is Captain Renée Féroce of FSF Warsub *Chasseur*, formally of FSF Warsub *Destructeur*."

So, that sub had been called *Destroyer.*

I continued. "Did I kill anyone on board your sub?"

"Do you actually have a conscience?" I didn't answer, and she said, her voice still hard, "Yes, actually. You killed one and seriously wounded three. And now you're going to pay."

I blew my breath out in a rush. It was a shame, but I had warned her. The alternative had been too scary. "You're going to have to kill me, Renée. You know that, right?"

"What do you think I'm trying to do?" she asked, her voice ice.

I glanced at the sonar.

Twenty kilometers.

"That's what I thought," I whispered. And I pressed the FIRE button. "Perhaps we'll meet again."

Then I cut the signal.

I'm sure alarms were ringing through the warsub at that very instant as their sonar detected the high shriek of the weapon streaking through the water, cavitating screws sending a stream of bubbles to the surface.

"Torpedo in the water," Kat said. "Running on a straight line to *Hunter*. Its speed is eighty."

That was the highest speed we could reach underwater, for any vessel or weapon, unless we used SCAV technology, which could go much faster—by a factor of ten or more.

"Close rear torpedo hatch," I said. It had been a new addition to *SC-1*—there had been no such hatch when Kat had first designed and built the seacar. Only the forward one, at the bow, just before the control cabin. "Prepare the next torpedo, Kat."

A press of a button automatically loaded the decoy weapon in the forward tube.

I watched the sonar carefully. "When it detonates at the halfway mark, we'll fire."

"Got it."

"Are they changing course?" Johnny asked from the living area.

"No," I replied. "They're heading straight for it."

"That's weird," Lazlow said. "Why head straight for a torpedo?"

"They've got plenty of time to react. It's still—" I checked quickly "—fifteen kilometers from impact. But the distance is closing rapidly."

We sat still and quiet in the seacar. Even Meg had returned from engineering. I glanced back at her and smiled. She returned it warmly. Ever since we'd reconnected and had started working together in this fight, things had been good between us. I had finally told her the truth about my past in the intelligence business, and now that she had joined the fight, we had a common goal and it had strengthened our relationship enormously. *Don't worry*, I mouthed at her.

The warsub was still on the same heading, at the same speed. I shook my head. Renée Féroce was determined, all right. She hadn't veered off in the slightest.

"Do you think she knows it's a noise bomb and it won't really hurt her ship?" Kat asked.

"There's no way she could know. It's never been tried."

"Still."

"What?"

She gestured at the sonar. "She's not moving away. That shows the exact same signal as any torpedo. Why wouldn't she at least evade and use countermeasures?"

I shook my head. This French captain was a conundrum.

The sonar screen abruptly flared white in the southern quadrant—directly behind us for a distance out to the limits of our passive mode—and the blotch remained there, flickering and pulsing as the noise bomb let off an unrelenting screech that would disorient and mask the audio signatures of any ships in the immediate vicinity.

"There it is," I said. "Launch the first decoy." Ten seconds later, "Launch the second."

The torpedoes were clearly visible in the water outside the canopy. The first shot out, trailing a stream of bubbles, and curved to the port, disappearing from sight within seconds in the dark water. It would send our fake acoustic signal northerly, close to our previous bearing. The second torpedo disappeared to the starboard. It would arc back to a westerly heading and send our signature on a bearing to the mainland.

"Close the hatch please, Kat."

I pushed the throttle forward and held it steady at fifty kph on our preplanned easterly heading. The thrusters vibrated the deck and the smooth hum filled the cabin. It sounded good.

I glanced at the white pulsing nebula on the screen. That noise bomb would be shielding all sounds in the ocean from the French sub. The same thing was happening to us right now as well, I realized. Our two weapons weren't showing on the screen at all.

I looked at the others. "The bomb will last five minutes. We have about four left. When it stops, we have to remain absolutely quiet."

"I actually programmed one of the torpedoes to broadcast an audio file of us talking," Kat said.

That made me blink. "Really?" I hesitated. "That's— That's—"

"Brilliant," Lazlow said with a smile. "Absolutely genius."

She shrugged. "We'll see."

"Now we have to be quiet," I said. "But first, any last words?"

There was no response; just nervous faces. No one laughed at my joke. I set the autopilot to maintain a steady heading, sat back, and exhaled. Sweat beaded on my forehead.

—••—

WITHIN FOUR MINUTES THE WHITE SPLOTCH that had occupied a massive portion of the sonar disappeared and the screen went momentarily blank. A blinking REBOOTING appeared in the top corner, and then it flashed once and the contacts in the passive range appeared again. I switched the VID on and looked left and right to find the torpedoes—

They were there. Each running straight and true, on the correct headings. Only they didn't look like torpedoes. They were seacars.

And on the projection, created by the computer and based on the sounds received, both looked suspiciously like *SC-1*.

The sonar confirmed it. Each signal on the scope had a label over it:

American Registry, US Colony Trieste
Database Identification: *SC-1*

A glance at the others showed their joy. *It was working!*

I realized an instant later I really should look into changing our own audio signature in some way. I wasn't sure how to do that however, because the engine output, screw shape, battery wattage, and fuselage/stabilizer form all determined a sub's signature.

We stared at the scope intently for long minutes. At that precise minute, Renée Féroce was no doubt watching three identical seacars sailing in three different directions, trying to figure out which to chase. The French warsub was 9000 meters behind us now, and we watched intently to see which way she turned.

West, north, or east?

If they picked east, we would need another strategy.

One that involved death, I thought.

—••—

THEY CHOSE NORTH.

Kat grinned. "That's the one that had the audio file of us." Her voice was barely a whisper.

Then three signals appeared on the screen simultaneously. Each was red. Torpedoes, sent out after each of the three *SC-1* signals.

And then, seconds later, three more.

There were now two torpedoes chasing each target, and they were 8500 meters away from us and closing fast.

Their speed was nearly eighty. Ours was fifty.

I sighed. I had expected it. The distance was so great, however, I hoped that the weapons would exhaust their power and sink harmlessly to the bottom before they could hit us. At the very least, we could avoid and launch countermeasures, but that would give our location away.

"What will the decoys do when those torpedoes close on them?" My voice was barely audible.

"Nothing. They'll stay on track, straight and true."

"Then we may have to do the same."

The depth was 2680 meters in this area. We might have to just bottom the seacar, pretend to be sunk, I thought.

Behind us the weapon closed steadily. I wanted to push the throttle forward, but if I did, the move would betray us. I gritted my teeth and stared at the screen.

Suddenly the FSF warsub shifted its heading to the east.

Toward us.

Damn. They'd had second thoughts, perhaps realized the audio file was too obvious a ploy.

"Will our decoy torpedoes change course?" Johnny asked at my back. "Can we make one look like it's us?"

Kat shook her head.

"Can we control them?"

"No."

"Then we wait," I said.

—••—

THE TORPEDOES ON OUR TAIL HAD closed steadily; they were now 2000 meters behind us.

To make things worse, eight kilometers behind them, *Hunter* was still on our tail.

Of the three targets to choose from, the French captain had picked ours.

I swore. We would have to fight.

But the two torpedoes on our tail weren't gaining anymore, and Kat sat up straighter when she realized this. We looked at each other with wide grins. They were running low on power.

Sure enough, the torpedoes started falling behind. Range 2020. Range 2029. Range 2038.

Range 2053.

A hand appeared on my shoulder. "Slow the seacar. Descend. Do it slowly, as if we're running out of power."

I looked behind me at Richard Lancombe and frowned. Then it hit me.

It might just work.

I began powering down.

Kat's face was grim, but she gave me a slight nod.

Over the next few minutes I continued to cut power. I also pushed the yoke away from me, bringing us closer and closer to the bottom. Soon the bathymetry of the ocean floor appeared on the canopy before us, white lines tracing the edges of features on the blue background.

Johnny pointed from behind me at a canyon straight ahead. It was a hundred meters deeper than the surrounding bottom, and it ran across our heading.

The trick was to make it look as if we were descending into it naturally.

The French warsub was gaining on us quickly. She was now less than five kilometers behind, at the same depth we'd been.

But still I pulled the throttle back and pushed the control yoke forward, aiming for the feature in the VID projected on the canopy around us. We sailed toward the yawning crevasse in the crust of the ocean floor—

We were over it now. Another few meters to descend—

And we were below the lip of the canyon.

I slammed the yoke forward and set us in a near vertical plunge.

Behind me were screams as people tried to hang on to something.

"Sorry!" I called. I wasn't worried about too much noise now; the lip of the canyon would cut it off from the warsub. I righted the seacar slightly and took on ballast. On the VID I could see boulders, rocks, ledges, rills, and ridges.

I picked a large feature against the canyon wall and positioned the vessel over it. Cutting power to the thrusters, we sank to the sandy floor. I kept the skids retracted; we needed to be as close to the seafloor as possible, to blend in as best we could.

We hit with a dull thud and a rattle. The hull creaked slightly, but I wasn't concerned. The vessel could take so much more pressure than the depth we were at: 2931 meters.

We flicked the lights off and sat in silence. They'd be up there.

Watching.

CHAPTER TWELVE

THE TRICK WAS TO MAKE THEM think we had just been a decoy torpedo that had depleted its batteries. We'd effectively sunk our own ship, made it negatively buoyant, and were hiding in a hundred meter-deep and fifty meter-wide canyon, nestled in amongst a jumble of boulders and ridges and ledges with the cliff at our side. The VID over my head showed the canyon above us, and the blue background was dark and ominous.

Blue so dark it was nearly black.

The white outline of the French warsub *Hunter* appeared far above.

—••—

WE WATCHED THE CANOPY IN DEAD silence. They were circling. They knew generally where we had gone, but I was still unsure if our ploy had worked.

But then mines started falling.

The VID displayed them as white stars.

And they were damned near to our position. Some were going to hit very close.

It was impossible to tell if the French knew our exact location, or if they'd just guessed and had started dropping bombs, like a WWII destroyer trying to damage a hidden U-Boat.

Those subs could only descend 200 meters.

We were at more than ten times that depth.

I spun to the others and mouthed, "Prepare the seacar—*quietly.*"

Meg and Johnny sprinted aftward. Meg collected tools to stow, and Johnny made sure everything was secured. If there were loose items about—wrenches, screwdrivers, cups, and plates for instance—and a nearby explosion sent them crashing to the deck, the warsub might hear.

They had a sonar operator, not to mention a computer with sensitive listening apparatuses, for just such a purpose.

The mines were only a few minutes away now. Eventually my people had sealed the hatches and the others were sitting in their places. Lazlow was gripping a mask and flippers, and it made me shake my head.

If we lost hull integrity, we'd be pulp in an instant. The surrounding pressure would collapse the bulkheads, and the incoming surge of water would be instant death.

Then again, I thought, if we developed a slow leak, not unheard of but extremely rare at current pressures, a rising water level might indeed warrant a mask.

Then I snorted inwardly. Nonsense. The pressure would just continue to rise—skyrocket in fact—until it compressed our chests like tissue paper.

The explosions began without warning. Pounding the cliff beside us, pummeling us with shock and compression waves.

The seacar rattled with each detonation. Meg and Kat had their heads buried in their arms, trying to stifle their cries. Lazlow was terrified—but he stayed silent, thankfully. Lancombe and Ng kept their faces impassive as the mines rained down on us.

Lancombe shrugged when he saw me watching him. He acted as though he'd been through it a million times. Perhaps he just didn't care anymore, after all he'd been through, after the life he'd lived underwater.

More explosions.

I gripped the arms of the pilot chair, knuckles white and palms sweaty on the leather. More mines were falling, but we were getting hit by falling rocks now as well. They were crumbling off the cliff that loomed over us, and showers of boulders streaked downward on the VID display. Everything from tiny gravel to basketball-sized rocks hit *SC-1* and ricocheted off the hull, peppering the ocean floor around us.

Well, I thought, grim. *They probably heard that.*

The console illumination flickered. The dim lights in the ceiling cut out.

Ventilation fans ceased.

Oh, shit.

This was bad.

And still the mines fell. Explosions shook the seacar, pressure waves cascaded over us. Equipment and tools rattled in their drawers and toolboxes. It was impossible to stop. Sweat soaked my forehead. I wiped an arm across it.

Drops of it trickled down my back.

If our lives ended right then and there, faster would indeed be better.

—••—

THE ATTACK LASTED FOR ANOTHER TEN minutes. The mines had fallen up and down the length of the canyon—at least within the five kilometers the VID could display—so I realized that the French captain didn't know precisely where we were. They were just dropping the weapons everywhere, hoping to take us out.

But finally it ended, and the enemy vessel churned serenely over the lip of the canyon to the west.

They were moving away, perhaps to chase down one of the other targets.

Still, I thought while chewing my lip, they'd been moving slowly.

I blew my breath out and looked at the others. The canyon afforded us some privacy because it cut off any noise we produced, but at the same time it protected the French warsub. We could no longer hear where they'd gone.

Johnny was shaking his head but there was a smile on his face. Kat looked terrified and Meg had a determined set to her jaw. Lancombe and Ng were impassive, as normal, and Doctor Manesh Lazlow was wide-eyed.

There was an odor of burnt electrical insulation in the air.

"It's okay," I said to him. "They've left."

He tried to speak but only a croak came out. Then he finally managed, "Thank God. I thought we were done for there."

"I've been through it more than a few times. It never gets easy."

But then I thought of Lancombe, who hadn't seemed bothered in the least.

The sonar was now dark. We had a lot of repairs to start on before we could get moving again. Meg and Kat would most likely be able to fix the systems without much trouble. If there were any major problems that would keep us from continuing to The Ridge, they would be structural, caused by compression waves and falling boulders.

We'd have to inspect the hull, when we reached a shallower depth.

Luckily there was no water flooding into *SC-1*, but the ship had taken a pounding.

—••—

SOME OF THE COMPUTER CONTROLS HAD shorted in the blasts. There was
a haze of smoke in the air. Kat made swift work of them, however, locating
the system outages and swapping out dead parts for new. Meg worked the
engineering side, tracing circuits and checking breakers and wiring for any
issues. Soon the consoles were lit again, the sonar was showing an empty
canyon, and the VID system was up and running.

But when we switched ballast to positive, blowing water from the tanks,
the vessel didn't move a millimeter.

Rocking us back and forth with the thrusters didn't work either. Both
operated normally and the churning sand outside was reassuring, but still
we couldn't move.

And, of course, the SCAV drive was down, and would remain so for another
two days.

There was no calling for help; the canyon would prevent all signals from
reaching a junction on a comm line.

I turned and looked at Johnny; his face was as grim as mine.

In the incredible deeps of the Atlantic, at the bottom of a barren canyon,
next to an unstable cliff that continued dropping boulders around us due to
new cracks and stress fractures, we were going to have to go outside and clear
the debris off *SCAV-1*.

—••—

I'D BEEN OUT DEEPER, ONCE BEFORE, and the punishment had nearly crippled
me for life. But I'd anticipated it happening again, and this time had stored
tanks of gases in the seacar so we could create our own mix. Because the
pressure outside was so great, we'd have to make a breathing mix that had a
very tiny percentage of oxygen. Too much oxygen under great pressures could
actually be toxic. There would also be nitrogen in the mix—but once again,
too much was a bad thing. The pressure would force more into our blood and
tissues and cause nitrogen narcosis, or *Rapture of the Deep*. It caused euphoria
and hallucinations. The rest of the mix would be an inert gas: helium. To make
the pressure outside bearable, we would have to breathe a mix that was at an
equal pressure, roughly 300 atmospheres.

Johnny swore when he heard my plan. He knew I'd done it before, but still
the thought was terrifying. But being prepared and confident could get one
through any manner of challenging problem, and Johnny and I had been

partners in TCI for years. He trusted my advice, and I knew that physically he could handle it.

It didn't prevent the fears from creeping in, however.

We were trembling as we climbed into the airlock.

Kat began to pressurize the chamber. Our ears started to hurt; we had to equalize constantly, squeezing our noses and pushing air into our ear drums to keep them the same pressure as the airlock—the *Valsalva* maneuver.

Kat monitored us through the closed circuit camera.

From this point onward, we'd have to depressurize when we returned from outside. It would take hours, perhaps the rest of the trip.

But it was a necessary discomfort. Survival was at stake.

Hell, the entire independence movement was on the brink. I realized with a hot pit in my gut that the people in that seacar were invaluable to it. We had to make it out of there. There were no other options.

The pressure continued to build.

—••—

THE AIRLOCK HATCH OPENED SLOWLY. IT was pitch black outside. Johnny and I had torches, which were high-wattage lamps, but even then they only illuminated a radius of a few meters. We stepped off the lip of the airlock and floated a meter to the bottom. It was hard rock at my feet; as we walked, we kicked up a few wisps of sandy clouds, but not a great deal. If we had been at a shallower depth, the visibility wouldn't have been too bad. There didn't seem to be much floating in the water with us. I'd been some places where there was so much life and churned up sediment that you couldn't see anything at all, even with powerful torches and the sun high in the sky.

"Kat," I said, swallowing past the lump in my throat. "Please turn on the exterior lights." I didn't worry about the vehicle being visible to anyone other than me and Johnny.

There was no one else around.

An instant later the seacar's lamps flared to life, illuminating a circle around the vessel.

Johnny and I gasped.

Then we swore.

There were a cluster of boulders on the hull of the ship, in front of the vertical stabilizer. Smaller ones were sitting on the horizontal support structures containing the two thruster pods. No wonder we couldn't move. There were hundreds of tons of extra weight on the sub. There's no way we could have ever hit positive buoyancy, and despite being under water, inertia was still a substantial force with that much extra weight on the seacar.

"Johnny," I said. "We have to get up there and start clearing the debris." There was no choice, no time to mull it over. I figured we had maybe an hour at most out there, possibly only forty-five minutes, before we had to get back to the sub. Our tanks couldn't hold much air at these incredible pressures, and going in and back out again was not something we wanted to tackle.

"Copy that," he said in a short voice.

Back to the old days, I thought. Planning a mission with a partner. There was no banter, no joking around. *Just get the job done, then move on.*

We had to grab the horizontal stabilizer to haul ourselves up. Fingers scrabbled at the hull plates, and gravel rained down on our masks as we looked up. But that wasn't the stuff I was concerned about. It was the large boulders we had to clear. I hoped we'd be able to move them. If not . . .

Finally I was standing on the seacar and I leaned forward in the direction I wanted to move. One foot after another, pushing stone chips and pebbles and rocks away, no doubt scraping the hull hundreds if not thousands of times. *Kat will be pissed*, I thought.

Still I pressed onward, Johnny at my side. His form was a shadow next to mine; the dim light barely showed him in his black wetsuit. But I could make out his face, and his eyes flicked to mine as we trudged along the top of the seacar toward the larger rocks.

Eventually we arrived—five meters had taken more effort than I'd imagined—and we began shoving rocks from the hull. We had brought two pry bars with us, and together we started to move some material.

The hull shifted under my feet, and I nearly lost my balance.

"Uh, Kat," I said. "Make sure the buoyancy is set to negative, please." I didn't want the seacar to suddenly float away from us.

A laugh, barely discernible. It sounded as though she were a hundred meters away from me, despite the headphones being right in my ears. It was due to the air in the facemask—three hundred times the amount than would have been in there at the surface. Then came a muffled shriek. "Mac! *Hunter!* She's right above us!"

I looked up but couldn't see her. She was dark.

We had nearly cleared the material off the hull. We had to get back to the airlock, *now*.

I turned to Johnny—

And a figure appeared out of the darkness, hurtling toward me.

My brain only recognized a flash before the diver hit me. A light blinking on his mask, and the shadowy image—a silhouette—of a long cable stretching upward toward the rim of the canyon. A gun in a hand, and a glint of a knife's hilt in a thigh holster, the deadly blade concealed within.

Shit! They were divers, tethered to the warsub, and they were trawling the canyon looking for their prey.

And they'd found us.

—••—

I CRIED OUT ONCE TO JOHNNY and then found myself sailing through the water, tumbling end over end, thrown away from the ghostly glow of the seacar and the hint of a cliff rising up into the darkness of the cold Atlantic waters.

"Mac!" I heard his reply. And then it cut off.

I focused on where I was going, which direction the seacar lay in, so I'd know how to get back. Landing on my tank, I bounced and skidded across the rocky bottom.

Pushing myself up into a sitting position, I saw a nightmarish scene: three figures streaked past the seacar, all linked with tethers, and all looking behind them as their sub continued through the narrow trench, hauling them along.

Their mouths were moving frantically, no doubt screaming orders at their crew, telling them they'd discovered us.

This French captain was driven. She wanted to kill me very badly, and she'd either inspired her troops to do something incredibly dangerous, or she'd ordered them against their better judgement.

Johnny had tumbled off the seacar in the collision; I could see him wobbling to his feet near *SC-1*.

I realized with a dull ache in my head we had not brought any weapons outside other than the pry bars, but I'd lost mine. We hadn't expected visitors while clearing the debris.

"Kat!" I yelled. "Get out of here, right now! Blow the tanks, take off! Dim the lights!"

"But what about—"

"You can come back for us. Fire a torpedo! They know where we are!"

There was only a second's hesitation and then *SC-1* started to move. Bubbles spewed from the ballast valves, and the thrusters started to churn. She pushed it up to full power, and the vessel powered away. The wash hurled Johnny and I even farther backward, and a surge of smaller rocks and boulders fell from the hull. Each time a rock fell from the vessel, the ship lurched upward.

And then it was free of debris. The ship righted itself—the ballast trim tanks took care of that automatically—and it disappeared into the darkness of the black waters.

I turned to Johnny. He was looking at me, on his knees as he shook the rock and sand from his wetsuit and blinked repeatedly to regain focus. Either the fall had shaken him, or the pressure was finally getting to him.

We were alone, way too deep, with nearby soldiers intent on killing us.

The sound of a torpedo launch reached my ears.

Kat had fired on the French warsub.

—••—

"MAC, WATCH OUT!" JOHNNY YELLED.

I spun slowly in the water and turned in the direction he was pointing. Three figures were swinging toward us again, tethers stretching up into the darkness. They'd appeared only a few meters from us. The darkness made it impossible to see much, but I realized it would be to our benefit; they held needle guns and were searching for a target.

Shots hissed out in the water, and the dim shapes of narrow, twenty-centimeter-long needles flashed between me and Johnny. I flinched back, swearing, and nearly lost my balance again. The last thing I saw as the figures disappeared into the canyon were hands grasping at latches and the tethers detaching as the three soldiers sailed free and arced into the depths.

Shit. They'd cut from the warsub as their ship tried to evade Kat's torpedo. I could still hear it in the distance, the pitch changing as it altered course repeatedly, attempting to intercept *Hunter*.

"Johnny," I said, breathless. "Do you have anything to use as a weapon?"

"No. I lost the pry bar." His voice was dull, lifeless. But I knew him well. He wasn't despondent; he was in a tactical mode of sorts. We'd been through situations like this before, infiltrating cities, fighting intelligence operatives, battling city security forces in other colonies of the undersea world. He was preparing to fight, and, like me, he was well-trained and deadly underwater.

"We have to kill these bastards now," I whispered. *Or be killed*, I thought.

That was often our lives, underwater.

CHAPTER THIRTEEN

THERE WERE THREE HOSTILES HIDDEN IN the darkness in front of us.

They knew where we were, and they had needle guns.

Our vessel had just departed the area and was engaged in a torpedo battle with a French warsub.

Johnny and I were not armed.

We only had a few minutes of air remaining.

We were under incredible pressure.

Just another day at the office, I thought with a shake of my head.

If Kat didn't score a hit against *Hunter* it wouldn't matter what happened in the hand-to-hand fight to come. If we survived and *SC-1* imploded, we'd still die from lack of air, or perhaps we'd succumb to the pressure and lie, catatonic and suffering, until the inevitable end.

Johnny was next to me. He was watching the darkness before us.

"No more voice contact," I whispered.

He nodded and I cut the comm with a press on the wrist band. All indicator lights winked out at another touch, and Johnny followed suit.

I went left, he went right.

A squeeze on the control valve injected a squirt of air into my vest, and I started to rise. When I hit the correct depth, I neutralized my buoyancy with another touch. We were not wearing flippers; we'd been walking on the surface trying to clear the debris from the seacar. Swimming was laborious as a result, and I worked hard, kicking to make some distance. Johnny had disappeared into the black water.

I had to trust that he was doing the same as I.

A distant whine sounded as I pushed myself along. It was the torpedo, and it was still shifting course constantly, altering depth and speed and course as it tracked the French sub. Kat must have selected HOMING as the function.

Another burst of sound hit me and I snapped my head left and right to peer around me. I was growing disoriented in the near blackness. But I recognized the noise.

Another torpedo in the water.

This one was likely French, and if they scored a hit—even a close detonation—it was all over.

The dream of *Oceania* would end.

Until the next idiot builds up enough courage, I thought. Enough drive to force the people of the oceans into recognizing the inevitable—that Earth's future belonged to them. That the people of the land superpowers had driven their countries into the dirt, literally.

That the oceans were the future.

I took a deep breath and stared below me, straining to see something on the seafloor ten meters away. Nothing.

After swimming twenty meters, I stopped and floated there.

Waiting.

The wail of the torpedo reached me again, and it continued to grow in volume. It was coming right for me. I made myself negatively buoyant and descended back to the floor. I crouched, and waited.

The shriek grew to unimaginable levels. The thing was right on top of me now, I thought. Fuck! What the hell was going on?

Another sound suddenly reached me. Another launch—only this one was *screaming* through the water.

I swallowed. It was a supercavitating torpedo. Had Kat launched it? A last resort to hit the warsub out there? Her only way out?

The volume was growing, and it was unnerving not being able to see anything.

The first torpedo abruptly pierced the veil of darkness and churned within five meters to my right. The screw cut the water and bubbles frothed from the low-pressure zone around the blades. There was a faint glow to the weapon as it streaked past. The wash of the four meter cylinder tossed me backward, head over heels. I spun crazily, arms outstretched to try to right myself, but it was hopeless. I collided with the cliff and floated motionless, trying to maintain regular breathing, but it was getting difficult.

Was I running out of air?

Probably.

I contemplated giving up. But there was no way I'd ever do that. It just wasn't in me.

I would fight until the bitter end.

An arm wrapped around my neck and I burst to life.

No time to rest! I screamed at myself.

I elbowed the guy behind me, grabbed the arm and jerked downward. The move hurled him over my shoulder, but things were slower in the water than in air, and I held on and pivoted him to the seafloor.

The torpedo must have dislodged his needle gun; it wasn't in his hand anymore.

He now had a knife, however, and he stabbed at me. I dodged it and maintained a grip on his arm, bending it backwards slightly, but it was difficult while floating. I couldn't get any leverage.

He thrust the weapon again.

I dodged it and bent my knee and pushed it into the back of his bicep. He was craning his neck back to look at me, to find me in the darkness, but I had the advantage now.

I noted dimly there were no obvious breathing tubes for me to pull or try to cut. They were hidden under a thick vest.

This was a member of a submarine infantry squad. A soldier trained to fight underwater.

But so was I.

I held his wrist and pulled with everything I had. He lifted his chin and screamed, bubbles spilling out from around his mask. His elbow was a weak link in his musculature.

And I was going to take advantage of it.

Resistance gave way and abruptly his arm bent savagely backward, the elbow a shattered spider web of bone. In one quick move I released my grip, grabbed his mask and regulator, and gave a sudden yank. It came free from his face, I planted my feet on the hard rock below, and pushed with everything I had.

The mask tore from his connecting tube and I rocketed upward, a stream of bubbles from his tank soaring past me.

He'd die in minutes now. Perhaps seconds.

An instant after the thought, a massive shockwave shoved me aside like a feather in a hurricane.

It was the supercavitating torpedo, churning up the valley at nearly 1000 kph, and it trailed a compression wave and a storm of sand and rocks and other debris that pelted me relentlessly.

I lost track of just what the hell was going on.

—••—

FINALLY I WAS ABLE TO SHAKE my head to clear my thoughts and reorient myself. My feet were floating free, and I had to make myself heavier again to sink to the rock below. Releasing some air from the vest did the trick, and I touched down a moment later.

There was a distant roar and I jerked to the left just in time to see a flash of light and a sudden image that disappeared almost immediately.

It had occurred just at the lip of the canyon a hundred meters above and a hundred meters behind me.

A large expanding ball of hot gases.

A flash of red from within.

Bubbles churning to the surface.

A dark metallic shape at the center of the void.

And a sudden implosion crushing the bubble around itself, collapsing steel plates and causing a rain of debris downward. The pressure from the depth was relentless, and the vessel had not been able to withstand it.

It had been the French warsub. I knew the shape of the *Liberty* class vessel. The three thrusters—two on each side, one at the top—and its twenty-one meter length.

Another explosion sounded then, but distant. Hollow.

A dim glow reached my eyes and I stared at it, thinking for an instant I had hit my limits, that I was at the end.

Should I call Johnny? I thought. Ask him what was going on?

But I didn't want to give my position away. I had to stay silent.

The light grew brighter until finally it was right on me.

A sound accompanied the light, and it was familiar. Reassuring and familiar.

It was *SC-1*. Kat was looking for me.

—••—

I COULDN'T WAIT ANY LONGER. I thumbed the comm back on and yelled out. My voice was a croak, and I realized dully that it was growing more difficult to breathe.

But she had heard. The seacar abruptly slowed to a halt, the lights a beacon guiding me in. The skids lowered, the whine of hydraulics piercing the water, and the vessel drifted slowly to the floor.

Johnny, if he was still around, would hopefully see the light and make his way to it. I looked around furtively. Was he nearby?

I called him. Again and again.

Finally I heard, "I'm here." He was panting. "Trying to get to you— Hard to—breathe—"

"Just a few more minutes," I said. "Hang on." I was struggling to get there too. The airlock was open now, beckoning. There was a light within, and there was a glow shining down from it.

It reminded me of pictures I'd seen of the sky topside.

They called it Jacob's Ladder. The sun cutting through holes in the clouds, hitting the Earth below.

I was growing delirious, I thought.

Time was running out.

Get back, now!

I was five meters away. The ship loomed over me, and it seemed larger than it really was. Kat had lowered the platform in front of the airlock. But I couldn't go in without Johnny. We'd have to depressurize together.

I wouldn't abandon him.

"On my way," he said.

A figure appeared from the dark to my right. "I see you—" Then I swore. It wasn't Johnny.

It was another French soldier.

And he was stranded now—his ship was gone.

His eyes were full of rage. There was a needle gun clutched in his right hand. He gestured to the airlock.

Johnny appeared at my side. We floated there, together, staring at the man in a stunned tableau.

—••—

"JOHNNY," I SAID. "DID YOU GET any of them?"

"One."

Which meant this was the only one remaining. And he must have seen the implosion as well. He knew *SC-1* was his only hope at survival.

He motioned to the airlock again.

I shook my head. "Kat," I said. "Are you watching this?"

"I see it. Barely."

"Close the lock."

She hesitated, then finally complied.

The man's eyes widened. I couldn't see much through the facemask; the dark wetsuit and vest protecting the air tubes and his tank made it difficult to see how big he was.

But I knew I had him. He was in serious trouble here.

I keyed a standard frequency for divers. "Drop the gun. Then we'll enter together. We'll take you with us."

Johnny glanced at me, a warning in his gaze.

But I couldn't leave the man here. He was only doing what the French captain, Féroce, had wanted.

He shifted his eyes to me and Johnny and back again. Finally, he nodded curtly and opened his gloved fingers.

The needle gun drifted to the seafloor.

I ordered him to drop the knife too, and he complied willingly.

The hatch opened again, and together the three of us entered the seacar.

—••—

THE WATER DRAINED SLOWLY AS THE pumps worked to clear the chamber. It took a long minute, however, due to the pressure outside, but finally it was below our shoulders and we pulled our masks off, gulping in the fresh, cold air.

The French sailor was shorter than Johnny and I. Floating outside, it was hard to determine height. But he was about 5⊠6⊠, and he was—

She.

It was a woman.

And when she spoke, I swore out loud. It was Renée Féroce.

Captain Renée Féroce.

—••—

SHE SAID SOMETHING IN FRENCH, RAPID and vicious. She spat the words.

I could speak Chinese, not French, but I got the gist of what she was saying.

"Sorry about your ship," I said. "Both of them."

"You fucking asshole," she finally hissed in English.

I clenched my teeth as I considered just what the hell I was going to do here. I sank to my knees and leaned against the bulkhead. There was a venting noise in the airlock now, as Kat slowly began lowering the air pressure.

Féroce was going to be with us for the rest of the journey. Unless we killed her.

A look at Johnny confirmed he was thinking the same thing. I snorted. This woman was hell-bent on revenge, and I'd saved her life, but we'd destroyed her new sub and the rest of her crew was dead. Thirteen more people.

There was ice in her eyes.

"Why are you sitting down?" she asked.

"We're going to be in here for a while."

"Fourteen hours," Kat's voice said from the tiny speaker in the ceiling.

"Damn."

"I can increase the pressure in the seacar a bit, however, and get you out of there earlier. Then we can decompress the whole sub slowly until we're back to four atmospheres."

"Kat," I said, my head hanging and my eyes on the steel grill beneath me. I was cold, and my head hurt, and my ears were aching. I was shivering uncontrollably too, but at least I felt better than the last time I'd been out really deep. "Take us up above the lip of the canyon. Set course due east for fifteen hours. Then head south." I did a quick calculation in my head. It would take just over seventy-two hours to get there. Then, "Can you turn up the heat in here please?"

"Will do. What are we going to do with our visitor?"

I stared at her. "That's up to her."

"Where are you going?" she asked, venom in her voice.

I offered a soft laugh. "Cut the hostility. You tried to kill me, we defended ourselves. I'm sorry, but it happened. Now you have to deal with it. Or we'll drop you off here."

She glared at me. Then, "Tell me."

I shook my head. "You're going to have to stay with us from now on. If you try to run, you'll die. If you resist, we'll have to chain you up or kill you." Her eyes widened, and I shrugged. "I'm sorry, but that's the way it is."

I looked up at the camera next to the speaker. "Kat, what happened outside?"

"I fired on them immediately after you ordered it."

Féroce glared at me, and I ignored her.

"They ran," Kat continued. "They evaded the weapon for a while. Countermeasures, evasive maneuvers. They ran up and down the canyon for a bit. Then they got a bead on me and fired their own torpedo. As we evaded it, I fired another. A supercavitating one. The warsub had no chance against it."

I nodded. Our SCAV torpedoes could go 1000 kph underwater. It was a missile that rode in a bubble of air, nearly frictionless in the water and harder than hell to evade.

Kat said, "We got away from their torp. Ran it into the cliff way up the canyon. Came back for you."

I looked up at the captain. "You had a tracker on our ship, didn't you?"

She pursed her lips. "You're so smart, you tell me."

"It's the best explanation for what happened. When the Ballard crews repaired SC-1 after the EMP, you snuck into the shops and put a tracker somewhere. It's how you knew to follow our signal and not the decoys. It's how you knew where we were in the canyon." I frowned. "But why lower yourself by tether at this pressure? That's insane."

"Don't tell me what's insane!" she shrieked. "After what you've done to me! After the things I've endured because of you!"

I mulled it over. "Did the tracker stop working? Did one of your mines knock it out?" She didn't answer and I sighed. "That's it, isn't it? You didn't know precisely where we were, so you tried to eyeball us in the canyon. Sonar didn't show us." I shook my head again. Desperate was the word I'd use to describe her. To push herself like that, just to kill one man.

She could have just waited for us, I thought, until we'd started moving again.

"Tell me where you're taking me now," she said between clenched teeth.

I glanced at Johnny. "To a secret facility in the Mid-Atlantic. We call it The Ridge."

She snorted. "Secret facility. Right. What are you doing there?"

I paused. And then, "We're preparing to fight a war of independence against the superpowers of the world, of course. And that's our base of operations, which you're going to see very soon."

INTERLUDE: QUESTIONS

```
Location:       The Gulf of Mexico
Latitude:       27° 34' 29" N
Longitude:      54° 56' 11" W
Depth:          25 meters
Vessel:         USS Impaler
Time:           2130 hours
```

FIRST OFFICER SCHRADER STARED AT DEPUTY Mayor Robert Butte as a sailor escorted him into the cabin aboard *Impaler*. Seaman Abernathy had brought him, as was the normal procedure.

Heller had still not arrived to the meeting.

Butte was wet from his swim outside the city to where a military scooter had picked him up for transport to the warsub. It was the new method of getting the man here, after he had put up a fuss the last time. This had been Schrader's decision, and Heller hadn't interfered, luckily. If it made Butte more comfortable, and helped keep this secret from McClusky, all the better.

Schrader dismissed Abernathy, who departed with a long and lingering glance at the Deputy Mayor. Schrader watched with disapproving eyes until the hatch had shut and the two men were alone.

Butte's gaze darted about the cabin. It was his third time in that particular room. Heller wanted him to remember what had happened to the double agent Rafe Manuel. The blood on the steel deck and the gurgling of the dying man. Schrader didn't agree with either decision—killing the man or bringing Butte back to this same cabin, just to torment him and keep him operating in a state of fear—and yet he was powerless to stop it.

"How are things in City Control?" Schrader asked in a soft voice.

The man was large and had had to duck through the hatch. Now he was standing there, awkward, as he crossed his arms before him, then unfolded them, put his hands in his pockets, then crossed his arms again. His legs were fidgety too; he shifted his weight every few seconds.

Schrader didn't blame him for being nervous.

"Mac isn't there right now," Butte said.

"Where is he?"

"He left on February 23."

Schrader's eyebrows lifted. "Funny day to leave. Especially for a McClusky."

Butte sighed and swatted the notion away; he then had to search for a place to put his hand afterward. "He's not like that, actually. He hates the day."

"Really."

"I think he was only fourteen at the time."

"So he left because of that?"

Butte shrugged. "I'm not sure. He just did. That evening."

Schrader thought back to that day. McClusky had spoken in the atrium of the Commerce Module; everyone in the region had watched, even sailors aboard *Impaler*. The mayor had spoken confidently and clearly about the efforts to colonize and how the city continued to press onward despite the hardships of labor. About the importance to the United States and humanity in general. USSF officers had vetted his talking points, and McClusky hadn't strayed from them. The rest of the city had celebrated the day. Heller had allowed them to, which surprised Schrader. It showed the first officer that Heller had some sense of the psychology in the situation, and knew that to stifle a celebration would only lower Trieste's opinion of the USSF and give them more desire to push for their independence. Heller was doing everything in his power to prevent that—hence the presence of the deputy mayor on *Impaler* at that very moment.

Schrader locked eyes with the man. "Were you aware when he left?"

He cleared his throat. "Yes. But it's because of someone else that I even noticed."

The hatch opened and Captain Heller stalked over the threshold and into his office. He barely acknowledged the deputy mayor's presence. He just sat down and rumbled, "Continue."

Butte glared at him. "As I was saying, McClusky left the city four days ago."

"He didn't tell you he was leaving?"

"No." Butte chewed the inside of his cheek. "He usually keeps me informed about city business. But not this."

"Interesting." Heller considered that, then said, "Continue."

"I was following this other person, who led me to the Docking Module. He boarded *SC-1* in the evening with several other people, and they left."

The captain's eyebrows raised. "Who else?"

"Mac. His girlfriend, Katherine Wells. His sister. There were three others I didn't get a good look at. And the man I was following, of course."

"Who was . . . ?"

"Professor Manesh Lazlow."

Schrader grunted. "The new recruit you told us about."

"Yes."

Heller tapped the steel table with his knuckles. "I researched this man Lazlow. He's an acoustician."

"Which I told you," Butte interrupted. Heller glared at him and Butte closed his mouth abruptly.

The captain continued, "He's not just an acoustician. He's been working in a field called acoustical engineering. He's from California, and the last couple of decades he was at Berkeley. A few associates of mine on the mainland did some digging. Within the last year he contacted Trieste on a number of occasions. There was mention of a video conference that happened, but we don't know when."

"The video wasn't logged in his account, the same as these emails?" Schrader asked with a frown.

"No." Heller turned to him. "Interesting, wouldn't you say? He must have felt compelled, for some reason, to conduct the video meeting secretly. With help, most likely." The captain sighed. "His wife died some twenty-odd years ago. He has nobody topside, apparently. Five grown children who have long since moved on, some have even retired from their jobs, and there is little contact between them all."

"So he has no reason to stay topside."

"No. And he's in a field that could be of use here."

"And he took part in some sort of untraceable video interview."

Heller nodded.

Schrader considered it all, but it still didn't add up. He wasn't sure where Heller was going with this, or if it was even suspicious at all. "It might all be innocent. He's old. He wants his last days or years to be in a different place."

Heller chewed a pencil. There were teeth marks all over it. So many, in fact, it surprised Schrader that it was still in one piece. "No. There's more to this man than meets the eye."

Butte said, "I've been following him, as you asked. He's done nothing suspicious. Toured the city. Katherine Wells has been taking care of him. He's seemed happy to be down here. Then the day of the celebrations, and—"

"He departs at night in a seacar with a mysterious group of people." Heller grunted. Then he looked up at the deputy mayor. "Which direction did the seacar go?"

Butte hesitated. "Uh, I'm not—"

"*Which way did it go?*"

The deputy mayor frowned and took an unconscious step back. A prickly sensation worked its way down Schrader's scalp. *Oh, shit.*

Finally, Butte said, "They went north."

—••—

HELLER LOOKED LIKE HE WANTED TO chew steel. There was ice in his eyes and his voice was gravel. "Are you sure? Remember what happened to the last person who said that." It wasn't a question.

The man sighed. "I know. Trust me, I know. I double checked the track. I asked Sea Traffic Control. The seacar went through the straits of Florida and then north, en route to Bermuda."

Heller snorted. "And Lazlow went with them." Schrader knew he was speaking to himself, internalizing this piece of news. "I wonder what you're doing, McClusky." Then he said in a much louder voice, "Schrader, tell our French friends to watch out for him to the northeast, near Bermuda. They might take care of this situation for us." Then to Butte: "I want to know when he returns. I want to know who is with them, and what heading they arrive from. Understood?"

Butte swallowed. There were traces of sweat on his forehead. "Yes, Captain."

PART THREE: PULSE

The Ridge

Latitude: 28° 05' 13" S
Longitude: 17° 23' 58" W
Depth: 3782 meters

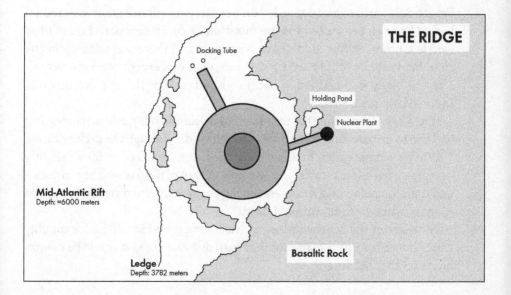

THE RIDGE

Docking Tube

Holding Pond

Nuclear Plant

Mid-Atlantic Rift
Depth: ≈6000 meters

Ledge
Depth: 3782 meters

Basaltic Rock

CHAPTER FOURTEEN

"You're really engaged in a fight for independence? You think you can beat the United States?" Captain Renée Féroce's expression was incredulous.

We had spent twelve hours in the airlock together, along with Johnny, and it hadn't been fun. She had announced several times that she'd wanted to kill me—those were her orders, in fact, and her reputation and future in the French Submarine Fleet depended on her carrying out her mission—and I'd had to keep an eye on her for the duration of decompression. I wasn't too worried, however. She didn't have a weapon, and there was nothing in the chamber that she could have used as one, with one exception: a scuba tank. She was likely well-trained in hand-to-hand combat though. Johnny was there to help me watch.

It had been impossible to stretch out or lie comfortably, and all three of us had had to urinate during the ordeal, which we did through the deck's grating.

When decompression finally ended, the hatch sighed open into a slightly overpressurized seacar cabin—so we could get out of the damned tiny airlock—and then Kat commenced depressurizing the seacar. When we arrived at The Ridge it would be four atms on board.

We were on the southward leg of the journey, and would be for roughly thirty hours before we made another turn due east. Then it would be twenty hours on that heading.

Meg and Kat had been hard at work on the SCAV drive, and they grinned when I asked about it. It was up and running. Tests had showed it operated perfectly, although they hadn't actually powered up. It made me relax a bit, knowing we had the option to run in case someone else discovered us and attacked.

After a quick shower in the tiny washroom and a change of clothes—it felt great to get out of the wetsuit—I gathered the group around me. Everyone was wary of the French captain, and she was looking around nervously too, wondering what exactly we were going to do with her.

"Relax," I said. "I'm sure you want to see our facility too."

She raised her eyebrows at that, and then gave me a curt nod.

"I trust you won't kill me before then. Deal?"

She frowned. "You're just going to . . . *assume*?"

I shrugged. "If I die, you die. How's that?"

She didn't say anything, she just glared.

"Besides," I continued, "sometimes the pressure is so great I kind of wonder what it would be like."

The others were staring at me, concern in their eyes. I waved it away. "Don't worry. I want to see the result of our efforts. I'm going to stay with this thing right to the end." I glanced at Renée Féroce. "As long as she lets me anyway."

Kat glared at her. "If you try anything, I will end you. And it'll be *painful*."

There was no response, but the two women had locked eyes, and the electricity between them crackled.

"Easy," I said. "No one's doing anything yet. I'm pretty sure our French captain needs to not only kill me, but to get back home to report it. Am I right?"

She paused. "I would be happy to just kill you. But to regain my position in the FSF . . ." She trailed off. "You're correct."

"Good. Then no one's killing anyone just yet."

Johnny coughed and I shot him a look. He said, "Remember when you had me and Lau prisoner? And you trusted us?"

I did indeed. Johnny had stuck with me, but Lau had run, warned the Australian authorities and his own government, and then Chinese agents had tried to kill me. I'd had to use a torpedo in Blue Downs to escape. "Your point is taken." To Renée I said, "Everyone here is going to watch you like a hawk. You are not to go in engineering or the control cabin. You'll stay here in this living area. You'll sleep on the deck. Understood?"

Her eyes were ice, but eventually she nodded.

I studied the group before me. I said, "The designer of this seacar. My sister, a sub mechanic. My former partner in TCI. Two freedom fighters. A French

captive who wants to kill me. And an eighty year old acoustician." I shook
my head as I stared at them. Renée Féroce was impassive, Meg and Kat were
staring at the others, Johnny had a quizzical expression on his face, Lancombe
and Ng were smiling slightly, and Lazlow sported a wide grin. "It's an eclectic
group of people all right."

"Circumstances have forced us together perhaps," Lancombe said, "but it's
for the best. We're all going to see this through to the end. Not just you."

"It might be a bitter ending," I said.

"No. I have faith."

I snorted. "We'll see." I poked my head into the control cabin and studied
the navigation screen. We still had quite a ways to go. I debated turning on
the SCAV drive in order to get us there sooner, but common sense struck that
thought away. I couldn't risk attracting attention to the site. We would stay
at seventy kph. Besides, I thought, there was plenty to do.

I stared at Lancombe and Ng. "Why don't we chat while we travel?"

—••—

THEY TURNED OUT TO BE A wealth of knowledge.

We discussed everything I had put in place following the disastrous battle—
from burying the nuclear plant, keeping TCI running with a much smaller
group of operatives, and setting up The Ridge and preparing our work there.
They still didn't know what it was, but they would find out within hours.

Lancombe said, "Trieste, like every undersea colony, is vulnerable."

It was late at night, the lights were low, and the others were in their bunks
or sleeping on the couches or the carpeted floor. Kat was in my bunk, Meg
had the other. Lancombe and I sat together in the control cabin, watching
the dark water outside the canopy.

"We're extremely vulnerable. When they killed my dad, they just cut their
way through a travel tube."

"Precisely." He nodded. "Any attacker can do that anywhere in the city."

"Except the plant."

"Yes. Good idea to bury it. Shanks should have done that years ago. The trick,
however, is to keep hostile people from getting close to the city."

"We use sonar to track every vessel that approaches."

"And those that don't have a transponder?"

"We send out an intercept vehicle."

He smiled. "Good. And what of the ones that have false transponders?"

That stopped me. "It's impossible to catch them that way, but our computer flags us on suspicious audio signatures."

He tilted his head. "Good idea."

"It's not foolproof, however."

He mulled that over. "So you're patrolling the area well. What about preventing people from invading your territory in personal scooters and entering through moonpools?"

I grimaced. "It's hard to stop that one."

"Because you don't want to infringe on the rights of Triestrians."

"Something like that."

"In war, things like that have to happen."

I didn't respond.

He continued. "What about attacks from the air?"

"You mean, a missile, a bomb, and so on?" I hesitated. "Those are harder. We've been talking about radar stations floating around our city. On buoys. Disguised. We can watch for air traffic."

He raised a finger. "Still. Seeing it is one thing. You have to be prepared to *deal* with the threat, before they bomb you."

I frowned. "You're saying shoot them out of the sky."

"Yes."

I had thought of that. "We're talking about submerged platforms that will rise at a moment's notice and launch surface-to-air missiles if need be."

He blinked. "Are they in place?"

"Not yet."

"Then we need to get on it." He leaned back and stared up through the canopy. "It's beautiful under here. I've spent most of my life underwater. I never want to be anywhere else."

The water sighed past the control cabin, white noise against the sounds of the seacar's systems operating to keep us all alive. The thrum of the thrusters, the whir of the ventilation fans, the random beeps from sensors and the navigation system.

"I agree with you," I said in a soft voice.

"I have another idea," he said abruptly. "Fish fences."

"What about them?" We had fish farms around Trieste, but they weren't nearly as large as Ballard's.

He grinned.

—••—

FINALLY, AFTER EVERYTHING WE'D BEEN THROUGH on that voyage—the French attack, the fight in the canyon, decompressing in the airlock with a potential assassin—we arrived at The Ridge.

SC-1 approached the rift zone—mountains that towered from the ocean floor upwards of five kilometers—slowly. Cautiously. Enormous upward currents buffeted the seacar as we moved past it into the mighty canyon piercing the mountain range along its massive length. It was longer than the Andes and Rockies and Himalayas together—70000 kilometers, snaking along the Earth like stitches in a baseball—and the central rift practically led straight to the Earth's mantle of molten rock. There, a thin five kilometer skin of crusted rock covered magma, but as the plates diverged and stretched and split and cracked, and the mountain range separated by a millimeter a day, molten rock pierced the thin skin to fill the gaps, creating new ocean crust in a steaming and fiery cauldron of churning and boiling water. Warm currents moved upward, tossing *SC-1* like an insect over a great abyss. The seafloor was now five kilometers below, a thousand meters past crush depth.

Should our systems fail and we were to plunge into the deep trench, the pressure would squeeze us like a flimsy soda pop can.

I watched the nav system carefully, settling over the proper coordinates.

The seacar lurched and heeled from side to side.

The passengers gripped the armrests of the couch; behind my pilot's chair, Meg held to the headrest tightly. Of course she and Kat had been there before, had even helped set it up, but the danger didn't escape her.

The dangers didn't escape anyone, in fact.

No one said a word. The displays cast images over our faces, the pulsating lights sending shadows up and down the darkened seacar interior. The hull creaked and the water sighed upward from the depths, murky with black sediment and warmed by lava.

I swallowed and pushed the ballast controls to negative.

We took on water, and began to sink into the dark clouds.

—••—

THE FACILITY LAY NESTLED AGAINST THE cliff bordering the rift on the east side. The trench was twenty kilometers wide. The dome was on a narrow ledge protruding out into the canyon, but the ledge was above our crush depth by 300 meters or so, sitting at 3782 meters.

"Set thrusters at station-keeping," I muttered as I stared at the instruments. Beside me, Kat pushed the appropriate button, and the thrusters worked to keep us at the correct latitude and longitude. It was difficult, however, because of the buffeting currents, and often one engine or the other would suddenly rev up, or switch to reverse abruptly, causing more shaking and rattling on board the seacar.

Outside, it was *black*.

We fell into the trench, toward the churning lava below.

—••—

AT 3500 METERS I SWITCHED OUR ballast to neutral and thumbed off the station-keeping. Pushing forward on the throttle, I increased speed to a quiet and steady ten percent thrust. The seacar vibrated with power now—restrained power—as if it *wanted* to move. Wanted to just get out of there.

Turn on the SCAV drive now! it screamed at me.

I shook my head to clear those thoughts.

This is why we'd put the base here, I told myself. *To hide it from prying eyes.* We needed to work in peace. There were fifty people here. Fifty people who had supposedly died in The Second Battle of Trieste.

I'd told Heller after The Battle that we hadn't been able to identify the meat churning through the waters following the explosions and collapsing bulkheads. Torpedoes had crushed our Supply Module and ruined our nuclear plant. Of course there were a lot of casualties, I had said.

And there *were* a lot.

Minus the fifty now at The Ridge, that is.

I smiled to myself as I thought about what I'd done. About the base we had constructed here without anyone knowing. Of course the USSF had asked around about the subs that had left Trieste and never returned. The ones that had carried the construction materials and the men and women who now worked here in secret.

I assumed that's why Rafe had died. He'd probably told someone on *Impaler* the subs had been going north, when they knew full well that the subs had been going *south*.

To this hellish location.

I leveled off at the correct depth and stared at the sonar. The east canyon wall was very close now. Flicking on the lamps, I turned the bow to face the sheer rock wall.

Have to be careful here, I thought. *One sudden current from below could slam us into that wall.*

I took in a deep breath and held it. The Ridge did not send out any signals to help direct traffic. It blended in with the rock. Anechoic tiles covered it—invented during WWII but modified constantly ever since—to absorb and scatter sound of different frequencies, rather than reflect it toward incoming subs.

There were no comm signals either. No one was sitting at a communications console to talk us in.

The base was still under four atmospheres, despite being at this great depth, so it was dome-shaped to help withstand the outside pressures. And the inner bulkhead was a hollow shield, devoid of air, preventing stray noise emissions from the factory equipment and the sounds of human life.

The people here had sacrificed more than other Triestrians had. They had given their immediate lives to this task, for they could not come or go until production had ceased.

The beam from our forward lamps barely cut through the water. There was rock just at its limits, and I struggled to keep the seacar steady and clear of towering basalt formations.

We turned slightly to the north, and I angled the nose down a bit—

And behind me there was a gasp. The dome of the facility was now clearly visible, on a flat ledge jutting out from the cliff. A travel tube extended from behind, penetrating the hard rock of the cliff face. That's where the nuclear plant was, protected by meters and meters of hard rock. Where a torpedo couldn't take it out with one blast.

On the north side of the dome, a cylinder lay on the rock ledge, connected to the facility with an airlock big enough for a seacar. It was the docking tube, and I powered SC-1 over to it and, nudging the ballast just a bit, descended another two meters and positioned the vessel perfectly before a large hatch.

There were two red lights on the rock before the hatch, impossible to see from more than ten meters away, but invaluable in helping guide the seacar into the tube.

It opened.

I brought us in slowly, ever so slowly.

There was a rumble as it closed behind us, and a set of floodlights suddenly flared to life.

Kat and I squeezed our eyes shut. We'd expected it, but still, it was a shock after staring into darkness for so many continuous hours.

The second hatch in front of us slid aside and we powered into the docking pool of The Ridge.

CHAPTER FIFTEEN

BEHIND ME AND KAT, THE OTHERS were incredulous. All but Meg, of course, who had helped build this place, but Lancombe and Ng and Lazlow and even the French captain were staring out the canopy, mouths hanging open and eyes wide. Johnny knew what it was, but he hadn't seen it before.

We were in a docking pool; there was a steel mesh catwalk beside the seacar.

I hauled myself out of the seat and moved to the ladder which led to the top hatch. "Shall we?" I asked with a half smile.

"What is this place?" Lancombe asked.

"The Ridge." It was all I said as I opened the hatch and crawled out onto the hull of *SC-1*. The metal was cold, and I stared down for a moment at the scratches and pitting caused by the avalanche of rock the French attack had caused days earlier in the water northeast of Bermuda. I glanced at Kat; she was staring at the damage, fury in her eyes.

I moved on before she could say anything.

Besides, it hadn't been my fault.

The pool was Olympic-sized, as some of the workers from topside had said before, though I wouldn't have ever known that, because the Olympics weren't such a big deal anymore. The ceiling was roughly five meters over our heads. It wasn't curved, for there was another level above this one. This "seafloor level" held the docking pool and most of the assembly machinery. The upper level of the dome, smaller with the curved bulkheads and ceiling, held the living and command quarters for the residents of The Ridge.

There was a man standing on the dock, the mesh sagging under his weight. "Hello, Mac!" he called out.

I couldn't help but smile. "Jackson. How are you?"

He was Jackson Train, an odd name for a man who had lived and worked underwater for the better part of three decades. He had been a Triestrian since just after my dad had died. He'd seen what had happened from his home in central United States, where the farms had dried to dust and blown away in the span of only a few years. If the greenhouse effect had destroyed the country, he'd often told me years earlier, then the humans who still lived on land were just insects in the glass house waiting for the walls to shatter. This had been while the two of us had worked the kelp farms, after I'd quit TCI. He'd immigrated to Trieste, where his experience as a farmer from a generation of farmers had helped him immeasurably. Just his work ethic was enough to get him a job where the labor was dangerous and grueling, in a place where scuba gear was a requirement. Underwater farmers risked death every single day. I had taken an instant liking to the man, and when we decided to start construction on this place, Jack had been the first person to come to mind.

He may have been a farmer, but his heart was that of an undersea worker regardless of the trade. I'd put him in charge of the facility, of coordinating the people who *were* construction and aquanautic engineers—like Kat—and gave him the job to get the place up and running. And I'd given Jack an impossible timeline: eight months.

Eight months. Not just for the dome. It had also needed a nuclear plant and a manufacturing line—mandates that would make any manager walk away.

But Jack had done it.

And he'd done it marvelously.

He and I embraced. "You're looking slim," I said.

"I think I lost an ounce or two last week," he said.

"I'm sure you'll gain it back. We brought some kelp beer."

The other man grimaced. "We're brewing our own stuff now. It's probably just as bad as what you've got."

"Probably."

He looked at the people clustered on the hull of the seacar, and I waved them over. "Let me introduce you," I told him.

He watched in fascination as I said their names. Lancombe and Ng especially caused the man to blink once and then open his eyes in wonder. Then he shook his head, knowing he would get the story out of me later.

Kat stepped forward and said to him, "Jack, this is Doctor Manesh Lazlow, the man I was telling you about."

He nodded and shook Lazlow's hand. "I'm excited to get you working, Doc. I can't wait to see what you've got in store for us."

I frowned and turned to Meg and Kat. "Why do we need an acoustician here at The Ridge?" I snorted. "Hell, now he can't leave." Those were my rules anyway. Any worker who arrived here to help out could not leave until the facility had fulfilled its purpose.

"Mac," Kat said, grabbing my arm. "He's here to help us build the *Swords*."

—••—

WE MOVED FARTHER INTO THE FACILITY, and once past the watertight hatch that separated the docking pool from the factory deck, the group of newcomers abruptly halted and looked around in shock.

The sound of machinery cut through the air, along with venting fans and torches and the yells of men and women piecing together components of seacars roughly the size and shape of *SC-1*. Workers stopped what they'd been doing—assembling a vertical stabilizer and moving it with a hoist over to a new hull—and called out to me. I waved and offered a smile.

"These are the new subs," I said to the others. "The upgraded version of the seacar you just arrived in." I studied them in a stunned silence. Then, "We're building a navy."

—••—

RENÉE FÉROCE WAS SCOWLING AT THE scene before her. "You're building subs here. Near the bottom of the rift in the Mid-Atlantic Ridge. But why go to such lengths?"

"Why indeed," I said as I stared at her. "To fight the superpowers of the world and win, one must *become* that which we fight." I glanced at Lancombe and Ng. "Wouldn't you agree?"

They stared at the factory, wide-eyed with jaws agape. "Incredible," Ng rasped. She could barely speak. "What you've achieved here . . ."

"In secret," Johnny said with a look of respect. "No one even suspects, do they?"

I shrugged. "The USSF does. They know I'm up to something." In fact, I was just doing what Shanks had done a year earlier. Only he'd done it at Trieste, where it had been impossible to hide. This, I hoped, was still a secret.

Renée glanced at me. "You mean to fight the USSF? Your own country?"

"We'll fight whoever opposes us."

She looked stunned.

"They won't let us live our own lives." I watched her as she soaked in the view. The thirty or so workers piecing together the *Sword* class subs. The machinery, the arc of electric torches, the flames of gas torches, the construction of thrusters and screws and control panels and ballast systems. The line didn't move fast; we didn't have enough people working it. We could finish one ship a day usually.

And we'd been up and running for seventy-eight days.

Renée said in a curt tone, "These ships have the SCAV drive that my country was trying to purchase from the Chinese?"

"And more."

"Explain."

"Also SCAV torpedoes, and a better VID display projection on the canopy."

"A faster drive, actually," Meg interjected. She glanced at me. "You're sure it's okay to tell her all this?"

I sighed. "She's here. What should we have done?" Meg raised an eyebrow and I groaned inwardly.

"You could just give me the plans to one of those—" she pointed at a *Sword* "—and then I will leave." Renée paused, and then, "After I kill you, of course."

"Haven't we been through this? You kill me, you end up dead. No one wins."

She glared but didn't say anything more.

I turned and looked at the militarized versions of *SC-1*. The two thrusters, two vents at the rear for the SCAV drive, slightly longer horizontal stabilizers, the flat hull on top, and the oddly-shaped—

"Wait a minute," I said, drawing it out as I stared at the seacars. "The bow is different." I turned to Meg. "That's not the fuselage we agreed on."

She grinned and looked at Meg. "Why do you think Lazlow is here?"

"I don't know. No one will tell me exactly."

Lazlow had a massive grin on his gaunt and drawn face as he stared around him. He looked like he had lost weight in the undersea colony and on the long voyage to get to The Ridge, but I had to give it to him, he was a trooper. He didn't seem to be suffering in the slightest. In fact, he seemed to be enjoying himself immensely. "I'm here, Mr. Mayor, to install some important equipment in that new nose on those subs, and it's going to do something marvelous. Something that's never been done before."

—••—

WE MOVED TO A CABIN ON the second floor, a lounge, where we could all finally stretch out on couches and enjoy the feeling of space for the first time in days.

Space.

I nearly choked at the thought. The ceiling was only six inches over my head, the bulkheads were only meters away on all sides, control consoles and sensor readouts filled the chamber, and even by Triestrian standards it was tight.

But it was better than things had been on the journey over.

I still couldn't believe we'd made it with so many people—including one who wanted to kill me—crammed into *SC-1*.

"We need to watch her," Johnny had whispered to me as we'd mounted the ladder from the factory level to the upper control deck. "She could swamp this place. Put an end to everything you've done here."

It was a possibility, I had to admit. However, something in my gut told me to just ride this out. Just let it be. . . . She would come around. Eventually. "We'll see."

Now we were in the cluttered cabin, while the newcomers sat with slack and stunned faces, marveling at what they had just witnessed in the deck below.

Except Lazlow, who had a layer of excitement in his expression. I studied him for a few long heartbeats as I tried to decipher this particular conundrum. He was an acoustician. Meg and Kat had recruited him to work on the subs at The Ridge.

His input had somehow changed the seacar bows.

And he had devoted his life to the seas and to the Triestrian fight for independence.

"What's your real contribution here?" I asked finally.

He turned to me and tilted his head. "I'm an acoustical engineer. I build things that produce sound. Tools that make use of sound, or use sound for our benefit. I'm not interested in just *listening*."

That had been my mistake, I realized. I'd thought the doctor had been brought to Trieste to use sonar in some way, or increase the passive listening range, or something along those lines.

Meg had an interesting look on her face. I'd come to understand it after so many years together. We were twins, after all, though I was a few seconds older. It was clear she was gloating about this surprise, lording it over me as if she'd tricked me.

"Come on, Meg," I said. "What's going on? Why bring the man here? He can't leave now. He'll have to stay for weeks, if not months."

Renée Féroce bristled at that, and she shot me a hostile glare, which I ignored.

"He's going to be a great help," Meg finally said, her lips in a half smile.

"You've said that before. But why exactly?" She remained silent and just stared at me.

I mulled over the situation, trying to make sense of it all. She was playing a game with me, hoping that I could figure it out on my own. Perhaps proving to me that her knowledge of aquanautic engineering was superior to mine. It wasn't a game I cared to play, but nevertheless, she was forcing me.

The bow of *SC-1* was blunt to facilitate the creation of a low-pressure zone. The fusion drive on the seacar flash-vaporized seawater, and boiler pressure pushed the steam out the rear vents to propel the sub forward.

Traditional submarines had a velocity limit of eighty kph due to drag and friction. But with the fusion drive using a jet of steam to force the sub along, it could achieve much higher speeds. And that blunt bow and the low-pressure trough caused what scientists called *supercavitation:* an area of water with such a low pressure that air bubbled outwards. This is why propellers—or *screws*—sometimes turned too fast and generated bubbles, leaving a trail behind. With supercavitation, the air at the bow stretched back to encompass the entire vehicle. This lowered the friction with the surrounding water. We called it the SCAV drive. *SC-1* could hit a speed of 450 kph. The *Swords*, we theorized, could hit closer to 460 kph. The double exhaust vent at the back was the reason.

But now Doctor Manesh Lazlow had complicated the situation. Changing the shape of the bow for something related to sound.

But not *listening,* as he'd said. . . .

I stared at him and furrowed my brow.

He'd said something about building tools to make use of sound.

To *generate* it.

My expression must have changed, for Meg's smile grew broader as she watched me.

"Yes," she said. "Lazlow has come up with the most marvelous idea."

"About using sound to increase velocity?" I frowned. I didn't see how that was possible. "Or is it to *absorb* sound, maybe? Make the sub stealthy?"

Lazlow gestured with his skeletal hand. "No. The anechoic tiles you use on this facility are the best in the world. My invention is not about absorbing sound." He smiled again, showing yellowed teeth and deep lines in his craggy old face.

I sighed. I was growing tired of this game. I just wanted this facility to continue making the newest and best subs to give us the edge in a fight.

Already we had the fastest in the world. The only thing we needed was to get the subs to go deeper, but the syntactic foam I'd sent the two TCI operatives out to get earlier would serve that purpose.

But deeper in the oceans was always better. We had been struggling with the depths ever since we'd first started exploring the oceans. Our cities were very shallow—only thirty meters. *SC-1* could go deeper than most warsubs out there, but still only four kilometers. Some areas of the oceans were eleven kilometers deep. There were untold riches out there, which we wanted to harvest for the benefit of our colony and for the whole human race.

Deeper was better.

If we could go deeper than any other colony or country, we would have a massive advantage.

Perhaps Lazlow meant to use sound to . . .

The breath caught in my throat.

Yes, I thought. *That's it.*

I spun on Meg and Kat. "Is it about depth? About pushing our subs deeper?" My face exploded into shock as I stared at them. "Using sound waves to dive deeper into the oceans?"

Lazlow nodded slowly, that impossibly wide grin still on his face. "That's precisely why I'm here, Mayor McClusky."

CHAPTER
SIXTEEN

"BUT HOW, EXACTLY?" I ASKED. JOHNNY, Renée, Lancombe, and Ng all sported quizzical expressions. We were completely focused on Lazlow now. And he was soaking up the attention.

"Sound is an incredible thing. It's actually a vibration that moves as a wave of displacement and pressure through a medium. The speed sound travels depends on the composition of the medium. In our case, that's water. But the composition changes continually."

Lancombe blinked. "It does?"

"Of course. It's still water, but the salinity is always changing. As is the temperature. These factors will affect how sound travels, but generally speaking, the speed of sound is quite fast underwater: fourteen hundred and eighty-four meters per second. But it's the properties of sound's movement underwater that has interested me for all these years, ever since . . ." He trailed off, and we watched him silently as his face grew slack. When he next spoke, his voice was a whisper. "For over twenty years now. I've always been obsessed with colonizing and traveling through the oceans. Living underwater. But the depths are what has constrained our movement outward on the seafloors. Not speed, nor the ability to take air with us. It's the sheer *crushing* force that has kept us from coming out deep for so many years." He pushed a bony hand against a bulkhead and held it there. He ducked his head slightly, as if he meant to push his forehead against the cold steel. But he seemed to catch himself in time, and looked back at us as if shamed by his moment of weakness. "Right now the forces outside would crush a man's chest paper-thin if he wasn't breathing air, or an oxygenated fluid, at the same pressure. It's immense. Tons per square inch. The slightest stress fracture or imperfection or broken valve on a seacar will cause instant implosion. We've seen such things happen before."

"*Thresher*," I said, and he looked at me, surprised. Kat also snapped a look at me; I recalled that we had had an argument about the sub when I'd first learned there were pipes carrying water in *SC-1*'s engine room—something extremely dangerous.

"Yes," Lazlow continued. "That sub is famous. But *Scorpion* is of more interest to people because of the conspiracy theories and mysteries surrounding her implosion."

I knew the story well, as did most people in the underwater colonies. It was one of those warnings taught in school. *Scorpion* had been a US nuclear sub on duty in the Mediterranean in May of 1968. On her way back to Norfolk, Virginia, US Atlantic Fleet HQ had ordered her to investigate a Soviet naval grouping in the Atlantic. The last contact with the sub had occurred while she was southwest of the Azores. There had been ninety-nine crew aboard at the time, and none had survived.

Investigators discovered the wreckage shortly after, and this created more mystery. The hull showed no evidence of detonations; rather, it showed an implosion event. Images from the scene displayed a warped and distorted hull, a debris field, and even a dead body lying on the sandy bottom near the wreckage.

Odd visual evidence compounded the mystery: a periscope was in the raised position, as were two antennae. Escape hatches in the aft and bow were ajar, and an exterior light was in the *on* position indicating that the sub had been at the surface at the time of catastrophic failure. The engine compartment had been *shoved*—by water pressure—fifty feet forward, and immense pressure had also crushed the control cabin. Some torpedo loading and exterior hatches were also ajar.

It was a puzzle.

Theories that circulated afterward included the obvious: Soviet attack. However, the lack of evidence of a torpedo explosion threw suspicion on this. Other theories included internal torpedo malfunction—such as what had befallen *Kursk* in the year 2000—a torpedo activation in a tube, a faulty trash-compactor, and a very believable hypothesis about a hydrogen explosion that may have occurred in the battery-charging compartment. Listening posts had heard ninety-one seconds of implosions as the ship sank below her crush depth to the bottom, three kilometers down. Whatever happened, ninety-nine men had lost their lives. There were ninety-nine families who never found out how their loved ones had died.

It made me pause to consider my surroundings whenever a topic like this came up. We were at great depths as well. We could all die in an instant, either during battle or simply in an accident that might baffle investigators for decades to come. Or, more likely, no one would even know what had become of us, like the *Scorpion* crew.

Being in a sinking vessel, knowing that implosion was only seconds away, would be one of the most terrifying experiences. I'd experienced some hazards in the oceans, there was no doubt of it, but true stories like *Thresher* or *Scorpion* had a massive impact on people who lived in the undersea colonies.

I watched Lazlow for a heartbeat. He seemed to be reviewing the events of *Scorpion* in his mind as well. I said, "You think sound can make a vessel go deeper?"

"I know it can."

"How?"

"Sound propagates as a pressure wave through a medium, causing displacement and pressure. So my theory, which I devised many years ago now, is that a soundwave with enough power behind it could compress the water as the sub drives into it."

Johnny frowned. "Compress it which way?"

"Away from the sub, directly before the vessel. Creating a *tunnel*, if you will. You see, my invention is a sonic generator in the nose of the *Swords*. The sound waves push out into the water, forming a compression wave."

"But the wave will propagate backwards too, into the sub. Isn't that even more dangerous?"

Lazlow grinned again. "You know your physics, Mr. Chang. Yes. But I've theorized that if the sub is moving during this process, it'll drive forward *into* the outward-moving compression wave, into the rarefaction zone, and away from the rebounding one behind it. So the sub is always in a low-pressure zone, avoiding the massive weight of the water above!"

He leaned back against the bulkhead now, and watched us with a satisfied expression.

But frowns were all that met him. Except Kat and Meg of course. They had heard it all before.

He realized we still didn't understand. "The rebounding wave is indeed dangerous, but the sub should slip right past it. The waves collapse together, *behind* the sub. They may even help push it along, like squeezing toothpaste from a tube."

I grimaced. It wasn't a good analogy to use underwater. "So when the wave returns to the source of the sound—"

"The generator in the blunt nose of the sub."

"—the sub is no longer there. It's . . ." I trailed off.

"It's continually moving forward, into the tunnel—or cone—of low pressure, created by the outgoing sound pulses."

"So the seacar has to be continually moving forward?"

He lifted his chin. "Yes. It's the major drawback of the Acoustic Pulse Drive."

I almost started asking more questions, but I stopped abruptly to think it over. Using sound to *push* the water away, essentially, and lowering the pressure around the vessel. It was incredible.

Brilliant, even.

"But what if the sub is too long, and the aft portion doesn't make it into the . . . into the low-pressure zone before the sound wave collapses back?"

"The rarefaction portion of the wave, you mean. Yes, that's an issue. But the length of the seacar will determine the properties of the sound wave. The wavelength will be inversely proportional to the frequency, so in essence the sub length dictates the frequency. A shorter sub requires a higher frequency, and a longer sub means a lower frequency."

That part went over my head. "What about the SCAV drive?"

"No," he blurted with a wide-eyed look. "You can't use the SCAV drive with this. The ship would overtake the low-pressure zone. You'd go right through it and into the higher pressures of deep water. You'd plow right into crush depth."

"So if we need to go deep, we have to go slow."

He frowned. "Around fifty kph is fine. You can start the Pulse Drive when you're near crush depth. For the *Sword*, that's forty-five hundred meters. Once the Pulse is on, pushing a frequency outward and generating a lower pressure in front of the sub, you can go deeper. But you can't stop. Don't ever stop."

"And if we did?" It was a silly question; I already knew the answer.

He grimaced. "You'd slow in the water and the rebounding compression wave would hit from all directions simultaneously. The sub would immediately hit a pressure greater than the capability of the hull to withstand. Instant crush depth." He shook his head. "You probably wouldn't even know what hit you. The hulls would collapse, the water would pound in, and you'd be . . . *mush* in an instant."

I thought of that body lying on the sand next to *Scorpion*, next to the wreckage at a depth of 3000 meters south of the Azores. The wreckage was still there; anyone could go see it. But the body the investigation team had discovered hadn't been jelly. In fact, the man had been wearing an orange life jacket, which had further compounded the mystery.

I shivered.

Looking at Kat and Meg, I said, "How did you find Lazlow to bring him to Trieste?"

Kat answered. "He had made some posts on the net about using sound to go deep. His comments were cryptic, but just interesting enough to make me research him a bit. I learned about his career. It seemed as though he might be able to help us. We spoke, and I invited him to Trieste. He sent specifications for the *Swords*." She gestured out at the manufacturing line, somewhere beyond the inner bulkhead of the chamber we were in. "We've been building the ships to his design. The snout, at least."

"Is that why you called them *Swords*? After swordfish?" The bow wasn't as sharp as a swordfish's snout, but it did protrude more than most other seacars.

She smiled. "Maybe. Sounds menacing too. After all, we're going to use them to wage a war, aren't we?"

"That's the plan," I said. She looked at me quizzically and I shrugged. The story of sailors dying at crush depth still resonated with me. Then I thought of something. "Lazlow, how deep can these subs go?"

He crossed his thin arms. "We haven't tested them yet, mind you, but I believe the limit is only dictated by the power of the sound generator."

"Meaning?"

"We can hit any depth in the Atlantic, as long as the sub is moving forward."

My jaw fell open. *"Any depth?"*

"Yes." He offered a smile, but this one betrayed a modesty I didn't expect. "Eight kilometers is the deepest abyss in this ocean. We should be able to go that deep."

—••—

DOCTOR MANESH LAZLOW SAID, "THIS IS all I've been thinking about, remember. This and colonizing the oceans. For the last two decades I've been working on this to help the people of the seafloor survive and flourish."

I stared at him. There was that mention of twenty years again. I wondered what was driving the man. What had made him work so hard for the oceans while he'd been living on land? There was pain in his face sometimes, a hidden suffering his amazement and wonder hid well, but twice in ten minutes now I'd detected traces of it.

"Manesh," I said in a soft voice. "Thank you for helping us."

He looked at me, his expression one of surprise. "It's quite the opposite, young man. *You're* helping me."

I snorted. I guessed after so many years, he might actually look at it like that.

I turned to the others as I mulled it all over. We currently had the fastest ships in the waters. No one could come close. Yet. But now we might have the deepest-diving subs as well. We could double the depth of any USSF or CSF or FSF sub in the world.

We would be a force to be reckoned with, that much was certain. We just had to keep building the subs.

And test them first, I reminded myself.

The thought of plowing through water at such high pressures was sobering.

Eight kilometers down.

The deepest areas of the Atlantic.

Untold wealth only the people of the colonies would be able to harvest. We'd be able to explore the deeps faster than anyone else. We'd colonize and build structures deeper than ever before, especially once we got our hands on the superior syntactic foam. We'd be able to run from our enemies if need be, or shoot at them from below, like having air superiority on land.

It was a monumental advance beyond any other nation in the oceans.

But first we had to gain our independence. Then we would show the world a new prosperity.

Unless they killed us all and took the technology for themselves.

I shot an unconscious darting look at Johnny. That's what he had done, after all, with Kat's SCAV drive. He had stolen it for Sheng City, and I had caught him. But it had started us on this incredible journey, and I wanted to lead the people of Trieste into a brighter future.

Actually, I thought, a *darker* future.

The dark depths of the world's oceans, where few dared to go.

And we were going to do it willingly.

CHAPTER SEVENTEEN

WE SPENT ANOTHER TWO HOURS DISCUSSING the Pulse Drive. Its benefits, drawbacks, and how exactly Lazlow had come up with the notion. The single largest flaw was that the drive's sonic pulses would essentially appear like a superhot flare on any sonar screen. The depths we'd achieve, however, would make up for it. He also made some comments about using sound for other tactical strategies, such as shielding a sub in a dampening noise field, using sound as a weapon, disguising a sub with a fake sonic signature, and so on. Lazlow impressed me. Sitting in the small lounge in the upper level of the manufacturing facility almost four kilometers under the surface, he spoke at length about his ideas and how he would be able to assist Trieste and our struggle against the superpowers of the world.

Afterward, we took a tour of The Ridge, and we got to see every facet of the manufacturing process, including the fusion reactors, where a powerful magnetic field fused hydrogen atoms to form helium and heat energy. The reactors were four-foot spheres circled with tubing and electronics and studded with injectors and sensors. Manufacturing them was the most difficult job at the facility.

I had wondered for many months after construction of The Ridge how the workers there fared. The isolation, the depth, pressure, and the lack of communication. I soon discovered they were jovial, friendly with one another, and there was a real sense of community in the facility. They were there for a common goal, and for many weeks they'd worked almost every waking hour, which they didn't complain about. It was incredible. I watched them as they talked to Lancombe and Ng—they'd recognized the names instantly—and asked them about my father and the early days of the fight for freedom. There was the odd glance toward me during those conversations, but I was okay with that. They were curious, and they had a right to be. They had sacrificed so much. They couldn't communicate with home, after all. They couldn't even contact me. People at Trieste thought they were dead, and we couldn't say otherwise. It would ruin our plans. When the construction phase was done, then we could move them back to Trieste, perhaps under assumed names. Then, and only then, would their friends and families discover the truth, and we would rotate a new crew in.

Unless we needed them for a fight. These fifty were also our pilots should another battle appear on the horizon.

There were of course conflicts, as in any close-knit community, but these were minor and usually solved within a day or two. There was also lots of sex, apparently—Jackson told me all about it—but as long as they built the seacars and maintained a steady production, I didn't care.

I considered another major issue facing me about The Ridge: Renée Féroce. I just didn't know how to solve the problem. She obviously hated me. She wanted to kill me. But for better or for worse, she was with us on this journey now, and I just couldn't bring myself to imprison her. Or kill her, for that matter.

I decided not to confine her, but she was our captive nonetheless. She couldn't leave the facility. I supposed she could sabotage it, flood it, cause it to implode, but I hoped that she had a sense of self-preservation.

I'd have to talk to her about it. Soon.

The men and women on the assembly line had grins on their faces and were thrilled to see us. They had a multitude of questions, but after a half hour of talking they eventually began to disperse and the sounds of machinery fired up again. The line started moving, in that open chamber within a camouflaged dome almost four kilometers down, and the militarized seacar construction continued.

—••—

WE SAW THE FINISHED *SWORDS*, FLOATING in an enclosed pool dug into the rock wall behind The Ridge, and it was a sight to behold. Our jaws dropped. We didn't quite know what to say. There were over seventy of them there, all painted black and covered in anechoic tiles and drifting silently in the darkened rock chamber. The roof was rough and jagged. Our engineers had used explosives to open the cavity, and it felt massive. There was an echo within, and it was cold and damp. It felt like a chilly wet day in there, and for some odd reason, a scene from *The Hound of the Baskervilles* came to me. *Weird*, I thought. I had very few memories of life on the surface, and yet here I was imagining a foggy scene on the moonlit moors of England.

—••—

FARTHER INTO THE ROCK OF THE cliff, a long travel tube led toward the facility's nuclear reactor. It hadn't been difficult to set up—they were contained units manufactured for underwater mining—and we'd purchased it through our mining interests group and adapted it to suit our needs at The Ridge. It ran our life support, pumps, pressure equalizers, and all the machinery and equipment needed for seacar construction. And knowing it was safe under the hard basaltic rock was comforting, after what had happened to ours during The Second Battle of Trieste.

We walked back as a group through the travel tube toward the dome. Again we passed the branch that led to the *Sword* storage pond, as the workers called it, and I noted Renée's eyes dart toward the vessels. "They won't work," I said. "Not until their systems are activated. Locked down right now." I had given Jackson those instructions months ago.

She shot me a stunned look, then stared ahead with that severe expression on her face. "I'm not going to be a willing prisoner."

Jackson blinked at that; he was still trying to figure out the relationships between all of us.

"Perhaps a willing tourist then," I replied. "Temporarily."

She sneered. "How temporary?"

I shrugged. "Until the fighting starts maybe? I'll have to see." I studied her as our feet rang on the deck's steel grating. "You could be useful here. A military person, putting her skills to use for us."

She snapped her head toward me. "To help *you*? The man who ruined my life?"

"I saved you. You were hell-bent on revenge. Going into the canyon like that, on a tether. Insanity."

"You killed my crew, you ruined my command, you caused problems with my superiors in the FSF."

I sighed. It was one way to look at it, I guess.

THE UPPER DECK HELD THE COMMAND cabin and the sleeping compartments for The Ridge's staff. Each berth was a small bunk separated by curtains that could be opened to speak with neighbors or drawn for privacy. The sleeping area occupied half of the level, its bulkheads were curved around the chamber as well as upward toward the ceiling. Jackson showed us to our bunks. We were exhausted, and we fell into our beds happy to stretch out on a comfortable mattress for a change.

Within seconds I could hear snoring around me. Lancombe and Lazlow, probably. I'd come to learn their sleep noises on board *SCAV-1*. I reached beside me and felt for Kat's hand. It was limp at first, but a second later it tightened momentarily.

The curved ceiling of the dome was comforting. It reminded me I was underwater. It was a pleasant feeling sometimes. At other times, during a TCI mission or an underwater battle, however, it could be terrifying.

Right then, with the sigh of the ventilation system and the chugging of pumps hidden behind bulkheads, the dim lighting and the sound of sub assembly still going on below, everything felt right.

The curtain beside me moved and I turned my head slightly to see who it was. I half expected to see Renée with a savage flash in her eyes and a blade in her hand, but it was Johnny in the bunk next to mine.

Renée was one bunk over, beside Meg and Jessica Ng, with the curtains opened, and I hoped she wouldn't try anything. She would wait. Plan. Calculate. Try to think of all the options.

Johnny said, "You're thinking about Renée."

I sighed. He knew me very well. "I guess. I don't know what to do with her just yet."

"I can't decide either. It's a dilemma." After a minute he said, "I can't believe what you've done in a year. This is . . . *incredible*."

I offered a grim smile in the half light. "I know what you mean. Being here is surreal. And back in Trieste, Heller is probably wondering just what the hell is going on."

"Trieste is a lot different than the Chinese cities."

Johnny had been gone for a year, dealing with the people of the Chinese colonies, trying to convince them to help us. "Go on."

"There aren't as many freedoms."

"Things are pretty bad for us too. The USSF is breathing down our necks."

I recalled how they had monitored my speech that day in the Commerce Module, and threatened me in case I tried to inspire dissent. And the two USSF sailors who had been so rude to our citizens in the lounge that day in the Living Module.

He shrugged, difficult to do since he was lying down. "I don't know much about that. I've been out trying to sell your plans."

"True."

"But the Chinese cities are tough. The whole time I was working for them, when you were our prisoner—" his eyes flicked to mine for an instant and I could see the regret there "—they didn't even let me walk around freely. Other operatives were always nearby, watching. And the people there are constantly informing on one another! It's ridiculous."

I frowned. "What do you mean? Informing on what?"

"If someone says something negative about their leadership. You know. Witch hunts and so on."

"And the people there don't like it."

"Not at all. They hate it."

I absorbed that for a long, silent moment.

Johnny finally said, "I've missed you, Mac. And I'm sorry again for what happened."

"We've been through that already. You made up for it. It's over. We have to move on, tackle this new challenge."

"Still."

"You feel guilty."

"Absolutely." There was a hesitation as he obviously picked his next words carefully. "I tortured you, Mac. Just to make my bosses happy."

"You did it for a reason. Shanks was torturing Chinese prisoners. You wanted to free them. You never thought they'd torture me in kind."

"Still," he repeated.

I reached out across the gap between our bunks and squeezed his shoulder. "Don't mention it again. I need you sharp for this. Things are going to get dangerous fast, and when they do, we can't be questioning each other's motivations or reliving emotional baggage. Got it?"

There was a prolonged silence, then, "Yeah."

I considered his words in the darkness. Soon his breathing grew regular and I knew he was asleep. Beside me, Kat was pressed against me, her chest rising and falling in silhouette against a blinking console on the bulkhead. Her long hair—a rarity underwater where most people kept theirs short—fell across my neck and chest, and I blew it away subconsciously.

She shifted and muttered something under her breath, then flung a leg across me.

Abruptly I pushed myself out from under her and ducked through the curtain to the area outside the ring of bunks. Renée Féroce's bunk was nearby, and I stepped inside her sleeping area and sat next to her. Her eyes snapped open and she yanked the blanket up to her shoulders. On either side, with curtains open, were Meg and Ng; both were sound asleep.

"Easy," I whispered. "I just want to talk to you."

"What do you want?" Her voice was quiet yet hard at the same time.

"We have a problem here. Do you know what it is?"

There was silence as the question hung between us. Then, "I'm assuming *I'm* the problem."

I grunted. "I want to tell you something. I understand why you're angry with me. But don't put me in a position where I have to make a sudden decision about you. I've been in the intelligence business a long time. The CIA assassinated my father. I've killed men and women before."

"Is that a threat?" Her eyes flashed.

"No. But I don't want trouble. Please." I sighed and made my voice soft. "Admiral Benning murdered my father, Renée. I found out just a few days ago."

She frowned.

"But I also found out that my dad sacrificed himself for the colony. For a future that might never come. It's hard to accept it all. But Benning . . . I want revenge for what he did." I clenched my hand into a fist. "I am going to have that revenge. But there is a time and a place. I know I can't rush it. There are other things I have to take care of first."

"Are you asking me to put off killing you? Are you crazy?"

I gestured at the dome over our heads. "Look around. If you're planning to try something right now, here, in this dangerous place, I could ask you the same question." I blew out an exasperated breath and stood up. "All I'm asking for is some time. I saved your life out there. Brought you into the safety of the seacar. Please return the favor."

I spun on my heel and left.

—••—

THE NEXT DAY I DEPARTED IN *SC-1* and powered away from The Ridge. I'd left Meg, Kat, Lancombe, Ng, and Lazlow to continue working on the seacars. Renée stayed as well, a prisoner of the deeps, but with the understanding she wouldn't be there forever.

Johnny sat by my side to return to Trieste. I was going to have to hide him there, right under the USSF's nose, but I needed him to help coordinate efforts.

Kat and I would reconnect later, after there was a more sizeable fleet of *Swords* ready at The Ridge. Our kiss before I'd climbed down the ladder into the seacar had been memorable. Her eyes had been sad and she'd stroked the stubble on my face softly. "Don't be too long," she had whispered.

"Don't worry. I just have to keep doing my job back home. I'm the Mayor, don't forget, and I didn't tell anybody where I was going. Not even Butte."

"I'm sure he has everything under control. You don't have to return so fast."

"I still have to make sure things are running smoothly. Keep the USSF off our backs. Or try to."

The docking pool was empty—Johnny was already in *SC-1* getting the systems ready—and we embraced beside the seacar.

"If you have to go," she sighed into my neck, "at least get the damage to *SC-1*'s hull fixed when you get back. Take care of the scratches and dings."

I smiled. "I'll make it happen, don't worry."

We kissed again, and I abruptly turned and descended the ladder. The hatch above me slid shut with a clang.

Johnny and I powered slowly through the airlock tube, the pressure spiking at the depth of 3782 meters, and when the outer lock hatch opened, I pushed the throttle to max and soared away from the facility, angling the nose upward and blowing a little ballast at the same time. There were no other contacts on the sonar above the Mid-Atlantic Ridge, so I descended once again into the rift and slowed velocity to zero.

Then I kicked on the SCAV drive.

SC-1 rocketed away from our manufacturing facility, which was now out of sight in the depths and camouflaged against the dark rocks of the cliff face, and we powered 1300 kilometers northward through the canyon in only three hours. I marveled at the power in my hands as I held the vibrating yoke tightly.

And the *Swords* would be even faster.

CHAPTER
EIGHTEEN

WE KEPT THE SCAV DRIVE ON through the rift all the way north past the Equator and beyond. The turbulence was less noticeable while travelling at 450 kph, but we had to be more vigilant when piloting at that velocity. Still, the rift was ten to twenty kilometers wide through the entire distance of the Mid-Atlantic Ridge, so the seacar was not in danger of crashing into the towering mountains.

We had to follow that track back to Trieste; if we arrived on a heading from the south, the USSF would notice we had left heading north and arrived from the south. So, we would go north first, back the way we had come.

As we were powering through the trench at 450 kph, an alarm sounded from the sonar and I glanced down at the scope. It could only have happened if a vessel was passing above us, but we were in a canyon, and out of the common sea lanes.

I instantly pulled back on the throttle and we dropped from SCAV. The details on the sonar shocked me and my heart strobed.

This was no ordinary seacar or warsub.

It was gargantuan.

The largest submarine in the oceans was the *Doomsday* class USSF nuclear missile boat. It was 232 meters in length. But the one overhead was a whopping 414 meters! There was no known sub in the world that size. It had thirty decks, which would make it a hundred meters tall.

Johnny and I stared at each other. The figure was just too difficult to accept. But even harder to comprehend was the vessel's velocity.

It was 467 kph.

It had a SCAV drive.

"Impossible," Johnny said as we watched the signal trace across the screen. Above, in the VID heads-up display, the vessel was shooting across the canopy faster than any other I'd seen, trailing a long white plume of swirling bubbles and turbulence.

Johnny and I couldn't say another word at that moment.

The vessel was just so damned huge.

The fusion reactor would have to be massive.

As it passed by overhead, the wake churned up the water hundreds of meters down. It tossed us like a bit of flotsam in a storm. Another hundred meters below us, it was churning sand from the bottom of the canyon.

And sure enough, on the screen, the label read:

**Unknown Registry
Database Identification: Unknown**

Not even the computer knew what this vessel was.

An hour later we decided to continue on our journey back to Trieste, and left the mystery of the largest sub we'd ever seen—*and with a SCAV drive too!*—far behind.

No one would believe what we'd come across.

—••—

USING THE SCAV IN THE TRENCH shortened our return trip markedly, but once we hit a latitude of thirty degrees north, we decided to cut the SCAV, crest the ridge, and turn due west toward Bermuda. Once at Bermuda, we would shift southwest and toward home.

The fact we had encountered the French warsub *Hunter* in that general area occurred to me, but only briefly. After all, we could have been any sub on a return course from Europe; we were back in the general sealanes, and there were quite a few subs and surface vessels in the vicinity.

Johnny and I spent the day theorizing about the supercavitating warsub that we'd seen, discussing where it could have come from, what military had created it, and so on. Then we switched to his year in the Chinese underwater cities, the things he'd seen and the people in charge there.

He asked me about the past year, and I spoke about the difficulties of being mayor, my relationship with Kat, her efforts at The Ridge, how my sister had helped out, and how Lazlow had entered the picture.

I also told him about my informant on *Impaler*, Rafe Manuel, and how someone had brutally murdered him on the USSF warsub. He grimaced when he heard the tale.

We were cruising at seventy kph in a deeper layer of water, to try to catch the southward flowing cold gyre from the North Sea, when a loud *ping* echoed through the cabin and reverberated along her hull.

It only took me a second to react. "Oh, shit," I said, and reached to turn our course. An instant later another ping hit us. "Johnny, we have to activate the SCAV drive."

He looked shocked. "But there are other vessels near—"

"*NOW!*"

I cut our speed to nothing and opened the fusion drive control panel. I powered up the reactor and soon our intake hatches had retracted, the reactor was flash boiling water to steam, and it was screaming from our rear thruster nozzle.

Our speed started to increase.

We couldn't hit supercavitation until the bubble of air had completely surrounded us, and I could see it out the canopy at the blunt bow, slowly beginning to form as oxygen bubbled from the cold water.

The sonar screen flashed; there had been a splash detected at the surface almost directly above us.

"Oh, *shit!*"

—••—

IT WAS THE SAME TACTIC THE French had used on me west of Florida. Send a ping and detect *SC-1*. Notify an aircraft of the location. Aircraft drops an EMP which detonates close enough to knock out computer circuit boards and chips.

And it was happening again.

This time, however, I planned to be long gone by the time the bomb descended to our depth of 1000 meters.

Then I stared at the sonar in shock.

It was a French torpedo, according to the database.

And it was accelerating.

—••—

SOON IT HIT THE VELOCITY LIMIT of eighty kph. I shot a look out at our bubble as it grew past the bow. It was just now hitting the front of the canopy. Friction was lessening already, and the fusion reactor was on full. The steam was *piercing* the water from the aft—it reverberated through the entire vessel and no doubt ships everywhere were now staring at their displays wondering what the hell was going on. We were climbing past eighty kph ourselves, so I breathed a sigh of relief. The French weapon would not catch us.

Then I glanced back at the sonar. The torpedo was at 200 kph and still accelerating quickly, angling straight down for us.

It was a SCAV torpedo. The US variety went over 1000 kph.

I resisted the urge to swear again, but the situation demanded it.

"Come on, come on, come on," I said, urging our SCAV. "Give me some speed."

Johnny triggered a ping of our own—active sonar—and a few seconds later the signal returned to us, reflected from any vessels within a hundred kilometer radius.

There was a large cluster of ships and submarines on the sonar, due east. We had emerged from the rift damn near to them—but not within the thirty kilometer range of the passive sonar.

My jaw dropped as I noted the ship classes. *Liberty, Republic, Fleur de Lis, de Gaulle.* Even a *Verdun.*

The collection of forty vessels represented every class of FSF warsub.

They were looking for the ship that had sunk *Hunter.*

They were looking for us.

—••—

THE TORPEDO ON OUR TAIL WAS gaining. Fast. We were only at 250 kph now and the reactor was roaring in our ears as the acceleration mounted. Water still slid past our hull behind the canopy, which was pitted and ragged after the damage caused by falling rocks in the canyon northeast of Bermuda.

I shook my head as I stared at the screen, my face tight. If the torpedo was an EMP, it only had to detonate close. The results would be instantaneous.

Systems down, sub lost.

"Johnny, look for deep water. *Really* deep water."

"Right." He pulled up a map on a second screen and stared at that depth finder. "Give me a second."

The torpedo was only a hundred meters away. "I have to evade," I said. "Release countermeasures!"

He pressed a button and the devices shot from the underbody of *SC-1*, simultaneously churning the water and releasing gases and emitting loud audio signals. They were meant to lure the torpedo in.

Make it detonate away from us.

I swallowed.

Putting the seacar into a steep plunge, I rammed the ballast tanks to negative and we rapidly took on water. We left the neutrally buoyant countermeasures far above as we powered downward into the depths at over 300 kph—

And the missile burst right through the cloud of bubbles and stayed on course, headed for us.

It wasn't armed yet.

"Dammit," I snapped. Leveling off and neutralizing buoyancy, I realized suddenly how effortless the yoke felt. The SCAV bubble had completely surrounded us.

Get us home, SC-1.

—••—

THE FRENCH MISSILE WAS SCREAMING ALONG behind us at 945 kph. It was going to overtake and detonate beside us. It was inevitable.

Unless I could disable it before it armed. Maybe turn our seacar into it.

No, that option wouldn't work. The torpedo would arm within a certain distance and explode right on us. I'd have to try a torpedo.

"Johnny, prepare a SCAV torpedo." I knew we had three left; Kat had used one against *Hunter* in the canyon.

He was staring at me.

I noticed his look. "I know. But it's either that or we die, here and now."

He nodded. "Got it." A second later, "Torpedo away. Homing on the other weapon."

I heeled the ship over to the port for a few seconds, then back to starboard. *Have to keep that torpedo off our stern*, I thought. It was so close.

I pulled back on the yoke and the change in course pressed us into our seats. We were *rocketing* to the surface. . . .

And then the torpedo detonated.

—••—

THE EXPLOSION FLASH BOILED THOUSANDS OF liters of water in an instant. The steam surged out in all directions, then shot toward the surface in a flowering blossom of white. The surrounding water crashed back in, and the compression wave snapped outward.

The shock wave slammed *SC-1* to the starboard.

"At least it wasn't an EMP," I said.

And then the bubble surrounding us collapsed and Johnny and I slammed forward into the seatbelts as the seacar rammed into a wall of water.

The second torpedo, ours, detonated an instant later.

I swore yet again.

And the systems flickered. Sections of the console winked out.

A spray of water cut through the living space from the upper hatch. The detonation had ruined a seal, and the water had found a way in.

Johnny leaped to his feet. "Pumps are out!" he yelled over the noise. "I'll go check them."

The water was flooding into the seacar—it was a waterfall now. The seal had given out totally, and the pressure at our depth was *shoving* the ocean into *SC-1*. Like a finger forcing its way into an orange, looking to peel it apart. Only in this case it would peel just a section open, then crush the rest.

"Remind me never to fire on a torpedo again," I said, purging our ballast. Dammit. *That had been stupid.* I was smarter than that, but I'd been worried it had been another EMP.

Maybe the French were too scared to detonate another one so close to the States.

Water was sloshing around my ankles now, and I turned to look at Johnny. He'd sprinted back into engineering, where he was tearing into the breaker panels and trying to get power to the emergency pumps.

"I'm going to have to seal the control cabin!" I called back at him. "You seal engineering! Can you get the pumps working?"

"Possibly," was the faint reply. "Good luck, Mac." Then the hatch slammed shut.

I sealed the hatch just behind the two pilot seats, and sat back.

There was nothing I could do now. The controls were out.

The living area, including the couches and bunks and kitchen and lavatory, was flooding. Only the control cabin and the engineering spaces were contained, but when the living space was full of water—

That would be a *lot* of weight.

We'd grow negatively buoyant.

And sink.

———••———

Already we were descending, and with blown ballast tanks too. I frowned. We should have been floating to the surface, at least until the cabin filled with water.

A look at the ballast displays hit me in the gut, however. They were flooded.

But how was that possible? We'd been positively buoyant before the detonations.

Unless the explosions had ruined the valves or pumps. Or both. Even if Johnny got the cabin cleared, we'd still hit bottom.

The depth finder was operating, but it was flickering. Three hundred meters. A stroke of luck. I'd been piloting at a depth of 1000 meters for hours before the attack. There must have been a rise in this area. We could survive the sinking, but if Johnny couldn't clear the sub, we were in trouble.

—••—

TEN MINUTES PASSED. THE PRESSURE MOUNTED as the sub sank, the hull creaked, and the air grew cold and damp. My feet were freezing—the water in the control cabin was up to my ankles, but no longer rising—and there were muted thumps coming from somewhere behind me. All systems were now out. Emergency lights were on, but that was it.

Another hour passed. I spent the time rooting through the control panel, and I found a few shorts and a few loose connections that I bypassed, but nothing had any impact on the status of the ship. I needed Johnny for that, back in engineer—

The lights flickered back on. The control panels came to life. Ventilation fans started whirring. But not because of anything I'd done.

A series of chugging pulses sounded from behind me—pumps were clearing the cabin of water. There were still major problems on the seacar—water kept spilling in from the top hatch, for instance—but at least the pumps could keep up with the flooding now. Our ballast was full, however, and I gingerly reached to the controls to change them to neutral. . . .

Nothing happened.

The hatch behind me opened and Johnny sloshed in. There was still a stream of green water falling into the cabin just behind him, which was more than a little disconcerting.

"Good job," I said, pointing at the top hatch, "but we're going to have to fix that."

He nodded. "We'll have to go outside. Flood the living cabin again, fix the seal. Then pump it out."

There was a sudden clang on the hull, and a dragging, scraping, screeching as something moved across the steel.

A glance at the sonar, then a look upward through the canopy confirmed my fears. There was a warsub settling over us.

They meant to tow us away.

—••—

VERDUN CLASS. TOP SPEED, 45 KPH. Almost two football fields long. A nuclear missile boat—we called it an SSBGN, or Ship Submersible Ballistic/Guided Missile Nuclear—it held twenty nukes, could hit a depth of 3200 meters, had one huge thruster on the aft end of the fuselage with five two-meter long screw blades, a crew of 113, and eight torpedo tubes as well as mines.

They also had grappling hooks.

I bolted to my feet. "Johnny, suit up, now! Flood the living compartment, fix the seal on the hatch." I started to gather my scuba gear.

His face was slack. "Where are you going?"

"We can't let them hook onto us. We can outrun this sub, but we have to get operational first."

"There are other warsubs with them!"

I snorted. "One thing at a time, partner."

The chain scraped across the hull again, and this time some links drifted past the canopy. Massive twists of iron. I grimaced as the screech hit. Kat was going to freak out when she found out about this. "Is the SCAV operational?"

He scowled as he pulled on his wetsuit and threw the tank over his shoulders. "No. It's out. And I don't know how to fix it."

So we'd have to run and evade with conventional tactics.

The thought made me stop in my tracks. My flippers were on and the mask was around my head. The tank was already across my back. I was standing in water and there was still a waterfall cascading from the top hatch. I shot a glance back to the control cabin. "Hold it." I frowned as I thought the situation over.

I had made a couple of big mistakes in this situation. One had been firing a torpedo at the French torpedo. But the other mistake had happened earlier. Returning to this area on our way back to Trieste. I had been trying to avoid the USSF tracking our path to The Ridge, but I should have known the French would be here. After all, Renée had put a tracking device on us. It wasn't operational anymore—we'd removed it long before—but it had led them to the canyon where we had destroyed *Hunter*. That canyon was to the east. . . .

They'd been waiting for us to return.

Shit.

They outmatched us completely. But they had made a terrible mistake too. Perhaps it was because they thought we were down and out—which we had been, for an hour or so—but now we had some systems back up and running, thanks to Johnny. The pumps were running full time, pumping the water flooding in right back out.

"Fire torpedoes first." I clenched a jaw as I thought about it. The underbelly of the massive vessel was right over us. They'd been hunting us, because they knew we'd destroyed two French ships already. I couldn't blame them for being mad, but I also couldn't go willingly with them. We had two SCAV and three conventional torpedoes left. "I'll go out the airlock with a welding torch. I'll cut the grapples off."

As if on cue, the seacar lurched to the side. The magnetic hooks had us.

"Prepare to fire three torpedoes into her underbelly. Set all three at impact detonation. Aim for the aft—engineering."

His jaw dropped. "Mac." His voice was quiet. "We've been through a lot together, but that's a nuclear missile sub out there. There are over a hundred sailors on her. We've never fired on a—"

"I know. But the situation is dire. When I give the order, fire the torpedoes. I'll be outside cutting off the grapples. Then we'll fix the hatch as that boat floods."

"And the other subs?"

"Like I said, one thing at a time."

CHAPTER NINETEEN

THERE WAS NO GOING OUT THE moonpool; we were way too deep. I grabbed a tank of the correct mix for our current depth and went through the airlock. Johnny would try to repair the hatch from inside, then he would have to pilot us away during our escape attempt. I would have to depressurize before I could enter the living area and control cabin; it meant another few hours lying on the airlock deck, wet and freezing—something I was not looking forward to. The hatch opened and I drifted outside cautiously. I was wearing flippers and kept my buoyancy neutral. The welding torch was heavy, however, so I had to lug it up to set it on the scratched and dinged-up hull. There was a stream of bubbles rising from the top hatch.

The warsub cut off my view, however. It had a flat underbelly studded with sensor pods, hatches, torpedo tubes, and airlocks. There were at least ten airlock hatches in view on the starboard side alone, for infantry and personal scooters. Four thick chains connected the sub to *SC-1*. They were attached to the seacar with powerful electromagnets. I would have to cut through each to release the vessel, and I'd have to do it fast. Once they realized what I was doing, they would try to stop me.

We were over the ocean floor by a few meters, and as I watched, the gargantuan screw blades of the *Verdun* class missile sub began to churn. Bubbles formed around the screw surfaces and joined the air escaping from

SC-1 on its 300 meter trip topside. The warsub was close enough to the seafloor that the giant thruster kicked up sand from the bottom, and a cloud formed behind, swirling counterclockwise. Fish caught in the maelstrom swam valiantly to stay upright, but the power of the current overcame them. They flailed away, helpless, as they disappeared into the darkness of the water.

The current was strong, but the ship had so much mass it would take a while to build up speed. Her max velocity was forty-five. As I watched, the chains stretched taut and *SC-1* hung back, like an animal straining at a leash. It became obvious I would have to sever the two chains at the rear first, and I quickly swam over to them, dragging the tools behind me.

"Johnny," I said into my facemask. "I'm starting now."

"They'll notice you soon. Work fast." His voice was small and tinny.

"Roger." I hesitated for a heartbeat, and then, "Fire all torpedoes, now."

With a burst of bubbles from the bow, the first torpedo lanced out. It quickly arced upward and soared straight and true to the warsub's aft. Then another torpedo emerged and followed a similar course.

An instant later the first weapon struck. I watched it happen from just fifty meters away. It plunged right into the thick steel of the armored vessel and a flare of white and concussion waves blossomed. A flood of water cascaded back in, and bubbles streamed from the puncture. Sharp shards of hull angled into the submarine, jagged and warped, like angry teeth intent on devouring French sailors.

Compartments flooded.

Men died.

Then the second torpedo hit.

I had to shield my face and eyes; material was shooting out from the blasts, and I was in danger of losing my grip on the hull. The detonations were so near and huge that they dazed me. My sight grew dark.

I was dimly aware of a third launch and a third explosion, but I pushed my facemask against steel, trying to shield my head from the shock waves.

The warsub had been completely unprepared. No countermeasures, no evasion, nothing.

They'd assumed we'd been permanently disabled.

Their screw kept spinning, but we had flooded sections of the warsub. It would slow her somewhat. Bubbles shot from the three punctures, each about five meters apart.

"Good shooting," I said.

Above, the warsub was shifting course to the northeast. The current was really picking up, and I had to hook a flipper through a rung in the hull. I had to be careful the welding tank didn't get thrown away in the swirling water.

The welder fired up instantly at my touch. More bubbles streamed to the surface.

It took two minutes to get through the first link. It actually took longer than I thought it would; the metal was not ordinary. It must have been a stronger alloy for the towing of larger vessels. But soon I'd made it all the way through, and the seacar lurched under me as the chain fell free and hung behind us, trailing into the darkness. The magnet was a large plate that peeled away and plummeted downward to the seafloor. Once I'd cut the connection, the magnetic properties had disappeared. There must have been an electrical cable sealed within the metal. And no electricity, no magnet.

They'd notice that, I thought.

"A hatch just opened on the warsub," Johnny warned. "Hurry."

I hauled the tools over to the next grapple and started to cut.

"Here they come," Johnny said.

"How many?"

"I see eight scuba—no, ten now—soldiers coming for you. They have scooters to help them against the strong current."

"ETA?" Sweat dripped from my eyebrows into my eyes, and I shook my head to clear the droplets.

"I'd say two minutes."

The second grapple fell away. I could do one more before I had to worry about the troops. I spun and began to pull myself along the hull toward the front magnets. I couldn't swim; we were now forging too quickly through the water. If I lost my grip, it'd be all over for me. Johnny would not be able to come back to find me.

"Careful," he said.

"I've got it." I finally arrived at the third magnet. The chain was tight as the weight of *SC-1* strained against the links. A risky glance up confirmed Johnny's warnings.

The troops were there, moving toward me. Each straddled a motorcycle-sized tube with a single nozzle at the aft end. There were no screws on these little vehicles—they utilized a pump-jet, with all moving parts inside the machine. A gimbaling nozzle angled the thrust, which controlled the direction the scooter moved. It was fast and maneuverable.

"They'll have weapons, Mac."

"I know." I focused on the welder. Another minute and I would have the third grapple severed. "Get ready to turn our thrusters on." I checked the direction the scooters were coming in from—the bow. "Turn on full reverse when I say."

The current would wash across the vessel toward the bow, hopefully disorient the troops, and perhaps even slow the warsub's progress.

"Okay. They've contacted us, Mac, and they're *pissed*."

The chain separated and *SC-1* lurched suddenly to the starboard. There was only one grapple left.

I ignored Johnny's comment about the French communication. "Get ready," I said.

"Ready."

I lunged over to the last chain and started to cut. Bubbles churned all around me. It was hard to see anything. I was breathing hard and my mask was fogging. Damn. You needed full visibility in an undersea environment like this.

Especially with armed people on their way to kill you.

"Do you have a gun?" Johnny asked. I could detect his worry.

"Of course." The holster was on my thigh. It was tight, and the strap was snapped on so the current wouldn't yank the weapon into the depths.

"Time to grab it."

A glint flashed before my eyes; twenty-centimeter-long steel needles ricocheted off the hull only inches in front of my mask. I pulled back and whipped my gaze toward the scooters.

I drew my gun.

Another swarm of needles shot toward me. Bursts of gas erupted from the weapons as the scooter operators gripped them tightly. But the current was too strong and the speed too great. I knew it would be difficult to aim in this situation.

"Turn on the thrusters!" I barked.

In an instant the screws started and *SC-1* jumped backward, hauling on the last remaining chain. We began to rise, and the chain stretched tauter than ever. It was quivering it was so tight now.

I studied it carefully, and something occurred to me.

Another flash of needles hit the hull and a cloud of something filled my vision before trailing away behind the seacar. Blood.

My blood.

The pain hit next. Strange that I'd seen the results before I'd felt the needle that had lanced through my right thigh—in and out without even slowing.

There was little evidence of the puncture, but the stream of blood from both sides of my leg gave it away.

Aiming at the tightest cluster of scooters—three of them, just to my left—I fired three rapid shots. Fifteen needles in all.

Then I ducked low, grabbed a rung, and pressed myself to the seacar.

The vessel was rocking in the water, swinging back and forth, and there was an enormous current whipping past me. The welding tank was slamming up and down against the hull, the tubes flailing in the water. I'd tethered it to a rung with a belt, but it wouldn't last long.

Then without warning the tank split. A surge of bubbles rushed out—

And it soared up and behind and disappeared into the distance.

"Shit."

"What's wrong?"

"Lost the torch."

"You got a couple of the guys though."

As he said it, I noted two riderless scooters spin away behind us, following the welding tank.

I could feel each beat of my heart in my thigh. Not a good sign. The blood continued to trickle out, but at least it wasn't spurting. Missed the arteries.

Another spread of needles shot toward me, and they ricocheted against the hull of the seacar, the bent steel flipping away harmlessly.

"Do you have ballast control?" I asked.

"No."

That's what I'd thought. The two torpedo blasts had damaged the pumps or valves—or both. "We need to rise a bit. Use the yoke—pull back a bit. *Slowly.*"

There was a hesitation and then he swore in realization. "Got it."

Behind me, the flaps on the horizontal stabilizer whined. I craned my neck as I clung to the ship. The currents were insane, and I couldn't take much more. The sweat in my eyes was growing unbearable, and my biceps were on fire. But I watched the flaps move, and the seacar began to rise.

Toward the warsub.

Our ballast may have been frozen at negative, and we were currently heavier than the water that we displaced, but with that velocity and the ability to angle our nose up and down, we could alter our depth.

We continued to rise.

And the chain leading to the hatch in the warsub's underbelly moved with us.

Toward the giant screw.

I held my breath.

Still it moved closer.

"A bit more," I said. "Just a bit."

"Get ready for a jolt!" Johnny cried out.

"Change thrusters to forward, full power!"

And then the chain came close to the churning screw of the warsub. Too close. In an instant the swirling current of the thruster hauled it in, and *SC-1* jerked forward suddenly. There was a pop in my shoulder and I ground my teeth against the agony.

The chain wrapped once around the propeller shaft, and—

It fell free. Severed by the giant blades.

"Turn to port, now!" I yelled.

"Hold on!"

There were more needles speeding toward me, but the swirling water washing past the seacar carried them away in random directions. Some flashed through the thrusters, but they were too narrow to cause any damage. Others rebounded off the hull, and still others were clear misses.

And then we were away.

The warsub disappeared behind us.

"We're still at negative buoyancy," Johnny said. He was warning me not to be too optimistic. It wasn't over yet.

"Keep us close to the bottom. Use the controls to keep us level."

"It's tough. We're really heavy right now."

"How much water is in the sub?" I was still holding tight, though my grip was tiring. I felt for my weight belt and grabbed the latch. Undoing it, I looped it under a rung before refastening it.

I finally relaxed, the belt straining against my waist. I could flex my hands and shake my arms out. Take a few deep breaths. Test my aching shoulder; I'd ripped the rotator cuff.

The water was rushing past my face, and I had to be careful not to let it rip my mask off or worm its way under the seal.

"Tanks are full. There's still a foot or more of water in the living area and control cabin. Pumps are keeping up. The engineering hatch is closed, but there's a bit of water in there too, which isn't good."

If water sloshed around too much, there were electrical components that could short.

"She's sluggish right now," he continued. "Hard to maintain level."

With the ballast full, the trim tanks didn't make much of a difference. And if we lost forward momentum, the control surfaces would not be able to keep us angled upward and at a constant depth. We'd sink.

"What's our speed?"

"Fifty-three."

I mulled over the situation. SCAV was out. Speed was lower than normal. The *Verdun* couldn't catch us, but there were other subs out there, hunting us. Subs that were faster. I debated risking an active pulse from the sonar, but didn't want to give our position away.

"Find a place to bottom the boat. Then we'll fix the hatch and hopefully avoid the French. But let's put some distance between us first."

There was a pause, and then, "I guess it's the best we can do. We can't go very fast until we clear the ballast and the water in the living area."

I remembered the time I had fired on the French ship *Destroyer*. I had damaged the ship, killed a sailor, and, as a result, Renée Féroce had devoted her life to hunting and killing me.

Now I'd just done it again. This time, however, it had been a missile boat that I had attacked. A nuclear launch platform.

Still, they had been trying to take me in, so I supposed I was justified in fighting back. Regardless, I had caused more damage than before, flooded more compartments, and possibly killed more French sailors. Hell, I'd killed at least two of the scooter operators just moments before.

I was supposed to be bringing people *together* in this struggle. Convincing them to fight as allies. And yet here I was making France more of an enemy every single day.

They would want revenge for this. More so than before.

And that thought scared me.

CHAPTER TWENTY

THE TRIP BACK TO TRIESTE WAS surprisingly uneventful, despite the twenty-four hour wait while the FSF subs searched for us. Johnny had set us down in a rugged field of boulders, and as I was decompressing in the airlock, he flooded the living compartment and set to work on the top hatch seal. It only took him twenty minutes, after which he pumped the living compartment out before the FSF subs could find us. I'd been worried about this: the constantly operating pump would have given us away. We'd had two choices: stop it and let the seacar flood, or fix it fast. Johnny had done the latter.

Afterward, he had a minor decompression protocol to follow, which he did in the living compartment. I had a much longer one, and once again, I curled up into a shivering ball on the cold steel deck of the airlock and endured it in a silent suffering.

But soon the sub was nearly fully functional, with the exception of the SCAV drive, yet again.

As the modules of Trieste appeared in the shallow waters of the continental shelf, I couldn't help but feel a thrill of excitement. I loved this place. It was my home, and I knew now that my father had given his life for it. It hadn't been a stupid mistake, or a thoughtless accident, or the careless naïveté I'd accused him of for thirty years. It had been a planned suicide with a greater goal in mind—to push me on a path that I may not have wanted or accepted.

But he'd taken a gamble, and it had paid off. I had accepted the journey after a long period of worry and bitter resentment, but now I—and the people nearest to me—had accepted the task with vigor.

At least, I thought my father's plan had paid off. We had to see what happened over the next few weeks, but for the first time in a while, I felt that things were finally progressing.

———••———

AFTER A FOUR HOUR SLEEP IN my cabin in Module B, I was back in my office outside City Control, looking at the sparse metal furnishings and the cold, bare bulkheads. I remembered the mayor's offices I'd seen at Ballard and Seascape; mine seemed very utilitarian in comparison. And the conditions back at The Ridge, where our workers were living with no comforts and working seven days a week for the benefit of the movement. . . .

I hoped they were doing okay . . . that Renée wasn't putting up a fuss and that Lazlow's efforts on the *Swords* would succeed.

Johnny was seeing to repairs on *SCAV-1*, and I decided to take the opportunity to address some mayoral business.

There were hundreds of messages on my comm. I shuddered when I saw that. They were mostly related to city business and complaints from the agricultural sector, especially after Heller's demand for more kelp. I pulled the first one up. It was Rebecca Hartley, the woman in charge of the kelp farms. "Are you crazy, Tru?" She was very pretty with short and spiky dark hair, but her informality showed she wasn't taking my request personally. Her eyes were hard and she was breathing heavily from the hard labor of her job. She had just come in from outside; she'd slung her tank over one shoulder, she wore a wetsuit, and she was using a public comm just inside the moonpool in her module. "We're already busting our asses to produce the amount that we do, and now you're increasing it by ten percent? At least give us more workers!" She slammed her fist on the button and terminated the call.

I sighed. "Shit." I hadn't liked doing it, but I'd hoped she'd understand. It was only temporary, after all, but I couldn't tell her that.

There were a variety of other similar messages, about malfunctioning equipment and needed repairs and safety protocols being broken in order to keep up with the increased workload, and I watched them all with a sinking feeling in my gut. This wasn't what the people of Trieste needed right now, especially with the USSF occupation going on. It was only going to breed more resentment.

There was a message from Cliff Sim, my security chief, and I brought it up eagerly and leaned toward the screen.

"Mac," he said. He was sitting in his cluttered office with a schematic of Trieste on the bulkhead behind him. He was stocky and big and kept his hair shaved to stubble because he was balding on top. He was tough, a product of Triestrian labor and work ethic. "Hey Boss. Where are you? You disappeared a few days ago and no one seems to know where you went. Butte has taken over while we're waiting for you to return." Then he darted a look off screen and lowered his voice. "You know, it's moves like that which are going to get the USSF curious about you." Then he tilted his head and swore. "But what the hell. Who cares about them, right?" He chuckled for a few moments then got right back to business. "I've been doing what you ordered, and I have some more video for you to see. It'll interest you. Also, the doctor has some information for us. Call me when you're back, we can go see her together." Then he switched off.

I chewed my lip. Interesting. More news, probably about Rafe Manuel's murder.

For the next few hours, reports from the various departments occupied my time. Sea Traffic Control, module and city maintenance, agriculture and mining. Many of the messages were maintenance requests or updates on ongoing repairs, and one, from Pressure Control, caused some alarm. Apparently, rising ocean levels were increasing water pressure on the colony. As a result, moonpool levels were rising. We had room to spare—the water was generally thirty centimeters or more below the edges of the decks—but as it rose on the surface, it rose down here as well. Of course we could compensate by increasing air pressure, but the world mandated a four atmosphere standard to enable easy movement between vehicles and colonies.

Finally, I checked in with Cliff in City Security, which was just down the corridor from City Control, and the two of us walked over to the hospital, also in the same module.

Doctor Stacy Reynolds greeted us without a change in facial expression, escorted us to her office, and called a young man in.

He was wearing a lab coat and stripping off gloves as he stalked in. There was blood on his shirt, apparently from a farming accident earlier in the day. He'd stitched a severed finger back in place.

"Hazards of kelp farming," was all he said when he saw us staring at the blood.

Doctor Reynolds's white hair was pulled back into a bun—difficult because it was so short, but somehow she'd managed—and as she spoke, her expression still didn't change in the slightest. "This is my intern, Jamal Ross. He's the one I mentioned to you earlier."

I frowned as I thought back to the last time I'd spoken with the doctor. She had mentioned the intern having had some experience in forensics on the mainland. Murder had been the topic of discussion back then.

"Hello, Ross," I said. "What news do you have?"

"Mayor." The black man had an interesting expression on his face. He was probably curious about Rafe's case; he was usually fixing minor injuries and dealing with water sores. Sometimes the staff there dealt with beatings or injuries from fights. This one was unique. "I looked at the body. Rafe Manuel."

"Go on."

"Definitely death due to head injuries, as Doctor Reynolds said. But I've had some experience with—"

"What did you find?"

He blinked and after a heartbeat rushed on. "I took photographs of the imprints. Boot imprints." He pulled them up on a screen beside us and he pointed out the details. "It had deep treads."

"Military?"

"Yes."

"USSF?"

"Yes."

I sighed. It wasn't news, but it was confirmation. Beside me, Cliff bristled. I could sense anger radiating from the man. He was constantly dealing with complaints about USSF sailors in the city, but the usual result to his investigations was just more paperwork. He couldn't do anything else. One day, he'd say to me, he wanted to see things set right.

I agreed with him.

"Thanks, Ross," I said.

"There's more."

That stopped me. "Go on."

"I've got a boot size for you. Thirteen. Whoever it was, the guy's big."

I considered that. Rafe was a smaller man. Wiry and short. He hadn't been a match for his assailant. "How big would you say the killer was?"

He frowned. "It wouldn't stand up in any court, but he's probably over six feet and more than two hundred pounds."

"Thanks for the report. It helps—"

Doctor Reynolds was staring at me. "Why are you limping, Mac?"

—••—

OUTSIDE THE HOSPITAL, IN A WIDE corridor filled with Triestrians waving at me as they marched past, I leaned against a viewport with Cliff at my side. I grabbed my thigh unconsciously and felt the tight gauze under my pants. The doctor's work. "What do you think?" I asked.

"It's pretty obvious what happened. But pinning it on one particular person is going to be a challenge."

I hesitated. "I have other methods of pinning it on someone."

He watched me silently. Then, "You have someone on *Impaler*."

I shot a look at him. "If I did, I'm not going to admit it."

"I see."

I turned and studied the activity going on outside the deck-to-ceiling port. Seacars and larger vessels, swimmers and maintenance workers, and even a class of ten-year olds on a scuba trip to the kelp farms. That sight made me smile, at least. The kids were getting a chance at seeing the most important function of our colony, and they were doing it away from the safety of a bus. They were getting outside for some real world experience.

"Things aren't going well topside. I'm not sure if you followed the news on your . . . your vacation."

He was watching me carefully, and I gave him a tight smile. "Watch it, Cliff. Don't make me think you're informing on me too."

The comment clearly bothered him. "I want to be a part of whatever you're doing. I don't want to work against you, Boss."

I raised a hand. "Easy. I know. I'm just ribbing you."

He relaxed slightly, but I could tell the comment had caught him off guard. It made me worry less about his loyalties. "I hate the USSF," he said.

I had seen it all with him. The beatings, the rape victims carried into the hospitals. I knew how he felt. "I hear you."

"I understand the French are after you about something that happened last year."

"They are. Now they're after me for something much worse."

He eyed me. "Really?"

"Yeah. They might try to attack us outright, just to get me in the collateral damage."

He nodded. "Good to know. I'll post more sentries, warn people about French strangers."

"Good plan."

He paused for a long moment, and then, "There are riots topside."

"What else is new?"

He turned to me. "No. Big ones. Tens of thousands of people protesting in every major city. Bangladesh is finally gone. Even the remnants. It's called Bangladesh Harbor now. The Baltic nations are at war, Canada is moving troops to her border, the Balkans are a disaster from the cultural clashes, and Russia is breaking apart as we speak. Again. And Africa . . . It's chaos."

I let it all sink in. Canada moving troops. It meant the US was threatening the border again. Made sense. The breadbasket regions were migrating north as the climate warmed. And no wonder Russia had been so quiet lately. . . .

"Cliff," I muttered, as if I hadn't even been listening to him. "What would you say if I told you that while I was . . . *vacationing*, I saw a strange warsub in the ocean?"

He was staring at me, but he'd raised an eyebrow and his face was blank. I noticed absently that there was a scar in his brow. "It didn't get a match in the database?"

"No. Sonar couldn't identify it."

He shrugged. "Must have been a privately owned seacar."

"It was four hundred fourteen meters long."

His jaw dropped. "Say again?"

"And it had a SCAV drive. It was going four hundred sixty-seven kilometers per hour. Over thirty decks deep."

"Bullshit."

I glanced at him. "Believe it."

"But—but—"

"Nothing like it exists. But if it *did*," I continued, "*who* could have built it?" Cliff had been in the USSF as a younger man, for a short spell anyway. He was familiar with the world's naval powers.

He frowned. "It's just impossible. It *can't* exist."

"Trust me on this. I can show you the sonar track."

He looked outside and lines traced across his forehead. "I would call it a *Dreadnought*."

I nodded. Like the warships that had contributed to the start of WWI. "Makes sense. But who built the thing?"

"A developed superpower for sure. It must be American, Chinese, British, French, or German. One of those."

I chewed my lip. "Tell me about the job I gave you."

He shot me a sly look. "I have some interesting video for you. I don't think you're going to like it."

I didn't.

—••—

BACK AT MY OFFICE, I CALLED up the Processing Module and within seconds Rebecca Hartley was on screen, glaring at me. "You got my message, finally. Where the hell have you been?"

I sighed. "Shit, Becky. I don't have to keep you aware of all my travels, do I?"

"You do when you hit us with a shitty order like that!"

"I'm trying, really. The USSF is pissing me off too."

"I don't doubt it. But if you want more kelp, we need more people. Plain and simple."

I blew out my breath. "What if I take some workers from the repair docks? I can spare ten maybe."

She frowned. "There's no equipment that needs fixing right now?"

"Of course there is. But if you have to work harder, so should everyone. Besides, I know they have a few former kelp workers there. Hell, I'll come and help if it comes to it. I've had enough experience."

She finally offered the hint of a smile. She had been my boss while I had worked the fields after quitting TCI eight years earlier. "I like the plan. Are you going to tell them, or should I?"

"I'll *ask* them, and I'll be really nice about it."

Her smile grew larger. "Thanks, Mac!" She cut the signal.

I grunted. Politics.

—••—

I TOOK CARE OF A FEW more calls of a mayoral nature, and forty-five minutes later my hatch slammed open and a large figure in a blue USSF uniform stormed in.

Captain Heller, of *Impaler*.

I rose to my feet. A prickle worked its way down my scalp.

He had a clipboard under his right arm and a pair of guards trailed him.

"They let anybody in these days," I growled.

"This is *my* city, McClusky. Not yours."

"It belongs to Triestrians. Not any one person."

He scowled. "Brilliant. Unfortunately for you, we occupied Trieste after your failed attempt at independence. There's no going back now."

I shrugged. "That's old news. That was George Shanks. He's long gone, thanks to you."

Heller sat in the chair before my desk without being invited. I sat as well, though I kept myself ramrod straight. His eyes were piercing and the look on his face was obvious. He'd tried to kill me before—during the chase from Australia and during The Battle—and I had escaped him both times. Now the people had voted me into power, and it had stymied him yet again. I was aware of his growing frustration.

"What do you want?"

"I don't need a reason to visit my office."

I gestured at the other two sailors with him. "Are these your goons? Why do you need them?"

"My escorts."

"Are you worried someone's going to hurt you?"

"Of course not."

"Then why would you need guards?"

He stared at me, silent, refusing to answer.

"That's what I thought," I said. "What do you want, Heller?"

"*Captain* Heller to you, McClusky, or do you want me to increase produce demands by another ten percent?"

"Oh, you can increase demands all you want. Whether you'll get them or not is another story entirely."

"We'd better get them."

"Things topside are rough I hear."

"All you need to do is watch the news." He sneered at me, "Or are you too busy?"

I shrugged. "Being mayor is a busy job."

"Which makes me wonder about your recent travels."

I frowned. "Investigating mining ventures. We need to increase output. You asked for it. I have to go and search out new prospects."

That stopped him for a moment. "You have people for that."

"I'm the mayor. The buck stops here, Heller. Can't send people to do jobs that are just too dangerous."

He glared at me in a bitter silence. I craned my neck and peered over the table. "What are you looking at?"

"What size boots do you wear?"

He hesitated. "Why the hell would that matter?"

I shrugged. "One of my men died a few days ago."

"Are you trying to give away his boots?"

"Good one." I offered a tight smile. "Whoever stomped him to death wore size thirteen, USSF issue."

He snorted. "I don't care about your internal issues like that."

I stared at the man; he returned my look intently, not saying a word. He was refusing to acknowledge that a USSF sailor had committed murder. He didn't even care. He just wanted more exports to go topside.

"You don't care that one of your men killed a Triestrian?"

"You Triestrians killed a lot of USSF sailors in The Battle. I care about that."

"That was Shanks, once again. Rafe Manuel was a sonar operator here in City Control. He sometimes went to *Impaler* for training."

He shrugged again. "I'll look into it. Anyone with size thirteen boot is a suspect. That should narrow it down."

"Thanks," I said in a dry voice.

"Where was your prospecting trip, McClusky?"

"North. Past Bermuda."

"Not south?"

"Not unless Bermuda has shifted hemispheres."

"What mineral?"

"Aluminum. Placer deposit."

"Worth mining?"

I shrugged. "Depends on the test results."

He stared at me, and I let the silence stretch on into a painful vacuum. I was sure I could hear the blood pounding in my ears, though that might have been my anger.

"Anything else, Heller?"

"Who was the Asian man who went with you?"

"Pardon me?" My insides quivered, but I kept my face like steel.

"We're still looking for Johnny Chang."

I laughed. "That fucker died in The Battle. Deserved everything he got."

He eyed me. "He was your friend. I heard you were seen with him before your trip. We're still looking for him. He played a role in the deaths of USSF sailors."

"You think every Chinese man around here is Johnny? There are a lot of Chinese Americans in Trieste. This one was a miner."

"Right." He stared at me. Then with a scowl, "Reports of your people antagonizing my sailors are on the rise. See to it."

I considered explaining the truth to him, but thought better of it. "I will."

He blinked; he had not expected the answer. Finally he said, "Did you have any trouble with the French?"

I let my forehead crease and I looked away as I processed the question. "No. Why?"

He grunted. "They've been causing problems around here. They detonated an EMP west of us, and caused some sort of issue near Bermuda. Where you just were apparently."

"I didn't see anything."

He pursed his lips and watched me for long minutes. "I hear they intercepted two of your people near the Seychelles."

It was like a sledgehammer to the gut. I tried my best to keep my face calm, but I wasn't sure I succeeded. "My people?"

He sneered again. "Triestrians."

I was worried he'd mention TCI, which wasn't supposed to exist anymore. "Who are they? Tourists?"

"I have no idea. I received the report from a French captain. She's been reported missing now." Then he abruptly rose and spun on his heel. "Get those export numbers up, McClusky." He and his guards left without looking back.

I watched him silently, my heart pounding.

INTERLUDE:
DECEPTIONS

```
Location:      The Gulf of Mexico
Latitude:      27° 34' 29" N
Longitude:     54° 56' 11" W
Depth:         26 meters
Vessel:        USS Impaler
Time:          1814 hours
```

FIRST OFFICER SCHRADER STOOD IN *IMPALER*'S docking bay and tried to swallow his nerves. His mouth was dry and it took several attempts to force a little saliva past the lump in his throat. Captain Heller was on his way back from Trieste, and as was usually the case, he was angry. He'd contacted Schrader as he'd boarded the transport in the underwater colony, and had ordered him to be there for a meeting.

Inwardly, Schrader swore. They could have just met in the captain's office, and in the meantime Schrader would have had some time to conduct ship's business, perform administrative work like assign crewmen new tasks for the following day, but here he was, standing in the cold and wet docking facility, waiting patiently for the increasingly angry man to storm aboard his own ship and start barking orders at his crew.

Even the sailors on the ship hated Heller. Schrader could tell. They watched him with disdain, they didn't trust his orders, they rolled their eyes when he screamed, and his constant drills were wearing on their patience. Schrader didn't know how much more they could take. At least they enjoyed being so close to Trieste, so they could relax and take in the sights of the underwater colony when on leave, but Schrader had been hearing stories lately of trouble with the citizens there. Fights, arguments, and so on. As far as he knew there hadn't been anything too severe—just men and women blowing off steam—but he didn't want anything to escalate past the point where it would make the USSF look bad. It would be better if *Impaler* were on patrol somewhere. That way the crew would have a solid couple of months of work, and no one could get into any potential trouble on shore leave.

The moonpool in the deck rippled for a moment and then a transport pierced the surface. It floated there as its thrusters powered down, nudging against the dock in the gentle swaying current. The hatch rose and Heller practically exploded out of it, stormed down the gangplank, and onto the catwalk grating that surrounded the pool.

"Schrader!" he called.

The first officer grimaced as he watched the man marching swiftly toward him. He wondered if he should pretend not to hear, just to annoy him, but it was too late. They had already locked eyes.

"Yes, sir?"

"Follow me!"

The first officer fell into step behind him. Trailing were the two men who had accompanied Heller over to the city: Abernathy and Sisko.

"How did the visit go?" Schrader asked in a soft tone.

"Terrible. I hate that man. I wish we could just arrest him and be done with it."

"The people would rebel. It would be the worst thing you could—"

He snapped a look back at Schrader. "Don't you think I know that? That's why he's still over there. That's why he's still mayor. That's why he's not dead."

Really? Schrader thought. *I thought he was still alive because you weren't able to kill him when you had your chance last year.*

Schrader held his tongue.

They wound their way through the narrow corridors, up ladders and underneath ducts, past sparks from work crews maintaining the warsub, and through the twisting artery along the center of the vessel toward the bow. Finally they reached the captain's office, and Schrader sat down with a sigh at the journey he'd just made. They'd practically been sprinting through the ship, and he could have just waited in the office for the captain to arrive. But no. Heller had insisted.

"What did McClusky say?"

The captain scowled. "That he was investigating a mineral deposit somewhere north of Bermuda."

"You don't believe him?"

"He's up to something. And not only that, I think I know the connection between the Chinese cities and McClusky. It was Johnny Chang."

"Why do you say that?"

"He was with Mac on his trip."

"Are you sure?"

"It's a hunch. But I bet that I'm right. I'll tell Butte to find out." He cursed under his breath.

Schrader said, "He's done a lot to help us."

The captain's brow furrowed and his eyes grew even harder. "He has? I've ordered him to *watch* what they are doing over there. He's the goddamned *deputy mayor* and he hasn't been able to give me anything."

"He told you who Lazlow is. He followed him to the seacar when McClusky left on his recent trip."

That stopped the captain. Heller stared into a distant corner, his mind clearly racing.

"What is it?" Schrader asked.

He picked up a pencil to chew. "Why would Lazlow go on a prospecting trip?"

Schrader frowned. "I don't see—"

"You're right. *Why would an acoustician go on that trip?* Why didn't I think about that earlier?"

"I guess he could have been there for some reason or another, possibly related to his field of study."

"But not related to a mining expedition."

Schrader had no answer to that, so he simply sat there in silence.

Heller remained quiet as well, fuming, until he said, "I planted a thread with the man. Some bait. I hope he takes it."

This made Schrader perk up. "What bait?"

"I told him that the French had captured two Triestrians. On the other side of Africa."

"Is it true?"

The other man nodded. "A French captain contacted me days ago. She told me she was looking for McClusky."

"Did you tell her where he was?"

Heller grinned, but there was no mirth there.

"And she traded this information for that?"

"Apparently two Triestrians were caught trying to steal something or other from a French base. They're prisoners now. She heard through command channels, told me the info, and in exchange I gave her some information on McClusky. Now I can use this piece of news to try and lure him in."

"To where?"

The captain growled, "I'm not entirely sure yet, but maybe if I know when he's going to leave, we can do a better job of following him. And I'm sure this time it's not going to be to Bermuda, or to the north, or whatever the fuck is up there. He's going south."

"How do you know?"

"Because that's what that little shit Rafe Manuel was trying to hide from us."

Schrader's insides quivered when he thought of that evening.

Heller continued, "I'm going to get a tracker on the sub, or follow it somehow, in order to see what's happening. To find out what that man is up to."

Schrader chewed the inside of his cheek as he mulled it over. It just might work, he thought. But what if Heller found something *bad*? Something that led to another conflict like the one the year before? He wasn't so sure that would be a good thing.

Outside the cabin there was a scrape and something clanged to the steel grating. Heller bolted from his chair and slammed the hatch aside. "What are you doing?" he screamed.

Just outside, crouching in the dimly-lit and narrow hallway, Seaman Abernathy was picking up a pile of electronics. He looked up and his face was white. "I'm sorry, sir. I dropped these. An officer gave them to me to get repaired. I didn't mean to disturb you."

"Your work today was to escort me to Trieste and back. It's done. Now get to your other duties!" Heller slammed the hatch and returned to his desk.

Schrader watched the confrontation in silence.

Heller said, "I'm going to figure out what McClusky is up to." And then his eyes lit up. "And once out in the open ocean, with no one around, we might finally have our opportunity."

The XO raised his eyebrows. "Pardon me, sir?"

"If we sink his little insect-like seacar, no one will ever know what happened. No one will ever find the wreckage, or his body for that matter. And then his precious city will be fully under our control, because the deputy mayor is one of ours."

The statement hung in the silence between them.

PART FOUR:
BAIT

CHAPTER TWENTY-ONE

I FOUND JOHNNY STILL WITH *SC-1* in the Repair Module. He was working on the SCAV drive with one of Meg's crew—people who were familiar with the seacar, had repaired her many times, and knew how to get the drive up and running.

Johnny turned to look at me as I entered the fusion compartment; he had a grin on his face. "It's just some wiring, Mac. Those two concussions knocked things loose. There's nothing wrong with the reactor."

I glanced at the chamber. Pipes along the ceiling carried seawater into the boiler just aft of the fusion reactor. It used magnetic fields to fuse hydrogen—deuterium and tritium, actually—to form helium and heat energy. We stored the helium, the energy flash-boiled the seawater to steam, and this provided our propulsion during supercavitation.

It was an incredible invention, and it was all because of Kat.

An ache settled over my chest when I thought of her. In many ways she represented this quest of ours. Before I'd met her, I'd been content to just farm kelp for a living. To stay out of the independence and the intelligence games. But when I met her and she convinced me that what my father had been doing had been the right path all along, and after I saw her invention in action, I realized I should be fighting for our rights and not sitting back and letting the world's superpowers walk all over us.

I shook myself out of it and pulled back to the present. Johnny was still grinning at me, and it made me happy. He had probably been miserable in the Chinese cities for the past year, negotiating and bargaining, and without much to show for it. Then again, he had offered them the SCAV drive and provided a solid foundation for an agreement, if and when they decided to join us.

"Good to hear," I said finally.

Johnny peered at me from under his arm. He was crouched next to a panel and was working on the wiring within. "You okay?"

"Yes. Just . . . thinking."

His eyes shot to the reactor, and his smile returned. "I've got it. No need to explain. You'll see her soon."

I nodded.

"What's up?"

I shut the hatch to the cabin and pulled a stool up next to him. The lights were currently dim, but he had portable lamps shining into the panel, sending twisting shadows across the deck beside him. They were almost hypnotic, and I stared at them as he continued working.

"I just spoke with Heller."

"Don't tell me." He stopped and looked back at me again.

"He suspects that you're here. He says someone reported that you boarded the seacar with me on our way out last time."

He snorted. "So he knows."

"I told him it was a miner on a prospecting trip."

"Good cover."

"I had to come up with it on the spot. I doubt it fooled him though."

Johnny frowned. "I can stay away from the USSF while I'm here at the city. Hell, I can live in here if I have to."

That's what I'd been thinking too. "He also says that the French captured two of my people. Though he didn't say 'operatives.' Just 'Triestrians.'"

There was a long pause. "And did you have two operatives out?"

"A few more than that, but I did have two on a mission to a French research facility. He had the location correct too."

"Damn." He stared at me. "What are you going to do?"

"I'm still mulling it over."

"Could be a trap."

"I know." I had already run it through my mind. I knew what I had to do—the syntactic foam was just too important to our people at The Ridge.

"He might be trying to see if you're still running TCI."

"Or he might just be trying to kill me."

"Or both."

I nodded. "Yes, there's that." I watched Johnny for a moment as he continued working on the wiring. "How have you been?"

"I feel good for a change, if that's what you mean."

"I guess it is." I hesitated, then, "I'm happy you're back too. I've missed you."

"Well, I guess I had to stay away for a while. Let things die down. And my trip to the Chinese cities was useful, if not very productive."

"It's a start. Baby steps. What we're proposing is a massive shift in politics. Hell, Seascape wasn't exactly thrilled with the notion, and they're American. They deal with the USSF every day too."

"Tourism is a different beast though."

Then I recalled my conversation with Cliff earlier, and I said, "I think we should wipe *SC-1*'s nav memory. Save the track we got on that mysterious warsub though."

"Already done." He tapped his forehead with a screwdriver. "Way ahead of you, partner."

I let the silence linger on for a bit. I really had missed the man. He was my best friend—perhaps my *only* friend—because everyone else at Trieste aside from Kat and Meg was a work-related acquaintance. True, Johnny had started out that way too, but we had gotten to know each other very well while on our missions in TCI. And the memories of my father around Trieste meant people felt they knew me before they'd even met me. Then when they did meet me, they weren't as genuine as perhaps they would have been otherwise. It was just hard to feel connected to people in that environment.

My father's legacy. It had created a bizarre and enigmatic situation.

"I'm thinking of leaving in a few days," I mumbled.

Johnny's head was buried in the wiring. "To rescue your people?"

"I have to."

"What they were stealing is that important?"

I nodded.

He sighed and withdrew his tools from the compartment, leaned against the console. "Then I'm coming too, of course."

"Of course." I offered him a small smile.

"Anyone else?"

"I do have someone in mind, actually."

—••—

Back in my cabin, I found the secret PCD in the clothes drawer and signaled my informant on *Impaler*. It took over ten minutes, but finally he responded.

"Go ahead." The voice was quiet and tinny.

"I need to know how Heller found out about the French captives."

A pause. And then the male voice replied, "He got the information from a French captain. She found out through command channels apparently."

I chewed my lip. And he had told me that the French captain had been missing for a while. Could it be the same person that I had taken to The Ridge? Renée Féroce? There was a possible connection between her and Heller—both seemed to be fixated on me.

"Do you know where the French are holding them?"

"No."

"Can you find out?"

"I highly doubt it."

"Can you get me any information on the French?"

"No."

Then what good are you? I wanted to say. But I held my tongue.

—••—

An hour later I met with Robert Butte in my office. He'd been leaning over Grant in Sea Traffic Control, peering at his screens, and I called him over to chat.

"You're back!" he said with a big smile on his face.

"Yes, it was an uneventful trip."

"Where were you?"

"Prospecting. The fellows over in the mining division had a tip."

He frowned. "Did it pan out?"

I nearly laughed at his use of the term, considering its origin topside had been for exactly what I'd claimed. "Not rich enough. Costs too much to mine that deep."

He nodded and didn't press me on it.

I said, "How were things here?"

He shifted in the chair before my desk. The chair was so small that he hung over it on both sides. He looked like a giant in it. "No issues. A few complaints from the aquaculture and mining people. You apparently requested more output." He watched me pointedly.

"I didn't request it. But yes, I relayed it to them."

He swore. "That's great. Fucking USSF."

"Heller wants ten percent more across the board."

Butte cursed again. "Doesn't he realize we're working damned hard as it is?"

"I don't think he cares, frankly." I paused and then, "Anything else happen worth noting?"

"A few more assaults. USSF sailors caused some property damage after heavy drinking in the Commerce Module."

"Did they pay for the damage?"

My deputy mayor scowled at me. "Funny, Mac."

"I try."

"It would be great if we could get Heller to admit that his sailors are a serious pain in the ass."

"Doubtful. He raised the quota on us. He doesn't care. He just wants to take more and more, send it topside, and make himself look better."

Butte was eyeing me. "Getting angry about that leads to dangerous thoughts and trouble with authorities. Just like your—" He stopped abruptly.

"What were you going to say there, Robert?" I watched him for a long minute.

He shook his head. "Nothing. Sorry I said it."

"There's no independence movement anymore. You know that, right?"

"Do I?"

I hesitated. "We learned our lesson after The Battle. It's over."

He stared into the distance, out the viewport over my shoulder. "If you say so."

"I do."

His face looked strained for a flash. "But if I wanted to talk about it, would you be the person to speak with?"

I hesitated. "About?"

"Independence." His voice was quiet.

I stared at him for a long moment. I had never spoken about that part of my life with him. About Trieste City Intelligence and our espionage network and about The Ridge. I'd picked him as deputy mayor for a variety of reasons. The people liked him. He got along with both intellectuals and the workers out in the fields and farms and in the Repair Module. He'd done those jobs before, as a younger man. But I had always wanted to keep this side of my life as secret as possible. Until it was too late, that is.

"I have nothing to say about it." My voice was flat.

He nodded and a look of disappointment crossed his features. "That's too bad. Because I've been thinking about it."

"Don't."

He looked abashed and we shifted to other topics.

He departed after a discussion of city business and a few other things that had transpired while I'd been gone on my "prospecting" journey. I watched him as he left my office. I wasn't quite sure what to think.

I stood suddenly and went out to City Control just outside my hatch. Grant Bell was still there, headset on and busy coordinating traffic to and from the city. I went over to chat with him and find out what had been going on during my absence. He smiled when he saw me.

"Hello, Mac."

"Got a minute?"

"For you, sure." He whispered a few commands into the mic and then set it aside. "What's up? How was your trip?"

"It was . . . okay. Could have gone better." I recalled what Grant had said to me when I'd asked for advice on what track to take heading out. I trusted him implicitly.

"That's too bad." He winced. "Hopefully things will work out."

"Maybe they will." And then I stared at him for a long heartbeat, not saying a word.

He tilted his head. "What's up?"

CHAPTER
TWENTY-TWO

THAT NIGHT I PULLED MYSELF INTO my narrow bunk and lay there quietly, listening to the sounds of the city in the steel hulls and decks around me. I had a cabin against an exterior bulkhead, with a small viewport to give me a view of the ocean. As mayor, I didn't want more than others, so I had kept my quarters in Module B. Flint, the former mayor, had occupied a relatively giant cabin on the upper deck, complete with a skylight and bulkhead viewports. I'd seen it in the days following the election. It had been twenty times the size of my current living space, before I'd ordered the space divided into multiple smaller sleeping areas.

The people of Trieste were happy I led by example, and appreciated the no-frills manner in which I did it.

I began to drift off to sleep, despite the thoughts churning through my mind. I saw myself wandering the corridors and travel tubes of the city, going somewhere with a purpose, on a mission, but not fully knowing what it was. All I knew was I had something to do, and I had to do it soon. My feet rang on the steel grates and decks. Happy voices echoed around me. What had I been doing? Where was I going?

Yes. . . . I remembered now. That was it. Kat's birthday was coming up, and I couldn't find anything to give her. Then I remembered that she'd lived on land for more than two decades, and although she loved the oceans, she did appreciate colorful flowers. In particular, their fragrance and delicate beauty attracted her.

I needed to find her some, and they were difficult to locate under water. We had plants and trees in Trieste, but not many flowers. Especially ones for sale.

Now, where could I find—

I suddenly appeared in City Control, and I looked around, confused.

"Problem, Mac?"

My jaw fell open. "Rafe? What are you doing here?"

He smiled, and the expression split his features. I'd missed that smile. "I work here, don't you know?"

"But—but you're—"

"I'm what?"

I swallowed. "This is a dream."

"Is it?" He continued to grin. "I think this conversation happened just a few months ago."

I thought hard, trying to locate the memory. "You're right. And you're about to tell me—"

"I can get you some roses. My cousin is on the supply run from Costa Rica to the US colonies. I can ask him to bring some. How many do you want?"

My brow crinkled. "How many did I get when this . . . when this really happened?"

He laughed, and it was warm and genial and heartfelt. My heart thudded in my chest and I realized how much I missed him. He said, "You asked for two dozen."

"Then that's how many I want."

"Done."

"But Rafe . . ." I muttered, staring at the man. Behind him the bulkhead map of the Gulf and the Caribbean framed his face.

"What?"

"You're not really here right now."

He tilted his head. "Where am I?"

I stumbled over my words. "I sent you to *Impaler*. For training."

"Yes. I need training if I'm going to work in Sea Traffic Control. Grant has been really good to me here too."

"Everyone likes you."

"And I'm enjoying it."

"But I asked you to listen for . . . for information over there."

He nodded. "I've been doing that. I've found out some good stuff for you too."

"And I asked you to leak something to Heller for me. It—" A sob choked its way up my throat and I clamped down on it. "It didn't work."

"Did he kill me?" That smile was still on his face.

A tear rolled down my cheek. "Someone did."

"Don't worry, Mac. I want to help my city. Don't blame yourself."

"But it's my fault, Rafe. I did this to you."

He was shaking his head. A voice called to me. I looked around in alarm. He said, "No. I volunteered. Don't you remember?"

"No. I don't."

"It's true."

The voice called to me again. I glanced around, trying to locate it. No one else was there. I turned back to Rafe.

He was gone.

My eyes snapped open.

The comm was beeping and I reached outside the bunk to flick the switch. "Go ahead." My voice was husky. I'd keyed *Voice Only*.

"Sorry to bother you, Mac." It was Grant Bell.

"No worries. What's up?" *Rafe had just mentioned you*, I wanted to say. I leaned back and stared at the ceiling just inches above my face. On the other side was my clothes drawer.

"I've got an odd signature coming in."

"What's odd about it?"

"It's a warsub. French. A big bastard. We don't usually see this type here, that's all."

I chewed my lip. "Let me guess. *Verdun* class."

There was a pause. "Yeah, how'd you know?"

"I had a run in with them." I thought the situation over for a long moment. Surely they wouldn't attack a US undersea colony outright.

Would they?

Would they be so brash?

I didn't think so, but still. . . .

"What's the distance?"

"An outer sonar array picked them up. They're still eighty kilometers away. We have some time."

"Speed? Depth?"

"Thirty-one kph, sixty meters."

"Grant, contact Cliff Sim. Tell him to meet me in my office. I'll be there in five. And . . ."

"Yes?"

"Better contact the USSF. Let Heller know what's going on."

"But what *is* going on?"

"I don't know, but it's a potential provocation. A missile boat being so close to the US coast."

"They might need help."

The thought our three torpedoes had caused tremendous damage to her hull and engine room occurred to me. They might have even considered it an act of war.

"If they do, we can offer it to them I guess. But their sailors are not to come over. Not with so many USSF here now."

"I can detect a problem with their screws. They're cavitating. Some sort of damage for sure. And the hull is creating a lot of noise."

It's because we put three holes in it, I wanted to say. But I settled on, "Carry out the orders, Grant, and thanks. Mac out."

I punched the comm and lay back with my eyes closed. Shit. This was not good. They were here for a reason, a good one. They would most likely not leave without me, and the USSF—Heller, mostly—would not defend me.

I hit the comm again in sudden decision. "Butte, where are you?"

Seconds later his voice drifted to me. "I'm sleeping, Mac. You?"

"Grab a bag of your things. Meet me in the Repair Module."

He immediately perked up. "Say again?"

"We're going on a little voyage. I want you to come with me. Are you game?"

There was a long pause. Finally he said in a confused tone, "I guess so. Where are we going?"

"I'm going to open your eyes to a much larger world, Butte. Are you interested?"

The response came sooner than the last one had. "Of course."

"Good. Meet me at *SC-1*." I keyed off before he could say anything. My next call was to Johnny aboard the seacar. "I have a visitor on the way. Let him in. Don't tell him anything, just say that I'll be there soon. We're leaving tonight."

—••—

A SECOND LATER, BEFORE I COULD lower my feet over the side and jump to the cold deck, the pressure alarm started to blare.

And it was *LOUD*.

The lights immediately flashed on—now a dazzling blue—and the alarm pierced the cabins and corridors of Module B.

"ATTENTION," a calm voice said over the comm units. I recognized it—Kristen Canvel in City Systems Control. "We have a pressure drop in Module B. Everyone get your emergency gear, evacuate immediately. Go to the nearest escape airlock or moonpool. Beware the rising water on the moonpool deck. Modules A and C, be prepared to assist with evacuations."

Luckily there were no children in this module; single men and women only.

I slung a bag over my shoulder, along with two items from my clothing drawer, grabbed my mask, tank and weight belt, and bolted from the cabin.

—••—

I HELPED DIRECT PEOPLE ON MY level to the airlock, though they already knew where to go. The timing of the pressure emergency—occurring right as the French warsub was closing on us—was not lost on me.

The moonpool was down on the seafloor deck, four levels below. I watched as people poured from their cabins and ran to the airlocks against the exterior bulkheads. Everyone was calm, there was no panicking. Instead, they had looks of determination on their features. Only a third of the people were in the modules at any time; the other two thirds were working or out engaged in other activities. Either volunteering or helping someone else out, or perhaps eating and enjoying an hour or two of recreation. But there were still a lot of people in the module. Thankfully we had time to get out, and we'd practiced it many times before.

I decided to go down to the moonpool, to see just how bad this pressure loss really was.

The blue lights were flashing in the hallway and the warnings continued to echo around me. Now it was Joey Zen speaking—she was in the Pressure Control division of City Control—and her voice was calm and soothing. Quite a contradiction to the flashing lights, I thought.

The steep ladder was metal grating and I looked down.

I couldn't see the lowest level.

My heart nearly exploded.

Water was rising up the stairwell, sloshing around and foaming against the bulkheads.

So this was no drill, nor a minor incident.

The water was nearly up to the second level, which meant water had totally flooded the first. Pressure was decreasing rapidly.

An instant later the airtight hatch slammed across the ladderwell, blocking it from rising any further. It would keep the flooding contained, but if the pressure loss continued, the structure of the module might be an issue.

The four atmospheric pressures inside balanced the weight of the water perfectly at our depth of thirty meters. It meant there was an equal pressure pushing upward on the ceiling and outward on the bulkheads as there was pressing inward from the water. But as the inner pressure decreased, the bulkheads would grow stressed, and they weren't built to manage much extra compression.

If a bulkhead gave *right now*, I thought, grim, the water would crash in and most likely stun or even knock me unconscious. And if that happened, I'd drown.

I spun on my heel and went up to the nearest deck. The airlock was at the end, and there was a line to get out. "There are other airlocks down the corridor," someone was yelling. "There are no lines there—move!"

I glanced where the man was gesturing; he was correct. The crowd dispersed rapidly. Down on the first level, all the airlocks were probably open—both inner and outer hatches—so people could swim out from the flooded area. They could also swim out the moonpool despite the rising water. I had no worries that people could get out; we were Triestrians, after all. If we could do anything well, it was *swim*.

—••—

WITHIN A MINUTE I WAS OUTSIDE in the water surrounding the module. There was a stream of bubbles coming from the second level and rising to the surface. The water was continuing to rise inside, but I couldn't tell if it had broken through the watertight hatch, or if that level were flooding from some other breach.

There were hundreds of people around me. Most had tanks on their backs, though a few had emergency breathers with only twenty breaths or so of air, and some were sharing with others as they swam to the nearest module.

My shoulder was in pain, and had been ever since the incident outside when the torpedoes had rammed the *Verdun* class warsub. Swimming was a challenge.

The biggest problem outside, however, was that many did not have weight belts, so their natural buoyancy, especially in the salt water, was lifting them up and away from Trieste. Because of this danger, there were guide wires bolted to the hull in case of emergency—for this precise situation, actually—and people could latch to them or hang on to keep from ascending toward a painful death due to The Bends.

People hung upside down as they pulled themselves along the guide cables. From what I could tell, however, it looked like an orderly evacuation.

People were nodding at me as they passed; some even grinned openly.

Just another day in the ocean deeps, I knew they were thinking.

If it wasn't for the French on their way, I might have returned the smiles.

I spun and found the Repair Module, and then started to swim to it, dragging my bag behind me.

—••—

I SWAM THROUGH THE ENTRANCE INTO the module. It was more difficult than a normal moonpool, which was just an opening in the deck of a module, because there was also a long tunnel large enough to handle most commercial and private seacars on the market. I didn't have flippers, so I had to half-walk, half-swim my way through the tunnel until I could look up and see the pool above me. I dropped my weight belt and floated up, appearing in the Repair Module's moonpool.

Nearby, *SC-1* floated serenely in the pool. People on the docks and on the hulls of other vessels, repairing steel plating and thrusters and performing general maintenance, didn't even know what was going on in Module B.

I hauled myself up a ladder and rolled onto the deck. "Shit," I said.

"Hey Mac, what's going on?"

A worker on a nearby seacar had noticed me. "Pressure loss in Module B," I said. "Had to evacuate."

His face registered shock. "Really?"

Things like this rarely happened.

"Yes." I dropped my tank and marched over to a comm on the bulkhead. I keyed it for City Control, and a second later Joey Zen was on the line.

"Status," I snapped.

"Who is this?"

"It's Mac. Now report." I hated to be curt with her, but I needed information fast.

"Sorry, Mac. Pressure has stabilized in B. We're still pulling people into the surrounding modules. We're monitoring on video; we don't see any casualties. We've got rescue divers with backup regulators just in case."

"Anyone slip to the surface?"

"No. A few close calls, but other people grabbed them and pulled them down before it was too late."

I breathed a sigh of relief. Then, "Transfer me to STC. And Joey—*thanks.*"

"No worries. Glad you're okay."

An instant later, Grant Bell was back on the line. I said, "Give me an update on the French warsub."

"Sonar indicates it's most likely *Lion*. She's got eight tubes, twenty missiles, mines—"

"Have they contacted us yet?"

"No. And we have no idea where Butte is. We've called."

"Don't worry about him. What about Heller?"

"*Impaler* is pulling out and putting themselves between us and *Lion*. If he's talking to them, we can't hear it."

"Any other weird signatures? Other French ships?"

"No." There was a long pause, and then his voice softened. "Mac, is this because of . . . of . . ."

"Don't worry about that," I said, cutting him off. "Please notify Cliff Sim that I'm not going to be able to meet him. He needs to protect the city. Don't let any of them come over."

"Why? They're damaged. It might be an innocent visit."

"Combined with a pressure loss in my module?"

There was an excruciating silence at that. Then, "Yeah. I guess you're right."

"Listen, Grant." I stared at *SC-1*, which was just over twenty meters away. Johnny was half out of the top hatch, watching. "I'm going to leave for a bit. I'm bringing Butte with me. I'll be back in a few weeks. Cliff's in charge until I return. Do you understand? Please tell him."

"Got it." There was no worry now; he was calm and professional.

"I'll be back. Until then, good luck."

CHAPTER TWENTY-THREE

SC-1 POWERED OUT OF THE REPAIR Module and we set course southeast toward the Straits of Florida. Johnny sat beside me in the control cabin and Butte stood behind us, watching over our shoulders. He had a look of intense curiosity on his face; he had no idea why I had suddenly called him from his sleep, ordered him to pack a bag, and meet me on the seacar.

I was hoping to appeal to his sense of adventure, and his implied desire earlier to join the independence movement. I couldn't predict what he was going to do, but I felt that I needed to bring him with us, to get him out of Trieste.

I had plans for him.

"But where are we going?" he kept asking.

I ignored my deputy mayor; there were more important issues at that moment.

"How's the SCAV drive, Johnny?" I asked.

"Repaired." He flashed me a smile. "Want to turn it on?"

I glanced at the sonar screen. *Impaler* was falling away behind us, and *Lion* was twenty-eight kilometers ahead, but we were closing the distance quickly. "Soon."

The comm beeped and I pressed the ACCEPT button, for voice only. It was Heller.

And he was furious.

"McClusky! Where the hell are you going?"

"Prospecting."

Johnny turned to me again, his smile even broader. I'd kept the video off so Heller couldn't see my copilot.

"There is a French warsub on approach to your precious city. They're demanding that we turn you over. And you're running away?"

I made my voice sound innocent. "What do they want with me?"

"They say you're a criminal. That you fired on their ship."

"And you believe them?"

"I'm going to damn well find out why they're so angry."

"I'm just going on a little trip. I'll be back soon."

"I'll fire a SCAV torpedo at you, you little shit! Then we'll see how soon your trip will be over."

That made me pause. Would he actually do it? I'd successfully avoided them before . . . but still, eventually something that he tried might work. There was no need to risk anything yet, but I couldn't just turn myself over. I had to fight. "Sorry, Heller. I'll be back in a few days. Until then, good luck with the French."

"How dare you! I'm going to—"

I disconnected the signal.

Johnny was looking at the sonar screen. "*Impaler* just flooded her torpedo tubes. Mac, they mean to fire on us."

"Get the SCAV drive ready."

He opened the panel and started the fusion reactor. Behind us, the hum of great power vibrated the seacar.

"I can stop this," Butte said suddenly.

I frowned. "How?"

"If he knows I'm here, he might not fire on us."

"But why?"

The large man behind me shrugged. "Just a hunch."

I considered the idea. Inside, I knew where he was coming from, but I wasn't sure what to say.

Johnny blurted, "They've opened outer torpedo doors!"

I said, "Lean over to the right a bit, Johnny. I don't want them to see you." Then to Butte, "Okay, get ready." I flicked the video on, and Heller's angry face filled the screen. His cheeks were flushed and there was a bulging vein in his temple.

"Have you decided to give yourself up? We're ready to fire."

Behind me, Butte leaned down farther and put his face in the image.

"Captain Heller, please don't fire. I'm here too."

There was an instant flash of something unrecognizable in Heller's features. He stared at the deputy mayor for what seemed an eternity. And then, "What are you doing there?"

"I don't know for sure. Mayor McClusky asked that I join him. It's a prospecting trip for the city. I'm not sure exactly where the site of the deposit is."

There was another long pause. "And why shouldn't I fire on the both of you? The French are angry as hell. McClusky's stunt could start a war! They're threatening Trieste, and both her leaders are running away? It doesn't make sense."

"I'm coming back soon," I said again.

Heller looked like he wanted to scream. "I order you to stop that seacar and return to the city!"

"Sorry, Heller. I can't comply. Either fire or shut the hell up."

Butte paled. He clearly didn't understand why I was goading the man.

But Heller had an odd expression on his face. His eyes kept flicking to Butte's.

And then something passed over his features that was hard to interpret. It seemed to be resignation, but there was something else there. *Expectation* maybe, but I still wasn't sure what.

Heller finally sighed. "I'll get the French out of here. I'll threaten to fire on *them*, maybe that'll work. But you're both in a shitload of trouble when you get back."

The comm abruptly went silent and the screen turned blue.

Johnny said, "Torpedo doors just closed. She's not going to fire."

I relaxed and flashed him a tight grin. "That's one down. One more to go."

He frowned for a heartbeat, before I pointed at the sonar screen. "There's still that French warsub out there. And we have to pass it on our way out of here."

—••—

I SIGNALED *LION*, VOICE ONLY. "ATTENTION French warsub. What are your intentions?"

The response came a second later. "Truman McClusky. You are to stop your thrusters and allow us to take you aboard."

"Why?"

The accent could not hide the indignation. "You fired on an FSF vessel! You killed crewmen. Now power down and prepare to be taken aboard."

"You fired a SCAV torpedo at us. You meant to kill me. You used an EMP on me in the Gulf of Mexico. And now you say that *I* attacked *you*?"

There was a long, drawn-out silence. "We did not fire the EMP. That was another FSF ship, a warsub that is now, coincidentally, missing, all hands feared lost."

"But your government ordered the attack?"

"You are the man who fired on our sub last year, no? You killed government officials. You are a wanted man."

"I admit to none of that."

"Then you're coming with us to face the charges."

"Sorry. I have other things to do right now. I'm mayor of Trieste after all, and I'm on a prospecting trip. If you fire on us, we'll return fire. Remember that. We have SCAV torpedoes too." I pulled back on the throttle and engaged the water pumps into the fusion furnace. A dull roar sounded from engineering.

Butte was staring behind him. I realized that he'd never been in a vessel with this method of propulsion before. "Oh my god." He was gripping my headrest; his knuckles were white.

"Best sit down, Robert," I said.

"What are you doing?" the French officer asked.

"I'm going to go right around you at four hundred and fifty kilometers per hour. I won't fire unless you fire first. And if you do, it will be a blood bath."

"How dare you threaten an FSF ship!"

"You're closing on Trieste with the intention of kidnapping her mayor. What the fuck are you talking about?" I slammed off the comm.

Johnny said, "Jesus, Mac."

"What?"

"What happened to diplomacy? You're a politician now, remember."

"Fuck politics. I'm getting sick of this bullshit."

A long silence fell over us as I watched the sonar. The warsub's distance closed rapidly. We were now traveling at 450 kph, and I'd made our depth 200 meters.

"Take us south a bit," Johnny said. "No need to get *too* close to her."

"You're right." I turned the yoke to the starboard and banked the seacar slightly. It pushed us into the chairs.

Behind me, Butte whooped. "This is incredible!"

"It's one of our tools."

"Tool for what?"

"For the fight, of course."

He fell silent while he processed that.

Johnny said, "She's coming up on our port now, Mac."

"What are they doing?" I was watching the VID closely. The projected image on the canopy showed the massive warsub sliding past us. She was 189 meters in length. The VID projected the bottom of the hull as fuzzy and indistinct white blobs; the sonar was picking up the noise of the water churning past the ruptures in the hull, but couldn't quite show the damage correctly. It compensated for this lack of information by making it indistinct and unclear.

"They don't seem to be doing anything."

"Torpedoes?" I swallowed. The last thing I wanted was to try and outrun more weapons that could double our speed.

"No sign of them. She's turning now though."

"To follow?"

"Yes."

I snorted. She was going to chase us, but I was going to keep the SCAV on high from that point on.

I pressed a few buttons on the comm system and Johnny watched from the corner of his eyes. He glanced at me in interest, but he didn't say anything. He'd noticed what I'd done.

We had to get to The Ridge fast. No more crawling through the ocean trying to be stealthy. We would follow a similar route as before—northeast to Bermuda, then east to the rift, then due south until we hit the secret facility—and once there, I was going to have a frank discussion with Captain Renée Féroce.

—••—

IN THE LIVING COMPARTMENT JUST BEHIND the control cabin, I sat on the couch and stared at Butte. His expression still showed his amazement with *SC-1*, but he was clearly concerned with the events he had just experienced.

"What's going on, Mac?"

"It's time to tell you what I've been doing."

His face registered shock. "What do you mean?"

I tilted my head. "Earlier, in my office, you implied that you wanted to join some sort of independence movement."

He remained quiet and watched me. I realized suddenly just how big he was. And it wasn't fat, it was muscle. He was over six feet and more than 200 pounds.

I continued. "I wasn't on a prospecting trip earlier."

"Where were you?" He frowned.

"Would you believe on a mission to our secret base in the Mid-Atlantic Ridge?"

He blinked. "Pardon me?"

"For the past year I've been secretly constructing a base. Fifty Triestrians are there right now, along with Kat and my sister, two of my dad's old friends, an acoustician, and a French captain who I saved after we destroyed her sub."

His face grew pale.

"I'm in charge of Trieste City Intelligence, Robert."

"What's that?"

"TCI. It's an espionage group. Spies. I send our people out around the world to protect our interests. To protect Trieste. I've been a part of the organization on and off for almost two decades."

"I had no idea such a thing existed."

"But you knew that Heller occupied us."

"Of course, but I thought it was because Shanks was leading an uprising."

"Yes. But he was also running TCI. And I was an operative, along with Johnny." I gestured at my partner, currently piloting *SC-1*.

"And this secret base . . . what are you doing there?"

"Would you believe constructing ultra-advanced fighter submarines to wage a war against the superpowers of the world?"

He leaned back and blew his breath out in a rush. "And you're taking me there now?"

"Yes." I considered how to word my intentions without giving everything away. "Maybe it's against your will, but I felt that you wanted to join up after what you said in my office earlier."

"But Mac, this is way more than what I thought."

I frowned. "You wanted to just talk about it? I'm *doing* something about it. Like my father did. All the USSF abuses and the troubles we experience *every single day*. You're deputy mayor, you know all about it. This ten percent increase is just another demand in a long line of thievery."

"But what are you planning? What do you mean, 'war'?"

"To lead the other cities of the world to independence. Hopefully we can do it without fighting, but if need be, we are going to fight to the death for this."

"But Mac . . ." He held his hands up, as if balancing the thoughts churning through his mind and not knowing which was heavier. "Your dad. He—"

"He sacrificed himself, Butte. He died for this mission. And now we're going to try to finish what he started."

"But, but . . ." He trailed off and just stared at me. Then, "What if I don't want to do this with you?"

I stared at him for a long, pregnant moment. "If you want, I can drop you off after and we'll never talk about it again. But you have to come with us now. You're going to see our base. And you're going to help us rescue our operatives from the French."

"What?" His eyes widened. "You mentioned a French captain at your base. . . ."

I nodded. "She tried to kill me. I have her now."

"And the French are after you because of that?"

"They're after me for a variety of reasons. But yes. They might be aware that I had something to do with the loss of her warsub."

"So they'll follow us?"

I glanced at Johnny. "We're going too fast right now. But they'll have other ships out there looking for us."

"They'll come back to Trieste then. Eventually. And they might do something to capture you there."

"What do you think just happened?"

He frowned. "What do you mean?"

"The pressure loss in Module B. Don't you see the significance?"

He hesitated. "It wasn't an accident?"

"No. There are probably French agents there already. They may have infiltrated a while ago and were waiting for me to return. Waiting for night time to make their move."

He winced. "I find it hard to believe that—"

"Robert." I leaned forward. "Trust me on this. *I've done similar things.* When I was an operative, Shanks sent me out to do exactly that, to other cities. There's nothing odd about it."

"You attacked other cities?"

I shrugged. "Sometimes."

"Killed people?"

"If ordered, yes."

His eyes grew hard. "You murdered people."

I raised a finger. "Only people who meant to harm Triestrians or who threatened the city. Or who'd already committed murder. Absolutely."

An image of Admiral Benning crossed my mind, unbidden. I thrust it aside. That would come, in time.

He swore. "I can't believe it, Mac."

"It's all true. And now you're part of it."

"I'm just not sure yet."

I considered the situation. He had indicated his desire to help, and I knew it was important that he come with us on this journey. It would all play out as it was meant to. Things were going to happen soon, and happen fast. And I needed Butte right next to me during it all.

I said, "It's okay. Come see the base. We'll rescue our people. And then you can decide. And if you say no, I won't hold it against you."

He stared at me for long moments, his expression fixed and his eyes harder than I'd ever seen before. Suddenly an image of Heller came to me, and the way he'd looked when he realized that Butte was on board the seacar.

I knew Butte was part of this now, whether he liked it or not. And he was going to have to make a very important decision, very soon.

CHAPTER TWENTY-FOUR

SOON WE ARRIVED AT THE MID-ATLANTIC Ridge and turned south for the long journey to the facility. It was thousands of kilometers away, on the other side of the equator, but traveling at nearly 500 kph made the journey easier. It did take effort on the part of the pilot to maintain focus and not crash into anything or descend faster than the hull could withstand. Traveling at that speed, should the seacar suddenly pitch downward, it would hit crush depth within seconds instead of minutes while under conventional drive. A bubble surrounded us, reducing friction with the water, but the air bubble exerted an equal amount of pressure as the water at that depth. Our crush depth remained the same.

The roar of the drive was constant and steady. It was loud, but it was a white noise our brains filtered out after a while. But it was working well, without even a stutter.

Butte seemed utterly bewildered. *SC-1* amazed him. He was used to conventional speeds, after all. Fifty kph. Even sixty or seventy. But certainly no faster than that.

And now, *this*.

He was experiencing the same wonder I'd felt when I'd first discovered *SC-1's* true abilities. Kat had tried to keep it secret, but I had been too clever for her.

The news regarding the independence movement had also clearly shocked him. It's as if one second he'd had a life he'd been happy with, and had only toyed with the idea of being part of something bigger than himself, and then suddenly he'd been sucked into a movement he hadn't known existed, and now he was having second thoughts.

I smiled inwardly at that. Then I stared at Butte.

Suddenly, I felt cold.

—••—

HOURS LATER, WHILE EVERYONE WAS ASLEEP, I decided to do something I'd been thinking about for days. Renée Féroce had been on my mind, and I needed to come to some sort of resolution on her. I thought I had a solution that would make everyone happy, but it would take a bit of massaging to get her to agree. But before I could, I needed to prepare for it.

I punched a command into the communications console and selected the French undersea city of Cousteau, the first one they'd settled in the previous century. Within minutes I had the mayor on the line, and the conversation was very short indeed.

—••—

WE WERE IN THE CANYON BETWEEN the enormous diverging mountain range. I'd descended so we were below the peaks on either side, essentially masking our sound within a long rift, and deep under us the churning magma and thermal venting rose in swirling torrents and buffeted the seacar, but we were moving so fast we pierced the currents easily.

Butte had heard about the SCAV drive following The Battle with USSF and Chinese forces. Part of him, he said, just couldn't accept such speeds were possible. After all, we'd spent our adult lives in the water with the belief the upper limit of travel was eighty kilometers per hour due to drag and friction. Now, Katherine Wells had not only broken that barrier with a crewed vessel— she had *smashed* it.

And if we were able to obtain the new technology from the French—the upgraded syntactic foam—and along with Manesh Lazlow's Acoustic Pulse Drive, we were about to prove there was no limit in the oceans, that we had the power and the right to dive anywhere, to explore everything, and to harvest whatever resources we wanted. It was within our grasp, and we were not going to let the USSF or any other power take what belonged to us. We'd been fighting for it for decades. Maybe not through outright hostilities, but from blood and sweat and pain and grief and suffering and joy.

It was ours.

Almost.

There were still some hurdles yet. Major ones. I knew not to be too brash, but we were on the verge of a major accomplishment.

When we were a few minutes out from The Ridge, we began to detect strange readings on the sonar—white nebulous clusters in the canyon. They seemed to grow and contract as if they had life. They were beating hearts in the ocean, materializing at random and then disappearing just as quickly. They seemed to follow trajectories—for the brief moments that they blossomed—and then they winked out, leaving faint wisps and ripples of sound that drifted through the water, rebounded off the cliffs on either side, and disappeared slowly as the seconds ticked on.

As we watched, the entire canyon filled with the white ripples. I imagined the ephemeral waves to be echoes bouncing through the canyon, overlapping multiple times, but growing dimmer and dimmer as they spread outward. Only these lasted far longer than echoes would, and they traveled much farther as well.

Butte watched the screen for long minutes, a cascade of confusion passing over his features. "It's hypnotic," he said. "Is it some sort of life? Whale song perhaps?" He glanced at the depth finder; we were at 3500 meters, close to our crush depth.

I pulled back on the throttle and powered down slowly. The envelope surrounding us began to withdraw; soon it was shrinking past the canopy and shriveling into a tiny mass of small bubbles emerging from the water at the blunt bow of the seacar.

And then we stopped smoothly, and the buffeting from below began to hit us. We rocked in the currents, and my stomach quivered for a moment before I clamped down on it, ignoring the discomfort.

Still the white clouds appeared and disappeared on the sonar screen; our passive system was picking up the sounds all right, and as each vanished, its ghostly embers lived on as the ripples reached out to caress the jagged and sheer cliffs, and then turned away to propagate farther outward into the canyons of cold and dark water, suffocating pressures and rising eddies of ash-choked plumes of outgassing thermal vents.

"No," I said to Butte, who was beside me in the copilot chair. "It's not living. It looks organic, but it's something else entirely."

He turned to look at me, shock in his eyes. "Is this something you're doing?"

"Not me, but my people, yes." At least I *thought* it was. And if I was right, it was a marvelous sight to behold. "Do you notice anything about the depth of those . . . those sound clouds?"

I didn't know how else to describe them. They appeared seemingly at random, and floated about the canyon until time and water stole their life.

Butte frowned. "They're all below a certain depth, you're right." He tapped the different clusters of white, and labels popped up on each one. "Four kilometers. They seem to appear at or near that limit, descend for a bit, then ascend again. And when they hit the four kilometer plane, they wink off."

"Yes. You're right."

"Could there be a thermal inversion here?"

"It's possible because of the heat rising from the tectonic activity down there at the bottom, but that's not the explanation."

"Why not?"

"Because the question still remains: what's creating all that noise there?" I pointed at the sonar. "All the echoes?"

He shook his head and swore. "I really have no idea."

I grinned tightly and powered up the conventional thrusters. Checking our coordinates, I saw that we were almost right on The Ridge. I descended another 200 meters using ballast, neutralized our buoyancy, and then snapped on the exterior floodlights.

They illuminated the central dome of the facility, the docking module, and the travel tube that speared into the rock of the cliff that loomed over it.

"Oh my god," Butte gasped.

—••—

ONCE INSIDE THE FACILITY, I STEPPED out onto the hull of *SC-1*. The docking pool surrounded us. I stopped suddenly when my brain had finally processed the scene. There were seacars all around. At least twenty. They looked an awful lot like *SC-1*—same size, thruster placement, canopy design and vertical stabilizer—but there were two marked differences. Firstly, the thrusters were slightly farther from the fuselage. Secondly, the bow was different, shaped more like the snout of a Bottlenose dolphin.

I smiled. They would still generate the low-pressure zone for the SCAV drive, but they also contained the audio generators for the Acoustic Pulse Drive.

They were *Sword* class seacars, equipped with the deep diving sonic technology that Lazlow had created.

They were the source of the white noise blossoms outside.

They were in the testing phase.

Butte and Johnny were looking around now too. Johnny had figured it out, and he said, "Fantastic, Mac. They've obviously installed some of the drives."

Butte turned to me and frowned. "How deep can they go exactly?"

I shrugged. "I guess we'll have to wait and see what Lazlow says. But his prediction was eight kilometers."

His jaw dropped. "But that's right to the bottom of the deepest part of the Atlantic. If you can go that deep—"

"That's right, Robert. It means the ocean's ours."

———••———

WITHIN A FEW MINUTES I WAS reuniting with Meg and Kat next to *SCAV-1*, and after a long and satisfying embrace and kiss with Kat, I shook Lazlow's hand. There was a grin on his tired face. He looked older than I remembered. The bags under his eyes were bigger and his cheeks even more hollow than before. But he was overjoyed at the circumstances. He clearly loved being underwater, and he was getting to use his expertise for something he'd been wanting to do all his life.

Jackson was also there, and he was more reserved but still happy to see us. We hadn't been gone long—only a bit over a week—but I explained I'd been forced to return because of the French.

"Where is Renée?" I asked.

"She's in the living area one deck up," Kat said with a shrug. "She doesn't say much. She just sits around. Whatever you said to her the day you left, it made an impact. She hasn't caused a fuss."

"I told her this was just temporary, that she was going to go home soon."

Meg eyed me. "And is that true?"

I sighed. "It's true, I just don't know how soon. I need her help with something."

Then it seemed as though they noticed Butte for the first time. Meg said, "Hello, Robert. What are you doing here?" Her gaze flashed to me; she'd known that I wanted to keep him out of TCI, to isolate him and not let him know what I was up to.

He gestured to me, but he was looking around, still wide-eyed and impressed. "Mac brought me. *Forced* me, more like it, but here I am."

"I see." Her voice was flat.

Kat said, "Have you joined our team?"

"I don't know yet."

Almost as one, they all seemed to grow tense. It was sudden and satisfying, actually.

"Then why are you here?" Kat turned to me. "Tru?"

I shrugged. "I made a decision. I thought it was necessary."

"But he *knows* now. There's no going back."

Butte's eyes lifted at that. "I'm not going to be forced into a decision, if that's what you mean."

I waved away his concern. "No, no. Don't worry. If you don't want to help, then so be it."

I turned to Lazlow, but I could tell the others were concerned about what I'd done. It didn't matter. We'd cross that bridge when we came to it.

"Lazlow," I said. "I take it you've succeeded."

"Indeed." His eyes were beaming.

"Tell us what you've achieved."

"The drive works perfectly. The generator vibrates the nose at a certain frequency, which in turn pulses the pressure back on itself, and a moving sub can enter the low-pressure tunnel before it closes again."

I blinked. "Fantastic. How deep have you managed to go?"

"All the way to the bottom here! Can you believe it? Six kilometers!"

I shook my head and exhaled. "Wow. Without any hull stresses?"

"Oh, there are still stresses, but the pressure decreases by the cube root of the square of the depth when the Acoustic Pulse Drive is activated."

"Meaning?"

"It simulates a pressure much less than reality. So a pressure of six thousand meters really seems like just under three thousand. The pressure doesn't increase proportionally with depth when the drive is on though. The acoustic waves lower the pressure, but it gets more difficult to resist the deeper you go."

"And our hulls can handle greater pressures."

"Yes. Just don't stop moving."

"Instant crush depth. I remember."

Butte was still shocked. "I can't believe this," was all he was saying over and over.

"We need to test it in the Pacific," I said.

"Yes!" Lazlow practically shrieked. "Let's try anytime."

I appreciated his enthusiasm. "How many ships are finished?"

Jackson pointed at the militarized seacars surrounding us. They had a black coating on them: anechoic tiles, to reflect sound waves of varying frequencies. "We have twenty in here right now. All are functioning, but without the pulse drive. There are twenty-six outside right now, piloted by the workers here, all functioning *with* the pulse drive."

I did the math in my head. "And there must be others as well."

The man nodded. "We have forty more in the holding pool. They're also functioning but without the acoustic pulse drive."

"But they all have SCAV drive, correct?" Johnny asked.

"Yes. But we haven't taken them out on trial runs yet."

"That's okay."

"When will we have that syntactic foam you were talking about, Mac?" Jackson asked.

I sighed. "That's partly why I'm here, actually."

—••—

I FOUND CAPTAIN RENÉE FÉROCE UPSTAIRS in her bunk. She was staring listlessly at the domed ceiling over her head. She turned when she heard me approach, and her eyes barely registered my appearance.

I sat next to her.

"Are you here to rub it in?"

"Rub what?"

"That you won? That I'm you're prisoner?"

"It's not much of a prison, really."

"Are you serious?" Her face took on a pained expression. "I can't run."

"Did you try?"

"No."

I nodded. That matched with what Jackson had told me. She hadn't tried to leave, but she hadn't helped either.

"And why not?"

She frowned. "You told me not to."

"True. But do you always listen to your warden?"

She sneered. "Like I said, rub it in."

"I'm just wondering why you haven't tried to run. Don't get me wrong—I appreciate that you didn't. I don't want to expose this facility to anyone. But why didn't you at least try?"

"Because I'm trapped here, asshole!" she snapped. "The pressure is too great. We're at the bottom of a goddamn canyon! There is no fiber optic junction anywhere near this place. We're totally out of the sealanes. And there's no comm at this station, anyway! Your experimental ships are zooming around out there making all kinds of racket—like flares in the night—and no one will notice unless they're close enough to pick it up with passive sonar."

"Still. You didn't even try."

She snorted. "Try what?"

"To steal a ship."

"You said they were locked out! That only your code could activate them."

"That's true. But you could have persuaded someone to give you the code, no?"

"I—I—" Her façade was starting to crack.

"You could have tried seduction. Or violence. Or torture."

"But you told me this was just temporary!" Her eyes flashed.

"I might have been lying."

"So was it a lie? Are you going to kill me now?"

I raised my hands. "I didn't say that, Captain. I'm just saying you took me at face value. You trusted me."

She seemed to deflate slightly. "I guess I did. I've been through a lot. It's been a hard year."

"Since I fired on *Destroyer*, you mean."

"You killed a man. You escaped. You, in a civilian seacar, and me, the captain of an FSF warsub. You humiliated me."

"And the FSF made you pay. They demoted you and sent you on a mission you couldn't win."

She set a laser-like glare on me. "I would have got you eventually, McClusky."

"But you didn't. You couldn't. You tried an EMP. You tried a kill squad. You shot torpedoes and tried hand-to-hand combat underwater. Then an FSF missile boat tried to take us out."

Her eyebrows raised. *"Lion?"*

I paused. "How'd you know?"

"They were in the area. I'd been communicating with them. They were the last ones I spoke with."

"They tried to take us with grapples. I cut them off and fired three torpedoes into her engineering section."

She swore. "You have a death wish, McClusky."

I shrugged. "Perhaps. But I'm not sure. I don't want to die—I want to fight. *Nothing* will keep me from this fight."

"Maybe it's suicide you want."

A sudden image of my dad strobed through my brain. My heart thudded. Could she be correct? Could I subconsciously be doing what my dad had done thirty years before? I didn't think so . . . but then again, the subconscious brain is one that the conscious doesn't fully understand.

They speak different languages.

I settled on, "I don't think so."

She snorted again. "Get it over with, McClusky. Do what you're going to do with me."

"I'm going to let you go."

She stopped abruptly and stared at me. She pushed herself up on her elbows. "Right now?"

"Not just yet."

"Figures."

"I need help. Then I let you go."

"And if I reveal this base?"

I looked around. "And what are the coordinates? Where are we right now? What depth are we at? Will you ever be able to find your way back here? Are we north of the equator or south of it?"

She eyed me. "You don't think I'll find you ever again?"

"I'm hoping not. But I'm also hoping that you'll at least understand our struggle a bit and perhaps even empathize with it."

"Doubtful. You are a criminal. You're an enemy of the state."

"I might be able to give you something that will change that perception of me."

There was a long pause as that sunk in. Then her eyes widened. "You'll give France the SCAV drive?"

"Yes. You can have it. I'll let you take a seacar with one. Back to France, but we'll leave you somewhere with the nav system wiped. You won't know where this base is."

"And what do you want in return?" Her eyes narrowed.

"I need help rescuing two Triestrians. Prisoners in your research facility in the Seychelles."

She bolted to her feet. "How do you know about that?"

I shrugged. "I have sources everywhere. That's the intelligence game." In fact, Johnny had contacted me months ago with the information about the base; he'd received it while in a Chinese underwater colony. "Your country gave China the superior syntactic foam. In return they were going to give you the SCAV drive. You're still going to end up with the drive. But I want my people back. And I want you to help me rescue them."

"I don't even know if they're there."

"How did you know to tell Heller then?" At her questioning gaze I said, "That's why I've come back so soon."

"To lead a raid on *yet another* French base? And how many more French are going to die?"

"With your help, hopefully none. *Without* your help . . . that's another story."
I exhaled. "Look, you know where they are. You told Heller. Someone told you.
I'm betting you've been to the facility at least once in your career. Even if you
haven't, I have the coordinates and you can at least help me when we get there."

"So you threaten me now with more death if I don't help?" she hissed. "That's
cruel, McClusky."

I shrugged. "Look at it this way—help me and you get the SCAV drive,
you get out of here, and you help prevent more French deaths. What's the
downside to all of that?"

She scowled and her tone was icy. "Maybe that you'll still be alive?"

I sighed. "There's always next time, Renée. When we meet again."

CHAPTER
TWENTY-FIVE

SIX OF US WENT ON THE mission.

Katherine, Meg, Johnny, Butte, myself, and the reluctant Frenchwoman, Captain Renée Féroce departed aboard *SC-1*, en route to a research facility in the Indian Ocean near the Seychelles off the coast of Africa. To get there we would have to pilot around the Cape of Good Hope—the southern tip of Africa and graveyard to countless ships. Where oceans met, massive currents swept from one to the other past the rugged tip of South Africa, hurricane-strength winds tossed the surface, and submerged rocks threatened even the most durable of hulls. The course we headed was dangerous no matter the type of vessel. Surface ships or subs, it was all the same.

We were at nature's mercy.

My face was tight as I piloted toward the stormy waters. I knew what was at stake, but we simply couldn't back down now. Heller and Benning and the entire USSF would not give up, so neither could I.

I remembered books I'd read as a child, stories of undersea cities and new nations and the countless resources on the seafloors we could harvest. Those tales had stuck with me throughout my adolescent and adult years. My dad's death had galvanized me, and forced me into the intelligence field and the quest for those resources.

Kat was next to me in the control cabin. She kept flashing me looks and smiles, and I tried to return them, but I was not as excited as she. There was great danger ahead. The French fleet was looking for us. I hoped we were leaving them behind to the west—the large grouping that had been near Bermuda, for instance, though there were likely others in the Atlantic—but I knew there were FSF forces in the Indian Ocean too.

—••—

WE USED CONVENTIONAL THRUSTERS; I DIDN'T want to attract attention on this mission. The trip took days to round the curve of Africa, and during it we spoke of current events and ate meals and even shared some drinks together. It was interesting and unexpected. Renée, for instance, was still standoffish, but she was under the impression she'd be going free soon. She was beginning to relax a bit. I caught her smiling a few times, especially with Robert Butte. He was personable and endearing—a politician in every sense of the word— and the two spent time sitting on the couch and chatting about life in the seas and how the FSF experience was different from the ocean colony one.

Kat and I were happy to get reacquainted, though we'd only been apart for slightly more than a week. We made love in one of the recessed bunks off the corridor just behind the control cabin. There were people only a meter away from us—piloting the ship and socializing in the living area—but we happily explored each other's bodies with hands and fingers and hungry tongues, and there were moans of pleasure and groans of delight, and frankly we didn't care what the others thought. Katherine Wells had brought me joy. She had shown me a future I could wholeheartedly dive in to. I had never had a long-term love affair before. I could see spending my life with her, and it was the first time I'd thought that in my forty-five years. She had also opened me to a broader future. I wanted both of us to live long enough to see it.

I had left Lancombe and Ng back at the facility, continuing the efforts to plan and build defenses for Trieste as well as The Ridge, and both seemed thrilled to be involved in the fight so intimately, once again.

Kat and I made love every night during the voyage. It was a distance of 9000 kilometers. Traveling at seventy kph, it meant a trip of just over five days. Each night after dinner and an hour or two of talking and socializing, we'd retire to the meter-wide bunk, make love, and fall asleep in each other's arms. With only a curtain pulled across the opening, and the voices from the living compartment drifting to us as we slowly moved together, the rocking of the seacar added to the motion, and each evening we climaxed multiple times.

"Love you, Tru," she'd whisper into my ear after each session.

I'd respond willingly; there was no holding back anymore. I was personally invested in this fight, and if I had to pick anyone as its symbol, it wouldn't just be me and my father—it would be Katherine Wells too. She had spent her teens and twenties caring for an ill father, and had put her dreams on hold. But when finally she could invest herself in our struggle, she had done it wholeheartedly.

Despite the enjoyable aspects of the mission, the days as we navigated the Cape of Good Hope were still stressful. The seacar rocked in the strong currents and it was difficult to keep her stable. The trim tanks were constantly pumping water back and forth, working to keep the vessel level. We could hear the whir of the pumps going off constantly every time one of the stabilizers caught a current and lifted or fell. But no one got sick; undersea colonizers were used to that sort of thing. Few ever got seasick after childhood.

But my hands were tense on the yoke, and my knuckles white, and sometimes it was a struggle to keep us driving straight and true.

It would be so easy to activate the SCAV drive and just power past these rough currents quickly, I thought.

But no. Surprise was more important, and soon we were past the rough currents and into smoother waters.

Butte grew more relaxed with every day that passed. Perhaps he felt that since he didn't have to make a commitment just yet, and I'd basically shanghaied him there, he wasn't bound to anything.

Little did he know.

But Meg worried about him, and rightly so. Once, while we were in the engineering compartment, she said to me, "Why exactly is Butte here?" She was looking over the work Johnny had done on the SCAV drive back at Trieste, but everything checked out. After all, her own workers in the Repair Module had helped with the system repairs.

"I wanted to force him to make a decision," I answered.

"What was wrong with the way things were?"

"He was beginning to ask questions," I said after a hesitation. "He was starting to push me." I had to leave it at that.

She stared at me for a long moment, then tilted her head slightly.

I sighed. Damn. She knew me very well. "I can't say everything yet, Meg."

"Why are you always hiding secrets from me? I'm your sister, dammit."

"Maybe I'm protecting you. You're my *little* sister."

"Stop it with that. We were born only seconds apart."

"Still."

She blew her breath out in huff. "Shut up. Why do you have to protect me?"

"Remember all those years I lied to you about what I was doing?"

"When you were in TCI and going on missions? And you told me you were working a menial job at Trieste?"

"It's kind of true."

"You totally kept it from me, until you showed up one day in a damaged seacar begging for help."

"I was hardly begging."

"It was either help you or let China catch you and hold you as a spy. Of course you were begging. *SC-1* was flooded, for fuck's sake. The vertical stabilizer—"

"No need to swear, Meg."

"Of course there is! When you continually lie to me, I need to know why."

"I'm just—"

"—withholding vital information. Same thing."

"No, it's not."

"Then tell me this: Why did Butte send a communication last night? You were busy with Kat, but I saw him do it."

That stopped me cold. I frowned. "When did it happen?"

"In the middle of the night. He went to the control cabin."

We were on autopilot at night since we were only using conventional drive. But I wasn't worried about what he'd sent. I knew he couldn't have given anything important away. "It's okay."

She clenched her fists and her neck tensed. "It's *not*! What if he told them about us?"

"He didn't."

She looked like she could chew steel. "Dammit, Tru! Don't be so trusting. *You're* the one who said we were going to keep him out of TCI, a year ago when you chose him as your deputy mayor."

I gave her a sly smile. There was a time, not long ago in fact, she hadn't wanted me to have anything to do with what had killed our father. It's why I'd spent two decades not telling her the truth about my occupation.

She would just have to wait a little longer.

—••—

Soon we were approaching the coordinates of the French facility that Johnny had messaged me about months earlier. I'd sent my operatives Maple and Bruce out to it weeks ago, and I hadn't heard from them since. There was nothing unusual about that, but Renée had said that command channels had made reference to the capture of two Triestrians near the Seychelles.

We timed our approach to occur at night. I kept thrusters at ten percent, hugged the sandy bottom as we moved toward it. No one spoke.

Soon the coordinates were within our thirty kilometer passive radar range. We stared at it intently.

Nothing.

A few surface vessels, churning slowly across the Indian Ocean between Indonesia and the Middle-East, but otherwise the undersea world was silent.

Still we closed on the coordinates.

Still, nothing.

"What the hell?" I whispered.

"Maybe it's stealthy," Johnny said at my side.

I glanced at him. "You mean like The Ridge?"

He shrugged. "It's possible. It's a research station, after all."

I thought back to the message he'd sent to me. He'd told me that the French had invented a better hull filler that could increase crush depth. I wanted the foam to give our subs a depth advantage now during SCAV or conventional travel, in situations where we couldn't use the Acoustic Pulse Drive.

I checked the coordinates again. "Maybe it's camouflaged." It was a sandy floor without much bathymetry. No real places to hide. No vessels moving about, entering or exiting a facility if it was there. "Let's try the VID system," I said. Maybe it would show a feature on the bottom that wasn't giving off any sound.

I snapped it on.

The canopy around us changed to blue. Darker shades represented depth. Any nearby subs would show as white outlines that the computer projected.

There was nothing.

Making our angle negative, I dipped the nose down until the seafloor came into view. It was flat, as the depth finder had showed, but the VID also highlighted the rising and falling features of dunes, shaped by the currents in the area. They weren't large, however—each was only about a meter or two.

But there was something on the VID image that sonar hadn't displayed.

A seacar, on the bottom, half obscured by the shifting sands.

—••—

I FROWNED. IT WAS JUST SITTING there.

It was only 200 meters deep, and I swung our nose toward the silent vessel, brought us in to just a few meters, then switched off the VID and turned on the exterior lamps.

Outside the canopy, we could see the vessel clearly.

There was damage to the hull. Some force had sheared the hatch off cleanly. The interior was flooded. Sand had drifted over the bow and aft of the vehicle. It covered the rear thruster, it drifted over the hatch threshold, and had collected inside the seacar and was building up against the starboard interior bulkhead. Fish swam in and out of the vessel.

In another few weeks, the sub would be lost, completely hidden by the sands.

"An explosion took the hatch off," Johnny said, pointing. "Look—there's some hull depressions and pitting there."

There was also a puncture on the other side, and the jagged hole was pressed *inward*. It reminded me of the damage I'd inflicted on the *Verdun* class warsub earlier.

The coordinates of this wreck made me gasp. They were identical to the ones that Johnny had given me.

I pointed it out to him and his eyes widened. "Jesus, you're right."

"Something's wrong here."

From behind me, Meg asked, "What's happening, Tru? Did you find it?"

I cursed under my breath. Then, "No. In fact, I think we're in trouble."

"Why?"

"This seacar is Triestrian."

Johnny frowned. "Are you sure?"

"Yep." I pointed at the serial number on the side.

On a whim I swung around and aimed the bright lamps into the control cabin, through the viewport. Shadows stretched through the interior and outlined the two pilot chairs. There were lumps of something in each.

Clothing, with piles of bone and rotting and flaky flesh within them.

The fish.

Oh shit, the fish.

They were feeding.

"Send out an active pulse, Johnny." I couldn't keep my eyes off the bodies. Or what was left of them anyway.

Beside me, Johnny swore. The sonar was lit with returns now, on all sides.

They'd kept their distance so nothing had shown on our passive screen.

But had we sent out an active pulse earlier, we'd have seen the clusters of French subs closing on us.

There were over two hundred vessels, representing every class of sub in the FSF. Some of them were French allies, including Belgian and Spanish ships.

The coordinates had been the bait.

And we'd sailed right into it.

CHAPTER
TWENTY-SIX

"RENÉE! GET UP HERE!" I YELLED. I almost slammed the throttle on full right there, but I held back. Johnny watched me nervously.

She leaned over my chair and looked at the sonar. Her face showed a glimmer of a smile.

"Don't be too happy," I said. "They'll sink us."

"Maybe I don't care."

"I think you do. You're a sub captain. You love what you do. You don't want to give that up."

"I'm not giving anything up."

I pointed at the coordinates. "There's no facility here."

"I never said there was."

"You said that the prisoners were here."

She shrugged. "I told Heller that I heard about the capture of some Triestrians."

"Who gave you that information?"

"It was on the command briefing weeks ago. It said, 'Near the Seychelles.'"

I thought furiously. Féroce had heard about a capture. She had told Heller. Heller had mentioned it to me.

But it hadn't been a total lie. After all, the seacar was there, complete with both bodies inside.

It was them. Maple and Bruce.

My operatives *had* been here. They *had* tried to steal something.

Unless . . .

Maybe they *had* stolen it. Maybe they'd succeeded, and the French had caught them in the act.

"Look at the coordinates. Are we at the correct location?"

She frowned. "No. We're a few kilometers from it still." She stared at me. She wasn't a willing helper, that much was certain.

"Johnny, these are the coordinates you sent me *months* ago."

He looked confused. "It's possible they were setting us up. Even that long ago."

It would mean the Chinese were still helping the French try to capture me, which wasn't impossible. After all, Johnny had mentioned that not every Chinese leader was on board with our plan. And it was very possible that the CSF had fed Johnny wrong information.

Just so the French could finally capture me.

And it had been a seed they'd planted long, long ago.

I snorted in frustration. Then I turned to Renée. "Where is it?"

"Sorry." She shook her head.

I stared at the crashed seacar out through the canopy, then glanced at the sonar. The warsubs were approaching. . . .

"Johnny," I said. "Let's go over to that sub. Let's take a look."

—••—

"YOU DON'T HAVE MUCH TIME," RENÉE said to me as I suited up. Johnny was next to me, also putting on his gear.

"You sound happy about that," I muttered.

"Maybe I am."

"We die, you die. Remember that."

She pressed her lips together tightly, but didn't respond.

Meg said, "Just what are you doing? The FSF fleet is nearly here. We need to run, *now.*"

"How long do we have?" Johnny asked. His expression was flat, but I could sense his excitement. This was the kind of thing we lived for. We had spent years doing this, and now we were back at it.

Kat replied, "The ships are all closing from a distance of between eighty and a hundred clicks. There might even be more outside of that range. At their current speed, they'll reach us in just over an hour."

So, they were running at full speed toward us. Made sense. They'd known we arrived at their bait. Perhaps an alarm system or a proximity detector on board the disabled seacar had sent a signal to their ships.

Kat said, "Get the nav chip. It'll give us an explanation."

I said, "Let's spend no more than thirty minutes out there. Then we'll have to decompress in the airlock. Meg and Kat can hit the SCAV and evade their forces."

"You hope," Meg snapped. "But you don't know. Let's just leave."

I grabbed her by the shoulders and pulled her gently to face me. "Meg. Sometimes we're going to have to take risks like these in this fight. I sent those operatives on a mission. I have to see if they completed it."

"But they're dead." Her eyes showed confusion. "Their seacar is exactly where the coordinates specified."

"Johnny sent me those coordinates months ago. A Chinese official gave them to him. I only sent Maple and Bruce out a few weeks ago. Maybe the French caught them somewhere else, and then they towed their disabled seacar here and scuttled it."

"But these are the coordinates you gave to your operatives, right? So how did they get caught? They came directly here. They couldn't have made it to the facility, since there is no facility here!"

I pursed my lips. She was right. I looked at Renée. "Captain, is the facility near enough for someone to find it easily?"

She shrugged. "If you waited around long enough, you'd see some ships coming to and from the dome. It's not totally covert, like your secret base."

I turned to Meg. "See? There's a chance. I can't just run without looking. Now, we're wasting time. Keep an eye on those approaching vessels."

She glared at me, but said no more. Kat hugged me and Butte wished me luck. It was clear he had no intentions of going out this deep. The thought made me laugh inwardly; 200 meters was nothing now. Like a swimming pool topside. I held the record for the deepest scuba dive ever, anyway, and I had no qualms about this.

"Watch the captain here," I said to Meg. "Take a needle gun, make her sit on the couch."

"You have nothing to fear from me," Renée said.

"You've made it clear you still want to kill me. Leaving us outside here would be an easy way to do it." I glanced at my sister. "Are you okay with the gun?"

She nodded. "No problem. We can hold her."

I turned to Butte. "And what about you, Robert?"

He blinked. "What do you mean? I'm not going out there."

"I know. But are you okay waiting for me in here?"

"Absolutely." His face was drawn; he seemed panicked.

"Don't worry. We'll get out of here just fine. We've got the SCAV drive, after all."

I barely kept myself from saying, *Unless they use an EMP again.*

—••—

JOHNNY AND I SWAM THROUGH THE rectangular opening in the flooded seacar's hull. The hinges were twisted and torn; an explosion had clearly detonated close and its compression wave had worked its deadly magic. It had caught the lip of the hatch and wormed its way into the seam. The hatch had only been as strong as the hinge, like the proverbial link in a chain. Water had pounded into the seacar, killing those inside. Had they been deep, the pressure wave would have smashed their skulls and torsos and killed nearly instantly. Had they been shallow and survived the initial wave, they would have drowned.

Inside there were drifts of sand piled against the far bulkhead. With each kick of our flippers, it swirled upward in a cloud that lowered visibility slightly. I noticed absently the viewports inside were not broken. Had it been a violent flooding, those ports would have shattered in the maelstrom.

There was a small living area. A couch against the bulkhead had been torn apart. I studied it for a few moments. There were two bunks; the mattresses and blankets were gone. There was nothing in the clothes drawers near the bunks, and they were all shut tight.

I gestured for Johnny to check engineering, and I turned toward the control cabin. A sharp kick and I drifted slowly toward it. The headrests of the two chairs were in silhouette against the forward port. Kat was holding *SC-1* just off the seacar's bow, and the bright lamps were shining inward through the port. The light sent long shadows along the deck, flickering and jagged. Fish attracted to the bright lights flashed in front of them, their shadows adding to the scene.

There were bits of debris floating up from the chairs. I slowly brought myself closer. I knew it was flesh. Fish were nibbling at the floating ichor, darting in and out and swallowing the meals in tiny bursts of speed. I nearly retched into my facemask, but clamped down on it.

That would end with me choking to death.

The sagging remains held within ragged clothes lay in clumps on each chair. Pant legs stretched downward under the forward console. White bone protruded from tears in the fabric.

I stared at the bodies for long moments. Then, "Johnny. Did you find anything?"

"There's evidence of a fire back here."

I grunted at that. A fire, underwater. I considered the evidence. Things just didn't add up. I reached for the navigation chip in the computer and stopped suddenly.

It was not there.

I said, "We need to get back, now."

"I'm just checking—"

"Now!"

We swam back to our own seacar and entered the airlock. The water rushed out and Johnny and I threw our gear to the deck and sat down for the short decompression. Kat was taking us through it already. I could feel acceleration as she turned *SC-1* to the south and started to power away. The roar from aft told me she'd activated the SCAV drive.

Meg said over the speaker, "Mac, what did you find?"

"This seacar was captured somewhere else."

"How do you know?"

"The fire, for one. There must have been a chase. Explosions. The evidence on the outside of the hull shows detonations. A fire started in the engine room. They were held prisoner somewhere."

"How do you know they didn't die in the chase?"

"They're dead in their seats. But they don't have belts on."

Pause. Then, "Say again?"

"No seat belts. Had the vessel suffered catastrophic implosion, or flooding from losing the hatch in a detonation, the rushing water would have crushed and thrown the bodies around. Even with belts on, the force would have torn them out and tossed them like limp dolls. But there they are, in that disabled and flooded seacar, just lumps of bones and rotting flesh in their seats."

There was a long pause. Then, "But why would the French do that?"

"A signal for us, perhaps. For me. A final insult." I shrugged. "It's a message. 'This is what happens to spies' maybe. Or, 'This is going to happen to Truman McClusky.'"

There was another break for a minute or so as I considered what had happened to my two people. Their true fate had crystallized in my mind now, and I didn't like the direction that it pointed.

I should have expected it though.

"What do you think the datachip will show?" Kat asked.

"There wasn't one."

"*What?*"

I sighed. "You heard me. The datachip was gone."

"But that would mean . . ."

"That someone pulled it intentionally."

"But Mac," Butte said. "Surely the flooding water could have done that."

"Maybe. But someone removed their clothing from the drawers. The water didn't do that. They were still shut tight. Someone placed the bodies back in the seats. Someone took the chip so we couldn't see where the two had gone. And how would that happen if Maple and Bruce had drowned from a hit? If the ship had sunk after a detonation?"

Meg sighed. "It doesn't fit, you're right. They must have been captured."

Butte said, "So they were captured . . . and killed. Then someone put their bodies *back* in the seacar, flooded it, and scuttled it at the coordinates you'd been fed. To lure you in."

"Yes." They didn't have the syntactic foam. The mission had been a waste. And now, we were in great danger. "How much longer for decompression?" I asked.

"Forty-five minutes."

"And you're heading south into the fleet?"

"Yes. We'll be hitting the first ship in just fifteen minutes."

I swore. I wanted to be at the controls for this. "Keep an eye on Renée. If she's going to make a move, it'll be right now."

There was no response.

"Kat? Meg?"

Still nothing.

I tried again.

Johnny turned to look at me.

Oh, shit.

———•◦•———

WE TRIED FOR ANOTHER MINUTE BUT still no one answered. The seacar's acceleration had stopped, and the roar of the drive had decreased as well. It seemed as though we were not moving quickly at all anymore.

I turned to Johnny. "We have only one play here."

His eyes were wide. "You think Renée made her move?"

"We have to open the hatch, right now."

His face showed shock. "But we haven't finished decompression."

Inside, my stomach churned.

The Bends.

Bubbles of air would surge from our tissues and enter our joints and vessels. They would course through our cardiovascular system and enter our brains. The Bends would disable us within minutes, and kill soon after.

And we were going to have to do it to ourselves, deliberately.

"We have no other choice, Johnny. If Renée somehow got a weapon and is in control right now, she's probably turned us toward an FSF ship. She'll surrender, or try to anyway. If you ask me, the French will just blow us out of the water."

"She might communicate a distress. Reach out for help."

"She can't." At his questioning gaze, I said, "I'll explain later." I blew out my breath in a rush. "This is our only chance."

Johnny had gone pale. "We've never tried this before. After everything we've been through—"

"There's a first for everything. We won't have long before the pain incapacitates us." I looked around for weapons. There was nothing. All our needle guns and knives were on the other side of that hatch. I gestured at the controls. "We'll have to bypass it. Order it to open early. Can you do it?"

"I wish I had to say no, but yeah, I can do it."

I stepped aside.

My stomach felt hollow. My heart felt like it was going to explode. But we had no other choice.

"Watch out for Butte. He might be with her," I said.

Johnny's expression showed horror. "You think so?"

"It's possible." I took a deep breath. "Now do it."

—••—

THE HATCH SLAMMED ASIDE WITH A blast of air into the cabin. We lay on the floor with our fingers through the grating to keep us from being thrown into the living area of the seacar. We'd known the explosion of air was going to occur; after all, we had been in an air pressure of over twenty atmospheres, and there were only four in the seacar.

The air burst out loudly. My sight grew dim and waves of dizziness overwhelmed me for a moment. Pushing myself up, I tried to clear my thoughts. *Dammit, focus, Mac!* I screamed inwardly.

I rose to my feet and lurched out into the corridor.

My tongue started to feel funny, but I thrust the thought aside.

I glanced right and left, trying to quickly locate Renée, but the moist air from the airlock had flash-condensed in the suddenly lower pressure. It was foggy on board now.

She was standing in front of the couch, with both Meg and Kat sitting in front of her. The rush of air had startled them, and they were looking around, momentarily stunned.

Air was fizzing on my tongue, I realized. Bubbling out of my innards.

Only a minute left, possibly less.

"Stop!" I yelled at Renée. I reached behind me and grabbed a needle gun from the rack next to the airlock.

She turned and brought her own weapon to bear. It was also a needle gun—the one Meg had had. Renée took a step back, toward the bunks, to keep us all in her sights. "Don't move any closer or I'll fire."

I realized that Butte was not there. Behind me, the hatch to engineering was shut.

"There are four of us and one of you," I said. My voice sounded fuzzy. My head was starting to hurt too.

Meg looked at me, concerned. "You have to finish decompression, Mac! You'll die."

"If need be." I took a step toward the captain.

"Stop!" she cried.

"You care too much about the oceans to do this," I said. It was sounding more and more garbled.

"I am French. I will not sit back and see you destroy French warsubs!"

"We're just going to run from them."

"What's Butte doing?" Johnny asked. He turned to the engineering hatch and tried to open it. "Locked from the other side," he said. I could barely make him out; his words were slurred.

"You could kill me right now," I said. "Shoot at my face and neck. It'll do the job."

She was staring at me, and her eyes were wide. "I will. I'll do it. Don't come any closer. After what you've done to me, I have the right to kill you!"

The fog swirled around her.

My head was swimming in it.

I continued to march toward her. The area was small, and I was only a few meters away. "I'm offering the world's oceans to the people who live there. To undersea colonists everywhere."

"And what of the world's superpowers?" she snapped. "What do we get?"

"You've had your chance, and you ruined it. You've ruined the land. Give us a chance underwater. We've earned it."

"Stop. I order you." Her voice faltered.

I lowered my weapon and walked until my chest was pressed against the square barrel of her gun. "Fire," I said. "You've wanted to do it for a year. Here's your chance."

Kat said, "Mac—don't let her—"

"Do it!" I yelled. "You hate me. You hate what I did to you."

She shook her head. "Don't confuse me. Don't force me."

"I'm giving you the opportunity to do what you've wanted for so long. I let you live. I saved you. And now you have the chance. Take it!"

"Tru!" Kat screamed. "What are you doing?"

Behind me, Johnny was hitting his fists against the hatch. "Robert!" But his voice was hoarse and raspy, and his pounding was growing weaker with each hit. He fell to his knees.

I turned back to Renée. I opened my mouth to speak and a sudden jab of searing pain shot through my brain. I threw my head back and a sound escaped my lips. At least, I think it was me. It was primal. A piercing shriek that echoed around us. Renée's eyes grew wide in horror.

I stumbled back and barely kept my balance. Then I slumped to my knees and clutched my head between my hands. The fog was thicker near the deck. I couldn't see anything. The pain between my temples was excruciating. My joints were locking up. I lay on my side and curled into the fetal position; it brought a tiny bit of relief, but not much.

Distantly, I heard the others arguing and then felt a pair of hands under my armpits. They dragged me into the airlock and left me on the cold and wet deck. My face was on the grating.

I was dimly aware the others had laid Johnny at my side.

The hatch closed and I heard rushing air.

They were pressurizing the lock.

I passed out.

CHAPTER TWENTY-SEVEN

I'M NOT SURE HOW MUCH TIME passed. I groaned periodically as the pain lanced through my head. Every joint was inflamed and sore. It hurt to breathe. Beside me, Johnny was in a similar state. He too had curled into a ball and was moaning softly.

But it didn't last long. Soon the hissing air had stopped, and my breathing grew steady. The gurgling wheezes from my lungs ceased.

Gingerly, I stretched my legs. They popped and creaked, but they still worked. I rolled onto my back and stared at the ceiling. Drips of water fell from it, hitting my exposed skin. It was cold and salty, but it felt good.

It felt like *life*.

I was still there. Still in the fight.

"Fuck," I said. I was a giant wound. When was it going to be so much that it finally just killed me? Already I had done things that a sane man wouldn't have. But I had justified every single instance with the quest for independence.

Because that's what had driven my father.

"Kat," I said, but it came out as a groan. I cleared my throat, swallowed, and tried again.

"How are you, Tru?" Her voice floated to me from the speaker.

"Alive." It was a rasp, but clearer now at least.

"We got you back under pressure. You'll be fine. I'm slowly bringing you down to four atmospheres. You've been through a lot worse."

"Have I?" My voice sounded hollow.

"Remember the time when you went out at forty-four hundred meters?"

I snorted. "Of course."

"This wasn't as bad as that."

"Seems like it." Hell, I had just willingly gone from a depth of 200 meters to thirty in a split second. Fish exploded from smaller changes.

I turned and looked at Johnny. His eyes were open and he was staring at me. "I don't want to do that again."

"Tell me about it." I studied him for a few heartbeats. "How's your head?"

"Don't ask."

I placed my hands on the grating to feel for vibrations. "We're not in SCAV," I muttered.

"Maybe the French got us."

"I didn't hear any detonations."

"I did."

I blinked. "Really?"

"Yeah. A couple. We performed maneuvers as well. Evasion. Countermeasures."

"Damn." I turned back to the speaker. "Kat, why aren't we in SCAV?"

"It's out," she said.

"Are we past the fleet?"

"Barely. They fired on us. We avoided the conventional torpedoes easily. The SCAV ones detonated close to us."

I frowned and closed my eyes. "Was the SCAV out before or after the detonations?"

"It went out at the first ones."

"Shit." I groaned. "And what's our speed now?"

"Full. Seventy. The fleet is on our tail."

This wasn't good. I pushed myself into a sitting position. Johnny did likewise. He was hanging his head and was having trouble focusing on me. "Easy," I said. "The pressure will take care of it."

The increased pressure would force the bubbles back into our tissues. Then, as Kat lowered it again, we would expel the excess gas normally through respiration. But the pain . . .

It would remain in my nightmares

"How much longer in here, Kat?"

"Another hour, just to be safe. I'm bringing you back, but slowly."

The events out in the living space were coming back to me. "Where's Renée?"

"Sitting on the couch. We're watching her. She's quiet. Passive."

"And Butte?"

"Won't respond."

I sighed. Dammit. "Can you patch me through to him?"

There was a brief pause. Then, "Go ahead."

I cleared my throat and shook my head to clear it. "Robert, it's me. I'm in the airlock decompressing still."

No response.

"Why are you back there?"

Still nothing.

"Robert, tell me, what's wrong?"

Finally, his voice, distant and faint, reached me. "Mac, I didn't want any of this. You forced it on me."

Did I? I wanted to say. *You sure about that?*

Instead I settled on, "Renée has given up now. We're past the fleet. We'll be okay."

"Until the next subs find us, you mean."

"Maybe. But there's no reason to lock yourself back there."

"Why'd you do this to me, Mac?"

"You were asking about independence. About the movement. You said you wanted in."

"I never said anything of the sort."

I shuffled over to the bulkhead and leaned against the steel. Water trickled down my back. I closed my eyes and thought. What had he said, exactly? He'd asked about the movement. About my father. He'd implied that he wanted to be a part of anything I was planning. "I'm pretty sure you did."

"Wrong."

"You wanted this. To be a part of the fight. Well, now you are."

"Bullshit. I didn't want this."

"Let's talk it over, Robert. You can't stay back there forever. Come forward and we'll hash it out."

"Hash what out? You're engaged in something I don't want a part of."

"How can you say that? Of course you want a part of it."

"No. That's wrong." His voice was gaining strength. My head was starting to clear, the ache was fading and my eyes were focusing again.

One look at Johnny confirmed that he was feeling better too. He returned my gaze, and his eyes were questioning. I raised a finger: *Hold on. I know what I'm doing.*

"Robert, I'll be out of the airlock in a bit. Then we'll continue the conversation together. And when we're done, you can decide what you want to do."

"You mean you'll take me back to Trieste?"

I hesitated. "I can't promise that, because we're going to have to deal with this fleet behind us. But afterward, I can arrange something. First, let's talk."

"We're talking now."

"No. We need to all talk, together. With Renée too." I frowned as I thought it over. "You can decide what you want after. I'll try to make it happen." I winced at the lie.

There was a long pause. I could hear him breathing heavily. Then, "All right. I'll listen. But you better be willing to let me leave when all is said and done."

I didn't reply.

—••—

AN HOUR LATER WE WERE IN the seacar's living compartment. Autopilot was bringing us toward the Cape of Good Hope, and we were making a speed of seventy kilometers per hour at a depth of 200 meters. There were over three hundred vessels following us at that exact moment. Meg wanted desperately to get the SCAV drive up and running again, but I held her back.

We had to talk.

Renée was watching me silently. Her eyes were wide and she couldn't take them off me. I gave her a crooked smile. "You almost got your wish."

"You *are* crazy."

"No. I'm driven. There's a difference."

"What for? Because your dad wanted this?"

"No. Because *I* want this." As I said it I realized how true it was. My dad had indeed wanted Trieste's future to be free. He'd wanted our efforts and work to pay off for her citizens, and not for the benefit of the USSF officers who oversaw us, or the economies topside that took our produce without any remuneration. I wanted that as well, but I knew there were other things that pushed me now. Every year I'd spent working for the city, every second that I'd harvested in the fields or out on missions for TCI, I'd done it for the people. For Triestrians. I had never done it for my father.

He was just a distant memory, one that haunted me every February 23. He was always in the back of my mind. I remembered that final argument, with me and him and Meg and Mother, fighting about the future of the colony and how the USSF would never settle for anything less than absolute dominance over us. But he resisted us.

Because he *knew*.

He knew what was going to happen the very next day.

He knew that it would be the last time we'd ever speak.

And he hadn't even said goodbye to me. Not even a hug.

I'd been fourteen years old, when every boy needed their father most. And he'd walked right into a trap, willingly, hoping that it would help the movement in the long run.

And now here I was, on a disabled seacar running from a French fleet that wanted to kill me.

But I was doing it now for *me*. Not him. Or his legacy.

"I want freedom for the people of the seas, Renée. For the colonies."

"You killed for that."

I nodded. "Yes," I said in a soft tone. "I guess I did. But it was for a good cause. It was for this." I gestured around me. "I needed to protect this invention."

"But now you're willing to give it to me freely."

I sighed. "You're right. I see you now as an ally. I know why you're mad at me. I understand. But I can't change it, and I can't kill you."

"Why not?" Her eyes were hard again.

"For the same reason you can't kill me. It's not in either of us. But we understand each other, I think. I've only killed in self-defense or for a cause. Never just on a whim."

She was quiet at that. I glanced at Butte. He was standing in the corridor with the engineering hatch at his back. It was open, and I had no doubt he would turn and bolt back into the chamber at the slightest provocation. "Come on, Robert," I said. "Let's talk."

"About what? Take me back to Trieste. Now."

"That's going to be hard since you sabotaged our SCAV drive."

A dead silence descended over us. Faces all around had gone blank.

"What are you saying?" Kat snapped. Her eyes flashed and her body tensed. She was sitting, but was ready to leap at the man and tear him apart with her bare hands.

I said, "Robert isn't telling us everything. It's why he's here right now."

"I thought he was here because you brought him. You called him to the seacar before you left."

"After the French sabotaged our city, yes. After the depressurization emergency."

"Why, exactly? You said it was because he wanted to help."

I shrugged. "I lied. He was fishing to find out what exactly I've been doing."

Butte was staring at me. His face was expressionless. "Why would you say that, Mac? I'm your deputy mayor."

"You're also a traitor, Robert. You betrayed Trieste, and you betrayed me. And you're going to be lucky to get out of this alive."

The hum of the thrusters vibrated the seacar as we churned slowly toward the tip of Africa.

With the French fleet directly behind us.

And a battle against an unknown enemy ahead.

INTERLUDE: THE LOOMING BATTLE

Location: The Atlantic Ocean,
                approaching the Mid-Atlantic Ridge
Latitude: 11° 12′ 50″ N
Longitude: 39° 45′ 10″ W
Depth: 150 meters
Vessel: USS *Impaler*
Time: 1305 hours

SCHRADER WAS STANDING ON THE BRIDGE of *Impaler*. Red lights illuminated consoles and crew stood at the ready. They were at battle stations. Their faces were tight, and no one spoke. Memories of The Battle a year ago still haunted them. Supercavitating ships and torpedoes churning across their path, impacts and imploding compartments. It had been a stressful fight, and though they had come out victorious, there had been many dead on both sides.

There was a large fleet with them. A glance at the sonar confirmed it; there were over a hundred warsubs to port and starboard traveling toward the submerged mountain range.

It was coming to a head, Schrader thought. Finally. They were going to achieve resolution, after all these months.

He glanced at Captain Heller.

For once and for all.

Heller turned to him, as if he could unconsciously feel his XO's gaze.

"Any word from Butte?" he asked.

Schrader glanced at the comms officer. "Nothing yet."

Heller swore. "What is he waiting for?"

"He must be occupied."

"That asshole. He went with McClusky so he could report on his activities. And the only thing we heard from him was that one brief transmission."

Schrader recalled it well. It had been a single set of coordinates along with a depth. It was in the rift of the Mid-Atlantic Ridge. Heller theorized that it was the location of McClusky's secret base, or wherever the man had been sending subs and had been spending his time during the past year. There was nothing at that location on the charts, however, so whatever it was . . . it was important.

Heller had set course for it immediately, calling every nearby USSF submarine to assist. They now had a veritable fleet steaming toward the location. Most USSF ships were currently in the Pacific dealing with The Iron Plains issue, but at least there was still the Atlantic Fleet nearby to help. If

McClusky was really there, then all hell was about to break loose.

And Heller would finally get his wish.

He would try to destroy the man who had tormented him for over a year.

It made Schrader shake his head. They had *won* The Battle. The USSF had occupied Trieste. They had even captured some of the supercavitating little ships, and they were in the process of making their own versions. USSF sailors wandered the halls and cabins of the undersea city. They controlled her economy. They made her decisions. They approved or vetoed City Council decisions. And yet, despite all that, still McClusky lived. Heller hated it, but there was nothing he could legally do. The mayor was like a cockroach that Heller just couldn't stomp on.

Until now.

Schrader glanced at the sonar again. They would be at the coordinates in just over two days.

The crew was running battle drills. They were preparing to drop their mobile troops and infantry and destroy whatever forces Truman McClusky had waiting for them.

Schrader was happy they had finally left Triestrian waters. He'd been hearing more and more about violent incidents in the city involving *Impaler*'s crew. Assaults. There was even rumor rape had occurred. Heller had taken care of the issues—or so he'd claimed. The reports made Schrader ill. He wanted the crew to be respectful over there. Professional. But now he doubted that that was the case. They were a reflection of their captain, he knew. And it disgusted Schrader.

Captain Heller's face was blank. His eyes were ice. But inside, Schrader knew, he was in a murderous rage. He wanted nothing more than to kill Truman McClusky and be done with these issues once and for all.

Schrader swallowed. He hoped that Heller wouldn't put his own vessel in peril in order to take the man down. That he wouldn't take unnecessary risks.

But then the XO shook his head inwardly. It was too much to ask. Heller simply wasn't thinking clearly. Butte's disappearance and the way McClusky had left Trieste behind so easily had pissed him off more. And then the French had further infuriated him with their display of force within US waters.

Rage consumed him now.

And he was going to keep going until either he or McClusky was dead.

PART FIVE:
THE STORM

CHAPTER
TWENTY-EIGHT

THE SEACAR WAS ROCKING IN THE currents as we powered toward the roughest waters in the world. Our depth was 200 meters, but even underwater swells collided and churned in a raging battle for supremacy. Differences in temperature between the oceans, varying salinities, and opposing densities caused unpredictable surges on all three axes. It was growing impossible to stand upright in the seacar.

Meg's eyes were concerned. "Mac, let me fix the SCAV drive."

"In a minute, Meg," I said in a soft voice. I was watching Butte; he was staring back, but he wasn't saying anything.

"I'm right, aren't I?" I asked him. "You're a traitor."

He shook his head and his expression was showing anger. "How dare you suggest that? I love the city."

"The only thing you love is your own life. You have no idea what it means to fight for your passion. To defend what you believe in."

"What are you talking about?"

Everyone was watching us now. No one spoke. The tension between Butte and me was electric. People were frozen, just waiting. . . .

"You know who killed Rafe Manuel, don't you?"

He frowned. "Rafe? I found out when you did, Mac. When those swimmers discovered his body in the sea grasses outside the city. It shocked me."

"Bullshit."

He stopped abruptly and threw his arms in the air. "Dammit, Mac. What are you implying?"

"I'm not implying anything. You know who killed the man. He was informing for me. He was going to *Impaler* and filling me in on what was happening over there. And when they found out, they killed him."

He was shaking his head. "But why would you think I had something to do with it?"

I paused, letting the thoughts crystallize in my mind. "Do you remember George Shanks?"

He blinked at the sudden change in topic. "Of course I do. He was leading the fight for independence. He's the reason the USSF occupied us."

"Shanks was my boss. Johnny and I were in Trieste City Intelligence for years together. George Shanks sent us out on missions. He loved the city. Despite his foolish arrogance, he cared about Trieste. He was passionate about protecting her."

"So?"

"He kept detailed files on the people of Trieste who objected to him."

The comment stopped Butte suddenly. He lowered himself to a chair, but I noted absently that he kept the engineering hatch to his back.

"He kept files on his own people?" His face showed horror.

"Cut the shit," I said. "He did it for a reason. He was scared of traitors. People like you."

"There you go again, accusing me. But you have no proof!"

"I have the files, Butte. And you're in them."

—••—

GEORGE SHANKS HAD KEPT DETAILED REPORTS on people who had objected to his plans. Anyone who had resisted his desire for independence was in those files.

On the day the USSF occupied Trieste, I had sent Johnny out on his mission to the Chinese undersea cities. I'd sent him in a supercavitating sub—as a gift to their leaders if they agreed to help—and then I'd had less than an hour before the invading forces had filled every important office and control area of the city.

After confronting Shanks in City Control following The Battle, I'd sprinted to his TCI office. By then he was long gone—I still didn't know what had happened to him, though rumor had it that a USSF soldier had arrested him after a bloody beating and taken him away. In his office were a variety of files, stored on paper so no one could hack into a system and copy data that could compromise Shanks or TCI. I destroyed everything I could before the USSF arrived. Anything about a former mission or a TCI operative, I burned. Anything about current operations, I added to the fire. And then I'd come across the folder. It wasn't big, but there were names in there. Names that I recognized. People I had worked with. Politicians. Workers in City Control. Farmers and miners and other citizens who had openly disagreed with George Shanks.

I hadn't paid much attention to it at the time. After all, it seemed a little too heavy-handed for me. There was nothing wrong with people having opinions, after all.

But Robert Butte's name had been there.

Robert Butte, who worked in City Control. He'd not only argued with Shanks on occasion about independence, but he'd outright threatened to turn him over to the USSF.

And when I'd read that file, I had known immediately what to do.

"You were in the files, Robert. You told Shanks repeatedly you didn't want independence. Why is that?"

He snorted. "What the hell are you talking about?"

I pointed at the drawer over my bunk. "I brought the folder with me. I grabbed it after the French decompressed the Living Module."

His eyes flicked to where I pointed, then back to me. "Fuck you."

"Swearing won't help you."

Kat said, "What does the file say, exactly?" Her eyes were wide, and her gaze was shifting back and forth from Butte to me.

"That he resented Shanks. That he fought him at every turn. Hell, I can understand that to a point. I hated that asshole too, after what he did to me. But no one can dispute that he loved Trieste."

"There must be more than that."

"There is." I sighed. "When the Chinese captured me, Shanks wanted to send a rescue attempt."

Beside me, Johnny bristled.

"And?" Meg prompted.

"Shanks asked for help. He approached Butte here. And what was your response, Robert?"

"What you're saying simply didn't happen." But his resolve was flickering. I could see it.

"You said that you didn't want the risk. The thing is, he wasn't even asking for anything too dangerous. He just wanted you to monitor Chinese frequencies."

I turned to the others. "You see, there were other Chinese spies in the city. We knew who they were, but we thought keeping them unaware that we knew was a better policy. That way, if they ever planned something major, we'd know."

"The enemy you know is less dangerous than the enemy you don't," Johnny said.

"Exactly," I replied. "So Shanks asked Butte here to keep tabs on them. After all, he worked in City Control in the communication section. Shanks felt it was important and might give us some information on when they could launch a rescue. But he couldn't just do something like that arbitrarily. After all, TCI was utterly secret. So he asked Butte for a favor. Butte turned him down cold, and not only that—" I looked at Butte "—you turned him over to Heller. You informed on him."

"Bullshit."

"Shanks knew. He suspected you after you refused to help. So he kept you under surveillance too, and he watched you meet with the USSF." I shrugged. "Eventually the Chinese released me in a prisoner exchange, but the damage had been done, Butte. The USSF knew about Shanks, and they knew about me when I tried to catch Johnny on the mission last year. Shanks didn't know to what extent you'd informed until I found out that the USSF knew everything. It stunned him. You single-handedly destroyed TCI, all because you refused to help when he needed it and you were upset that he even asked you."

Butte was glaring at me now. "You have no proof of any of this. It's ridiculous."

"I have the files. There are even dates and times of your meetings with the USSF from years ago."

"Bullshit," he repeated.

"But there's more," I said. My resolve was starting to break too. I was angry at the man. "I've been keeping tabs on you too, Butte."

He blinked. "But why? That doesn't make sense. I'm your deputy mayor for fuck's sake."

I looked at Johnny, who said, "The enemy you know is less dangerous than the enemy you don't."

Butte's eyes narrowed. "You gave me the job even though you thought I was a traitor?"

I smiled, but there was no warmth there. "Absolutely. And it worked."

"Why would you do that?"

Everyone was watching, their faces drawn and pale. They couldn't believe it.

"When we found Rafe Manuel, I gave Cliff Sim specific orders. Not to investigate the murder, but to investigate *you*. To follow you."

"That's ridiculous," he spat. "Why not find out who killed—"

"I already knew that. It was simple. He went to *Impaler*, Robert, and someone over there killed him. And the problem for you is, *you were with him.*"

—••—

"BULLSHIT," HE SAID, BUT IT JUST wasn't as vociferous as before.

"I know you went to *Impaler* with Rafe. I watched you board the transport. It's on security video. Cliff showed it to me. I also know you went back to *Impaler* a few days later, also on a transport, while I was visiting Ballard and Seascape. And I know that later you went out the moonpool and boarded a vehicle outside the city, just so we wouldn't see you. But Cliff was watching the whole time."

His face was frozen now. He couldn't say anything to dispute this.

"I knew you asked Sea Traffic Control about my heading when I went to The Ridge. Grant told me. He's with our movement, you see. I asked him what you wanted."

Still nothing.

I pressed on. "I know you were following Lazlow too, before he came with us to The Ridge. Why was that? Was it because Heller ordered you to? Was it because Heller wanted to know why Lazlow had come to Trieste?"

Nothing.

"I watched you on video follow Lazlow to the Docking Module. You saw him get into *SC-1.*"

"But why wouldn't you ask me . . ." he tried in vain.

"Because I already knew why you were doing it. But I had plans for you too, you see."

He was staring at the deck now, but he finally lifted his eyes to meet my gaze. "Why?"

"So I could play you. Don't you see that?" But then I swore. "But it backfired on me too. You gave up Maple and Bruce, didn't you? You were following them, I'm guessing. You told Heller they'd received orders from me, and the USSF gave them up to the French. *And now they're dead.*"

He shook his head and opened his mouth, but nothing came out.

"Two Triestrians dead, probably tortured for information, and it's because of you."

"You don't know that," he rasped.

"There were holes in their clothing. The French tortured them."

"No. . . ." He trailed off.

"You almost got me killed too, Robert."

"How's that?" Meg snapped. Her eyes flashed.

"When I went to visit Ballard and Seascape. Somehow the French knew I'd left. Someone had told them. They tried to take me out." I turned back to the deputy mayor. "Is that true? Did you turn me over then too?"

He didn't reply. He was just staring at us now.

But his eyes were wide and scared.

He was panicked.

"And finally," I said, "I know you sent a message from this seacar. Two nights ago. Right? Meg saw you."

He hesitated for a moment, then finally gave a quick jerk of his head. "I told Heller where I was."

"The coordinates to The Ridge?"

"Yes. I sent them."

"Which means the USSF will be on their way."

Meg rose to her feet. "Holy shit. Are you serious?"

"I am."

"But that means that the French and the USSF are going to meet right over our secret base in only forty-eight hours!"

"That's right, Meg," I said.

She was glaring at me. "You don't seem too surprised or upset by this little fact!"

I sighed. "I'm not. I've been expecting it, and not only that, I've used Butte here to arrange it for me. The war for Oceania started last year. We lost that battle, but the next one will occur in the Mid-Atlantic Ridge, thanks to Deputy Mayor Robert Butte here." I gestured at him. "Thanks to you, Heller is on his way, hopefully with a large fleet." I turned to Renée, sitting on the couch across from me. "And thanks to you, the French are following us, hoping to capture me, and they'll meet us there at precisely the same time."

I smiled. "And the upcoming battle is going to test our *Sword* class ships for the very first time. And if we win, it'll be the first step toward Oceania."

CHAPTER TWENTY-NINE

THEY WATCHED ME FOR LONG HEARTBEATS, eyes wide and jaws gaping.

Meg finally whispered into the silence, "Are you aware of what you've done?"

"Yes."

"You've arranged a massive battle right over our secret base. A base which won't exactly be so secret anymore!"

I shrugged. "We'll see. If any of them try to escape with knowledge of the facility, I guess we'll have to decide what to do. But I'm hoping that we won't have to worry about it."

She looked horrified. "Dammit Mac, these are two of the most advanced submarine fleets in the world! You're putting not just our lives on the line here, but the entire movement! If we die here, the independence movement might too." She frowned. Then, "Are you doing what dad did? Are you willingly killing yourself for this? To make martyrs out of all of us?"

I sighed. "Geez, Meg. You don't think much of me. I would never do that to us."

"Dad did it!"

Suddenly a rage that I hadn't known existed bubbled to the surface. "Well I'm not Dad, am I?"

My booming voice filled the seacar. Everyone was still staring at me.

I continued. "Dad had a plan and he carried it through. I disagreed with what he did, but it was a different time. They didn't have the technology we have today."

"So you think we'll just wipe through those forces easily?"

"No. But we're faster and we can dive deeper. We'll adjust our strategies. And we'll have them in a confined space. Inside the canyon." I paused and wondered if I should tell them the rest yet.

"Dammit Mac, all this time you've been arranging this, and you didn't let on!"

"I couldn't risk it. I knew about Butte here, and I had Cliff following him and studying his movements, and it helped, but I needed to use him to set up this battle."

"Well, you've done it. We have just over ninety vessels, but only fifty pilots, and they'll probably have a force of almost four hundred ships!"

I shrugged. "It has to happen sometime. It's why we built The Ridge. Now we're going to find out if we're up to the task."

Renée was horrified. "But McClusky, people are going die. Because of this quest for independence."

I nodded after a long moment. "I'm sure of it. French, American, Triestrian. There will be casualties."

Butte said, "Mac, I don't want any part of it."

I spun on him. "You made that choice when you participated in Rafe's murder!"

"What are you talking about? I didn't do it."

"You were there. You went over with him. You watched it happen. Who was it? Heller? Or was it you?" I stared at his feet. "It was someone over two hundred pounds with size thirteen boots. Do you fit that bill?"

"I didn't do it!"

"Then who did?" I stalked up to him and pressed my face close to his. "Did you watch Heller do it? Pound a man to death on a cold, steel deck? Stomp on his face and head until brain spilled out?"

"I—I—"

"But what's worse is that *you kept informing on us*. You kept giving him stuff."

He hesitated. "Just little things, Mac. Nothing major."

"Like Lazlow's identity?"

"No, I never said—"

"Stop lying!" I screamed. I was beginning to lose it, even though I knew I couldn't afford to. I had to keep my cool. I took a deep breath. "I know you did, because I have an informer on *Impaler*."

His face paled. "You have an—"

"Someone who cares more about life than you do."

Renée swore. "Look at you. You say you care so much about life, and yet you've triggered a massive battle. It's already started and the warsubs haven't even arrived."

"The USSF and the FSF are the aggressors. We're just defending ourselves. And I certainly don't crush people's heads under my boots."

"You attacked a French warsub last year. *My* sub."

"You were going to take me in. The French delegation was going to prevent me from getting the SCAV drive back."

She huffed and turned away from me. "You can rationalize all you want, but this war that's coming . . . people are going to *die* because of your actions."

I didn't answer that. I just turned back to Butte. "Now. The question is, what's going to happen with you?"

He frowned. "What do you mean? You said you'd take me back to Trieste."

I snorted. "To let you keep informing on us? That's not going to happen, Robert."

His eyes narrowed and he stood a little straighter. His fists clenched at his sides. "So what now then? You keep me captive in your facility? You think you're going to keep me there like a docile little lamb?" He gestured angrily at Renée. "I'm not going to be like her."

"That's not good news for you then, I'm sorry to say."

He glanced at Johnny and then back to me. "You're going to have to figure something out then, because I'm not going to be so easy to—"

In a flash I struck out at him. He was bigger than I was, but I hadn't given him warning. My strike sunk into his throat and he fell back with a gurgle. He lurched toward the hatch to engineering and I grabbed him to keep him from running.

And then he fought back.

———••———

HE WAS FASTER THAN I'D EXPECTED. I had assumed that his size would slow him, but I had to block one punch after another in quick succession, and they were coming from all sides, seemingly at once. I turned to present a smaller target to him and continued to block. His breathing was getting heavier, and I studied him closely. . . .

Then when he went to throw a right cross, he dipped his left arm too much. I blocked his right and swung with my own. . . .

And clipped his jaw.

He staggered back as though hit by a truck.

The blow had dazed him.

I took another step toward him and threw three more punches. He managed to block the first two, but my third was an uppercut and I tagged him with a swift snap to his lower jaw.

His teeth shut with a loud *click*.

Meg yelled, "Mac! Don't kill him!"

I ignored her as I grabbed him around the neck and shoved his head down toward the deck. Butte swore and spun to the side. He wrenched out from my grip with brute strength, then suddenly stood upright, and struck me in the chest with a high and fast front kick.

It pushed me back and knocked the wind out of me. I wheezed as he stepped toward me. He grinned. "Think you're going to play me the fool?"

"You've done that well enough yourself," I said between breaths. His kick had hurt me.

"There's no way you're going to take Trieste from the USSF."

I blocked three more kicks and swung with my own straight arm to his neck again. He ducked it and came up with a solid left hook which caught me under the eye. I lurched backward.

"I helped Heller because I know he offers the best future for Trieste."

"Servitude?" I threw a quick combo and landed two hits to either side of his face.

"Stability," he gasped. "He offers stability for Trieste."

"And meanwhile the people suffer. His sailors torment us and he takes our hard work and sends it away. We need to be working for ourselves. All underwater cities do."

He feinted with a punch and then delivered another one of those front kicks. It caught me again, this time in the gut. I fell back and grunted.

Johnny, who had been standing behind me, stepped up and caught me under the arms. "Want me to finish this, partner?" he asked.

"I've got it," I said.

I took a big step forward and blocked two more kicks: one aimed at my head, the other at my groin. I grabbed his foot and wrenched him toward me, pulling him off balance. Then I jumped and kicked at his face. My heel connected with a dull *slap* and he fell to his knees.

"You've been informing on us for a year," I said. I threw another series of punches, and he barely managed to block them. It was only a matter of time now. He was gasping for air and bleeding from his nose and a cut under his eye. My own eye felt swollen and sore; no doubt it'd be black in the morning.

My shoulder hurt too. I thrust the pain aside and focused on Robert Butte. He was on his knees. "What are you going to do? Kill me?"

"I'm going to make you suffer the way Rafe suffered. Make you feel the pain that he felt, while your boss kicked him in the head until he drowned in his own blood and his skull peeled apart and his brains dripped everywhere."

"I told you, I didn't—"

"Shut up!" I yelled. "You stood back and let Heller murder someone who loved Trieste!"

I swung harder and connected with his cheek. His mouth was hanging open now and bloody saliva dribbled out and spilled down his shirt and onto the deck.

"Mac!" Kat yelled. "Don't do it!"

I threw one more punch and then stopped and looked back at the others. Meg and Kat were watching with worry on their faces. Renée choked back a gasp. Then she shifted her gaze to me.

Johnny watched impassively. He agreed with what I'd done. Butte, however, looked like a nightmare. He was on all fours, wheezing, staring at the deck, blood and saliva and tears falling to the steel. I felt a pang of regret. I'd more or less walked him right into my trap, and he had now paid a painful price. There was more to come, however, but not torture. I had bigger plans for Butte than simply physical pain.

I straightened and took a step back. I said, "Don't worry. I'm not homicidal."

"Seems that way," Renée said from between clenched teeth.

"I'm done," I said.

Before me, Butte remained slumped to the deck.

"He got off easy," I said. "He's still breathing." Other nations would have executed such a man. He was a traitor, plain and simple. I didn't have any respect for him. "He's been informing on Trieste for years. He's the cause of the USSF occupation. He's exposed TCI to Heller. He had a chance to help rescue me, and he chose not to."

Meg came up and put her arm around my shoulders, guided me to the couch. "You seemed to lose it there," she said.

"Maybe I did." The seacar was rocking and I practically fell into the cushions. An image of Rafe came to me. Murdered because of a traitor. "But he deserved it."

"What are you going to do with him?" Kat asked. She too was helping me get adjusted. She had a cloth and was wiping the blood from my face.

"I'm going to make him fight," I said.

"Bullshit," he groaned, staring at the deck.

"He's going to step up and join us. Or he'll pay the ultimate price."

He finally lifted his head and made eye contact with me. His face was swollen and both eyes were turning black. "You want me to fight for you?

After what you just did?"

"You got off easy, Butte," I said. "You even got some good hits in on me. And I didn't kill you. So yes. You owe me now, and you're going to fight. It's the only way you'll ever see Trieste again. Do you understand?"

Renée said, "Is that what you're going to do with me?"

I turned to her. "What do you mean?"

"Hit me? Beat me up?"

I somehow gathered the energy to laugh. It made my ribs hurt. "No. I'm going to keep my promise to you. I'll let you take a *Sword* and go home. Take it to your people in France. See if any will join us. Explain what happened last year at the guyot." I took a breath. "And hope that they understand why I'm doing this."

—••—

WE PILOTED THE SHIP AROUND THE curve of Africa, through the buffeting and roiling currents that had killed many sailors and hulled many vessels over the past centuries.

The next day I watched the water outside the canopy as I held her course against the forces trying to push us this way or that, up or down, back or forward. At times our speed surged by a couple of clicks; at others, it felt as though we were flying into the wind.

The water was dirty, laden with debris and vegetation and junk from the surface world.

The seacar may not have been on autopilot, but I was; I couldn't stop thinking about what I had done to Robert Butte.

I had pretended to be his friend. I had brought him into the cadre of elite in Trieste, pretended to respect his opinions, only to crush his spirits and physically destroy him in front of the others. True, the match had been slightly closer than that, but the end had never really been in doubt. Despite his larger frame and mass, I was a trained operative. I had killed in hand-to-hand fighting before. I'd come up against some of the best trained fighters in the world, and I'd won every time. Or at least held my own.

He was sitting on the couch behind me, staring at the bulkhead. His face and knuckles were bruised and battered. He sported a split and fattened lip, two black eyes, and a cut over his left eyebrow.

Sullenly, he glanced at me, then turned away. He was ashamed. He probably also hated my guts.

But why was I so concerned about him? He had created this situation himself.

Gave himself up to the enemy. Betrayed the only thing he claimed to love.

And he'd watched Heller brutally kill Rafe Manuel, and he hadn't done anything to stop it.

He was complicit in the murder.

"What are you looking at?" he muttered at me. We were past the Cape of Good Hope now, steaming toward The Ridge, with the mass of FSF subs trailing behind us, neither gaining nor falling back. I was on the lookout for ships in front of us; after all, the French Indian Ocean fleet might have called for help. Someone to stop us. We had to be vigilant.

"I was just thinking," I said.

"About what? Humiliating me some more?"

"About killing you, actually."

He stared at me for long silent minutes, his bruised raccoon eyes boring deep into my psyche.

I had to look away.

"You really want to kill me?" he asked.

"For what happened to Rafe, I feel that way." I shuddered. "But I'm not going to do it. You got what you deserve. But it won't end there."

"So you *will* kill me."

I shook my head. "I'm not a monster. But you are a traitor. I'll give you one chance tomorrow."

He frowned, which was hard to make out because of all the swelling. "What do you mean?"

"If you fight with us. Defend The Ridge. Help us. It might change things."

He slumped back in the couch. "You think I'll fight Heller now? After what you did?"

"Tell me honestly, Robert, do you think you deserved what I did to you?"

He hesitated and couldn't respond.

I said, "Maybe you don't know how to answer that. But think about it hard. Because of you a man died a few weeks ago. But what about what you did years ago? You told Heller about Shanks. How many people died because of that? How many operatives did he and Benning catch? What happened to Shanks because of your actions? What about me? Tortured by the Chinese for four months while you could have offered a little assistance. Shanks asked you to monitor Chinese communications at Trieste, that's all."

"It was illegal," he nearly spat. "I had a problem with it."

"And meanwhile they tortured a loyal Triestrian."

He sighed. "Maybe you're right, but I thought what I was doing was noble."

"Not to me. And when I found out you were informing on me, I realized that I'd done the right thing making you deputy mayor. I was able to keep a really close eye on you."

He was quiet for a long time. I turned back to the controls and checked the gauges and readouts. Then he said, "I'm sorry, Mac. I know you are doing what you think is best for Trieste. Maybe it's because of the way people look at you . . ." He trailed off.

"What's that?"

"The people look at you with awe in their eyes. They don't just respect you, they *revere* you."

"Stop it."

"They worship you. Because of your dad."

"I said stop."

"Maybe I did what I did because I was looking for someone to treat me with just a little bit of the respect you get every single day without trying."

I snorted. "Did Heller give it to you?"

"At first. Years ago. But lately he's changed."

My forehead creased. "In what way?"

"He's consumed and driven by rage. I don't think he'll rest until he gets what he wants."

"Which is?"

He remained silent for a long, slow series of heartbeats. And then, "He wants to kill you, Mac. And he won't stop until he does. It's as simple as that. Tomorrow you're not just fighting for Trieste. You're fighting for your own life. He'll do everything in his power to kill you."

"And are you going to help us? Or do I have to chain you up in The Ridge and leave you to wonder if the dome will implode around you?"

He shook his head. "I don't know."

I stared at him before I turned away.

But I couldn't stop thinking about what he'd said.

And it wasn't the Heller bit that bothered me.

CHAPTER THIRTY

WE WERE ONLY AN HOUR FROM The Ridge when Meg finally gave up on the SCAV drive. Robert had shorted the computer control somehow and Meg had finally conceded that it simply could not be fixed until she had a couple more days to devote to it. There were two fleets en route, and she had to focus on other issues.

Namely, our defense and battle preparations.

Butte wasn't able to help. He had ripped wires out and cross circuited the system, causing an electrical surge, but he had no idea how to fix electronics. Only destroy them. Meg and Kat were both furious with him.

"But Mac," Meg said, hands on her hips and nostrils flaring. "We need this seacar in the battle. We can't *not* use her."

"I agree."

"But the SCAV drive. We won't be able to run in an emergency."

"Then we'll have to sink everyone in our path."

"Dammit Mac! This isn't funny!"

I shrugged. "What else can we do? It's either use *SCAV-1* and deal with it, or don't."

Her eyes narrowed. We were in the living area of the seacar, and Butte was sitting right next to us. He looked miserable with his black eyes and swollen face, but he didn't say a word.

He probably didn't want to attract the two women's wrath.

"Kat can pilot her," I said. "You and I can each take a *Sword* and we'll work together."

She frowned. "How will *that* work?"

"I guess we'll find out." I grinned, and a second later she followed suit. I turned to Butte. "So, are you going to help us?"

He frowned. It looked as though moving his facial features had hurt. "If I help you, Heller will kill me too."

"If you don't, you might wish you had died."

"Another threat, Mac?"

"No." I snorted. "You're going to wish you had helped though."

"Why?"

I left him stewing and didn't answer.

—••—

WE FINALLY APPROACHED THE DOME AND entered the docking area. I stared at the sonar screen; there was nothing there. After all, the enemy subs were out of our passive range, and the last time we'd sent an active pulse they'd been roughly seventy kilometers distant. Once we'd ducked down into the canyon, however, the rock walls had shielded our noise and rendered us practically invisible—until they entered the same rift, that is.

We had a bit of time.

We couldn't call ahead either, which made it difficult. We'd constructed the facility that way. No one could call in, no one could call out. There were also no fiber optic cable lines nearby, nor were there any junction boxes to receive and transmit calls. The nearest one was not only hundreds of kilometers away, but it was up on the shallower seafloor and well north of us up the rift.

Once we'd docked at The Ridge, we basically exploded from the seacar and raced to find the others. Jackson was already there on the dock, looking curious about the results of our mission, but Lancombe and Ng were busy somewhere else.

Meg and Kat sprinted away to help get the working *Swords* ready, and I quickly told Jackson what was going on. At first he looked shocked, then a cunning smile flashed across his face. "This should be good," he said.

I felt the same optimism as he. The *Swords* with the new acoustic deep diving system, along with the SCAV drive, would be a huge surprise to the USSF and FSF.

"We need to have a meeting with every single person here. Can you arrange that, Jackson?"

"Sure. We can meet near the line. That's where everyone is right now. Building ships."

"I'm afraid those ships won't be finished before the battle." I grunted as that thought crystallized in my mind, and the notion that within an hour we were going to be involved in a massive battle without much preparation. I wondered if perhaps I shouldn't have been so strict about isolating The Ridge and preventing all contact with its crew. I hoped it wouldn't end up being a fatal mistake. "Make it happen." He grinned and turned and then I said, "Wait a minute."

"What?"

I glanced around at the ships in the pool. "Do any of these *Sword*s have SCAV but not the Acoustic Pulse Drive? One that's also unarmed with an inoperative navigation and communication system?"

He looked pained. "Yes to the SCAV, but they all have nav systems and communications, Mac. We've been trying to get the APD installed in as many as we can, but—"

"Pick one and please unlock the console for me. Destroy its nav and comm system."

He frowned for a minute, then shook it off. He pointed at one in the pool. "There."

"Okay, go do it, thanks. Oh—which one can I use?"

He pointed at another, right next to *SC-1*. "You can take that one."

"Thanks." I looked at Renée, who was standing by my side. She was peering around, obviously not happy to be back in that place. "Are you ready?" I asked.

"For what?" She nearly spat the words at me.

"To leave."

She blinked. "What?"

"It's time for you to go, Renée. The battle is about to happen."

"The battle that you caused."

"No. I didn't cause it. I just arranged for it to occur at a certain place and time." Though I wished we'd had a few more months to prep. I shoved that thought aside. "Not the time, actually."

"You're not ready."

"Not fully. But I have plans that no one knows about."

"Such as?"

I shook my head. "Sorry. You are not part of this, unless you want to stay and find out."

"Not on your life."

I pointed to the *Sword* sitting in the pool Jackson had just debarked and sprinted from. "You can take that ship. Go now, before the fleets arrive."

She looked stunned. She didn't understand.

I said, "I told you I would. Right?"

"I thought maybe it was a lie."

"I meant it. Take the ship and see if you can convince French authorities."

"The incoming fleet?"

"No." I sighed. "Leave them. They're desperate to get their hands on me. There's no way you'll be able to convince them, and I need you to get this ship back to the French colonies."

"But I can—"

"When the battle starts, ships will be sunk. Do you want to lose the SCAV drive?"

She clearly looked conflicted. "But I can stop the fighting. Maybe."

"But I don't want you to."

"You hate the French that much?"

"It's not that." I exhaled. "I have to start dealing with this issue. We need to begin the fight, and it's about to happen here. I also want to take care of Heller, once and for all." I shuddered at my euphemism, but pressed on. "You have a choice to make. Stay and try to convince them to stop, or run and get this technology home."

Her eyes flashed.

"I'm giving you the tech you wanted a year ago. I just dropped it in your lap. Now go."

She stared at me for a long heartbeat but said nothing.

"What?" I asked in a quiet voice.

"Why do I feel like I should thank you? After everything you did to me?"

I said, "I'm sorry about firing on your ship last year, and about killing your crewman. I really am. I'm sorry about your career."

Her eyes softened and she lowered her gaze. "I don't think I've misjudged you, but—but—"

"Yes?"

She exhaled in a rush and then suddenly swore. "Dammit! Why do I feel this way? It's absurd! It's Stockholm Syndrome or something!"

I nearly laughed. "It's not Stockholm Syndrome. It's because you know that I'm part of something more important than what you're concerned with."

Her eyes bored into me. "I wanted to kill you. I *needed* to. I tried to. But then you saved my life in the canyon and held me prisoner here."

"I told you I'd let you go."

She almost said something, then stopped herself. Then she tried again and couldn't. Then she blew her breath out and swore, "Damn you, McClusky! You drive me mad!"

I grabbed her around the shoulders. "Just get out of here safely. Get the ship back to France." Then I hesitated. "But do me a favor?"

She snorted. "What?"

"Don't take it to the French mainland. Please take it to Cousteau." That was the largest of the three French undersea colonies.

She frowned. "Why?"

"They'll make better use of it than the French mainland government can. I've already contacted her mayor." I turned from her and marched away. "Good luck, Renée. I hope you can get away before the USSF traps you here."

I didn't look back.

——••——

BUTTE WAS RIGHT BEHIND ME AS I stalked toward the assembly line on the main deck, just through the travel tube and into the main dome.

It was a short walk, and our feet rang on the metal and echoed around us. Otherwise it was quiet, and I could feel the tension within me increasing with each step.

Within minutes the battle would begin.

The French and Americans against us Triestrians.

But it wouldn't be on their terms.

It would be on mine.

Behind me, Butte said, "Are you really going through with this, Mac?"

"Of course I am. What do you think this base is for?"

"I know why you built it. But is this struggle really that important?"

"My dad died for it."

"He was murdered for it. But is it worth it?"

I stopped. "The superpowers of the world oppress us. They steal our produce. They attack our people. You know it better than most. You've dealt with it, as deputy mayor."

He sighed. "Yes, but you're setting the city up for more hardships."

I raised my finger. "Only if we lose, Butte. Only if we lose. And we're not going to. We've lost too much already."

"How can you be so sure?"

"The new subs are going to shock them." And then I smiled inwardly. It was a monumental understatement.

—••—

I STEPPED INTO THE ASSEMBLY LINE area and stopped abruptly. There was a large group of men and women standing there, waiting. They didn't say a word. They were completely and utterly still, and their faces were frozen.

But they weren't angry or mad as I had feared.

They were happy.

They were smiling.

And then, as one, they began to applaud.

I said a few words to Jackson, and he gestured at Butte and took him away. He would put him in a cabin somewhere and lock him in. Temporarily, at least. I would deal with him after the battle, as long as we survived.

I turned to the group of people before me. They had been in this place for months, working every single day without a break. They had not been able to leave or even communicate with the outside colonies. They were completely and utterly secluded from the rest of the world, and I owed them everything. And, I knew with a hundred percent certainty, they were all loyal.

Off to the side I saw Meg and Kat, Lancombe and Ng, and Lazlow. They were smiling too, especially the older three. Lazlow looked more gaunt than ever, and I wondered how he had survived for this long. He'd thrown himself into the saturation environment and had been working nonstop now for weeks to get the *Swords* prepared and ready for battle. Last I'd heard, more than thirty seacars had his Acoustic Pulse Drive, which would represent the majority of our force today.

We only had slightly over fifty pilots, after all.

Pilots.

Funny, I thought of these fast-moving and highly maneuverable ships more as airplanes than as lumbering submarines.

And our force would shock the invaders.

—••—

"HELLO," I SAID TO THE ASSEMBLY before me. "I wanted to thank you for the work you've done over this past year." I looked around at the machines and the tools and equipment and the lines of partly-finished hulls still suspended by chains and surrounded by robotic riveters.

There was no reply. But still the smiles met my gaze.

"I said hello!"

"Hi, Mac!" came the enthusiastic reply.

"I'm sorry to spring this on you, but the battle is less than an hour away. The FSF and USSF ships hunting us are entering the rift right now. We need to get our *Swords* ready and armed and prepped for battle."

"The ships are mostly ready, Mac," Jackson yelled. He'd returned after putting the injured and sullen Butte in a cabin somewhere else in the base. "We just have to bring a few more out of the storage pond."

"You've done a fantastic job here," I said. "But it won't be easy." I sighed. "We're facing off against—give or take—four hundred warsubs."

There were some uneasy looks at that. Smiles faded and laughter subsided. The shared glances were not hard to decipher.

"Four hundred, Mac? Did I just hear you right?" a voice called out.

"You heard it." I studied them for long heartbeats. "But we have a few advantages. First, we have the SCAV drive. As best we can tell, they still don't have it."

"We won't be able to say that for long!"

"True. They definitely don't have Lazlow's pulse generator either. We're going to dive deeper than they can and evade them faster than they can imagine."

"We've been working on strategies," Lancombe said. "They won't know what hit 'em!"

His enthusiasm was obvious and I silently thanked him.

My gut was still quivering, but I couldn't let them see I was nervous.

I recalled images of my father, and tried my best to emulate his fervor.

"There's also something that no one else here knows yet."

"Mac, hurry up—we have to get ready!"

I searched the voice out and found her in the crowd. "I hear you, but let me finish." I found Johnny and singled him out. "You remember the command I gave the seacar's comm, Johnny?"

He looked confused for a second, then realization dawned on his features. "I remember, Mac."

"Tell them."

He nodded and turned to the group. "Earlier, while on our way here from Trieste, Mac programmed it to send the wrong information should someone make an attempt to signal the USSF."

Dead silence met the comment. No one understood.

"What he's saying," I interjected, "is that I ordered our computer to send incorrect coordinates should someone try to call for help."

I watched Meg closely, and her eyebrows lifted. "Wait a minute!" she cried. "Robert Butte made a transmission from *SC-1*. I was worried that he'd given us away."

"He tried to," I said. "But the thing is, I anticipated it. I already knew he was informing on us at Trieste."

The group was looking around, perplexed. They had watched Butte enter the dome, and had seen Jackson take him away. They still weren't aware why the deputy mayor was even there. They must have thought that he was with us.

Little did they know.

"What are you saying, Mac?"

I sighed. "You see, I knew that he was spying on me. And I wanted the battle to occur here, in the rift, confined between the two sheer rock walls, where no one else will know what's happening. But I didn't want anyone to discover our base, so I made sure that when Butte tried to give us away—which I knew he would—he would mistakenly give the wrong coordinates."

Their looks still showed confusion.

I added, "The computer substituted the real coordinates with fake ones. The USSF thinks this base is at a different location."

—••—

THE GROUP WAS SILENT FOR ONLY a split second and then it erupted into whoops and screams and applause.

"They're going to attack somewhere else!" was heard over and over.

I grinned.

And when the USSF struck, it would be at a location over twenty kilometers to the south.

Where the FSF was probably already gathering.

And then *we* would be the ones to surprise *them*.

CHAPTER
THIRTY-ONE

THE GROUP WENT BACK TO WORK preparing the seacars. They worked without speaking and their faces were stone. They were hopeful about the upcoming fight, but they were aware of what had happened at the last two battles: the short conflict thirty years ago between my father's movement and the USSF and CIA, and the Second Battle of Trieste last year, when many had died.

We had surrendered then, but it was to prepare for another day.

This day.

But it wasn't Shanks leading them this time, nor was it Mayor Janice Flint.

No Triestrian knew where those two were anymore, and that was telling enough. The Second Battle of Trieste had not been a success, but it had laid a strong foundation.

I glanced at the people around me. In the large pool, there were over fifty seacars ready to depart and forge twenty kilometers to the south. As soon as we exited the dome, in fact, we would probably pick up signals of the waiting fleets.

We would home in on them, moving in silence, and then strike. Then we'd dart into the dark depths, where they could not even travel.

Most of my people would be in his or her own seacar. We would abandon the facility until the battle had ended. We needed every single person on this.

I locked eyes with Johnny where he stood next to the seacar. He was ready,

I could see it in his face.

Meg was nervous. She had never been involved in anything like this. My news had shocked her, but she had smiled and given me a thumbs up when I checked on her a moment before.

"You should know by now that I'm not dumb," I'd said.

She'd thrown herself at me in a hug at that.

Kat and I had also shared a special, private moment. While the others were preparing the seacars, we'd embraced in *SC-1*.

"I can't believe what you did!" she said, throwing her arms around me.

I kissed her and held her tight. "Are you going to pilot *SC-1*? Or do you want your own *Sword*?"

She pulled back and her eyes flared. "How dare you even ask that! Of course I'm going to be in *SC-1*. I missed the last battle, I'm not going to miss this one!"

I grinned. Last year, she had been in Trieste listening to the fighting over the comm and watching it on the sonar displays instead of in the middle of the action.

She looked around at the interior of the seacar. "And this is my baby. I can't be in any other ship."

"But the SCAV is down."

She shrugged. "I guess I'll make do."

I stared at her for a long heartbeat. Of course I'd known it, and I gestured to the control cabin. I had to go and prepare my own ship. "Ready?"

—••—

I'D GIVEN STRICT ORDERS TO STAY off the comms and remain silent. No vessel was to enter SCAV or use the APD until the battle began.

Lancombe and Ng were inside *SC-1*. There was no way they were going to miss this either, or stay in The Ridge while the battle went on twenty kilometers away.

Meg was in her own vessel, and Johnny and I were in one together, along with Lazlow. Neither of us had trained with the Acoustic Pulse Drive, so Lazlow was going to demonstrate on the job, so to speak.

There was a small piece of paper on the pilot chair. I reached down and grabbed it with interest.

It was a note.

From Renée.

Scrawled on the scrap were a series of coordinates, with the following next to them: *Find the syntactic foam. Good Luck.*

I smiled.

She may have hated me, but at least I had turned her to our side, even if it was just a little bit.

Johnny was watching me silently. Then, "What is it?"

"A note from a friend. At least, I *think* it's from a friend."

He frowned but didn't say anything else.

I pulled the seacar outside the dome and waited for the others to collect nearby. There were fifty-three vessels in total, thirty with the deep-dive technology. Workers from The Ridge crewed fifty of them; Meg had one, Kat was in *SC-1*, and I was with Johnny in another. All but *SC-1* had functioning SCAV drives.

There was no one left in the facility except for Robert Butte, trapped in a small, bare cabin on the second deck, with only water to keep him alive until we could return.

And if no one did, he would die there, all alone.

The *Sword* Johnny and I were in was sparse inside. The interior bulkhead had weld marks tracing hull plate seams, there were rough and sharp edges, and there were zero comforts. It was bare bones, built for war and basic in every way except for the engineering of its drive systems, sonar, and weaponry. The underbelly of the console was fully exposed with wires hanging loose and computer chips exposed. I felt dismayed at that. *There better not be any flooding*, I thought.

When all fifty-three seacars were outside, we pointed south and powered through the rift toward the fleets that were searching for a secret base that was not there.

The twenty-three subs that did not have the acoustic generators slowly angled up and crested the ridge more than a kilometer over our heads. *SC-1* was with them. They used ballast only to rise, so they made little noise. They disappeared from sonar and continued the journey, on low power, cruising quietly southward.

I stared at the display, waiting.

Waiting for the FSF and USSF warsubs to appear.

We were only using passive sonar, which had a range of thirty clicks, but there was nothing on the screen.

I frowned and glanced at Johnny. It was weird. "Where are they?"

"Who knows?"

He chewed his lip and stared out the forward port. There was nothing to see, of course; it was too dark at this depth. I switched on the VID and the canopy turned blue. The canyon wall was to the port, and the twenty-nine seacars were just aft of us, projected in white.

Our force was a spear, and our seacar was the point.

When we were five kilometers from the false coordinates we had transmitted, I said to Johnny, "Prepare the SCAV drive." I pulled our throttle back to zero.

"Really? There's no one—"

"They're here. They're just silent. Waiting for us. Hovering there. Let's blow through them at full speed."

He frowned but flipped open the panel for the drive. The *Sword* was based on *SC-1*'s design, and the controls were nearly identical. The only real differences were the shape of the bow—for Lazlow's acoustic generator—and there was no carpet or comfortable couch in the living area. Lazlow was back there, in fact, sitting in a steel chair and readjusting every two minutes in order to protect his back.

Johnny pressed the buttons to initiate the fusion reactor in the engineering compartment, and it roared to life. The vibration through the ship was reassuring. It spoke of *power*. Real power.

Unbridled power.

"They would have heard that," I muttered.

"Initiating steam flow."

The roar at the aft of the ship began to grow, and the bubble at the bow formed within seconds. It began to stretch backward.

Soon we were at 400 kph and still accelerating.

I stared at the sonar display. "Come on, come on, come on. . . ."

Before us, white flashes began to appear as warsubs frantically tried to move out of our way.

"Ships!" Johnny cried. "Ten—no thirty—no . . . *hundreds*! There are hundreds of ships in the canyon!"

"Get ready," I said.

Red flashes appeared on the screen as one by one the enemy subs fired torpedoes at us.

I couldn't count how many there were.

Johnny said, "Mac! There are—"

I hauled back on the throttle and we crashed back into normal water. "SCAV off!" I barked. "Lazlow! We're activating the pulse generator!"

He was at my back in a second. "Take us down, and keep an eye on the depth."

I watched silently. The hull creaked as we plummeted. Our ballast was neutral, and I was using the diving planes to guide us on an angle downward.

The torpedoes were closing fast, however. They were less than 1000 meters in front of us.

I made our descent quickly. Nearly straight down.

Our depth increased.

We were at 3800 and falling—

"Now!" Lazlow said. His voice was ragged and his bony hand clutched my shoulder. "Keep your speed at fifty—that's key."

I leveled off and made our velocity fifty. I pressed a red button on the console at my side, and instantly a THRUM! THRUM! THRUM! started to echo through the ship.

The SCAV was off though, and the noise caught me off guard for an instant.

It was Lazlow's invention.

The high-powered generator in the bow vibrated the outer hull, and the outward-moving compression wave transferred its kinetic energy to the surrounding water. The water surrounding the bottle-nosed projection moved away in all directions from the generator, lessening the immense pressure. When the sound rebounded back to the seacar, we'd already moved forward into the next outward-moving pressure wave.

The vibrations were coursing through the vessel now, and I dipped the nose down once again.

Toward the dark depths, 6000 meters below.

On the sonar screen, the area around us—directly in the center of the scope—was a flare of white. It was pulsing and oscillating, broadcasting noise in all directions. It was a magnet calling out to all nearby vessels. It was the opposite of stealthy.

The depth gauge read 4300 and it was still climbing. . . .

I swallowed.

"Don't worry," Lazlow said. "She can take it now, better than you can imagine. There's less stress on the hull than when you were at 2500 meters!"

I shook my head at that. Amazing. Checking our speed, I concentrated on keeping it at fifty. "What happens if we go too fast?" I asked.

"You'll punch out of the low-pressure zone and back into high pressure."

I stared back at him. "Crush depth?"

"You won't even feel it." There was a grin on his skeletal face.

I snorted. "You seem excited by the notion."

"Death, no. Depth, yes."

Johnny suddenly blurted, "The torpedoes are coming right at us!"

I glanced back at the sonar. Behind us, the rest of our forces in the rift had backed off and were waiting to see what happened. Before us, the red lines marking torpedoes were all angling toward us, on a downward path.

It made me smile, for I knew what was going to happen.

If a ship couldn't make deeper than 4400, neither could a torpedo.

"Read out our depth for us, Johnny."

"Forty-four fifty. Forty-four seventy . . ."

He continued to call out the depths as I made our angle even steeper. Soon he was calling out numbers in the five thousands.

I said, "Careful, Lazlow. You're not belted in."

He was leaning against the back of my chair now, his full weight on it. "I'm okay," he said.

It made me frown, but I said nothing.

"Look!" Johnny yelled.

One by one, on the sonar, the red streaks began to wink out. There had been *hundreds* of them only seconds ago. Now they were disappearing faster than we could count.

"What depth are they at?" I asked.

"Nearly 5000 meters."

"They couldn't handle it," I said. "They imploded." And the explosives had failed to detonate.

The missiles were now chunks of steel, pushed into odd, twisted shapes, falling like metal rocks into the deep ocean below us.

I laughed.

—••—

BEHIND ME, LAZLOW HAD A GRIN on his face. The drive was pulsing the ship around us—the rhythmic hum was actually quite pleasant, and not even that loud—and we were powering through water deeper than I ever had before.

"It's amazing," I said. "Lazlow, I didn't quite believe it would work, until now. Well done."

"All the tests have succeeded over the past few weeks," he said, the lines in his forehead deeper than ever. "Why would you doubt it?"

I shrugged. "I guess I had to see it to believe it. It's . . ." I trailed off.

"You're welcome," he said finally.

I turned my attention back to the sonar. "Time to engage that fleet." I triggered the comm system, audio only. "Attention USSF and FSF forces. You have fired on our seacar without provocation. Care to explain?" As I said it, I leveled off and maintained a depth of nearly 6000 meters.

The reply was instant. "McClusky! This is Captain Heller of USS *Impaler*."

"What are you doing here?" I asked.

"I'm here to arrest you for treason and conspiring to betray us to the French."

I frowned. "Explain."

"Why should I? The French attacked Trieste and depressurized an entire living module."

"In an attempt to kill me."

"Well they put thousands of lives at risk. Then they threatened me while you ran away!"

"So I understand why you're angry at the French—I am too. They've been trying to kill me for weeks. But why are you firing on me?" I tried an innocent tone.

"You've been conspiring with them and the Chinese and I want to know what is going on! What are these vessels you have with you? All the noise? How are you able to dive so deep?"

"You'd like to know, wouldn't you?" I adjusted my course slightly, turning to stay under the USSF forces. My sonar was labeling the ships as it intercepted their signatures. The French ones were located in the rift a kilometer south of Heller's group.

I nearly gasped out loud when I saw the sheer number of vessels in the canyon. Granted, it was ten kilometers wide, but there were 387 warsubs there, in two massive, distinct groupings.

"McClusky!" Heller screamed. "You are to lower your speed, ascend to our depth, and surrender your vessel. Order your other ships to turn around."

"Sorry, Heller. Can't do it."

There was a long pause, then, "You've been building up a force preparing for this, haven't you? Where did these ships come from?"

"I don't know," I said. I knew it would anger him.

The comm suddenly crackled and another voice came on the line. "This is Captain Laroche of the FSF. Truman McClusky of Trieste, it's our intention to either take you in for the murder of French military and government officials or kill you in this canyon. The waters here will be your grave."

"How poetic."

"You will not joke with me, McClusky."

"You've been trying to kill me now for weeks. All that's happened is more French sailors are dead."

"So you admit to killing our people in the Gulf of Mexico?"

"After you detonated a nuclear device in US waters? Yes, I guess I admit to it."

Heller bellowed, "You have no right to use such weapons in our territory!"

"We did it to capture the man you also want. We were justified. He is a renegade, a rogue, an intelligence operative who knowingly killed our people to keep technology out of our hands."

"Technology that the Chinese stole from us," I said.

"Regardless." The voice had changed slightly—it was contrite, and I could almost see the shrug from the other end of the audio transmission.

"So you think stealing is okay?"

"It's what you were trying to do at our base near the Seychelles, was it not?"

"I don't know what you're talking about."

"McClusky!" Heller said. "You're operating TCI again, aren't you? The two Triestrians the French killed, they were your people?"

I laughed. "Don't feign ignorance, Heller. You killed our man Rafe Manuel. *You* should be on trial for murder! You killed him because he wouldn't tell you what you wanted, isn't that right? And you also used Butte to spy on me. But I know about you now, Heller. And there's no way you're going to get out of this. You tried to use that information to trap us here. Instead, we've *trapped* you here."

He paused. Finally, "What are you talking about?"

"I guess you'll find out."

The French captain: "I'm not going to say this again. Surrender or die."

"Not a chance."

"So be it." The French signal clicked off.

"What are you going to do, Heller? Are you going to keep firing on me? Your weapons don't have much effect this deep."

"Our mines might."

I glanced back at Lazlow, and he screwed up his face. "It's possible," he said. "Spheres are structurally more sound than cylinders."

"I guess we'll have to see," I said. I flicked the mic off, and Heller swore profusely.

"That fucking asshole! He's signed his own death—" And then his voice cut off too.

I studied the sonar for a heartbeat. *Impaler* was the largest ship there. The rest were *Houstons, Cyclones, Typhoons,* and there was one *Matrix* and one *Trident.* He had ninety-eight warsubs, 3000 meters over our heads.

I pulled back on the yoke and pitched our nose up.

Behind me, Lazlow stumbled back and barely got into his chair before he tumbled into the rear bulkhead.

"Uh, Mac," Johnny said.

"Don't worry." I kept a close eye on our depth. "Get the SCAV ready and prepare a torpedo. Impact detonation."

"Got it."

When we hit 4000 meters depth I rammed the SCAV throttle to full and cut the acoustic generator. I blew ballast and we started to soar up from the depths. We left a tremendous wake behind us—a cone of steam churning up from the depths, and we were the tiny metal seacar balancing on its tip, pointed up and surging toward the mass of enemy warsubs.

"I'm aiming for *Impaler*."

"Got it. What about the French?"

"They're a kilometer away still. Let's worry about Heller first." I triggered the comm and sent a single order to our *Swords*. "Go." I turned to Johnny. "Fire the torpedo."

It was a SCAV weapon. We shot up from the depths, and at our bow a hatch slid open and the missile rocketed out. Its speed was so great that the bubble formed around it nearly instantly, lowering its friction, and it headed straight for *Impaler*'s underbelly just above us.

The warsub was banking hard to starboard and it was launching a multitude of countermeasures.

"You have no right to fire on us!" Heller said, back on the comm.

I ignored him.

The sonar screen flared white all around, but I kept my eye on the VID screen and the ship directly above us.

The torpedo would ignore the countermeasures, for I had chosen IMPACT detonation. Not HOMING. The drawback was that you had to make sure your aim was perfect, otherwise it would keep on powering through the water, never deviating from its straight-line course.

Our bow was steady and *Impaler* was directly in our crosshairs.

The torpedo lanced out, shrinking rapidly.

And then it crashed into the warsub and flared into a ball of white and crimson fire. The sea around it flash-boiled to steam and the crushing waters pounded back into the cavity.

Direct hit, to *Impaler*'s lower decks.

Air expanded out of the hole and the ship shuddered massively from the impact. The sound of the detonation hit us and we were so close that even the compression wave shook the *Sword* we were in.

The sonar screen turned white from all the noise.

Everywhere around us, *Swords* were turning on their sound generators and diving deep, torpedoes were *everywhere*, mines were dropping, and explosions were pounding the waters and their echoes were rebounding off the cliff walls on either side of the canyon.

Bubbles churned and rose to the surface, mixed with debris and bodies and oil and blood.

The battle had begun.

CHAPTER
THIRTY-TWO

"EVERYONE, FIRE AT WILL!" I CALLED. "Stay deep to avoid their torpedoes—their weapons can't go below 5000 meters."

"Got it," came an anonymous response. It might have been Jackson, but I couldn't tell for sure.

The thud of explosions reverberated through the hull of the *Sword*, and I glanced around to find their source. Our own fleet of vessels had already fired and their torpedoes were hitting USSF ships. Some of the torpedoes were SCAV weapons, and had quickly accelerated to 1000 kph before slamming into large warsubs, such as *Impaler*.

Heller's sub was limping already, trailing debris which fell into the depths, and a stream of bubbles rose to the surface high above.

But she wasn't out of the fight yet; torpedo after torpedo shot from her tubes, along with countermeasures and mines.

The ocean around us was full of weapons and ships and debris and bubbles; it was almost impossible to find a place to move without ramming into something. There were just so many ships around.

"Everyone go deep now, while you can," I said.

The response was instantaneous; *Sword*s plunged and flared into white pulsing hearts on my sonar display.

"Do it," I said to Johnny, and he punched on the pulse drive while I pushed the stick forward and made our velocity fifty. "I hate going this slow."

Torpedoes were crisscrossing the scene from port to starboard and starboard to port, on random and haphazard angles across the canopy above me. Large warsubs continued to take impacts, and countermeasures were churning everywhere.

"I don't think they've hit a single one of our vessels!" Johnny said.

I did a quick survey of our ships on the screen. It was hard with all the noise interference and the throbbing of the pulse drives, but I thought he might be correct. "Let's keep it up."

Our *Swords* were now cruising at the 6000 meter mark and torpedo after torpedo angling down at us simply disappeared from our scopes as the pressure wormed its deadly tendrils into the seams and casing flaws and circuitry of the missiles as they punched downward into the depths.

Not one exploded.

Mines were falling now too, and I watched as these worked their way downward. They appeared as white stars on the VID, leaving flickering and fading trails as they plunged.

They passed the five-click depth plane and continued to fall.

"Watch those mines," a voice called. "Keep an eye out."

The good thing about being so deep, where the water was a little less crowded, was that we could predict the path a mine might take and avoid it easily enough.

Suddenly a torpedo appeared on my screen from far above. It had lanced out from the French fleet, and it was not headed at us. It was powering toward the USSF forces.

"A USSF boat hit a French sub a minute or two ago," Johnny said. "Now those two fleets are going to go at it."

Sure enough, a barrage of American missiles emerged from numerous warsubs, all headed south toward the French.

"If they can't hit us, they're determined to hit *someone*," I said.

The torpedoes were a mix of SCAV and conventional weapons, the former accelerating quickly and darting deep into the French forces before detonating. Several explosions lit the area and one warsub immediately imploded, a shock of bubbles and debris crushing in on itself before the churning maelstrom began to float upward and a dead wreck of a hull spiraled downward. It collided with the nearby canyon wall in its death throes.

The USSF forces were ignoring us and facing off against the FSF.

I hit the comm. "Everyone, make your angle positive and prepare a batch of homers. Get ready to fire."

"We can't fire from this depth though," came a reply.

We were circling the battle, below it, maintaining a constant speed of fifty kph.

"I know. We're going to aim upward and fire simultaneously at 4000 meters. As soon as the weapons are away, use the pulse drive and go deep again."

It would be a wall of steel and explosives ascending from the deeps.

I couldn't help but feel the thrill of excitement.

Our plan was working.

—••—

A GLANCE AT LAZLOW SHOWED HE was feeling the same thing. He was finally seeing his invention in action; his eighty years of life had culminated in this. His eyes were dancing as he traced the sight of the explosions in the canopy and on the sonar screen, and as the distant sound of explosions vibrated our vessel.

His life had turned sideways two decades ago, and now he had nothing on the surface to return to.

This life was his home now, and he had dedicated himself to seeing this through.

I spun back to the controls and checked our depth.

It was time.

"Fire, Johnny."

We shot a homer nearly straight up and then curved around and activated the pulse drive. The distinctive thrum of sonic pulses came to us again, and I welcomed the sound. I found them comforting and calming.

Fifty torpedoes were on their way up to the fleet above us. Some of our ships had fired multiple weapons.

But before there was an impact, a *Sword* ventured too close to a slowly falling mine. It must have had a proximity fuse, for the explosion occurred while the ship was still twenty meters away, but it was enough. The detonation was sizable and the concussion waves pounded the little seacar. A wrinkle traced across the top of the hull, just aft of the canopy—

And in the blink of an eye the vessel folded in half, the central portion of the fuselage warping inward, the bow and canopy bulging outward, and a bubble of air burst out and floated serenely upward.

Inward... outward... upward...

I swallowed.

The ship crumpled in on itself and it tipped over, heading down. Strangely enough, however, the two thruster pods remained intact, and the screws turning under battery power corkscrewed the wreckage around as it plummeted into the depths.

An image of *Scorpion* came to me right then—pictures of the dead ship following its discovery. The engine compartment had been *shoved* fifty feet forward into the rest of the sub by the power of the imploding water.

I turned back to the battle and stared intently at the screens, watching every single detail.

A shiver traced down my spine.

—••—

OUR WALL OF TORPEDOES SOARED UPWARD from the depths and multiple weapons detonated early upon hitting a layer of churning and bubbling countermeasures. The explosions rocked the entire area, steaming layers of frothing foam rose from the blasts, and water pounded into the naked cavities to fill the voids. Concussion waves rocked outwards. But many torpedoes passed through the line undeterred, and just beyond, they began to impact the warsubs.

There had been just under a hundred USSF ships engaged at the start of the battle, but now there was half that number. Some were powering away slowly, limping along, listing to port or starboard and trailing streams of bubbles from gashes and holes in their hulls.

Some were hovering silently, seemingly dead, without any maneuverability or power. They were sitting ducks.

And some were sinking through the line of countermeasures, toward crush depth, listing aftward or forward as they took on water and their crews sank to their deaths.

I shuddered when I saw that. The barrage of French torpedoes combined with our own weapons had damaged some warsubs beyond their engineering capabilities.

Our flood of torpedoes finally impacted their warsubs, and there was a wall of flowering eruptions flaring across our sonar.

"Holy shit," Johnny mumbled, watching the screen. "I've never seen anything like that."

Even The Battle last year had not shown that kind of success. We had just hit thirty targets simultaneously.

And we had only lost one.

A point of light appeared on the sonar, heading straight for us. The VID system projected it on the canopy; it was a *Houston* class, or a *Hunter-Killer*. Small and fast and highly maneuverable. I heeled us around and prepared to go deep. That type of warsub could exceed our conventional speed, however, and I had noticed it too late. It was at seventy-eight kph and arcing down at us.

Our depth was just over 3000 and I pushed the stick away from me and punched the SCAV drive. "Hold on to something," I said.

The roar built and the steam started to churn out of our aft vents, but it was going to be too late. He had us dead to rights, and in his sights. It took too long to build up to supercavitation.

Our depth was 3300. . . .

And something occurred to me.

That class of ship's max depth was only 2100 meters, and he was already well past it.

I spun our *Sword* around and curved back up and toward it.

"Uh, Mac . . ." Johnny said. "What the hell—"

"Hold on!"

Our SCAV was on full as we moved toward the *Hunter-Killer*.

His torpedo door was open.

I could almost see the nose of the weapon nestled in the tube, ready to fire and kill us all.

And end the movement.

I pointed the ship closer to it, then heeled around and yanked the throttle back close to zero.

He didn't want to fire and risk damaging his own ship in the explosion, as Captain Renée Féroce had experienced with me a year earlier. She had regretted not acting.

"What are you doing?" Johnny asked.

"I've got it," I said, calm.

We were so close now I didn't think he'd fire. I pushed the vessel just a bit closer—we were only *meters* apart now—and I thumbed the Acoustic Pulse Drive on.

Lazlow said, "We're not deep enough—"

"Don't worry about it!"

Our bow generator started to pulse and throb and compression waves began to resonate outward from it.

I spun the yoke to the port, just slightly, and our bow nearly touched the outer hull of the other vessel.

The compression waves continued to vibrate out. . . .

In the ocean depths, water pressure was always working to expose the slightest flaw in our fragile vessels. Our ships were always just *barely* able to withstand the deadly environment.

And in a blink the ship's hull, only a meter beside our bow, imploded.

A seam opened in the *Hunter-Killer* and water flooded in, turning everybody within to bloody pulp in an instant.

I imagined I saw the flash of fear in the sub driver's eyes as he realized what I was doing, but of course it was not possible. Our VID couldn't show that kind of detail.

The thought would haunt my dreams.

But there'd be time for that later.

The ship crunched into a ball before our eyes and tumbled downward and out of sight; bloody bubbles rose before us to the surface.

Johnny's expression was shock. "Oh my—" And then he shook his head. "Wow."

The acoustic drive was actually an effective weapon. At certain depths, that is. It had simulated a higher pressure and taken that *Hunter-Killer* straight past crush depth in an instant.

Explosions continued to rock the sea around us. I wondered absently what the surface far above resembled at that moment. We were too deep for explosions to ripple the water up top, but the flood of air and vaporized water would be churning the surface like a storm.

Johnny pointed at the sonar. The French forces had pressed their attack. There were over two hundred of them still, and they were coming.

—••—

OUR COMM SYSTEM BLINKED AND I pushed the button to receive audio only.

"McClusky!" Heller said. "What the hell is this?"

I touched the *transmit* option. "What's wrong, Captain? Can't take the heat? This is something you caused."

"What are you talking about?"

"You chose to occupy us. You chose to steal our produce and take our ore and our fish without proper payment. Now *this* is your payment."

"You are terrorists!"

"We're Triestrian, Heller. American citizens. And it's about time you realized it." I had no ill-will for the people topside. They hadn't asked for us to be treated the way we were.

But the USSF had harmed us. They had killed us. They had repressed us. They exploited us and raped us and hurt our citizens.

They'd killed my father.

And I didn't feel sorry for Heller.

Not one bit.

"You killed Rafe Manuel," I said. "*You* did that, didn't you, you son of a bitch?"

"He was a traitor."

"He was a patriot."

"He was lying to me!" Heller was screaming now, and Johnny painted me with a worried look.

I said, "He was following my orders, and you killed him."

He hesitated, then said, "So what? Why do you care? He was a casualty of war."

I said in a soft voice, "He wasn't the only informer, Heller."

"What? What's that?" A series of nearby explosions muffled his voice. I thought I could hear water spraying into the command deck of his warsub.

"I know about Robert Butte. I fed him false information, or no information at all. I used him to bring you here."

There was no reply.

"And there's more," I added. "I have an informant on your ship still. Someone who's been giving me information about *you*."

"Bullshit!"

"It's true." I steered us deeper and kept an eye on the scope to make sure there were no warsubs or weapons nearby. Then I said to Johnny, "Get another torpedo ready. We'll ascend and fire again."

"Got it," came the crisp reply.

I said, "Heller, he's on your ship, *right now*." I cut the signal.

Let him stew on that.

Johnny said, "Is that true?"

I nodded. "He's given me some good intel. He's helped me over the past year. Told me what Heller was doing and how much he knew. I used Butte to feed him information, then got my informant to tell me what was getting through, and if Butte was really a traitor. He confirmed it, sadly."

"And who is it?"

I sighed. "A friend. Someone who might not make it through this battle." I put my finger on the scope and *Impaler* zoomed on the display. She was badly damaged, taking on water, barely moving, and there were multiple holes in her hull.

She was foundering.

———••———

"FIRE," I SAID.

Johnny pressed the button and another torpedo shot from our bow, trailing a stream of cavitating bubbles. "Away," he said.

I keyed the comm for my sister. "Meg, are you there?"

"I'm here!" came the instant reply.

It brought a smile to my face. A year earlier she'd been totally against this type of thing. Against war. Against the fight for independence. Against what our father had wanted.

What he'd wanted more than life itself, apparently.

But now Meg was enthralled with the activity, with the undersea action, with the realization that each day brought independence closer for us.

"Be careful here," I said to her. "This is getting really dangerous. Stay deep."

"Tru, aren't these *Swords* incredible? The Acoustic Pulse Drive . . . it's *magnificent*!"

"It is. Take care of yourself and stay away from those warsubs."

"I have four torpedoes left. I'm taking my time with them!"

Other calls were coming in and I listened silently to the battle as we evaded missiles, dove deep, ascended, fired, then dove deep again. There was a barrage of overlapping signals, all workers from The Ridge, some men, some women, some I recognized, and some I didn't.

"Jane—that *Matrix* is almost out! Take another shot at her!"

"Got it!"

"That rock outcropping over the *Typhoon*! It's ready to go. Can someone fire on it?"

"Just did."

"It's crumbling onto the ship! The damage is— Whoa! The *Typhoon* just imploded, everyone! The rock must have ruptured the hull!"

"Watch out for that homer! It's a SCAV!"

"Get out of there!"

"That *Trident* is trying to use his grapples for fuck's sake! Does he think we're slow-moving or something? I'm taking him—"

"Another USSF warsub just left the battle!"

"Another just imploded!"

It continued for another twenty minutes. We'd lost eight more *Swords*, each one hit by nearby concussions from explosions that might have been avoidable. There were just so many ships, so much debris, so many countermeasures, and white blotches from our own ships performing deep dives past conventional crush depth crowded the scope. Sometimes collisions with weapons happened accidentally.

"Is there a way to filter out our own ships' noise?" I yelled back at Lazlow. "From our own fleet? To clear this scope?"

He was frowning. "I see the problem. Perhaps. I'll have to think about—"

A massive concussion hit our vessel and water began to spray in from the airlock hatch.

Johnny turned and swore. "The lock is flooded. Outer hatch might be gone."

An image of the flooded seacar near the Seychelles came to me, with my two operatives dead in the command seats while fish fed on their rotting flesh.

It made me want to retch.

I didn't want to end up like that.

Then our screws stopped turning.

And our nose tipped down.

We were plunging into the deeps.

CHAPTER
THIRTY-THREE

"TURN ON THE SCAV," I SHOUTED over the spraying water. Lazlow was behind me, trying to see what he could do, but he was too frail to do much more than maintain his balance in the wildly-rocking seacar.

"It's out," Johnny said.

Our nose was angled down, we were taking on water, we were negatively buoyant, and our screws were not turning.

The hull creaked and popped ominously, and I stared at the depth readout. We were at 4200 meters and descending fast.

"Oh, shit!" We were nearing crush depth.

I punched the acoustic pulse and thankfully the generator started smoothly and its throbbing filled the cabin. There was an instant and jarring groan ratcheting through the vessel.

Lazlow called from the back, "Mac! You have to be going fifty for that to work! We have to be able to move *into* the low-pressure cone that the sound waves create!"

He was right. We were only going thirty. Otherwise the compression waves would rebound and increase pressure on our hull. We had to be out of their way when they turned back on us.

I pushed the yoke forward.

"What are you doing?" Johnny asked.

"We need speed to stay this deep, right?"

He looked horrified. "But you're diving deeper!"

"We need the speed," I repeated. Still, we didn't have enough, for the hull was creaking and cracking each second. I slammed the ballast to take on more water, making us heavier.

Increasing our speed even more.

Pointed straight at the ocean bottom, nearly two kilometers below.

We plummeted down now, our thrusters and SCAV out, and ballast tanks full.

—••—

WE WERE AT NINETY DEGREES STRAIGHT down. Our seacar was flooding and we were beyond crush depth. Only the acoustic generators were keeping us alive at this point, but our drive systems had no power.

When we hit bottom, either the collision with rock would implode us, or the sudden cessation of the acoustic pulses would.

We had 1800 meters to go, and we were traveling at fifty-three kph. That meant we were going 883 meters per minute.

We had just over two minutes of life remaining.

Lazlow was lying on the back of my chair, and the belt was holding me in place; my head hung toward the canopy in front of us.

The big problem right now was that we couldn't get back to the engine compartment to see what was wrong—it was straight up, behind us!

"I'm going to level the seacar for just a second or two."

Lazlow screamed, "But we need the speed!"

"We're not going to wait like this for two minutes to die!" I swallowed. "I'll right the sub and Johnny, you run back to engineering. Lazlow, you get up here and get your head under the controls." The console underbelly was completely exposed. The flooding in the seacar had splashed water down into the control cabin and it was rapidly filling.

Water and computer circuitry didn't mix.

"We're only going to get one shot at this!" I said.

"What should I try to repair—SCAV or thrusters?"

I snorted. "Doesn't matter. You see what the problem is, you decide." I took a deep breath. "NOW GO!"

I hauled on the yoke and the ship labored to right itself. We started to pull up from the vertical fall and the water in the control cabin began shifting back to engineering. Johnny lurched to his feet and tried his best to move backward, but it was still too steep a climb.

"Hurry!" he yelled.

I pulled with everything I had and angled the stern planes to tilt the aft section of the seacar down, to level us. Then I hit the ballast controls and cleared the nose tanks of water, but it was laborious due to the depth.

Lazlow cried out and pointed at the displays.

Our speed was decreasing!

Fifty-two!

Fifty!

Forty-nine!

Our hull began to pop and groan. New water fountains started, this time from the viewports in the living area.

Oh, shit.

The sounds around us were chaotic. Water spraying in, water sloshing backward toward engineering, the acoustic generators pulsing rhythmically, all three of us swearing profusely—

Johnny finally managed to stand and stumbled back to engineering, weaving from side to side as he did so. Finally he called out, "I'm here!"

—and I pushed forward on the yoke and flooded the bow tanks simultaneously.

We were vertical again, and speed was steady back at fifty-three.

My stomach was in knots.

900 meters.

One minute of life left.

———••———

ABOVE US THE BATTLE RAGED. FRENCH and USSF forces were now openly firing at one another, and the FSF had the advantage because of the damage we'd already inflicted on Heller and his group of warsubs. White explosions danced around the sonar screen—they were churning countermeasures and falling rocks from impacts with the sheer canyon wall to our east.

Lazlow's head was buried in the console, water mounting around him, and he was struggling to trace the circuits to the SCAV drive.

The ship still had power, after all. Why were the propulsion systems out?

Johnny's voice called over the racket, "The thrusters *are* turning!"

"What?" That didn't make sense. Parts of our console were dark, however, so we may have had some RPM—I just couldn't tell.

"The screws are fucked! The concussion wave must have bent the blades! We have to fix the SCAV!"

We had only seconds remaining.

"Uh, Lazlow," I said, staring at the VID. The rough rock of the bottom was on the screen, and we were approaching a house-sized boulder. "You have twenty seconds."

"It's on me, is it?" he asked.

His stick-like legs twisted out from the console and water washed around his torso. He must be freezing, I thought. The water was only four degrees Celsius at this depth.

"Unless Johnny can find the problem back there," I said.

I thought of Dad on that last night before he died. The argument we'd had. Why he hadn't told me what he'd been planning. Why he hadn't at least hugged me, or looked at me, or even given me a smile and told me that he loved me.

He'd died leaving so many things unsaid between us, and the thing that haunted me was, *he'd had a chance*. He could have said it to me, but he chose not to.

He'd just let me go on, for thirty years, without knowing the truth.

It made me angry.

Lazlow said abruptly, "Loose wires!"

Before I could react, the SCAV panel lit up.

I didn't even think. I punched the reactor control and started the water flow through the reactor.

But I couldn't hear the roar from the engine compartment. There was too much other noise.

"You did it Lazlow!" I said. I hauled up on the yoke, but it was difficult to move. "Blowing ballast!"

The boulder was only fifty meters in front of us now, and there were also plumes of ash rising from the tectonically active seafloor—

I hauled on the yoke but I was leaning down *into it*—we were still vertical.

It had been easier earlier, but now there was more water in the bow and we were heavier than before.

Lazlow reached up from his position and pushed on the yoke, shoving it *toward me*.

Our nose started to come up.

Our speed was steady. I had to struggle to keep it slow—only fifty—for holding the fusion reactor and the SCAV drive back was like hauling on a team of angry horses.

And we arced upwards, just three meters from the bottom.

We'd made it.

—••—

WE POWERED UP FROM THE DEPTHS, our acoustic generator turning the pressure back on itself and our SCAV barely on and keeping us at fifty kph. Soon we were at a depth of 4000 meters and I increased velocity to 400 kph, leaving a trail of steam behind that bubbled and frothed upward.

The sonar screen showed the ongoing battle, and it did not look good for Heller's forces. Many were leaving the scene, some *barely* moving due to damaged screws or engineering sections, and many warsubs had imploded or been blown to bits and were now on their way to the bottom. The FSF forces were faring better, but they had lost a sizable number of warsubs too. They were down to just over a hundred, but they had targeted the USSF fleet and were taking them out, one at a time.

Then around us, in the cabin of a flooding and damaged seacar, we heard a *PING!*

It was louder than any ping I'd ever heard. We almost had to cover our ears from it.

"What the hell?"

Johnny was staring at the sonar. On it, flares of white had been pulsing from our *Sword*s that had gone deep and were in Acoustic Pulse Drive mode. They were winking out, one by one.

PING!

Another one.

I frowned.

"Oh shit," I said. The French had realized what we'd been doing. I keyed the comm frantically. "Everyone get shallow, NOW! The French are using a loud sound blast to disrupt the pulse drive!"

It should have occurred to us earlier, but if turning the pressure backward was a result of loud acoustic pulses, then a similar pulse of noise could stop that process and cause the compression portion of the wave to rebound faster.

And our *Sword*s that were deep would instantly implode.

They were making the ascent now, but the ones closer to the French sub that had broadcast the powerful signal were already gone. The ones farther away were not as affected by the ping.

"Target that sub there," I said. I touched the sonar, identifying a French *de Gaulle* class warsub—103 meters long with a crew of thirty—and transmitted the coordinates to our forces.

"Got it," came a quick reply. "But don't go deep."

I shook my head. Our tactics would have to change now. They'd figured out a way to keep us from going down.

I thumbed the comm again. "Kat, are you there?"

"Right here," came the quick reply.

"It's time."

And from over the canyon wall, two kilometers above the battle, Kat in *SC-1* and a force of twenty other *Swords* crested the ridge, angled down, firing everything they had.

It was a cloud of torpedoes—both conventional and SCAV, from above and below—and they had the FSF and remaining USSF forces dead in their sights.

The French were in no-man's land now, and they were in trouble.

—••—

ONE AFTER ANOTHER THE FRENCH FORCES lost ships to torpedo strikes, nearby concussions, or flooding that became too difficult to overcome.

Our own seacar was in trouble as well. We could not stop the leaking from the airlock, as we'd lost the outer airlock hatch. Soon we were going to have to turn back to The Ridge.

From a large *Verdun* class vessel, a surge of smaller one-man ships emerged. They were a swarm of bees, and they were circling the area quickly, trying to attract torpedoes and lure them away from the larger warsubs, each carrying a torpedo of their own.

"Mac!" came a call from the comm. It had been Kat.

"What's wrong?" I looked for the source of the call on the sonar screen.

"Torpedo on my tail!"

"Hit the SCAV!" I cried. "Get out—" I realized belatedly that her drive was down.

There was a red line tracing a path through the water toward *SC-1*.

It was a supercavitating torpedo, and it had already hit 1000 kph.

Lancombe and Ng were in the seacar with her, and I could picture their faces in that moment. They had probably been enjoying the battle—listening to the cascading and overlapping voices on the comm with an antenna thrust over the lip of the canyon—and were experiencing something they'd waited more than thirty years for.

And now a torpedo had them in its sights.

Kat pulled away quickly, dangerously near the canyon wall—

But the SCAV was closing.

As Kat pulled away from the sheer rock cliff, and the torpedo made its closest approach, its onboard computer must have sensed that it was now or never.

It detonated.

The entire cliff wall beside *SC-1* collapsed in a cloud of boulders which showered the seacar.

Kat screamed.

There was a sound of flooding, of water spraying into the control cabin.

The seacar wobbled as rocks hit the hull and rolled off. Kat had to hold tight to maintain control, and I could hear her breathing heavily over the comm. She had to push *SC-1*'s nose down in order to dislodge the last of the boulders, and they scraped the already-damaged hull.

"More flooding!" she shrieked. "The canopy this time."

"Stay calm," I whispered to her. "Watch where you're going." Johnny pointed at my sonar screen and I followed his finger. "Kat, there are some of those one-man fighters on your tail. Watch out, they'll—" Red lines suddenly appeared. Three of them, following the seacar.

Dammit.

I angled our own vessel toward her to see if we could help. "How many torpedoes do we have left?"

"Two, both conventional," Johnny said.

"Set them to homing and select those fighters."

He nodded and his fingers flitted across the weapons board.

Kat's voice: "Mac, these guys are on our tail!"

"I'm coming. Launch countermeasures."

We had only SCAV drive and I pushed it to full and angled toward *SC-1*.

Johnny said, "Mac, we can't fire while at this speed!"

"I'm just getting closer to them, then we'll slow."

The vessels were hugging the cliff on the east side of the rift. Three torpedoes were clearly on her tail, projected on our VID, and she was weaving from side to side to throw them off her course. Countermeasures were churning in her wake, and one of the torpedoes went for them and detonated.

"Damn!" Kat cried out.

There were still two more.

Another red line appeared on my sonar, heading for *SC-1*, and coming from directly in front of her.

"Kat! Dive or go shallow! Get off that course, now!"

She began to pull up—

And the torpedo detonated against the rock wall, right in front of her.

She screamed again, and then, nothing.

—••—

I STARED AT THE SEACAR ON the VID and waited. *SC-1*'s SCAV was down, and conventional thrusters were on. The two torpedoes following her had also detonated simultaneously. It was miraculous that the seacar hadn't imploded.

It was limping to the north, barely at ten percent thrust.

"Kat," I said. "Are you there?"

Nothing.

"Kat."

I shook my head. Dammit. I'd have to wait till after the battle to find out what was happening.

The surprise attack by our forces from above had made a devastating impact on the FSF, however. More warsubs were sinking and others were running to the south. Our last two torpedoes had hit two different vessels; each scored an implosive-force detonation.

Two more FSF warsubs, out of the fight.

Ten minutes later, the few remaining USSF forces were purging ballast and going shallow and heading west.

I blew out a breath and leaned back in my chair. I would have to give an order that I did not want to give

But there was no choice. We had to protect the movement.

I gave the order.

I would never forgive myself.

The battle had resulted in the destruction of over three hundred warsubs. The remaining French ships were lumbering—or barely moving—away, wary of our *Swords* and eager to try again another day.

"Wait until they're gone, everyone, then begin north to The Ridge," I muttered. "If possible. If you're in dire straits, go now."

There was a long silence over the comm, and then someone cheered. And then someone else.

And then suddenly the speaker was a cascade of screams of joy and whoops of excitement. The hard year's work had paid off. The militarized seacars had done it.

We'd finally won a battle.

The Third Battle of Trieste in the Mid-Atlantic Rift.

INTERLUDE:
OBSESSION'S END

```
Location:      In the Mid-Atlantic Rift,
               Heading West
Latitude:      27° 55' 12" S
Longitude:     17° 35' 58" W
Depth:         2780 meters and descending
Vessel:        USS Impaler
Time:          2133 hours
```

FIRST OFFICER SCHRADER WAS STARING AT Captain Heller, who was screaming at the crew around him. He was furious that they had lost the battle, that so many torpedoes had hit them, that the ship was flooding, and that they were about to lose the engine room.

Water was spraying in from multiple directions now, the lights were dim, and the looks on the faces of the crew said it all.

They were losing not just the engine room, but the entire warsub.

They'd sealed multiple compartments to contain the flooding.

Many sailors had died in those compartments. Others had died during torpedo detonations, and the rest were sitting rigidly at their stations as Heller raged at them and blamed them for the loss.

Finally, Schrader could take it no longer. "This is your fault," he said in a strangely calm voice.

Heller turned to him and the sight made Schrader shudder. The captain's face was red and the veins at his temples were bulging.

But the XO pressed on. "You shouldn't have attacked them. You should have waited to see what they were doing. And by engaging the French, who had superior numbers, you've ended up with a shattered force and a dying sub."

"Shut up," Heller said. His voice was a rasp.

"No. This is because of you." Schrader pointed at the depth gauge, where the numbers were increasing despite the crew's best efforts. *Impaler* was a *Reaper* class warsub, 250 meters long with 400 crew, and they were losing her. Her crush depth was 3850 meters, and they were now over 3000.

"I said *Shut. Up.*"

"I won't. You have to know that your anger at that man has changed you. That you've let it cloud your judgment. You killed Rafe Manuel because you were mad at McClusky, *not* because of something he did."

Heller glanced around to see the crew staring at him. Their eyes were hard.

Heller said, "McClusky did this. Not me."

"It was your hate that drove you to it, because you couldn't kill him last year. Because the citizens of Trieste revere him, and it drove you crazy. You've wanted nothing more than to kill him, but you just couldn't do it. And now you've ended up killing all of us."

"How dare you?"

"What?" Schrader stepped forward. He was a large man, and he didn't shy from a confrontation. "How dare I tell the truth? You're *obsessed*. You're not rational or reasonable anymore. You don't care what our sailors do over in Trieste, but the fact is that our poor behavior over there has driven Triestrians to this! To fight for their independence. It's not because of McClusky—it's because of *you!*"

Behind the captain, Crewman Abernathy was watching with wide eyes. Schrader had seen him around a lot lately.

The XO continued, despite the captain's increasing anger. Schrader just didn't care anymore. He could see the end coming.

The depth gauge was flashing red and said 3733 meters. They were sinking fast.

"You are an idiot. You can't think clearly."

Heller could barely control himself now. He was looking around at his crew. "Who among you has been informing on me? Who is the traitor here?"

His eyes searched everyone around him. He studied each person for a heartbeat or two before moving to the next.

No one looked away.

Then his icy gaze settled on Abernathy.

Heller's eyes narrowed. "*You.* You were always there. You were always escorting Butte to my office." A light seemed to go off in his head then, and his forehead flattened. "You were outside my office last time too, carrying electronics that fell to the deck! It was an excuse to listen to what we were talking about!" He stepped forward and grabbed the smaller man around his lapels. Heller's face was beet red now. His bald head was covered in sweat. "You are the spy here!"

Heller drew his fist back and prepared to strike the man—

And Schrader grabbed it and hauled the captain around. "No. It's not him."

Heller looked outraged. "How dare you—" He stared at his XO in complete and utter silence. No one spoke. The only sounds were the spraying water, distant yells echoing up from below decks, and alarms in other compartments.

Flashing lights glimmered in the captain's wide eyes, which showed mostly white.

He said, "It's not you. Tell me—it *can't* be you."

Schrader smiled. "Right under your fucking nose. And you missed it because you can't think clearly."

The depth read 3934 meters.

The hull groaned.

Abernathy crouched against a bulkhead, cowering from the captain.

Schrader reached into his back pocket and pulled out a PCD. Heller watched with wide eyes. The XO keyed it on. "Are you reading me, McClusky?"

It took a moment, during which the hull creaked ominously, and then a voice: "I'm here."

"I don't think I'm going to be able to help you anymore."

"I appreciate all you've done. The people of Trieste will remember. You're a good man, Schrader."

"I put on a good act, didn't I?" His voice was soft.

There was a long pause. "You did. When we first met last year, you made me think you hated us."

He shrugged. "I'm in the USSF, but I don't hate anyone. I'm to follow orders. Only I didn't agree with the ones I was given."

"I know."

Heller screamed and leaped forward. Schrader stepped sideways and avoided the captain. "I'm going to leave now, McClusky. Good luck to you. I think we're almost done here."

The captain said, "How dare you? I'm going to kill you, McClusky!"

Schrader pocketed the device and squared his broad shoulders. "Now. You're good at killing weaklings. How about you try me?"

The two men circled each other for a moment before Heller reached in to grab his XO's neck. The two large men grappled in silence as each tried to gain the upper hand.

The crew around them couldn't believe what was happening.

The depth gauge read 4560 meters.

There was a creak of metal, a sound of tearing bulkheads, and a flash of gray steel.

And then, nothing.

I LOWERED THE PCD AND STARED ahead. On the scope between Johnny and I, there was a loud signal coming in from the west of us. From *Impaler.*

"It just imploded, Mac," Johnny said. He was staring at the readout. "Bulkheads collapsing. Descending rapidly. It's way past crush depth."

"He was a madman," I said. "And now he's dead."

For years we had dealt with *Impaler* hovering just outside Trieste, her sailors menacing us and abusing our citizens.

And now she was gone.

Finally.

And Schrader too.

He had first contacted me after The Battle in the Gulf a year earlier. He'd confessed Heller had been growing more and more angry, and that the election which had put me into office had made things worse. "He's unhinged," Schrader had said. On that day, we had agreed he would help keep me informed in an attempt to prevent Trieste from suffering *too* much under the USSF.

Schrader had been a good man, with good intentions. He had helped us enormously.

And the fact he had died in this battle saddened me. He hadn't deserved death.

—••—

ONLY TWENTY-THREE VESSELS RETURNED TO THE Ridge. We had lost thirty in the battle, most of which had fallen victim to the French audio pulse which had disrupted our Acoustic Pulse Drive. It still bothered Lazlow, who felt that he should have seen it coming. He vowed to create a defense to it, which he said was possible, and I grabbed his shoulder to give it a squeeze. "It's okay," I said. "Because of you, we won this battle. Your tech was crucial."

He waved that off. "You arranged it. We had total surprise and a confined, deep location so they couldn't call for help. They were cut off. Your decisions were brilliant, Mac." He shook his head. "You father would be proud."

I paused. "Thanks, Lazlow. That means a lot."

"Why didn't you tell anyone?"

I sighed. "There were too many unknowns. Informants, spies, and espionage. It's too much sometimes. I had to play it close to my vest." I shrugged. "Different people knew different pieces of the puzzle, and all they had to do was get together to share all the necessary info. But of course, they couldn't do that because they didn't even know what was important and what wasn't." I thought of Grant Bell in City Control, who had a general idea of where The Ridge was, but not precisely. Meg and Kat, who knew about Manesh Lazlow and what he was attempting. Hell, they'd known more than *I* had on that piece. Lancombe and Ng, whom we'd recruited to help, but whose real contributions would have to come later, when Triestrian defense became the priority. Johnny, who had begun the first attempt to take my message to the Chinese underwater cities. Then, from *Impaler*, I only knew what First Officer Lieutenant Commander Schrader chose to tell me. There was Robert Butte, whom I had used to feed information to Heller, which may or may not have been true, in order to manipulate the USSF into doing what I wanted. Maple and Bruce, whom I had sent on a secret mission, which Butte had figured out and given away to Heller. Cliff Sim, who'd helped with the investigation of Rafe's murder. And Renée Féroce, who had revealed the capture of the two operatives at the secret French facility near the Seychelles and had given this vital piece of information to Heller.

It had been a delicate tapestry of lies and secrets and truths and manipulations, and it had worked out for Trieste.

Finally.

In 2129 we'd lost almost 2,000 people in the Second Battle of Trieste in the Gulf of Mexico. Today the USSF and FSF had lost a similar number, along with 300 warsubs.

We'd lost thirty.

It had been a near total success.

Inside The Ridge we emerged from our seacars and hugged and cheered and smiled and screamed in joy. There were some casualties, which saddened us, but we couldn't help but realize how successful the day had been.

I couldn't be completely happy, for I was still worried about Katherine in *SC-1*. I still hadn't heard from them, but based on the sonar scope, I knew they'd been with us on our journey back to the base.

Then *SC-1* rose sluggishly to the surface nearby, and I leapt to the seacar to make sure all was okay.

Inside, I found an odd scene. Lancombe and Ng were in the living area, standing frozen in place. They watched as I threw open the top hatch and practically fell into the seacar.

"Where's Kat?" I snapped, ignoring pleasantries.

Lancombe pointed to the control cabin.

She was in the pilot chair.

Pinned to the pilot chair.

—••—

I CLAMPED DOWN ON AN INHUMAN gurgle of rage, a swelling of fear and rasping roar of anxiety. There were no words, simply a stringing together of sounds and angry gasps.

Pieces of steel protruded from her face. Her eyes were open in a lifeless and black stare.

The shrapnel had pierced her in multiple places and had penetrated deep into her brain. In her torso, there was more steel pinning her to the chair. Pieces of the console that had exploded in a torpedo detonation.

I grabbed her around her neck and pulled her to me. "No, no, no," I hissed. "*No.*" I couldn't think of anything else to say. I pressed my face to her neck and began to cry.

Katherine Wells had steered me to the path that I'd abandoned years before. My father had started it, and I had deviated after my experience in the Chinese undersea cell and the months of torture. But after meeting Kat and seeing her wonderful invention—the SCAV drive—she had turned me back to independence. She had brought love to my life, a love I had never experienced before.

And now it was gone.

A second later Johnny and Meg appeared at my side. Their faces said it all. Horror and grief.

We knelt there, beside Kat's body, for long, painful minutes.

We may have won the battle, but this one hurt a hell of a lot more.

—••—

HOURS LATER, I STOOD NEAR THE assembly line in the main dome at the conveyer with the unfinished hulls of several *Swords* halted and waiting for completion. Jackson was at my side, and he still had a grin on his face. I couldn't match it.

He noticed and put his hand on my shoulder. "Mac, I'm sorry."

"It's okay."

"It's *not* okay."

"We won. That's what counts."

He stared at me. He knew I didn't fully believe it myself. He gave my shoulder a final squeeze and turned to look at the motionless tools and hulls. "We really did it, didn't we? We fucking did it."

"Kind of."

"What do you mean?"

I shrugged. "One battle. We crushed them. But Trieste is still vulnerable. And we still need to forge alliances to win this war."

"I'm sure you'll do it." He had a glint in his eyes as he stared at me, and that smile was back on his face. I'd seen the look before. Many Triestrians shared it whenever I saw them in the city.

It always made me uncomfortable.

"I'm not sure," I said finally. "It'll be harder than it seems." And there was still so much to do. Chinese and French undersea colonies. Hell, not even the American ones were fully with us.

But I knew I would keep trying.

I had to.

There was no other option for me, especially after this day. I had to see it through.

Or die trying.

Meg appeared next to me and gave my hand a squeeze.

"Hiya, sis."

"Tru." She paused and shifted silently on her feet for a few soundless heartbeats. Then, "I'm so, so sorry. I loved her too."

I looked at her. Tears were spilling from her eyes. "Don't cry, Meg. It'll make it hurt too much."

"We have to accept things like this, not bury them. That'll just turn into hate and resentment."

I thought of Heller at that moment. I wondered what suffering he'd dealt with in his life. If something personal had made him the way he was. "I know," I said. "But it's too raw right now."

"I understand." There was a long pause then. We just stared at the unfinished hulls on the assembly line. She said, "What are you going to do with Butte? He's still here."

"I don't know. I think I'd like to kill him."

She stared at me. "You don't mean that."

"I kind of do."

"You're better than that."

"You must not know me very well."

"Come on, Tru. I know you. I know you planned to kill Johnny last year, but you held off. You realized you just couldn't do it."

"It's not because I *couldn't* do it. It's because I saw a better way." I sighed. "I don't think you really know what I've done in my life, Meg, when I was an operative with TCI. I've killed before. A lot of people."

"You did it for Trieste. You were on missions. But we're not on a mission right now. It's over. We won the battle. You don't have to kill Butte."

"He betrayed the city. He turned over information. Rafe died as a result. He almost gave away this base. And he continued to give away information, even when he saw what a psychopath Heller had become." I shook my head. "I think he really does deserve to die."

She hesitated. "How will you do it?"

"I'll put him in an airlock and open the outer hatch."

"The pressure will crush him."

"That's the point."

"It'll be fast though. Too fast."

I stared at her. "You agree then?"

She tilted her head. "No. I'm just helping. Why don't we slit his wrists and let him bleed out?"

"Come on, Meg. You make it sound like I'm an—"

"Or how about we use one of those riveters there to shred his liver. We'll tie him to the line and let him bleed out slowly, right there."

"Meg—"

"Or how about a needle gun to the gut?"

"I don't—"

She spun on me and grinned widely. "Or we can strap him to *SC-1*'s bow and fire a torpedo through his body."

I couldn't help but chuckle. I knew what she was doing. "That doesn't even make sense. It would explode in here, and if we took him outside to do it, the pressure would kill him first."

She stopped and stared at me. She wasn't smiling. "If you're going to go savage, Tru, you might as well go full out."

Then she turned and walked away.

— •• —

RICHARD LANCOMBE AND JESSICA NG WERE celebrating with the rest of the workers. I found them drinking kelp alcohol in the sleeping area. They were grinning and dancing as I ascended the ladder, but when they saw me, they immediately stopped and approached.

"You don't have to stop celebrating," I said.

"We'll miss her too," Lancombe said.

I waved his concern away. "Want to chat for a minute?"

"Sure." We sat on a bunk and spoke while the rest of the group celebrated the night away. Music played and people were laughing and cheering.

It was surreal.

I said, "Have you been working on your ideas?"

Lancombe said, "Yes. When we get back to Trieste we'll start implementing them immediately, as long as you're willing.

"I'm definitely willing." I wasn't going to give up on this fight.

He and Ng sighed noticeably. "Good," Ng said. "We were worried."

I blinked. "Really?"

She shrugged. "Kat. It's obviously going to affect—"

"I'm fine," I snapped. It came out too harsh, however, so I paused and said, "I'm sorry. I'm okay and we'll continue the fight. We have to develop new relations with other undersea cities and make allies. Hopefully we'll have a break from the USSF. For a while, at least."

"Hopefully."

Lancombe said, "The defenses will take time to set up."

"Tell me your ideas."

He nodded. "We'll use fish farm fences to disguise torpedo launchers. We'll arrange them around the city domes."

Those fences were streams of bubbles that held the fish in. They would also make the launchers invisible to prying eyes. It was a brilliant idea.

"Go on," I prompted.

"We'll cover the domes with anechoic tiles."

"But everyone knows where Trieste is."

"True, but the tile will make it harder for torpedoes to lock on. We'll also place countermeasure launchers around the city, in case torpedoes are inbound."

"Good one."

Ng said, "We're going to put radar stations on buoys on the surface."

I frowned. "New buoys? Or the ones that are already there?" There were markers on the surface to keep ships from passing directly overhead.

"The ones that are already there. We'll have to do it secretly at night."

"At the surface." I whistled. "That'll be tough."

"Yes. But we can do it. We also want to add torpedo scooter ships, like what other navies have."

They would be one-man scooters, fully open to the water so operators would be wearing scuba gear, with a torpedo slung underneath.

"Okay. Go on."

"We need to build underground shelters too."

"In case the base is attacked?"

He nodded. "Under the living domes. We'll have to carve them out and line them to make them watertight. It's difficult but possible."

I sat there and thought it over for long minutes. "It all sounds good. We should start this soon."

"Don't you want to at least have a drink first? Enjoy the taste of victory?"

I glanced at the vile stuff within his glass. "Victory?" I mumbled.

Lancombe realized what he'd said. "I'm sorry."

I waved it away. "No. It's okay, Richard. It *is* a victory. A big one."

Ng said, "It really is, Mac. Your dad would be so happy right now. This is something that he knew he'd never see in his lifetime."

"So he set me up to do it for him."

She nodded. "He did. And it worked, didn't it?"

I frowned.

—••—

A BIG CHEER SUDDENLY SOUNDED AND the music ramped up. I glanced at the revelers and several of them waved me over. I forced a smile and waved back. Jackson had just told them they were going to be able to go home. Back to Trieste. We all would, soon. And then I'd have to send another work crew to keep building militarized seacars.

We needed more. *A lot* more.

Lancombe and Ng went back to the celebration, and Johnny appeared at my side. "You okay, Mac?"

"Yes." I rose to stand with him. "I'm okay."

"I'm sorry about Kat. I really liked her."

I couldn't help but offer him a small smile. "She wanted to kill you when you first met."

"I can't blame her for that." He laughed. "She was possessive over her invention, and rightly so."

I said, "I have to go talk to Robert now. Want to join me?"

He stopped and stared at me, concern in his eyes. "Are we going to kill him?"

"I don't . . ." I trailed off. "I want to, but I'm not going to."

"Want me to do it?"

I knew he would if I asked. I waved the notion away. "Naw. That's okay. Meg talked me out of it. Let's go have a chat instead."

We found him in a small and bare cabin. He was chained to a bed and it smelled rank in there. There was a bottle of water next to him, and a bucket for his waste. The sound of the party filtered into the chamber, and Butte could hear the racket.

He offered me a sheepish smile. "Sounds like success, Mac."

My nose wrinkled. "Yes. A big one. Heller's gone."

He snorted and sat up in the bunk. There was a single sheet over him. A makeshift shackle and chain attached his right arm to the bunk. I unlocked it with the key Jackson had given me, and sat next to him.

He stared at it and rubbed his wrist. "Time to kill me, Mac?"

"You're not dying today."

He frowned. "Prisoner forever?"

"Not that either." I glanced at Johnny. "I hated what you did, Robert. I still don't fully understand why you were informing on TCI, on Shanks, on me, and on Trieste."

He looked suddenly frantic. "I love the city, Mac! I don't want you to take it down a path that will lead to pain and death."

"We were already on that path. Caused by Heller and the USSF."

"That's not the way I see it."

"So the beatings, the rapes, the theft of our produce is okay?"

He blinked. "No, of course not."

"So what were you doing to stop it?"

He couldn't answer that.

"Exactly," I said. "Nothing. Instead you fed Heller information which just hurt us more. Got our people killed. You watched him murder Rafe and didn't do anything."

He held his hands out. "Mac . . ." But he couldn't say anything to that.

"I'm letting you go, Robert."

Johnny shot a look at me, but I ignored it.

Butte's eyes were wide. "Pardon me?"

"You heard me." I stood up. "I'll give you a seacar. We'll dismantle the nav and communication systems. It'll have conventional thrusters only, nothing else. Get out of here."

"Just like that? I can leave?" He was utterly shocked.

"Pretty much." I turned and began to march away. Then I looked back at the man. "Oh—one more thing. You can never go to an American undersea colony again. Not Trieste, not Seascape, not Ballard."

His face paled. "But Mac, that's my home."

"You betrayed your home. You betrayed Oceania."

"There is no such thing!"

My face grew hard. "There *is* such a thing! I'm fighting for it. So are others. I told you there would be a consequence for not helping us. This is it. You should be happy I don't throw you into an airlock and flood it, or let the people out there tear you to pieces, which they gladly would." He jaw snapped shut at that. "Now go, and find a new home."

"But—" He stopped and a sob rose up his throat which he was not fully able to stop. It was like a choking gasp. "You're banishing me?"

"Find a new path, Robert. You obviously wanted one. Now you've got it."

I stalked out, Johnny at my side.

Robert Butte left The Ridge later that evening.

I hoped I'd never see him again.

EPILOGUE

EPILOGU

THE FOLLOWING DAY, ALL WAS QUIET in the facility. I rose early and pulled on worker's gray overalls and surveyed the base, examined the remaining seacars, stood on the assembly line and once again stared at the half-finished hulls hanging from their harnesses. We would need many more of these ships. Hundreds more, with pilots to drive them. And defenses around Trieste.

And alliances with other cities.

And freedom to do as we pleased, away from prying eyes.

I sighed. My heart was pounding and I had to take several deep breaths. The road ahead made me worry for our future; it made me anxious. There was too much on my shoulders. It was almost impossible to process. There were too many obstacles before us, and frankly I wasn't sure I knew precisely what to do next.

But I had no choice in the matter. I would keep working, keep trying, keep motivating my people.

I marched to an exterior bulkhead and pressed my hand against the cold steel. On the other side was an ocean full of resources and a frontier that we had barely explored. I was on the front line of that exploration, and the thought calmed me somewhat. It pleased me to be in this place. Living underwater and creating new technologies and fighting for our rights.

My dad had brought Meg and me to Trieste when we were children, and those early years had been wondrous. Staring out the expansive viewports with wide eyes at the undersea vista, watching the seacars and scuba divers and fish, I'd felt happy that I was working hard to forge a new future for humanity. Topside, people were suffering with a changing climate and crashing economies. I was lucky to be underwater.

The same feeling coursed through me now, and I welcomed it. It was a feeling that I hadn't experienced frequently, because of the difficulties I'd had as a TCI operative and while engaged in this fight for independence.

But the whole future was open again to me, and it made me feel content.

I took a deep breath, and the weight of the oceans above seemed to lift from my shoulders.

Kat was gone, and I'd have to get used to that. It would take time, but I knew she had given us the greatest gift to help win the fight: the SCAV drive. It had opened the frontier for us, and although other nations would soon also have it, it had given us the advantage.

For now, at least.

We had to keep pressing.

Admiral Benning had killed my father thirty-one years ago, and I knew I would not be satisfied until Trieste and all the inhabitants of the oceans were not only free, but until I had completely dealt with my dad's murder.

His sacrifice, for our future.

Soon Meg and Johnny appeared on the lower deck with me, along with Lancombe and Ng. We smiled at each other as we drank kelp tea and talked about the previous day, reliving the action with excited expressions and gesturing the maneuvers that our seacars had been engaged in during the fight.

As Johnny was talking about our dangerous journey to the very bottom of the rift—without propulsion and only the acoustic drive to keep us alive—an image flashed through my mind of the massive warsub we had stumbled across in the Mid-Atlantic Ridge weeks earlier. Four football fields long and one high. The crew of that vessel could number in the hundreds, I realized with a start, and the fusion reactor for its SCAV drive would be the size of a house that could also power cities. Its armaments had been shocking.

I still didn't know what nation had built that mammoth dreadnought, and I was not looking forward to finding out either.

The group of people standing with me were still smiling and relating the events of the battle, and I had to pull myself out of the reverie and back to the present. Their company made me smile, but the journey ahead was still so dangerous.

But at that particular moment, three kilometers under the cold and dark water in a steel dome, standing with the only family I had left, I felt happy.

a note from the author

Thanks to my agent Carolyn Forde, and also to Sandra Kasturi and Brett Savory of ChiZine Publications for publishing this underwater thriller series. A special thanks to Leigh Teetzel, my editor on this book, as well as Klaudia Bednarczyk for a thoughtful proofread. Thanks also to Erik Mohr of Made by Emblem for the cover art, and Jared Shapiro and Errick Nunnally for the wonderful interior design.

Any errors in regards to the physics of cavitation and supercavitation, the effects of water pressure, sound propagation underwater, and SCUBA diving are mine alone.

I would like to also extend my thanks to Ian Martin, a physicist who helped me with the concept of the Acoustic Pulse Drive. Although the drive would have deleterious effects on wildlife of the oceans, I find it to be an interesting concept which was fun to investigate and write. It provided a great deal of dramatic opportunity for me, especially during the battle sequences in this book.

The Jacques-Yves Cousteau quote is from his preface "Our Planet's Life Belt" of:

Earle, S., & Giddings, A. (1980). *Exploring the Deep Frontier*. Washington, DC: National Geographic Society.

Once again I pushed Mac hard and had him out in the water at incredible depths. I realize this portion of the tale requires suspension of disbelief. I did it for tension and drama. The current deep record dive for a person is just over 300 meters. I pushed beyond it by a factor of ten. However, the method is in fact based on reality. Our bodies are mostly water and therefore don't compress, but the air voids inside will. Lungs, sinus cavities, ear drums. If we breathe air at the same pressure as the outside environment, the two forces cancel each other out. James Cameron's fantastic movie *The Abyss* got around this by having the protagonist breathe an oxygenated fluid, so there were no air spaces in his body to compress. In the movie, Ed Harris's character plunged into the abyss to a depth of over 5600 meters. Once again, I apologize for asking for extreme suspension of disbelief, but the end result was fun to write and I hope also fun to read.

—••—

I'D LIKE TO TAKE A MOMENT to tell you about the novels and films that inspired me to write this series, The Rise of Oceania.

When I was a youngster I read quite a bit of YA Science Fiction. Lester del Rey wrote *Attack from Atlantis* (1953) which I embraced along with his other YA stories. His submarine USS *Triton* utilized a similar method of propulsion as the SCAV drive in this series. Monica Hughes wrote *Crisis on Conshelf Ten* (1975) featuring a shallow city and a rebellion involving "Gillmen." Frederik Pohl and Jack Williamson wrote *Undersea Quest* (1954), *Undersea Fleet* (1956), and *Undersea City* (1958) featuring an undersea navy and colonization of the oceans amid corporate competition and national interests. In my adult years I discovered Tom Clancy's *The Hunter for Red October* (1984) and Frank Herbert's *Under Pressure* (1956). And of course films of underwater colonization and adventure included: *The Deep* (1977), *Das Boot* (1981), *The Abyss* (1989), *Leviathan* (1989), *Deepstar Six* (1989), *Crimson Tide* (1995), and *U-571* (2000). Not all are great, but the undersea environment contains a vast amount of resources and is largely unexplored and I find stories in this setting compelling. In many ways the environment is more dangerous than outer space. Science Fiction authors tend to set their tales on land or in space, and although some novels take place underwater, they are few and far between. I wanted to explore this next frontier and make it exciting and engaging with new technologies to ramp up the adventure and action. Thanks for reading this novel, suspending your disbelief, and voyaging with Mac and his group to carve a future for themselves in a fascinating and dangerous underwater environment.

During my research I came across the story of *Scorpion*. *The War Beneath* involved a discussion of *Thresher* and I wanted to include another such cautionary tale in this novel. I have the utmost respect for the people who are actively engaged in exploring the next frontiers, at great risk to their own lives for the betterment of humanity.

I chose the name "Truman McClusky" because in his heart Mac is a blue collar man, true to his word, with a strong sense of ethics. I spent six summers in manual labor (mostly forming and finishing concrete) to pay for my education. The people I met and worked with were of the strongest character and are among the most honorable men and women I've ever met. I wanted to pay tribute to them with this series. McClusky's nickname, *Mac*, is a reference to one of my favorite films, *The Thing* (1982)—the character that Kurt Russell immortalized in R.J. MacReady.

—••—

MAC WILL BE BACK, OF COURSE, in Book Three: *Fatal Depth*.

—••—

PLEASE VISIT ME AT FACEBOOK @TSJAUTHOR and Twitter @TSJ_Author. Also visit www.timothysjohnston.com to receive updates and learn about new and upcoming thrillers, and also to register for news alerts.

MY FUTURISTIC MURDER MYSTERIES INCLUDE *THE Furnace* (2013), *The Freezer* (2014), and *The Void* (2015), all published by Carina Press.

THANKS AGAIN FOR INVESTING YOUR TIME in this novel. Do let me know what you think of my thrillers.

Timothy S. Johnston
tsj@timothysjohnston.com
30 June, 2019

ABOUT THE AUTHOR

TIMOTHY S. JOHNSTON IS A LIFELONG fan of thrillers and science fiction thrillers in both print and film. His greatest desire is to contribute to the genre which has given him so much over the past four decades. He wishes he could personally thank every novelist, screenwriter, filmmaker, director and actor who has ever inspired him to tell great stories. He has been an educator for twenty years and a writer for thirty. He lives on planet Earth, but he dreams of the stars. Visit timothysjohnston.com to register for news alerts, read his blog and reviews, and learn more about his current and upcoming thrillers. Timothy is the author of *The War Beneath* and *The Savage Deeps*. His futuristic murder mystery/thrillers include *The Furnace*, *The Freezer*, and *The Void*. Follow Timothy on Facebook @TSJAuthor and Twitter @TSJ_Author.